THEY WERE LOCKED IN DEADLY COMBAT— FIGHTING FOR THE LIVES OF MILLIONS . . .

LIEUTENANT SKEET MERRILL. He was an American, a Pacific submarine commander, and one of the best. His courage and skills made him the perfect pawn in World War II's deadliest game.

SIGI PETERSEN. A provocatively beautiful—and highly dangerous—Norwegian spy. Only she knew the mission's *real* purpose.

SS COLONEL SCHILLER. He was the Nazis' top manhunter. Savagely clever and bitterly cruel, he'd give the enemy spies just enough rope . . . to hang themselves.

KAPITAN DIETER LOEWEN. This ace U-boat commander was vulnerable to the charms of a beautiful woman—but merciless to any enemy of the Fuehrer.

The fate of the world, victory or defeat, depended on the men and women who risked their lives in the . . .

Tides of War

TIDES OF WAR

DOUGLAS MUIR

JOVE BOOKS, NEW YORK

"I'll Be Seeing You"
By Sammy Fain and Irving Kahal
Copyright 1938 by Williamson Music Co.
Copyright renewed. All rights administered
by Chappell & Co., Inc. International copyright secured.
All rights reserved. Used by permission.

"The White Cliffs of Dover"
By Nat Burton and Walter Kent
Copyright 1941 Shapiro Bernstein & Co., Inc. New York.
Copyright renewed. Used by permission.

TIDES OF WAR

A Jove Book / published by arrangement with
the author

PRINTING HISTORY
Jove edition / October 1987

ISBN: 0-515-09182-0

Jove Books are published by The Berkley Publishing Group,
200 Madison Avenue, New York, New York 10016.
The name "JOVE" and the "J" logo
are trademarks belonging to Jove Publications, Inc.

PRINTED IN THE UNITED STATES OF AMERICA

10 9 8 7 6 5 4 3 2 1

This one's for Sharon, Dave, Eric and Todd

The U-boat attack was our worst peril. It would have been wiser for the Germans to stake all upon it.
                                        —WINSTON CHURCHILL

Prologue

"Your armed forces sweetheart has another special dedication from Northern England. It's from Mum, Dad, Peggy, and Little George."

The fourth officer–radioman of the United States Navy ammunition tender *Cape Cod* adjusted the volume on the transceiver. Young, alert, and always interested in what was going on outside the ship's confining radio shack, he liked to pick up the latest war news or music from London, Lisbon, or Paris. Admittedly, when off duty and not monitoring the vessel's official convoy wavelength, he enjoyed fooling with the auxiliary receiver. Tonight, as his ship approached the English coast, it was the 57 megacycle band of the BBC that captured his interest. Vera Lynn's dedications continued, her soothing voice echoing in his earphones. She started to sing:

"I'll be seeing you, in all the old familiar places
That this heart and mind embraces, all day through.
In the——"

The explosion came suddenly, so quickly the radioman saw for only a fraction of a second the red blur of his own body shattering before him. There was a tearing scream of iron, an enormous belch of fire and smoke, and then the roaring inrush of the sea. One moment there had been Vera Lynn, the next, absolute, terminal nothingness.

1

Chapter 1

THE BLACKOUT CURTAINS were askew and the window open. London's night air was still heavy with the smell of destruction: smoke, charred rubble, spent explosives.

Lieutenant Skeet Merrill, USN, winced and groaned inwardly. Whenever he thought about the new German pilotless weapons his mood darkened. Merrill would be the first to admit he could use some of that inborn English pluck and calmness in the face of adversity.

Molly Tremayne's two-room flat was inviting enough, by British wartime standards. The little brunette's khaki Wren service cap was still perched jauntily on the top of the bedpost where she had tossed it before dinner. Merrill hadn't slept since the buzz bomb attack a couple of hours earlier. Trying to settle down, he'd shifted repeatedly, side to side, face to back, but he wasn't able to doze off. His athletic body was full of annoying aches, thanks to a few of Molly's friends who had introduced him to Rugby the day before. Merrill had welcomed the diversion, though the romp was far rougher than he'd imagined, even for a jock like himself who had played a little football in college. The friendly competition had been one more improvised pastime while waiting for D-Day and his own hush-hush pre-invasion assignment. Merrill pounded the pillow with his fist. His attractive English companion stirred beside him, but she didn't awaken.

Again Merrill felt a vague uneasiness over his upcoming mission. The job had yet to be fully explained, and it had been a long time coming. Too long, and he'd become rusty. Rumor had it that the Secretary of the Navy or Roosevelt himself had made a personal appeal to Churchill to take Merrill on board at G-10. Under the circumstances, SHAEF Commander Eisenhower's endorsement had been a mere rubber stamp. Despite all the high-level maneuvering, Merrill felt uncertain over his role. He was, after all, a submarine commander; he'd never asked to be taken off his Pacific Theater pigboat and thrust into the role of a land-based spy. Merrill's discomfort during the past several days had compounded itself into a puzzling anxiety. Why had there been so many postponements?

He glanced toward the open window. Somewhere off toward the river, a dog howled mournfully, its master, no doubt, one more casualty of the night's V-weapons. Merrill glanced at his watch. One o'clock, double-daylight war time. Beside him, Molly Tremayne lay on her side, cuddled against his muscular shoulders. Merrill rolled over and raised himself up on one hand. In a mood of protectiveness, he slowly combed her fragrant brown hair with his fingers. Molly wore patriotic pajamas of pale blue, piped in navy blue and embroidered with an RAF emblem. The fashionable, sought after nightwear had cost her eight clothing coupons. When he gently kissed Molly's forehead she snuggled closer, her smooth hand slowly and methodically slipping up his thigh. Merrill quivered with anticipation.

A frayed and soiled white cap proclaimed the *Kapitan Leutnant* the U-boat's commander. Dieter Loewen wasn't tall, but handsome and solid, with strong shoulders; he'd just turned thirty-nine, but his corrugated face, weathered by the elements, made him look older. Loewen's head, thatched with premature strands of gray, was set on a sturdy neck, around which hung an Iron Cross, First Class, with Oak Leaves and tiny Silver Swords.

"God in heaven!" Loewen rasped as he stared into the periscope eyepiece and scanned the horizon. The torpedo had run slow but was directly on target. The sudden explosion near the flank of the convoy was a white-hot holocaust, a scene from hell. Loewen's hands trembled. The merciless blast—far larger than expected—could only have been an ammunition ship. A green flare shot into the sky and Loewen quickly noted the destroyer escort's position. "Dive! Emergency!" he cried, dipping the periscope.

Less than a minute later the destroyer ran over the U-601 like a roaring express train. Again and again the depth charges detonated. Like a gigantic fist, their fearsome pounding shook the deck plates.

"Emergency speed," snapped Loewen. "Drive her as deep as you can."

Only when his U-boat reached a depth of five hundred feet did he permit the engineer to halt the descent. The steel hull groaned under the intense pressure, and for twenty minutes the nerve-shattering explosions continued overhead. At last they stopped. Loewen mopped away the beads of sweat coursing down his face and looked at the others. His crew was taut-lipped, each man fighting off the dreaded *Blechkoller*—the tin can neurosis that often strikes when a U-boat is pinned down by the deafening depth charges. Their eyes were all riveted to him, expectant, as if he were about to pull off some miracle. One man was praying.

The navigator looked up from the hydrophones, "Nothing but silence, sir."

Only after an hour's additional time was Loewen satisfied that he had eluded the destroyer.

When the danger was over and the inferno above had died down, Dieter Loewen once more had to fight back a familiar empty sensation inside him. Though he was a man committed to action, he had a sense of privacy about him, and again he felt it—the loneliness more frightening than death; the painful, gut reaction that he alone was responsible for the God-awful terror that had just been inflicted on the enemy. It was a rotten war, the ambiguous morality of which once more tore open all the scars the Battle of the Atlantic had left on him. *Attack, attack, attack.* Always attack, whatever the odds. Then pray you are not destroyed in return. Simple rules. Nazi rhetoric and self-delusion aside, it was the terrible price he paid for being the last of the great U-boat aces and acknowledged as one of the Fuehrer's favorites. Loewen's men called him the *Lion of the Atlantic*—the lucky one. Even his name was derived from the German word for lion.

* * *

The tobacco smoke hung as thick as Thames fog in the Prime Minister's conference room at 10 Downing Street. The rectangular chamber was almost filled by the massive, felt-covered table surrounded by chairs. Field Marshal Montgomery, General DeGaulle, First Sea Lord Admiral Cunningham, along with their aides, had departed, but SHAEF Commander Dwight Eisenhower hesitated at the exit. Winston Churchill, his usual pugnacious manner betrayed by weariness, remained seated alone at the head of the table, his back to the fireplace.

General Eisenhower exhaled sharply, then said, "About that blade threatening our jugular, Prime Minister. I suggest . . ." He paused, rubbing his chin. "I should save it for tomorrow. It's late and we're all bleary-eyed."

"No, quite all right. I know what you're after," Churchill grunted, not bothering to look up. "Indeed, you seem to have the man with the qualifications. Monty and I won't fight you on the matter. I only regret that young Dutch woman—Erika Vermeer, I believe—was unsuccessful at the U-boat base at Wilhelmshaven."

Eisenhower nodded. "As luck would have it."

"Give us a few more hours to prepare our G-10 for this Lieutenant Merrill of yours, General. Curious nickname you've given him—*Cowboy*." Churchill paused to toss his cigar butt backward over his shoulder. It missed the fire bucket but fell in the dying embers of the hearth. "If we get away with this spectacular movement of over twenty thousand men and God knows how much material, it will go down in history as the most astonishing feat of this war or any war. But if we fail, General, the channel tides will run red with the blood of our youth, the beaches choked with their bodies."

Eisenhower's eyes lowered briefly. "President Roosevelt has asked for a clarification of the U-boat problem. I can't stall much longer before cabling your reply."

Churchill's eyes twinkled. "Indeed? Once again the polite pirate grows impatient. He'll have it shortly, I promise."

"Good night, Prime Minister." Eisenhower grinned and left the room.

Almost immediately Mrs. Churchill entered and hastened to the window sash to let out the stale, smoky air. "It's after three, Winston," she said in her authoritative manner. She dropped a pair of felt slippers beside his chair.

The PM ended his contemplative scribbling on a note pad, looked up at her, and sighed. "I'm sure of it, Clemmie. Doenitz will send in his wolf packs. His U-boat commanders will put up a desperate, if not suicidal battle. Their German conqueror complex will compel them to do so."

She looked at him askance. "I had thought the submarine war was being won," she said softly, sitting down beside him.

"Not won, my dear. Only temporarily contained. With the new snorkel devices, we've a new problem." Churchill scowled, held up his fountain pen, felt its shape, and waved it before her like a sorcerer's wand. "One small, protruding shaft now enables the blighters to suck in fresh air and recharge their batteries while remaining submerged. Our radar was good enough to catch the Heinies wih their lederhosen down when the entire sub was periodically forced to surface. But now the U-boats can approach anywhere, stay underwater and unde-tected—unless we're virtually on top of them."

Clemmie nodded. "The Channel?"

"Precisely. The invasion troopships will be plump, sitting ruddyducks."

"And still you insist on personally tagging along?" she asked, anxiously.

"I suspect you agree with the King. He's been listening to Eisenhower as well on the matter."

Clementine put a firm hand on Churchill's wrist. "Observing the D-Day landings from the deck of the destroyer is far too risky. Your leadership and immediate availability are needed within the sheepfold."

"Now, now, my dear. Every Englishman has to overextend himself these days." Churchill thought for a moment. "The water maybe cold, but I still feel it's my duty to plunge with the others. His majesty is wrong."

"Cheer up, Winston. We can at least go down to Southamp-ton to see the boys off."

Sitting up stiffly, the PM pushed the papers before him away. He took off his shoes and slid his tired feet into the slippers. "Apparently Eisenhower wins again. Clemmie, there is only one thing worse than fighting a war with Allies, and that is fighting a war without them. I may not see the invasion first hand on the coast of Normandy, but I fully intend to end this new U-boat menace once and for all."

Clementine looked at him seriously. "Provided there's time and luck isn't with that madman Hitler."

Skeet Merrill stared wearily out the window, waiting for the first tendrils of dawn to end what remained of his sleepless night. He knew the morning sky would be anything but cheerful, for the weather forecast was for a heavy storm front. Already the rain had begun to fall steadily. From the street below Merrill could hear a milk cart making its rounds.

Merrill was startled by the sudden clamor of the telephone beside the bed. The mattress springs creaked as Molly Tremayne slid nervously away from him. He picked up the receiver.

"This is Lieutenant Merrill. Yes, Sergeant." For several seconds Merrill listened to the terse, very specific instructions being given at the other end of the line. "What? Sure I hear you, but it happens to be five-thirty in the morning and I haven't had my java yet. Tell the Colonel I'll be at the Maritime Museum at ten if he wants to check on me. And you might also tell him I can already recite forward and backward the contents of those files. Right now I know more about the German navy than my own. All right, I understand. I'll be ready by tonight. Yes, *on time*, dammit. The fat man with the cigar can count on it."

Replacing the phone on the hook, Merrill turned to Molly and exhaled sharply. "Sorry, Mary Poppins. It's official. The vacation's over." He stared at her and frowned. "Do you have to chew gum so early in the morning?"

"Sorry, love. One of my bad habits."

"What flavor is it?"

"Skeet—" Her big brown eyes blinked in confusion as she put aside her wad of Wrigley's. She looked up at him and asked, "The assignment . . . you're leaving now?"

He gently tapped her chin. "No, but damn soon enough. Tonight, after dinner."

Molly shook herself awake and smiled beautifully. "'Methinks I hear the wanton hours flee. And as they pass, turn back and laugh at me.'"

"Shakespeare again, Miss Tremayne?" he asked.

"Hardly. *Villiers*. The second Duke of Buckingham."

Merrill scratched his ear. "Yeah, to be sure," he replied in an offhand manner. Smiling, he traced her full round lips with one hand and gently cupped her breast with the other.

Shivering with pleasure at his touch, Molly tilted her head and gave him a brief worried look. "Did you sleep well?"

Merrill told the truth. "No." He looked at her soberly, trying to decide whether to turn on one of his ice-melting smiles. Considering the hour of the morning and the message he'd just received, he was a long way off from mirth. Merrill guessed it wouldn't matter; Molly was good at changing his moods. She knew well enough how to get the crinkles working around his serious hazel eyes. Methodically, slowly, her arms entwined around his chest and shoulders. He shivered as her tongue delicately probed into the folds of his ear. Then she found his hand and pressed it deep within her thighs.

In southeastern France the day broke clear with a brilliant sun poking over the tops of the Rhone Alps. Erika Vermeer woke a half-hour later than usual and peeked out the crack in the shutters. It would be a perfect day, she thought, for taking the children on a hike. But she'd have to hurry; the others were already downstairs.

Erika had sought not only employment at the remote orphanage two weeks before, but refuge. Her work in *Het Verzet*—the Dutch Resistance—followed by her espionage activity in the German port city of Wilhelmshaven, had put her at the top of the Gestapo's wanted list. Erika had at first sought sanctuary in Paris, but her employer there—the *patron* of a Left Bank bistro, had suggested she would be safer at his provincial orphanage run by his cousin.

Izieu was one of the most pleasant villages in the Lyon district, and Erika had found happiness here. Still, she was restless to get back into serious resistance action. She intended to remain here a month, possibly a little longer. If she were smart, she'd stay until the Allies finished their planned liberation sweep across France. But how long might that take?

While waiting, at least Erika had the children to supervise. In the pastoral setting it didn't seem that the world was at war at all, except when the boys and girls wrote sad letters to their incarcerated parents. Today again she would help the orphans forget their troubles; they would climb to the top of a local mountain and look down on the beautiful Rhone River.

Erika hurriedly put on a pair of dungarees and a man's striped shirt, not bothering to tuck it in around her wiry frame. She went to the mirror and brushed the curly, reddish brown hair she kept as short as possible. Examining her boyish face with its freckle-covered pug nose and petulant mouth, she decided more sunshine was definitely in order; she'd grown pale spending so much time in hiding. Beneath her lashes, her eyes, at least, were clear and sparkling, unlike those of the older women at the orphanage who drank too much wine. Erika smiled at her reflection—the wide, empty, doe-like eyes. Revealing eyes. She'd been especially secretive with them since her arrival at Izieu, careful that others might not learn of her sexual persuasion. To admit that she was a lesbian would only complicate an already precarious, dangerous situation.

Erika was about to go downstairs to help serve the children breakfast when she heard heavy vehicles approaching the building. She hurried to the window and threw open the shutters. *German trucks and SS men!* She stood there, frozen. Had the enemy followed her and caught on to the masquerade? Or had they discovered that the children sequestered in the orphanage were Jewish, sent to Izieu by distraught parents who hoped the young innocents might escape the chimneys of Birkenau and Auschwitz?

Heart fluttering, Erika dashed downstairs to the kitchen at the rear of the building. The Gestapo gangsters had already entered and despite the outcries of orphanage personnel, proceeded to herd up the fearful boys and girls sitting in ranks at the kitchen table. Their breakfast cups of cocoa went spilling as the children, along with several teachers, were hustled outside and thrown like packages into the waiting trucks.

Erika was aghast. When she tried to interfere, she was held roughly by a glowering SS sergeant.

"Your papers," he commanded in thickly accented French.

She answered him in German. "They are upstairs in my room." Now she would feed him the lie: "My name is Erika Vermeer." How he would light up if she were to tell him the truth, that she was the very much wanted spy Erika Krager.

The SS man warily followed her up the tile stairway, his pistol held in readiness. Moments later, apparently satisfied with the forged Dutch documents that she provided him, he left her and locked the door from the outside. She heard his boots tramp back downstairs, then shouting and truck tailgates slamming closed.

Chagrined, Erika went to the window. The Germans were ready to leave with their cargo. As the trucks bumped their way out of the orphanage courtyard the tearful occupants sang a French patriotic song: "You will not take Alsace and Lorraine."

Erika swallowed with difficulty and fought back tears. Immediately, she made up her mind. She didn't belong here in an Alpine retreat. If danger was everywhere, she'd just as well be in the thick of it. Paris was as good a place as any. She'd ask Pierre Roger to take her back on at his bistro. Regardless of the risk, after what she'd witnessed today, Erika Vermeer had to work even harder for the Allied espionage cause.

Chapter 2

EYES TURNED, stunned by her beauty. Quick stepped and confident, the intense blonde in the form-fitting woolen suit threaded her way along the crowded station platform.

Ignoring the hungry stares of the servicemen around her, Sigi Petersen hurried past one coach after another, searching for an empty seat in one of the compartments. The London-bound express at last appeared ready to gather itself and pull out of the Manchester station. A conductor shouted up the line. Most of the cars were filled to capacity with departing men in khaki, and a ragtag civilian band brought in to see them off played an off-key version of *There'll Always Be An England*. Several frilly women on the platform wept quietly, blotting their tears with damp lace handkerchiefs.

Turning down a cup of tea offered her by one of the volunteers at a refreshment cart, Sigi walked faster. The sweating RAF flight sergeant bearing her luggage pointed to a coach door that was still ajar. The compartment being half-empty, Sigi climbed swiftly inside and claimed one of the soiled, red leather seats. The sergeant flung a heavy valise up into the compartment after her and closed the door. Somewhere up the line a shrill whistle blew.

Sigi cranked down the window and reached outside for the RAF man's hand. "Goodbye, Sergeant Davis, and thank you," she said simply. She winked, wondering vaguely if she would ever see the sexy Ringway parachute instructor again in her lifetime, then just as quickly dismissed the thought. It didn't matter. His job was finished. Sigi had also found Davis a trifle inquisitive, and she disliked inquisitive men.

11

The express jerked, then rolled forward in a shroud of escaping steam. Sigi waved from the open window as the train gathered speed and moved out of the station. When the flight sergeant's face became lost in the shouting, waving crowd, she tucked her head back inside the coach and wearily slumped into the seat. Ignoring her companions in the compartment, she kicked off her shoes, fumbled through her purse, and withdrew a tattered copy of the humor magazine *Punch*.

Back on the station platform, RAF flight sergeant Hugh Davis turned on his heels and rapidly picked his way through the crowds to the exit. *Blimey, peculiar business*, he thought. Asking a bit much to train anyone to parachute properly in only two days' time, not to mention the distraction caused him by a charmer of the opposite sex the likes of Sigi Peterson. He was sure this mysterious, close-mouthed bombshell had not been top-priority trained for anything routine. Not by a jolly long shot. Whatever the hush-hush involvement, it had to be big—very big.

Davis knew only a little about her. Sigi was a young thirty-one, with flaxen hair and well-defined features. Her bones were well-structured by Teutonic measure; she had penetrating glacial blue eyes, a few blemishes which she tried to keep covered with makeup, full lips, and a narrow nose. The rest of her contours were as close to perfect as any man could desire.

Operations at Ringway had provided only her basics: the personal background, health profile and her orders, oddly lacking in detail. Her credentials, what Davis had seen of them, made impressive reading: Sigi Petersen had just passed her twenty-ninth birthday when G-10 first made contact with her, three months before the Nazis overran Norway. Before that she'd been an instructor in linguistics at the University of Oslo. Promoted four times by G-10; fluent in four languages; recommended for Special Service Order of Merit. The profile ended there, with no mention of her assignments. There was also the standard physical data—height, weight, color of eyes, blood type, allergies, and so forth.

So much for another expedited jump school graduate, he reflected. One more two and a half day wonder for the RAF stagers to worry over. Davis found the sandbagged telephone box he was seeking and checked his watch. Precisely as instructed, he would ring up a specified number in London and report that Sigi Petersen was en route. His part of the project was finished.

It had been a tedious morning in the basement of the Maritime Museum and Skeet Merrill's eyes were exhausted from the fine print. Except for the photographs and curious illustrations, he would have been bored to the point of nodding off, especially after the wakeful hours he'd endured the night before. There was absolutely nothing more he could learn about the development, technology, or strategic deployment of the *Reichskriegmarine's Unterseeboots*. Or the damned personnel who manned them over the past three decades.

Merrill was hungry when he left the museum. He'd wanted to have lunch with Molly, but for the past week the Admiralty Planning Room had been a hornet's nest of action and most of the Wren staff had been making do with twenty-minute breaks. Instead of meeting her, Merrill took a cab to Arthur's Attic, one of his favorite cafes located off Piccadilly on St. James Street. There were two other American officers in the restaurant, both bomber pilots. Merrill exchanged only a few civil greetings and took his own table at the rear of room. He checked his ration coupons, then ordered kidney and vegetable pie with a pint of Guinness. Following the meal and a second brew, he wished he'd had a double whiskey instead—this to anesthetize himself against the pain of separation he and Molly Tremayne were about to undergo. Merrill smiled to himself. If a man could endure the hangovers, the life current of Scotland was good at numbing sorrow. He'd be leaving Molly, possibly tonight or tomorrow. When and if he saw her again was pure speculation, and it saddened him.

Merrill paid his lunch tab and left the cafe. Outside, the rain had let up and he didn't need his umbrella. Strange, he mused, how umbrellas for officers were taboo in the States but here in London they were so commonplace.

Merrill thought again about his whirlwind relationship with Molly Tremayne. He'd known her for all of a month; why had he waited until today to turn over in his mind the meaning of their relationship? Until now he'd rationalized their wartime encounter as just that—companionship, shared laughter, and a little non-obligatory action under the sheets. Merrill suddenly hated himself for being so calloused, but hadn't she too, preferred a loose involvement? Women—it was hard to know what they really felt.

Passing a bombed-out building, Merrill hesitated and stared with the rest of the crowd. Its macabre, twisted steel and brick rubble still smoldered from the wrath of a V-bomb the night before and firemen were gathering up hoses that littered the pavement. Merrill shook his head in dismay as he surveyed the empty space suddenly created in the block. Despite his sophisticated knowledge of explosives, each time he saw the destructive force of the German rockets, he was awestruck. Until the Nazis were stopped, Molly Tremayne would be just as vulnerable in London as he would be when he went into action across the Channel.

Merrill walked faster, heading back toward Piccadilly where he hoped to find a flower stand and taxi. The least he could do was get back to Molly's early, clean up the flat, and set a pretty table for their planned farewell dinner. If there was time, he'd also try to pick up some rare vintage wine on the black market. Hang the cost; where he was going, greenbacks would be worthless.

It was a grim day on the coast of Brittany. From out of the gray vault of the sky over St. Nazaire, two seagulls dove repeatedly at the lifeless form hanging from the gallows.

The woman looked up, arched her eyebrows, and shivered. Marie Selva had a round, pinched face, a slightly hunched, short build, and thick brown hair shot with gray that was parted in the middle. She wore a maroon kerchief around her neck, a black topcoat, and carried a worn gray leather purse. From her matronly appearance, few might suspect she was the top operative in Brittany for the French Resistance.

A gust of wind carried the scent of rotting flesh swirling around Marie's nostrils. Above her, the bloated body swung slowly in circles, the rope around its neck creaking with a nerve-grating groan. Left to ripen in the elements, the face of the accused spy had become barely recognizable, a grotesque mask of purplish pulp. The greedy gulls had plucked out the eyes the day before but still the birds menaced the body. Wiredrawn and wary, Marie grimaced at the odor and backed away from the gibbet. In her dual role as an operative and an undertaker—a career she had inherited from her deceased husband—Marie Selva was all too familiar with German punishment for any St. Nazaire shipyard worker suspected of subversion or sabotage. With increasing frequency the local SS detachment had used this wooden gallows at the entrance of the fortress-like, underground U-boat base and then left the bodies to rot—ominous warnings to other French workmen. Marie knew that sooner or later the German guards would relent, particularly when the stench became unbearable. Then once more, as St. Nazaire's mortician, she would have the odious task of disposing of the latest corpse.

Each time the Nazis made their grisly point, Marie Selva's sense of patriotism boiled within her. Distressingly, most of the Frenchmen she interred were friends and neighbors who had been providing her with vital intelligence on Reichskriegmarine U-boat activity. In the past twelve months, one by one, most of these contacts had been eliminated by the vigilant Gestapo, while those remaining, fearful of reprisal, had become conspicuously silent, drawing their pay from the enemy occupiers and waiting out the end of the war. Despite their conviction that the great battle had reached a turning point and France would soon be liberated, the base workers knew their lives and those of their families still hung precariously balanced every day they punched the German time clocks.

Marie quickened her step away from the foreboding walls of the submarine base and headed back up crater-pocked Rue d'Anjou toward her undertaking parlor. Her hands felt clammy and sweat formed on her forehead despite the cool breeze coming in off the Bay of Biscay. As each day passed, her fear intensified. If the mighty Allied invasion and liberation didn't come quickly, the next bloated body on the end of the rope might very well be her own.

Sigi Petersen dropped her copy of *Punch*. She was tired, far too weary for the dry satire in British humor magazines. Staring vacantly out the train window at the passing Cheshire countryside, she thought again about the peril that lay ahead. She knew, instinctively, why London had chosen her, sparing nothing to qualify and prepare her for the upcoming assignment. It was all part of the master plan. Only a month before she'd been given the opportunity to read her own Special

Services annual review. She'd been described in the dossier as *the consummate professional—methodical, capable, and reliable, an operative knowing exactly what she wants and able to go after it by the shortest route. Her voice is brisk, precise, decisive. Sigi Petersen is more than clever; she is cunning.*

Sigi smiled to herself at the recollection; she knew that the profile was accurate enough. Indeed, in some respects she went about things more like a man rather than by the hidden and circuitous routes often used by women. There had been other items in the dossier that pleased her. She'd received high ratings for intelligence, operational skill, and emotional stability, not to mention an underlined reference to her *magnetism* —something cryptic about an *intangible and pervasive gaze in her eyes that seemed to attract followers.* True, she mused. She did enjoy having men at her fingertips; she was especially good at handling macho animals who behaved like dogs after a bitch in heat. Admittedly, men challenged her and she enjoyed going through them as one would a *smorgasbord*: sampling, testing, choosing, rejecting at whim.

While in attendance at the RAF Parachute School, however, she'd been specifically ordered not to fraternize with either the fellow students or instructors. She'd found it all damnably annoying. The gin, the pints of stout, the jars of rum had all been offered and, dutifully, they'd been turned down. Still, the security provisions of her stay at Ringway may have been a blessing in disguise, for she'd really not been up to socializing. The expedited training had been rigorous, more so than her worse expectations. Sigi had been determined that no man would show her up, and she'd succeeded, despite her carefully hidden fear. Backward and forward somersaults, Japanese rolls to the right and left, drops from a giant trapeze, the actual jumps from an aircraft flying at 125 knots—she had learned to do them all. Not well, perhaps, considering the time element, but the techniques would be remembered; with luck she could now leap and kiss French dirt without breaking her precious neck. Sigi had assumed that with each succeeding lollop into the pastoral English countryside there would be a gain in confidence, but not so. Acrophobia or whatever, Ringway had been a frightening experience from beginning to end.

Taking out her silver and pearl compact, Sigi examined her face in the mirror. There wasn't much she could do about the

the look of fatigue, but at least she could touch up the lipstick. Frowning at her reflection, she resolved to beg London to send her over to the continent by submarine or motor torpedo launch, and not aerial drop. Possibly the journey could be made by Lysander, the small, lightweight army plane that was able to put down on an airstrip the size of a postage stamp. Hell didn't frighten her at all, but the *jump* into it scared her more than she was willing to admit.

From the train's seatbench opposite a young sailor, at least a dozen years her junior, had been observing her since they left Manchester. His watchful eyes skitted nervously from her face to her legs then back to a magazine he made only a pretense of reading. Sigi smiled seductively and he took the crumb by grinning back and lowering the magazine.

"Just a visit to London, ma'am, or is it home for you?" His voice was uneven and nervous.

"Just a visit, I'm afraid. I'm originally from Oslo."

The callow, wide-eyed sailor looked even more delighted on hearing her Scandinavian accent. "I'm based in Newcastle. See a lot of your boys up there," he said enthusiastically. "I assume you're caught up like the rest of them, here in England for the duration."

"I suspect you're right, sailor."

"My name's Clifford, ma'am." His eyes danced as he looked at her. "Are you married?" The others in the compartment stared at him but he awkwardly continued, "I mean, you're very pretty."

"Thank you," she said, enjoying his blush. "My name is Sigi." *He's cute, but too young; probably as clumsy as he is oversexed.*

The sailor leaned forward. "May I buy you a toddy when we arrive in London?"

Sigi sighed and said with finality, "I'm flattered, Clifford. But I expect to be met at the station. I'm also miserably tired, and need to get a few winks now, before arriving." Smiling demurely at him, she pulled her wool skirt down properly over her knees, and burrowed back in the seat. Totally exhausted, she dozed off. Her eyes didn't open again until an hour later as the express slowed down at the outskirts of London.

It was almost dark when the train clanged across several points and glided quietly into Euston Station. The disappointed young tar across from her said goodbye and disappeared with the other passengers from the compartment. Sigi got up, stretched, and rolled down the window, surveying the crowd on the busy, sandbagged platform. As instructed, she'd make no effort to leave the train.

Suddenly her eyes were drawn to a tall, heavily sideburned individual in a khaki uniform with three chevrons and a king's crown on his sleeve. The sergeant came nearer, his serious eyes gazing into all the coaches with an air of expectancy. When he was opposite her compartment, he stopped abruptly and looked straight at her.

"Miss Petersen, I suspect?"

The red-haired army sergeant had a rich Scottish accent and was ruggedly handsome, despite the exaggerated sideburns. Sigi felt a compulsive urge to flirt with him, but she bit back the impulse. "Yes," she said firmly. "And you are Sergeant Cummings?"

The tall man nodded. "Aye. Come along with me if you will. We'd best hurry and not keep the Colonel waiting."

Chapter 3

CONSIDERING THE London food shortage, Molly Tremayne's candlelit, farewell dinner turned out to be a bacchanalian feast. Earlier, Merrill had been lucky, finding an enterprising cabbie with a black market connection to a bulging larder. Molly had prepared Beef Wellington with all the trimmings and they'd washed the lot down with a liter of Portuguese wine and brandy-spiked coffee. The entire dinner scene had a distorted kind of reality.

"Now what?" Merrill asked with a grin.

"Could we go to the cinema? There's an American mystery in town. *Laura*, with Gene Tierney and Dana Andrews."

Merrill shook his head and pointed to his watch. "Sorry, not enough time. You've got a precious forty-five minutes left."

She looked at him askance, then smiled. "It's sad. You never seem to have time to pause and smell the flowers. Hurry, hurry, hurry."

"Your fragrance is enough for me, ma'am."

Laughing, polishing off the rest of the coffee, they adjourned to bed where they now sat nude, facing each other in the lotus position. With Molly Merrill felt as uninhibited as with himself. The young Englishwoman was always yielding, ever easy-going. Merrill reached over to the nightstand and picked up his harmonica. He managed to sound off with a half-dozen bars of *Mairzy Doats* before Molly pulled the instrument away from his lips.

Eyes sparkling, she purred softly, "Time we made some music together, love. Mind if this little bird perches on your hairy chest?"

"I'd be right proud and honored, ma'am," he quipped, toying with a little Texas twang. Merrill's eyes slid slowly over her body. As usual, what he saw excited him.

With a look of annoyance she said to him, "Wait, please. Move your ruddy butt, Lieutenant."

"Now what the——"

"My Aunt Samantha, bless her soul. She'd never forgive me if we left pecker pudding all over the hand-stitched quilt."

Merrill laughed. Molly's nonchalant, melodic voice was country Cornish, charmingly accented and as pleasingly homespun as the pink and yellow quilt they struggled to remove from the bed. She let the bedcover drop to the floor then instantly, aggressively climbed on top of him. Merrill lay there for a moment, pretending helplessness. They laughed. Then they made serious love.

Five minutes later they lay prostrate, breathless, and completely satisfied. For a long time neither of them moved. Finally Molly laughed and Merrill kissed her once more, slowly and tenderly. Rolling over, he grabbed his watch from the bedside table and checked the time.

Merrill pulled himself together, sat upright on the edge of the bed, and rubbed his chest. Grumbling unintelligibly, he whispered, "Sorry, kitten, that appears to be it." He rose and shuffled over to the porcelain washbasin in the corner of the room. "You want that quilt back on the bed?"

"I'll take care of it," Molly said sadly. She sat up on the pillows and tucked her knees up under her chin. Shaking the hair away from her face, she flashed one of her winning smiles. "I suppose it had to end sooner or later."

"Pessimistic little imp, aren't you? Think a minor thing like a war will keep me away forever?" Merrill looked back into the mirror, examining himself. Tight muscles rippled under his embarrassingly white skin; he'd been in overcast England too long. In his military dossier he'd been given high marks for keeping himself in prime physical condition. They'd also passed him with flying colors in his personality profile, rating him as *alert, self-reliant, resourceful, sardonic, and slightly cynical.* Merrill had twice questioned his superiors about the last entry, which he'd heatedly contested. The evaluation remained, along with an added notation, *occasionally argumentative.* Under a category called *General Appearance*, a personal, more flattering notation had been added by his last commanding officer: *A lean, six-foot-two, rangy character with brown wavy hair, a strong chin, and clean-cut handsome face, Skeet Merrill has the look of a man who ought to have a saddle between his legs. Definitely the kind to get things done.*

Merrill covered his face and neck sparingly with suds from their last bar of Palmolive and splashed water on himself. He felt invigorated now and wide awake. At last they were letting him get back to work. Though the espionage business consumed him completely and the pay was excellent, for the past month things had been quiet, too quiet for a man of his stamp and know-how. Lacking an immediate challenging assignment, he'd even asked to be transferred back to line duty on a submarine. Merrill had been refused by SHAEF Command, assured once more that something eventful was in the wind. He thought again about the past, his battles in the South Pacific. He'd been drawn to the brine, though not blindly, like some men. Merrill simply took fierce pride in his submarine service background and the twin dolphins on his Navy jacket. He longed to be back in command of a pigboat again, more than he was willing to admit.

Merrill finished rinsing his face and groped for a towel. Anxious to help, Molly leaped from the bed and found it for him. She pushed it into his hands, at the same time pressing herself against the back of his nude body and running her fingers through his thick hair. Merrill briskly dried his face, and tried to reach into a nearby wardrobe cabinet for a clean shirt, but Molly's hands were moving, swiftly and lightly, down his neck, across his back. Her fingers finally came to rest on each side of his muscular hips, and he felt the sensual curves of her body lean into him.

"No time," he said, hating the words. He found the shirt and hastily slipped into it. "Have to run."

Molly looked at her Yank naval lieutenant curiously. Skeet Merrill not only looked like a cowboy, he often talked like one. She watched him lay out a pair of civilian pants. "Urgent business, I suppose, Skeet?"

"Very."

"You're tight-lipped, as usual. This time it's the real thing?"

Merrill nodded hypnotically as he buttoned his pants.

Molly was glad he'd chosen civilian clothing. As long as he

left his officer's uniform in her closet there was a good chance he'd return quickly enough. Molly knew she had a bit of a war hero on her hands; the row after row of ribbons across Skeet Merrill's dress blues told her that. When he'd been close-mouthed about them to the point of rudeness, her curiosity had driven her to the library. The ribbons, she discovered, were more than good conduct, theater of operation participations, and sharpshooter medals. Most significant were the Distinguished Unit Medal, the Navy Cross, one star, and the Distinguished Service Medal, two stars.

In her WRNS warrant officer position at Admiralty Operations she'd come to know a great deal about certain naval officers, British and American, more so than Most Secret Security would permit her to divulge, even to Skeet Merrill. Often she'd listened in amusement to his various cover stories, patiently nodding but all the time knowing the reason for the sham. Perhaps that was one of the reasons they'd gotten it on so well—her patience and understanding of Skeet's need to come and go, and his closed, super-secret manner.

"Let me help," she said soothingly. "Why I put up with a clumsy lout like you is beyond me." Her hands moved expertly up the front of his shirt, securing each button. Her fingers hesitated at the top collar snap as she frowned slightly, tilting her head like a considering cockatoo. "How old are you, Skeet? I mean *really*."

Merrill ignored her, moving to the wardrobe and retrieving his wallet.

Molly went back to the bed, sat restively, then sprawled, bare bottom up, across the rumpled sheets. "We lie around up here, God knows, making war babies, and I haven't the foggiest how old you are, where you were born, or where you went to school. Nor do I know who might be waiting for you back in the States. Fair's fair, love." She shot Merrill an anxious look.

"Thirty-four. General Hospital, Albuquerque, New Mexico. Graduate of the University of Texas. And I'm not married, as I've told you a half dozen times before. Divorced before the war started."

A likely bit of bumpf, Molly thought, knitting her eyebrows.

"Ended the affair back in Galveston," Merrill added as an afterthought.

"Where's Galveston?"

"Down south, on the Gulf," he mumbled with a bored look.

Molly could believe everything thus far, but now she waited for the mistruths. It was a short wait.

"I have to go down to Southampton temporarily. Fleet business."

"Will it be a matter of days? A week, or a fortnight?"

Merrill shrugged. "Who knows? Don't count on anything, Molly." Winking, he sat on the bed beside her and groped under it for his shoes. "Let's leave it at that and both be surprised. It's a rotten, unpredictable war."

In the tactile silence that followed, Molly slid out of bed in a smooth, snakelike motion, picked up her underpants from the floor, and climbed into them. She turned off the overhead lamp, then glided across the room to the bay window and pulled back the blackout curtain. Moodily, she gazed out into the blackness of the London night. Somewhere off in the distance a hickboo siren began its mournful wail. Closer sirens took up the air raid alarm until the neighboring canines joined in with a depressing chorus of their own.

"You don't look over thirty," she said, idly, withdrawing from the window and securing the blind.

Merrill laughed, pleased with the compliment. He looked at her in the darkness. "You'd better get that ducky ass of yours down to the shelter. I've got to run."

Molly turned the light back on. "You forgot something." She picked up his harmonica from the table and brought it to him. "I've never seen you go anywhere without this."

He smiled and pocketed the shiny silver instrument.

She hunched her shoulders. "Do you love me, Skeet?"

"I said so, didn't I?"

"But war small talk is one thing. For the duration, and all that tommyrot." She smiled at him and started to sing:

"There was a fair maiden the sailor adored
    Who he left all alone on the moor
And all she could find to ease her sad mind
    Was to go to the lighthouse door, oh,
And wait all alone by the shore."

Hesitating, she gave up a shrug. "It must be ancient. A jolly old fisherwoman in St. Ives used to sing it to me when I was a

child. I'll never forget the hair on her chin and nose. Want to
hear the rest, love?"

Merrill grinned. "Definitely, but save it for later, okay?"

She felt disappointed. "All right, I will. Please be careful,
Skeet."

Merrill grabbed his overcoat and hesitated in the doorway.
He saw Molly once more in the reflection of the wardrobe
mirror, sitting on the edge of the bed, very alone, and
undeniably *boing-boing*. She also looked a little afraid. Molly
Tremayne's naïveté was genuine; she was innocence without
the simpers, yet she also had an independent, self-reliant streak
he found fascinating. Merrill bit down on his lip. He wanted to
talk, to make love to her again, but there wasn't time.

The real passions in Merrill's life were simple enough:
submarines, football, women, and on Sunday mornings, Joe
Palooka and Dick Tracy. College football seemed light years
away now, and as for women, he'd already warned Molly that
if it came to deciding between staying with her in England or
being reassigned to a pigboat, she'd come out the loser. At
least until the war was wrapped. Merrill had one more passion:
good sourmash. But like most Yanks stationed in England he'd
managed to acquire a taste for twelve-year-old Scotch when
ever he could find the prized stuff.

"Smile, kitten," he whispered, finally. "You're beautiful
and I'll miss you."

Molly hastened over to the door and he kissed her again,
passionately. Brushing the hair back from her face, Merrill
gently cuffed her under the chin, winked, then abruptly turned
and ran down the flight of stairs that led him out into the
London night.

Merrill looked briefly skyward then quickened his pace. No
planes, no sweep of searchlights, no anti-aircraft fire. But then
he heard the familiar, unwelcome buzzing sound. Zzzzzzzz.
Coming closer and closer. Zzzzzzzz. An air raid warden
stopped Merrill and flashed a blue torch quickly over his street
permit. Zzzzzzzz. Neither of them spoke, their attention
riveted to the ominous sound overhead. The grim-faced
warden waved him on.

Suddenly the buzzing cut out. Merrill pressed into the
pathetic cover of a shop doorway, waiting out the few seconds
of terrifying, apprehensive silence before the explosion. It hit

two blocks away, a sickening, reverberating blast that pained his ears and made the street beneath him tremble. Merrill hurried on, knowing that in just five minutes another V-1 would come over slightly to the left or to the right of the first, the pattern not complete until five of the buzz bombs had played havoc in the area. Then the Germans would change the pattern to another part of the city.

Merrill knew better than to look for a taxi. He'd have to hike to his designated rendezvous at a strange address off Grosvenor Square. A fire pumping rig, followed by a jeep bearing white-helmeted rescue workers, roared past and turned up a side road just behind him. Merrill started across the deserted street.

Suddenly, from a parked vehicle less than a block away, the blinding glare of headlights focused on him. *Fool*, Merrill flashed. How could the driver have forgotten the blackout? Before Merrill could shout, the vehicle accelerated rapidly. He heard the squeal of tires fighting the pavement for traction as it headed toward him at full speed, the headlights bearing down on him like long white lances.

Merrill stared in disbelief, his breath catching in his throat. He hurtled over the cobbles and up onto the sidewalk, but the headlights swerved, following him. Merrill cursed and lunged into a shop doorway. The vehicle—a Wolseley saloon—roared past, just missing him by inches. It careened back to the street and screeched to a halt at the corner. The driver reversed gears, turned around, and came at him again, but this time Merril had plenty of time to retreat farther back into a shop alcove.

The Wolseley didn't try again, instead disappearing around the corner.

Confused and angry, Merrill clenched his teeth and leaned against the storefront. He slowly shook his head and wiped the film of sweat from his face. *What the hell?* His heart pounded so heavily his chest hurt.

Once again the street was strangely quiet.

Merrill listened to the unsettling silence for a full minute, then he heard again the ominous sound from the sky.

Zzzzzzzz. Zzzzzzzz. Zzzzzzzzz.

Chapter 4

As long as the buzz bombs were active in another part of London, the Prime Minister was determined to get on with business rather than sit it out in a damp cellar. At the moment Churchill was dining by himself and listening to a replay of a radio program. Curiosity alone drove him to listen to the censor-approved broadcasts of Edward R. Murrow of CBS and Fred Bates for NBC. The PM was interested not only in the content of the news commentaries, but in their emotional tone and any possible hyperbole. If the American public was either given the facts or bamboozled, Churchill was determined to know about it immediately, not later. Churchill knew that Congress, President Roosevelt, and his Cabinet were all highly motivated political animals who listened carefully to the folks at home; the American public, in turn, listened to their news correspondents in London.

When Murrow's program concluded, Churchill turned off the wire recorder and turned back to the lean lamb chop that had grown cold on his plate. He was eating alone, for his wife had gone out to attend a War Orphan's Benefit at the Savoy Hotel. A servant entered the dining room and replenished Churchill's wine glass.

Churchill waggled a finger. "Wrap up that recording and put it in my briefcase. I'll take it with me when I visit Eisenhower."

"Sir, will you have some rice pudding for dessert? Or strawberries, perhaps? We've a little fresh cream today."

"No. My mind isn't on food tonight. Bring in the telephone, please."

The waiter obliged. A minute later the switchboard made the connection with a non-governmental number Churchill had read from a pocketed scrap of paper. Churchill sipped his wine while waiting for the ring to pick up at the other end of the line. Finally he heard a familiar voice. "Hello?"

"Colonel Foster?"

"Yes, sir."

"We haven't met, but you do recognize my voice, of course?"

"Certainly, Prime Minister, as would any Englishman. But I hardly expected you to ring here directly, sir. Something extraordinary come up?"

Churchill nervously rolled a still-wrapped cigar back and forth on the linen tablecloth. "Second, third thoughts, call them what you will. Our new man on this Operation Storm Tide business. You've had a chance to look him over?"

"No, sir. He's due in tonight. Buzz bomb activity in the neighborhood may have held the American up. We expect him momentarily."

The PM took off his glasses and sharpened his tone. If he couldn't build a bonfire under the entire G-10 Department, he'd at least plant a thorn in the ear of the colonel who ran the show. "The First Sea Lord tells me he has reservations, Foster. I want the facts myself. Have you people covered every conceivable situation that might arise?"

"Front, flank, top, and bottom, sir," came the prompt reply. "Beyond that, it's a matter of operative initiative."

"And improvisation," Churchill added, with a cough. "How can you be sure the feisty Yank will accept our provisions, the woman in charge?"

"He's an officer. Like it or not, he'll follow orders. If not, we'll bloody well find another man."

"Eisenhower and I have already pursued that. There's no other man with his qualifications, Colonel. In either of our shops. You will make this Lieutenant Merrill understand. Flatter him if need be; tell him it takes a fox to catch a fox. Or a hound to catch a lion, if that's more appropriate. But remember, the *reason* for the woman being in command must remain proprietary. That is a matter between you, the First Sea Lord, and myself only. Agreed?"

"Yes, Prime Minister."

Churchill lowered his voice. "The U-boat facilities in

Brittany must be crippled, but the *other element* is of even
greater importance; the fate of our invasion fleet—the entire
damned armada—hangs in the balance. If not the very outcome
of the war. Are you with me, Colonel?"

"Yes, sir. I'm listening."

"And as for the matter of Dieter Loewen—the importance of
this part of the mission as well is beyond superlatives. Foster, I
must remind you to instill in your operatives the staggering
facts. This one German officer has been directly responsible for
the loss of thirty-seven ships—over 250,000 tons of Allied
shipping sent to the bottom. And now that demented Pharaoh
in Berlin is about to honor this U-boat ace again. The Iron
Cross with Oak Leaves and Crossed Silver Swords, apparently,
isn't good enough for the blighter. My arch-foe Hitler intends
to do him one better; a Diamond Cluster!" Churchill paused to
take a sip of wine, then snorted angrily. "The Fuehrer and his
infamous heroes—Lion of the Atlantic—bah! We've had
enough of this demigod U-boat ace. Quite enough of Kapitan
Loewen. Do we understand each other, Colonel?"

"Perfectly Sir. Admiral Ramsey has already reminded me
that you are particularly concerned on that point."

"*Adamant* is the word. Adamant and angry, Foster. Good
night and good luck."

Foster glanced nervously across the room at her. Sigi
Petersen was an island of serenity as she continued filing her
nails, waiting for him to ring off the line. Finally ending his
cryptic conversation with Churchill, Foster hung up the phone,
folded his hands before him on the replica Louis Quatorze
desk, and exhaled sharply. The hotel room that served as his
temporary office fell into an awkward silence as he tugged on
his copious moustache and thought for a moment. Glancing
impatiently at his watch, Foster edged back in his chair, trying
to avoid the intoxicating perfume that repeatedly assaulted his
senses.

Foster liked a tidy, well-organized desk. Even in this
improvised facility he had brought along his wife's photograph, a tin box for tobacco, a polished walnut mail tray, and
the brass nameplate that had been given to him as a gift at his
last promotion. Foster picked up the nameplate, polished it

with his sleeve, and examined his moustache in its glistening surface.

Colonel Stuart Foster, Royal Marines, ostensibly adjutant to a key officer at Admiralty Operations, but in fact the head of British Special Services, was distinguished looking enough for his late forties. He had graying temples, a jutting battleship chin, and a well-groomed, but a trifle bushy moustache. Beneath Foster's thick eyebrows, intense brown eyes probed constantly when he spoke, for he was clearly the sort of individual who understood the why of things. He understood the personal why, the military why, and the political why of every facet of his profession, and he understood that they were all different and often contradictory. Foster's business at Section G-10 was espionage and it consumed him. Not being ambitious and having no hopes or illusions beyond running his own department, he worked with a nervous efficiency, and because he never promised the First Sea Lord or the PM more than he could perform, his efforts gave satisfaction. Foster spoke his mind, took his orders, gave orders in return, accomplished some of the greatest spy coups of the war, collected his pay, and finally—whenever he could manage a few hours of sleep, slept reasonably well.

Although it was just past nine-thirty in the evening, Foster suspected he had many hours ahead of him before he'd catch any sleep on this particular night. Shuffling through the documents on his desk, he felt another warm wave of the attractive blonde's perfume sweep over him. He looked up and their eyes locked again. Foster couldn't help wondering how many men had been devastated, held helpless and captive by her sweet sexual thrall. Stiffening in his chair, he said slowly, "I can offer you anything, Miss Petersen. Highly qualified assistants, all the francs and reichsmarks in the world, the most sophisticated radio equipment, and the best contacts on the Continent. I can supply you with everything but *time*. Not nearly enough of that. Unfortunately, the ——"

"Call me Sigi, Colonel," she interrupted. Again, the provocative smile, the flashing eyes. "Anything, you say? Find a way to slip me into France *other* than by parachuting."

"Sticky business, that," Foster grunted, reaching for his briar and sniffing its capacious bowl. Avoiding her eyes, he proceeded to fill it from his tin box. "Mind if I smoke?"

"Not at all." Sigi dropped her emery board and withdrew one of her own Players cigarettes.

Smiling, Foster struck a match, lit her cigarette, then skillfully consumed what remained of the flame in his pipe. Once more he studied her at length. Sigi's eyes focused back on him as if to yank out by the roots the thoughts behind his inquiring stare. Foster quickly shifted his gaze away. Their meeting had thus far convinced him that Sigi Petersen had both sex and intelligence and she readily turned them on and off at will. She was a trifle too hard, a bit cool for his taste, but for purposes of the mission she was perfect. Sigi had an unquestionably good figure, a dramatic voice, long golden hair, and very intense eyes. *The eyes*, Foster reflected; it had to be the glacial blue eyes that made her opponents squirm. And certainly, considering the male society Sigi moved in, their focus contained an edge of worldly perceptiveness.

Foster was certain now he'd made a splendid choice. Indeed, it was because of this combination of intelligence, conspicuous Teutonic visage, and a marked proficiency in the enemy language, that Sigi would be sent to infiltrate the German camp. It was a challenging assignment, one Foster suspected would be fraught with peril of the worst kind; but this headstrong Norwegian woman had a reputation for being one of the cleverest agents in the Allied cause. Foster alternated his silent gaze between Sigi and the antique clock on the wall. Where was the other half of the team, the American? The clock ticked monotonously on, the pendulum behind its closed glass no longer distracting, but offering relief.

Sigi lifted her chin and took a long, theatrical drag on her cigarette. "Tell me, Colonel. I'm curious as a Cheshire cat. What's Lieutenant Merrill really like?"

"Good looking chap. Knows his business."

She frowned. "I'm familiar with his appearance. We met at an Embassy reception, though only briefly. I was referring to his *personality* profile."

Foster grinned. He suspected assaulting men's senses at parties was routine for Sigi Petersen. "Skeet Merrill's quite the ladies' man, I hear."

Her eyes were vacant as she coolly replied, "I honestly don't remember."

"Merrill's a trifle on the stubborn side; that should give your Nordic temperament a run for its money. At times he can be arrogant, but he has his soft spots. You'll have to find them. Most important, Merrill's all genius with explosives and knows submarines like the back of his hand; he speaks only fractured French, but you'll find his German is flawless." Foster watched Sigi's face carefully. It was obvious that she smelled a clever rival. Her eyes were wary.

"How well does he take and follow instructions?" she asked.

Foster shrugged. "Testy, testy, my dear. We'll both find out soon enough, won't we?"

Sigi stared at him, waiting for an amplification, but Foster retreated into silence. Curiosity, apparently, continued to clutch at her, for she asked, "Is that all you have to tell me?" Her wool skirt slid up as she crossed her legs. "Supposing, Colonel, Lieutenant Merrill doesn't approve of my methods?"

"You'll make a splendid team," Foster retorted, with an air of finality. He smiled at her. Foster knew that here was a woman who was instinctively aware of her own dramatic effects, for she didn't press him, instead pulling her skirt back over her knees and calmly picking up several documents from the desk. Ignoring him, she buried herself in the papers and began to read.

Foster waggled a finger menacingly. "You'll destroy those in the fireplace, of course, when finished. Preferably before our American friend arrives. I repeat, that information is for your eyes only, and not for Merrill." He watched her finish reading the documents, then rise and float with infinite grace to the small metal fireplace at the opposite end of the room.

Sigi said nothing to reveal her thoughts as she set the papers afire with a cigarette lighter. After idly watching the flames for several seconds, she took the fire iron and poked at the gray ashes until they crumbled to unrecoverable fragments of dust.

The V-weapon blast had been close, too close. Skeet Merrill couldn't remember how long he'd sat on the curb, his tortured head feeling like bedrock was being drilled inside it. The street he'd just passed through was a scene from the *Book of the Damned*. From somewhere in the distance he heard a woman screaming in pain. Grim-faced rescue workers were converging on the rubble and he was in the way. Merrill unwound for a moment longer, then unsteadily climbed to his feet, retightened his nerves, and proceeded up the street. German buzz bombs were bad enough, he thought, but what rankled him more was the vehicle out to do him in. Someone in England wanted him dead, at least incapacitated. Why?

Six blocks later he approached the Heathcliffe Hotel, instinctively slowing his pace and turning to see if he had been followed. The street was deserted. He strolled quickly up to the sandbagged entrance, flung aside the blackout curtain, and opened the door. Inside, a British army sergeant was slouched at a sidebench reading the Daily Express while the night clerk, a frail old man, swept up the remains of a shattered chandelier. The clerk, still rattled by the closeness of the V-1 explosion, looked up anxiously at Merrill, but continued to sweep at the broken glass as if in a trance.

"You have a single room with a bath close by?"

Before the distressed hotel clerk could answer, the sergeant was at Merrill's side. "You're bloody late, Lieutenant, sir. And you won't be needin' a room. The Colonel won't be keeping you here long." He offered his hand. "I'm Sergeant Hugh Cummings, sir. You'll be seeing me along on the mission."

A match for Merrill in height, Hugh Cummings was a redhaired Scot with a broad, imposing face made even more so by tufted sideburns running down his cheeks. Merrill looked at Cummings askance, considering his casual, unmilitary manner. It suddenly dawned on Merrill that he was out of his Naval officer's uniform and didn't deserve a salute. Still eyeing the sergeant suspiciously, Merrill extended his hand.

Cummings shook it, smiled, and continued in his rich brogue. "Recognized you from a photograph, sir. Come along this way," he said affably, motioning for Merrill to follow him up a narrow flight of stairs. "Och, it's one bad night out there," he said.

"Yeah. Helluva night, considering," Merrill replied, finally smiling in an impersonal way. "The colonel in a good mood?"

"Aye. Hardly prooper if he wasn't, considering the company."

"How's that?"

Cummings grinned. "Not up to me to spoil the surprise, sir."

The second floor hallway was dim. Several electrified sconces, with short mock candles and red parchment shades, glowed at half their normal intensity. Fallen ceiling plaster littered the carpet. At the end of the corridor Sergeant Cummings halted and nodded to the corporal standing attentively outside Room 12. Cummings inserted a key in the lock, then pushed the door open for Merrill and held it. "I've been asked to wait outside," he said softly. "It's your show now, mon."

Merrill stepped stolidly through the entry and felt the awkward silence of the hotel room envelop him.

"He's here, sir," said Cummings, copping an admiring glance at Sigi Petersen before closing and securing the door behind Merrill.

Standing silent and attentive, Merril's eyes swept around the room.

"Come in, Lieutenant, we've been waiting."

His bid of welcome had not come from the man in khaki behind the Louis Quatorze desk. It was a sensuous, slightly accented voice, and it belonged to a woman leaning against the fireplace; it was a pretty face Merrill recognized from the past. He looked across the room at her, feeling a strange rushing of time against him. The Embassy party—it had been over a year since he'd seen Sigi Petersen. Once more, he liked what he saw. Her hair, plaited in two braids, and piled like a small crown on the top of her head, was the color of moist straw; her eyelashes too, were very light. Her lips were full and sensuous, just as Merrill remembered them. There was no sign of her appearing older; she was severely and cunningly as pretty as before and aware of it. Their eyes held and instantly he knew she was sizing him up. He smiled without embarrassment and she finally dropped her stare.

Merrill had never worked with Sigi Petersen, but he knew of her reputation. The word was out that she was hard as a diamond, practical from head to heel and mistress of every form of coercion necessary to the gaining of her own and G-10 needs. From across the room Merrill's sensitive nose caught the fragrance of her light but musky perfume.

Sigi came forward and extended her hand gracefully. "We meet again. You're looking good, Lieutenant Merrill. The European battle hasn't left any visible scars on the Pacific war hero, I see." Her slightly accented voice had an almost melodic quality.

A trifle theatrical, he thought, suffering her a broad, cowboy grin. "After three years of war, Miss Petersen, the name of the game is not to look good but merely to stay in the saddle."

Merrill smiled and turned to the equally familiar face behind the desk. Stuart Foster immediately extended his hand. "Welcome aboard, Lieutenant. Beastly bit out there from the Jerries. Trust they didn't find you too close by. Seems everyone else in London is down in the undergrounds—nearly 400 thousand sheltered there last night, I hear."

"They struck close enough," Merrill replied impatiently, eager to get beyond the platitudes. "Not the buzz bombs making life risky for me, Colonel. Bad driving on someone's part almost put me away for keeps."

Foster shot him a quizzical look.

Merrill held his gaze. "Appears that I'm on a hit list."

"You'd better tell me about it."

"I will. After I find out precisely what's on your agenda."

The colonel smiled in gold-toothed effusion, shoved his briar back into his jacket pocket, and pointed to a pair of wingbacked chairs facing his desk. "Make yourselves comfortable, please."

"I assume you plan to have us work together on an assignment?" Merrill asked bluntly, trying to decide whether to be taken aback or pleasantly surprised by the presence of Sigi Petersen. Always before he'd been a self-reliant, one man show, free of encumbrances that slowed him down. Now, suddenly thrust before him without warning, calmly sitting there, smiling and filing her nails, was a female encumbrance.

Foster seemed to be reading his mind. "She's prepared, Merrill. Exceptionally well-trained."

"Sorry, sir," he replied stoutly. "Maybe my instinct rebels against partners. I've learned that when the danger is highest, all the sharpened reflexes and intellect, all the preparations and training in the world count for nothing. It's pure *instinct* that counts when there's no time for rational intellectual thought. Or team decisions."

Sigi looked up in annoyance. "Your vaulting pride doesn't become you, Lieutenant."

Ignoring them both, Foster sat down, blew some tobacco off a piece of blue paper and pencilled a note on its margin. It was a copy of a decoded radio transmission—Merrill recognized the secret format. Pushing the communiqué aside, Foster looked up at him sharply. "You seem to have a bee in your bonnet tonight, Lieutenant."

Merrill looked away from Foster, turning to Sigi Petersen. She bore a slight frown and her eyes, for a change, were vague and distant. Merrill tried laughing, but the contrived effort only increased the perceptible chill in the room.

Colonel Foster leaned forward. "File the sexist nonsense away, Merrill. You're too astute for that. Sigi wasn't picked by plucking straws. In fact she's one of the most qualified operatives in Europe—male or female. Forget personal preferences. This one's a team effort. Your special handles make you the only suitable partner to assist her. You proved your capability to me on Chariot."

Sigi looked at Foster quizzically, exhaling a long column of smoke through her nose. The ashtray she held in her hand was filled with lipstick-stained butts from half a dozen Players cigarettes.

"Sorry, Sigi," Foster offered. "Neglected to tell you our American friend was with us on a 1942 commando raid we sent to France. Mission called Operation Chariot. Lieutenant Merrill, like yourself, wasn't picked at random for this assignment; he picked up a British medal for that one."

Merrill shook his head. He tried for a cheery grin, but all he managed was a wince. He had his own ideas about that former mission. "Facts were, Colonel, I damn near had my ass shot off. If ever a one-way ticket was dreamed up by the Admiralty, blowing up the drydock at St. Nazaire was it."

"Tommyrot!" snapped Foster. "You made it out, didn't you?" He shoved his pipe back in his mouth and sucked it deeply. "Caught the blighters completely unaware. Beautiful operation, both in concept and execution. And unprecedented valor, I might add, on your part."

Merrill disagreed. He'd been lucky, damned lucky. Whatever, he wasn't about to press the point now; Stuart Foster's feelings were obviously bruised. "So much for Chariot, Colonel. You didn't hustle me up here top secret to swap commando stories. What's cooking now?"

"You're going back to St. Nazaire."

Chapter 5

ADOLF HITLER HAD a passion for large vaulted rooms with plush carpets and tapestries. The great hall at the Berghof, with its sense of space and magnificent mountain views of the Bavarian Alps, particularly pleased him. It was well after eleven and the evening meal long past, but still the Fuehrer sat beside the big fireplace surrounded by several of his guests. Eva Braun relaxed at Hitler's immediate left, while his Alsatian Blondi, the only one in the room daring to nod off, lay curled at his feet. The conversation had once more lapsed into one of Hitler's tiresome monologues.

An aide entered the room with a tray of peppermint tea. The Fuehrer, his secretary Fraulein Schroeder, and SS Reichs-fuehrer Himmler were the only ones to imbibe. Hitler pushed the dog off his wool-lined slippers, rose to his feet, and took his cup over to the window. Staring out into the star-studded, peaceful night, his voice droned on, continuing his lecture.

"It is a matter of manipulating statistics. For five months our enemies have been claiming to have won the Battle of the Atlantic, but they are wrong. Yes, miserably wrong." Hitler turned, gazing across the room at his assistant Martin Bor-mann, whose advice seldom displeased him. "Tell me, Herr Reichsleiter. Our operatives report the number of ships is staggering. The largest fleet the world has ever assembled. Will this armada come at Calais or Normandy?"

Bormann stiffened. "Your military·intelligence staff is still divided, my Fuehrer, but I favor your own intuition. The main thrust at Pas de Calais."

Hitler nodded sagely and looked around the chamber.

Observing that Heinrich Himmler had visibly flinched and pursed his thin, colorless mouth, Hitler snapped: "The SS Reichsfuehrer apparently disagrees?"

Himmler remained tight-lipped in deference to Bormann.

Hitler frowned and continued: "*Intuition*, our friend Bormann claims. Indeed, a good leader never has enough of it. I could use a measure more. That sot Churchill is predictable enough, but I still can't read Eisenhower's mind or that annoying, expressionless face."

"We shouldn't underestimate the English and their influence on the mindless Americans, my Fuehrer," Himmler said quietly. "Churchill's years of naval leadership experience will always be a bone in the throat of our Kriegsmarine. The man has a peculiar streak of luck running for him."

Grimacing, Hitler interjected, "Again you are the lecturing schoolmaster, Himmler. Still, I'm intrigued. Proceed."

"In the Orkneys one of our U-boats fired three torpedos at the battleship *Nelson* while Mr. Churchill was on board. All three torpedos failed to explode."

Martin Bormann added with a smile, "And despite the Luftwaffe's efforts to level the vicinity of Downing Street, the Prime Minister's reputed to sit out the blitz without retiring to the shelters. The man has the arrogance to claim he's gifted by providence."

Hitler sipped his tea and shuffled his feet. "He wasn't so lucky at Gallipoli."

Frau Schroeder shrugged. "That was another war, my Fuehrer."

Hitler scowled. "All gamblers have good and bad streaks of luck." His voice raised several decibels. "I say the Jew-lover merely plays the odds!"

The room fell silent. Hitler went back over to sit by Eva Braun; he gently placed a hand on her wrist. "Soon, Eva. I will introduce you to a man who is truly gifted by providence."

She looked up at Hitler curiously, but suppliant as ever, kept her silence.

The Fuehrer continued: "When we return to Berlin we will honor the Fatherland's number one military hero—a man whose exploits surpass even those of Baron von Richthofen."

Martin Bormann's wife, always the most talkative of the women present, glanced up. "Already, the children are collecting the U-boat ace's pictures as though he were a national folk hero."

Hitler laid his head back on the chair and closed his eyes. "Good. Excellent. We'll do his Iron Cross with Oak Leaves and Silver Swords one better. Diamond inlays!"

Shrugging, Heinrich Himmler began polishing his eyeglasses. "I beg to remind you, my Fuehrer, that Kapitan Leutnant Loewen has still not joined the Party."

Hitler opened his eyes. "Yes, I know. Older dogs don't take easily to housebreaking. I will work on that."

An SS aide slipped quietly into the room, handed Heinrich Himmler a priority communiqué, and departed. Himmler stared at the message though his steel-rimmed glasses, frowned, and promptly passed it on to Hitler, who examined it with an annoyed look.

His face reddening with displeasure, the Fuehrer rose to his feet. There was a silent pause, the momentary eerie silence before an avalanche. He beckoned to Martin Bormann, who immediately came to attention. At Hitler's feet, the dog too, had become suddenly alert.

"Bormann, get a message off to OKW in Berlin. Have Grand Admiral Doenitz join me here at the Berghof as quickly as possible." Hitler turned to the others, trying to suppress his mounting rage. "Continue, if you wish. There are critical matters I must attend with Himmler." Cursing Winston Churchill in monosyllables, Hitler strode briskly out of the room, Heinrich Himmler and the dog Blondi scurrying after him.

Skeet Merrill groaned. *St. Nazaire again.* Colonel Foster's stony words had burned him like the hot lead from a ricochet. He watched, dumbfounded, as the Englishman withdrew a creased map from his briefcase and carefully unfolded it on the desk.

Merrill couldn't resist another parry. "Pardon the prairie-talk, Colonel, but I'll be a snake-eyed sonofabitch. Need I remind you that Chariot was itself a daring repeat of Zeebrugge in the First World War?" Merrill had spat out the words. "Pressing our luck for a *third* surprise is asking too damned much of Nazi incompetence! You can't be serious about another expedition to Brittany."

Foster nodded, glaring back at him. "The Germans are hardly incompetent, Lieutenant, and mind you, neither are we." He picked up a pencil and drew several bold arrows on the map in the vicinity of the English Channel. All the symbols pointed to France and Belgium. "D-Day, we've tagged it. The invasion of *Festung Europa*," he said, tapping his pencil. "The greatest armada the world has known and let's pray it will be the last one. Over four thousand ships. The Jerries would give up their pure Aryan blood to know just where we plan to strike. Deucedly so, the exact time. I can't give you the date and hour now, but let's say the departure is imminent."

Merrill was still thinking about the hell some eighteen months back that had been St. Nazaire. Flippantly, he asked, "My draft board okay this operation?"

Foster showed no sign of being amused. "Your orders were cut at SHAEF. All the thunder and lightning may be coming from the PM, but Ike's handling the strategics."

Warmed that a fellow American was pulling the strings, Merrill's eyebrows wavered. Until now he'd felt like an interloper on a foreign soccer team. Even the Colonel's pronunciation of *leftenant* for lieutenant had begun to grate. "What's my assignment?" he asked quietly.

"Simple enough for an operative with your expertise. You're familiar with St. Nazaire, you speak fluent enough German. Most important, you have a handle on explosives and know submarines." Foster hesitated, then added: "You blow up the underground sub base at St. Nazaire and bring Germany's top U-boat ace, Dieter Loewen, back to England."

Skeet Merrill's heart skipped a beat. He suddenly felt smaller than his six-foot-two. *Loewen!* The all-too familiar name had struck him like a well-aimed torpedo. The infamous Lion of the Atlantic! There wasn't a seaman in the world who wasn't awed by the infamous German's reputation. And the fortress-like U-boat pen. Merrill looked at Foster askance. "Jesus Christ almighty, Colonel. You said simple? What's the RAF been doing, sitting on its ass for the last six months?"

"The concrete roof is 16 feet thick. Lord knows we've tried to penetrate it. Blockbusters aren't big enough."

Merrill's curiosity consumed him. "Why the hullaballoo over what's left of the pigboats? Now, on the eve of the big push?"

"Improved anti-U-boat measures withstanding, you're a sub

man, Lieutenant. Snorkels; the flank of the D-Day fleet; a suicidal German high command. Need I go on?''

Merrill slumped back into the wingback chair, stared at Foster's implacable eyes, then rolled his focus to the alluring woman perched on one corner of the desk. Staring at the map of Europe, she'd been quiet for a long time, letting Foster draw him out. Or was she daydreaming? Merrill's eyes narrowed in judgment, taking her in slowly as she restlessly crossed her legs. The gently rounded curves seemed to slither together prophetically under her green skirt as she looked up at him. A contradictory, but cozy assignment, Merrill thought. His eyes darted back to Foster. "And *her flank*, Colonel? What's the charming lady got to do with this proposed cliff-hanger? Why Sigi Petersen? And tell me more about this enemy hero we're supposed to Shanghai as easily as a drunken Chinaman.''

Sigi looked up, spared Merrill a brief glance of bored disapproval, then put out her cigarette and strolled over to the mirror by the fireplace.

Merrill watched her swing across the room. She was letting him know that it was definitely a take-a-hold-of-me bottom.

Sigi glanced in the mirror and read his thoughts. She withdrew a tube of lipstick from her pocket and looked at him sharply. "You just might try cocking your ears instead of your Colt, cowboy." Her tone was cold, not at all like the red lipstick she applied to accent the contour of her full, round lips.

"Yes, the details," intervened Foster, refolding the map before him. "The PM is livid over these new V-weapons. They have no strategic effectiveness beyond demoralizing and undermining the national resolve. Fortunately, that madman on the other side of the channel underestimates British fiber. The question posed by Downing Street—and it's a reasonable one in my book—is what countermeasure, beyond routinely bombing Berlin and other cities, can we employ against the German civilian population? Psychological warfare, mind you." Foster pointed his pipe at Merrill, then swung it over to Sigi.

Merrill waited expectantly. Sigi again appeared to have slipped into some private reverie. She asked, this time in a soft voice, "The word *civilian* still has a meaning in war?"

Circumspectly ignoring her, Foster continued, "Despite Dr. Goebbels' efforts to anaesthetize the population, most Germans place less faith in their foot soldiers than you might expect, for their supposedly invincible field armies and Panzer

Corps have let them down too many times. But they do believe—like the Fuehrer—in the superiority of Third Reich technology: rockets, advanced jet airplanes, and the new submarines on the shipways. The pesky U-boats, that's where the two of you come in. Our French operatives have tried to destroy them and failed. Now then, here's the new approach. Germans can move in and out of the pens without being searched. Our Norwegian maiden here not only looks German, but like you, Merrill, speaks it with perfection. She also, undeniably, has other assets that may prove an effective distraction.''

Merrill kept silent. He turned from Foster and watched Sigi's unfriendly eyes in the mirror; they were still as cold as slivers of ice.

Foster continued: "The Fuehrer and Dr. Goebbels have a penchant for publicizing national military heroes, particularly pilots and U-boat aces. Propaganda to stimulate the home front—or what is left of it. The Prime Minister wants G-10 to strike a blow at the very nerve center of this morale machinery. There is *only one* U-boat ace remaining. *The Lion.* That puffmonger Goebbels knows this and is making Dieter Loewen out to be a folk legend! The Kapitan is also a favorite of the Fuehrer.''

"That's a ton of weight to put on my shoulders," grumbled Merrill. "I suddenly feel cold and lonely.''

Sigi turned away from the fireplace. Eyes thawing, she smiled seductively at Merrill. "I'll try to keep your toes warm, Lieutenant. And share part of that load.''

Merrill smiled back at her. He liked her stance; it reminded him of a pose he'd seen in a Tallulah Bankhead movie. He couldn't remember which one.

The colonel scowled and relit the pipe. "Destroy their snorkel refit capability. At least pinion the bloody operation for ninety days until we get a foothold on the Continent. And bring Loewen back to England. We've done it before; a German general from Cairo, a colonel from Berlin. Give the mission the old college try. The mission's code name is Operation Storm Tide. You'll have help from the French Resistance, but how you'll get the frogs inside the facility is another matter. I wish you luck with your resourcefulness." Foster gestured toward Sigi. "There, let's trust, is your ducat of admission, Merrill. Her name will be Anna Schramm, ostensibly a journalist working for Goebbels' DNB in Berlin. Charm, Lieutenant, or should we admit to sex appeal?''

Merrill had to work hard to maintain his unruffled, professional mask of detachment, for his real feelings bordered on disbelief and incredulity. Suddenly, his patience broke and he complained, "Expecting a bundle, aren't you? The lion beds down with the lamb only in the parables.''

Ignoring him, Foster patted two large manila envelopes on his desk. "Miss Petersen's documents are flawless, like your own.'' He winked at Merrill. "Sorry, chap. You're obliged to take a cut in rank for this one.''

Merrill flinched for what seemed the umpteenth time. He waited for Foster's explanation.

"You'll be a Wehrmacht photographer assigned to assist journalist Schramm. Your name will be *Schmidt*. Sergeant Burger Schmidt.''

"What makes you think I'm a photographer?''

"I've already seen your work. Amateur, but sufficient.''

Merrill shook his head. "Damned resourceful. Who dreamed this masquerade up?''

Sigi smiled enigmatically. "I've a strong feeling we're going to make a splendid team, *Sergeant Schmidt*.''

Merrill watched her kick off her shoes, then perch, a trifle too dramatically, on the corner of Foster's desk. The colonel's eyes sparkled in boyish delight. Merrill steeled himself, ignoring her pose. "Can't say I appreciate the name Schmidt. A trifle pedestrian. As for the sex aspect, the siren's song sounds just a little off key to me.''

Sigi straightened her legs. Her flirtatious manner vanished. "Business is business, Lieutenant, if that's what you prefer. You take care of yours and I'll properly take care of mine.''

Bunk, mused Merrill. Her trite analysis was disgustingly prudent. All Sigi Petersen needed was a steeple bell to put a ring to her sudden respectability. Ignoring her, he turned to Foster. "Chivalry, equality aside, as I see it, Colonel, can a lady spy—and God, I grant you she's beguiling—pull her own oar when the rapids get rough?'' Merrill turned, giving her a quick, appraising look. There was soft contempt, stitched with envy, in his voice as he said, "No offense, Sigi, but I speak from field experience. The action's going to get dirty and tough. As I see it, the mission sounds like a shit hole.''

Her face flushed, not from embarrassment, but resentment. "God, but you're an egotistical bastard, Lieutenant Merrill. Kindly remember you're not taking one of your Southern seminary girls on a tour of Pigalle. If you want to ride in my canoe, fine. But I can paddle quite nicely by myself."

Foster intervened. "Please, please. To get on with it. The itinerary. Your mission will begin not in St. Nazaire, but in Paris."

Merrill managed a marginal grin. Paris. This news, at least, put a brighter glow on the operation. Though he'd never been to *La Ville Lumière,* his old man had been there in the first war, and for years, back on his Texas spread after a fourth round of bootleg whiskey, the senior Merrill had slipped into the same verse like a broken record.

> The general got the croix de guerre,
> The son of a bitch, he wasn't there,
> Hinky dinky parlez vous.

"*Lieutenant Merrill?*" Sigi's sharp summons shattered his reverie. "Our quarry will arrive in port tomorrow and head for Paris," she said. "Apparently a rest leave before reporting to Berlin."

Merrill looked at her. "You suddenly know one hell of a lot more about this operation than you've let on. And that canoe of yours will be a damned sight cozier if you call me Skeet."

"She's read this," Foster interjected, tossing a copy of the decoded radio transmission into Merrill's lap. "From our Paris operatives." Foster waited patiently while Merrill examined the message, then added, "Our folk hero is to receive Germany's highest honor. As journalists, you'll interview Loewen and his crewmen inside the U-boat base. Take pictures, perform as skilled propaganda experts would be expected to do under the circumstances. But first, you'll have to get the blighter—who'll probably be behaving like a Wagons-Lits tourist—temporarily back to his home port. And you may not have a good many hours before the Jerries catch on to our ruse. Time is of the essence."

"Anything else?" Merrill asked impatiently.

"The plastic's waiting at Chatham Airfield. If you select dynamite instead, our resistance woman Marie Selva has access to a half ton of it, cached in a barn outside of St. Nazaire."

"Any of the French operatives good at swimming underwater?" asked Merrill.

Foster pointed toward the door. "Sergeant Cummings out there is a skilled diver. He'll parachute into the St. Nazaire area later and meet you."

Sigi asked, "How do we get back, Colonel?"

"Still being arranged," Foster replied impassively. "Sergeant Cummings will set you up with your return contact."

Merrill sought for a throwaway remark but smiled instead. He may not have cared for the mission's prospects, but he was impressed by Foster's thoroughness.

The colonel wasn't finished. "Our people in the costume loft have packed your suitcases. You'll have ample currency in your belts. These envelopes contain the names of your Paris contacts, German identification papers, photographs, and other material to implement your individual cover stories. For God's sake, polish this information; your lives depend on it. Sergeant Cummings will chauffeur both of you to Chatham Airfield tonight."

"Do we go into France by Lysander?" Sigi asked hopefully.

"Sorry. Far too risky. You jump," replied Foster.

Foster studied his charges carefully. He had no qualms about the woman. He looked at Merrill, searching the American's expressionless face once more. Foster's mind as well as his eyes focused on it. Though he'd have preferred to have a fellow Englishman playing first string with Sigi and Sergeant Cummings in the upcoming action, no one in Special Services had come close to matching Skeet Merrill's unique qualifications. Foster had listened to Merrill's contrived cleverness with practiced tolerance, and had been solicitous enough to make the American feel valuable and needed. Having lapsed long enough into silent thought to give weight and importance to everything the Yank had questioned, Foster now leaned forward and made his final thrust, earnestly and quietly.

"Two more things, Lieutenant. There's a reason we've met here in secret instead of in my office at the Admiralty." Foster lowered his eyes and exhaled sharply. "There's evidence that Naval Affairs G-10 has been infiltrated somewhere along the line. Keep your wits about, for you can bet your last guinea if we've got a double-agent on our hands, the bugger's every bit as clever at his job as you are.''

And deadly, reflected Merrill. His mind swung erratically as the brush with death on the London street an hour earlier came back to him. When he could get the head of G-10 alone, he'd pass on the information. But he wouldn't inform or worry Sigi. Not yet. "Is there anything more?" he asked Foster.

The colonel finished relighting his pipe and leaned forward. "Collectively, you both have the experience and the intelligence; I only pray you have enough time and enough luck. My final point: for the duration of this short mission *Fraulein Anna Schramm* is not only ostensibly in charge of the team as far as the Germans are concerned, but from my standpoint, representing Allied Joint Intelligence, she will in fact be in command.''

Thunderstruck, Merrill reared up like a wounded animal. He stared back at Foster, speechless.

The colonel's face was as cold as carved bedrock. "You do understand, Merrill?"

"May I ask why?" his question had come out as a choked whisper.

"You may not. Later, I promise you'll understand."

As much as Merrill wanted back into action, he suddenly felt bewildered and cheated beyond measure. "I'll be damned," he stammered, before his voice locked in his throat and he could say no more. Merrill wanted to protest, to ask the *big why* once more, for in the spy business the why sometimes took the smell from a rotten assignment. But he knew better than to push it. Not now. They wanted the moon but they were handcuffing him and she had the key. Merrill felt like Houdini in a trunk.

His eyes drifted to Sigi. It was obvious she wasn't feeling the least uncomfortable; the Marlene Dietrich half-smile on her face was as near to that of pleasurable anticipation as she could permit herself in the colonel's presence.

All Merrill could do was bite back his disappointment and slowly shake his head.

Chapter 6

IT HAD BEEN a tiring journey from the south of France, partly by train, the rest of the way in the back of a produce truck. Erika Vermeer was exhausted. Her former employer and resistance friend Pierre Roger had at first given Erika a lukewarm welcome back to his Paris bistro, but after she'd explained what had happened at the Izieu orphanage, he'd become agitated and immediately begun making plans for her. Definitely she could make a few centimes by performing again at La Reine Bleue, but more important, Roger had an immediate use for her sensitive fingers—important skills she'd picked up from her locksmith father in Holland. She had only been back in Paris a few hours and already the *patron* had a resistance assignment for her!

But first, she would get a good night's sleep, and that meant the familiar straw mattress in the bistro cellar. Erika didn't mind the dampness; it was the omnipresent silence of the cellar's other resident that had unsettled her during the previous stay. The bistro's deaf-mute custodian, Maurice Duval, made up for his silence by constantly writing notes. Erika grinned in spite of herself as she headed down the rickety staircase. She was determined to explain everything to Duval, fill up one of his notebooks if necessary, tomorrow at breakfast. Tonight she would ignore him, for she desperately needed sleep.

In OKW's underground command bunker in Berlin, the number one man in the Reichskriegsmarine apprehensively gathered up the morning reports. Grand Admiral of the Fleet

Karl Doenitz, who had come up through the ranks as a U-boat commander himself, was a slight man with a full head of gray hair, a sharp nose, and steel blue, inquisitive eyes. Scanning through the incoming data, Doenitz scowled, left the communications room, and stepped briskly down the corridor to his office. He sagged behind his desk and read over each of the teletypes from the U-boat bases in Norway. Then he went over the reports from Brest, Lorient, and St. Nazaire in France. Biting his lip in annoyance, he turned and placed two more ominous little red flags on the Atlantic grid chart above him. The flags were accumulating rapidly, particularly off the coast of France in the Bay of Biscay.

"The problem, *Herr Gross Admiral,* is that your *Unterseeboots* chatter incessantly." The calm, authoritative voice from the doorway belonged to Generaloberst Alfred Jodl, Adolph Hitler's OKW Chief of Staff. "All this uninhibited radio traffic will compromise you, I promise."

"Reichskriegmarine Intelligence concurs with the general," grumbled Doenitz. "But Goering is stubborn. Without reconnaissance from his Luftwaffe, we have no alternatives to radio transmission." Doenitz glanced down at the last of the teletypes and managed a measured smile. "One bright piece of news. Our illustrious sub ace has struck again and successfully eluded his pursuers. An ammunition ship, the *Lion* reports. That alone should make a considerable dent in the Allied supply line."

Jodl ran his palms up and down the broad red stripes on his pants and smiled affably. "Good. The Fuehrer will be pleased."

Doenitz considered. "As will Dr. Goebbels and his propaganda experts. You'll see Kapitan Loewen's face in the morning newspapers again."

The Generaloberst nodded and handed Doenitz a teletype. "The Fuehrer and his top aides have decided to stay on at Berchtesgaden several more days. He requests you join him there immediately, a secret matter of utmost importance. You will arrange for the first available Luftwaffe plane for Bavaria."

Back in England at Chatham Field, the morning was gray and dismally wet. The weather was worsening. Skeet Merrill looked out the window of the sparsely furnished officers' billet and watched the driven rain. The wind had increased to near-gale strength. There was a knock on the door and when he opened it Sigi Petersen stood there, water coursing off her raincoat, her face forlorn.

"The official word," she explained, handing him a communique that officially postponed their departure for twenty-four hours. "Every plane in the south of England is grounded."

Merrill cursed, oblivious to the presence of Sergeant Cummings, who had come up behind Sigi. "What now?" Merrill asked. "We waste the day playing Rummy or Poker?"

Sigi grinned, ignoring his intractability. She replied, "Later, possibly. Right now the sergeant here insists we review our cover stories. One more proficiency test."

Hugh Cummings stepped forward. "Colonel Foster's idea, not mine, lass. Drill and drill again, he insists, until we run out o'time."

Merrill glumly shook his head. "What does he take us for, cretins?"

"War is a series of mistakes," Sigi said calmly. "Avoiding them, Skeet, we've a chance at staying alive." She looked out the window at the rain, sighed, and turned back to study him.

Merrill smiled at her. He had the impression she was a clever tiger pretending to be a kitten.

Softly, she asked, "May I get personal? Like have you learned anything from the war? I mean, other than its usual futility and folly?"

"Yes. Patience."

She mewed again. "The sooner that invasion armada sails, the sooner I'll get home to Norway. And you, Skeet. What does home mean for you?"

"I haven't decided. I'm still working on it."

Hugh Cummings politely coughed. Closing the door, he placed his locked briefcase on the bed, opened it, and looked sharply at Merrill. "Last time through, sir, you did hesitate badly on two questions. And Miss Petersen forgot her mother's birthplace." Cummings sent an admiring glance at Sigi and she smiled back. "Let's begin again," he said authoritatively. "Your bloody lives depend on the correct answers."

* * *

Minding a fishing hand-line at the end of St. Nazaire's avant-port jetty, the little Frenchwoman waited patiently. Marie Selva seldom fished, for there simply wasn't enough time in her day. The undertaking parlor had been a husband and wife operation, and since her mate's passing, she'd carried the load herself with only what part-time help was available. Most of the able-bodied men in St. Nazaire were working for the Germans in the shipyards or out in the fields.

While making a pretense of fishing for the past two hours the French widow had caught nothing. Nor had she observed any U-boat movement across the bay.

Merge into your background, Madame! Conduct yourself like a very clever insect. These and similar exhortations from the espionage master-minds in London were etched on Marie's brain. But the most believable and comfortable background was the green tile-lined embalming chamber at the rear of her funeral parlor just off Rue d'Anjou. French Resistance operative or not, Marie was definitely a creature of habit. Despite her mannered dress and obsession with cleanliness, Marie was a nervous woman and suspected she carried with her the faint scent of formaldehyde; she had a disconcerting habit of sniffing her palms. At least today, she fretted, if there were a lingering odor about her, it would be wafted away by the brisk breeze blowing across the Loire estuary.

Marie shivered. She wasn't about to question orders from London, but she'd give anything to be elsewhere. Once more she considered her assignment. Before her, the gray river stretched over a mile wide as it met the sea, a flat expanse of shallow water dotted with mud flats, but penetrated by a single deep water passage, the Charpentiers Channel. Thus far her vigil of the harbor had been uneventful; neither of her objectives had been realized. She'd been unable to photograph a Series Nine U-boat equipped with the revolutionary new snorkel breathing device, and secondly, there was nothing to report regarding the return from sea of one particular U-boat with a crouched lion painted on the side of its conning tower.

Two factory whistles blew almost simultaneously. It was getting late. The shivering Frenchwoman diverted her watchful eyes back toward town where industrial chimneys belched columns of smoke and the great soaring cranes of the shipyard crept back and forth beneath the ever-present umbrella of barrage balloons. Fumbling in her purse for her watch, Marie looked up suddenly as she heard the faint but unmistakable sound of diesel engines. The noise grew louder. Farther up the channel the long silhouette of a U-boat came around the bend into sight.

Marie quickly withdrew from her purse the small pre-war Leica the British had air-dropped to her, along with other supplies, just one week earlier. She waited patiently, ready to snap the shutter when the U-boat passed by. Once beyond the shallows and breakwater, the sub's commander would waste no time in submerging, for it was still daylight and the sky above St. Nazaire was by no means secure from brazen Allied aircraft.

Marie had selected her fishing spot carefully. Behind her was a meter-high pile of cobblestones waiting for a workman's trowel and replacement in the storm-damaged quay. The granite blocks would obsure her from the prying eyes of other fishermen or high-power binoculars back on shore. Pre-setting the Leica's focus and exposure, Marie selected a shutter speed of two-hundredths of a second. The submarine, hull 531, was now opposite her, less than fifty meters distant. Her patient vigil was at last rewarded, for protruding above the conning tower behind the periscope shaft was the ugly, unmistakable serrated shape of a newly outfitted snorkel!

Marie managed three good shots before she heard the abrupt, gruff voice from behind. Panic gripped her as she turned and glanced up. A Mauser 7.65 pistol was pointed at her heart and the hand that held it was disturbingly steady. Dressed like a fisherman, the surly figure who had crept up on her undetected had a disjointed, orangutan frame, an outsized jaw, and wore a woolen stocking cap that crowned piercing brown eyes.

"The camera. I'll take it now." The man ordered in French. His coarse, uncompromising voice had a heavy German accent.

Marie Selva swore repeatedly to herself. *Holy Mother of God, had she been followed out on the quay or was her discovery a fluke?* Her mind flashed. She suddenly saw cankerworms gnawing through one of her very own caskets, and she was in it. Marie reluctantly pulled herself to her feet, the uncompromising Mauser intimidating her every inch of the way. She glanced up the quay, noting that there was no one else in sight. They were hidden behind the pile of stones. To seaward, the U-boat had cruised off in the distance. Her adversary insists on the camera; *very well, he'll have it then*.

Marie smiled and abruptly tossed the Leica. Her startled captor tried to make the catch with one hand but failed. The momentary confusion was just what Marie wanted; her sudden, unladylike kick deflected the Mauser into the nearby pile of cobbles.

They both dove for the weapon. Her opponent was closer and far stronger, but his fingers never closed around the gun, for Marie's carefully aimed six-centimeter square of granite dropped him instantly to the ground. He shook his head, trying desperately to gather himself to come back at her.

Marie quickly retrieved the Mauser, but noted it bore no silencer. A gunshot would bring company she didn't need. She tossed the weapon aside and grabbed another cobblestone. There was an ugly cracking sound as she struck her groggy assailant again. The ape-like stranger slumped to one side and lay still. Marie felt for his pulse but all she sensed was her own heart fluttering in panic. Before her was the sprawled shapelessness of death she'd seen all too often in her own and during her husband's lifetime.

Overhead, the sea birds—having held their breath during the battle—began to caw again. Marie gathered her wits. She hurriedly wrapped two cobblestones several times with fishing line and secured them to the body. Beads of sweat coursing down her face, she pulled and shoved, finally managing to roll the heavy, weighted corpse over the lip of the quay. Several curious ducks approached, mechanically stroked the water over the place where the body disappeared, then swam off.

Marie picked up the Leica and examined it. The lens was broken, but the case and valuable film were intact. Retrieving the dead man's Mauser, she patted it thoughtfully and shoved it inside her coat pocket. Who was this individual who had posed as a fisherman and accosted her?

The sky darkened as a wide front of clouds moved in from seaward. Nightfall would come soon and Marie knew that no citizen of St. Nazaire was permitted on the jetty after dusk. Already in the distance she could see two German footsoldiers coming to warn the fishermen that it was time to leave. Gathering up her fishing line and bait pail, Marie began the

hike back along the quay. Although she'd have no information
to relay to London concerning Dieter Loewen's U-boat, she did
have the important photographs of Germany's new snorkel
equipment.

Marie thought about the critical hours ahead and the
impending invasion. As darkness fell, she would pass on the
responsibility for monitoring U-boat movements into the
French port to old Andre Chaban, tender of the swing bridge at
the inner basin. Although Chaban made a conscious effort to
do what was expected of him, Marie knew her night replacement had a problem. Not the poor eyesight one might expect in
a man of seventy-three, but rather habitual drowsiness, the
extent of which seemed directly proportionate to the amount of
Beaujolais Chaban quaffed at dinner. Only this morning she
had explained to the bridgetender the importance of special
vigilance in the days ahead.

Marie quickened her pace as she neared the two German
soldiers strolling toward her along the quay. Gazing at her
indolently, the patrol passed by, swinging in stride, carbines
slung. Thinking of what had happened back on the quay, Marie
walked faster. She would radio London that St. Nazaire was
turning from hot to scalding. Colonel Foster and the other fools
at G-10 were asking too much of her. Earlier this year
Combined Operations had pleaded for total destruction of the
bomb-proof U-boat pens. Accordingly, she had arranged for a
resistance team from Paris; two times they had attempted to
penetrate and sabotage the underground facility, and twice the
fortress, like an angry animal, had driven them off. Now once
more, terse messages from London and Paris were querying
her on the possibility of another assault. Marie's mind felt
boggled. The incident at the end of the quay had been too
close.

Reaching the end of the long jetty, she turned and fearfully
glanced behind her one more time, then hastened up Rue
Durand toward her undertaking parlor.

Chapter 7

THE RAIN HAD continued into the darkness and still fell in torrents outside the airbase billeting quarters. In the mood for company, Merrill rapped softly on Sigi's door. Getting no response, he knocked harder. The latch was ajar and the door swung open, but the room was empty. A distinct smoke odor greeted his nose—not Sigi's cigarettes, but pungent pipe tobacco. Cummings had been here recently. Merrill thought for a moment, then closed the door and walked back down the hall to his own quarters. The rain on the Quonset roof continued to rattle like a snare drum.

That London night in December, it had been raining then too. Merrill's mind began backtracking like a film run in reverse. The holiday embassy reception fifteen months ago, a memory he had deliberately suppressed since meeting Sigi for the second time in Colonel Foster's office. Now it all came rushing back to him in infinite detail. They had danced two numbers and lingered briefly over the punch bowl, but her eyes had been on him all evening.

Merrill snapped on the lights in his room, their sudden brightness bringing his thoughts back to the present. He turned on the radio, waited for it to warm up, then turned to the U.S. Armed Forces Network. They were broadcasting a replay of last week's Lucky Strike Hit Parade, and *Besame Mucho* had moved up in the rankings. Merrill was pleased. He liked the song. Idly pulling out his wallet, he examined the picture of Molly Tremayne. His recollections of Sigi the year before vanished. He suddenly wanted to call Molly, to say goodbye one more time, to let her know he was in his own bed, alone, but he suspected the Chatham communications officer would refuse his request for security reasons. Merrill placed the wallet, photographs, and his wrist watch in a large envelope, for as of tomorrow he'd carry only his forged Wehrmacht identity and personal items of German origin.

Merrill had the feeling of being watched. He turned and saw the tall Scot standing in the open doorway, grinning from ear to ear and gesturing with an upraised bottle of Johnny Walker Red Label.

Merrill smiled back at Cummings. He eyed the precious bottle with relish, but his thoughts still jarred uncomfortably between Molly and Sigi. *Booze.* Not a bad idea, he mused; wash down the guilt. Besides, his teeth were still on edge over the mission's prospects and a decent belt would numb his misery.

"Join me for a bedtime tooch, Lieutenant?" the sergeant asked, winking. "Off the record, of course, sir. The delay's giving you the rats properly, I suspect."

Merrill lowered the volume on the radio. "Where I come from we call that red eye." Cranking up a wolfish grin, Merrill nodded toward a chair and grabbed a coffee cup from his night table. "Why not? I'm off duty. And also *off the record*, have you seen the lady?"

Cummings popped the cork with his teeth and poured a generous level of Scotch in Merrill's cup. He took a long swig from the bottle before responding. "Haven't seen her, mon, since supper." Cummings avoided Merrill's eyes. "Probably down at the radio shack, I suspect."

Sitting on the edge of the cot, Merrill sipped his drink and looked at Cummings through narrowed eyes. "Ever been on a job with Sigi Petersen before?"

"No, mon. Not that I wouldn't like to. Envy your spot, I do."

Merrill laughed. So much for fencing with Cummings. He obviously wasn't about to admit having been in Sigi's room. Merrill idly wondered about Sigi's attitude in bed, how many men during this war had used her, making up for lost orgasms. "She's a sex pistol and then some," he said flatly.

The Scot beamed from one sideburn to the other. "Och, loaded and ready to fire, no doubt." Calmly, he withdrew a large pipe and proceeded to fill it. "I suspect she's goin' after bigger game than usual this trip out."

Merrill nodded and mimicked, "Aye, lad." He was about to say something clever about the U-boat ace, but he suddenly remembered that Cummings knew only the partial details of the mission. "Your job is to get us out, I understand," he said instead.

"I'll do just that, God willing."

Merrill swilled down the Scotch in his cup and slowly shook his head. The sergeant immediately poured a refill.

Their conversation drifted over British airpower, Cumming's stint in the Cameron Highlanders, and then to Merrill's South Pacific adventures in submarines. As they aimlessly talked, Merrill's mind again wandered. He thought of Sigi and felt the chilling mantle of a new kind of responsibility fall on him. A bullshit assignment if he ever saw one. A glorified bodyguard, he reasoned, with the job of keeping a sex goddess—or whatever she was—out of trouble. The Hit Parade program began blaring the number three song of the week, *Mairzy Doats*. Cummings looked at the radio quizzically but said nothing.

With the drinks in his belly, Merrill felt less of the anger he'd brought with him to Chatham, the seething annoyance at Sigi Petersen's assignment to head up the mission. He'd gone over her qualifications more times than he could count, but still the colonel's decision made no sense to him. She'd never been to Brittany before. She knew nothing, absolutely nothing about explosives. And she sure as hell didn't look the type to belly-crawl around a filthy U-boat.

Merrill hated himself for being such a male chauvinist, but he didn't like being forced into a corner by any woman. And Sigi Petersen was definitely like no female he'd ever experienced before. Her stare was almost violent, her words sultry, her pose and walk openly defiant. In a way, Merrill felt mentally raped by a mysterious new entity in his life, an entity stronger than himself. But at the same time Sigi's words sometimes struck him as curiously submissive, and it was this ambivalent quality that kindled what remained of the brute in him.

Merrill turned off the radio and for a long time merely sat with the mug of Scotch whiskey between his hands. Closing his eyes, he tried to unwind, to get rid of the drawn and tense feeling. He could feel a familiar twitch—the small muscle beneath his right eye trembling involuntarily.

Merrill vaguely heard Cummings calling to him. He stiffened and looked up.

The British army sergeant appeared ill at ease. "I said, Lieutenant, that bloody few sailors pick up a Navy Cross. How did you come by it, mon?"

Merrill exhaled sharply. "Forget it. Medals mean nothing to me, Sergeant. By the time the war is concluded, we'll all have a surfeit of this madness called heroism. Excellent Scotch, I might add."

"Modesty or privacy, have it your way." Cummings poured again. The big Scot's face looked drawn and pinched. His eyes seemed to have taken on a special intensity as though to penetrate inside Merrill's head.

Sensing his drinking companion's disappointment, Merrill offered, "Medals. Melt them down for shell casings and we'll all be better off. I just do my job."

Cummings sucked on his curved brown pipe and blew out a thick cloud of Dunhill tobacco smoke into the room. "You're too modest, my friend. In London these days they like to say *keep your pecker up.*" Grabbing the bottle of Johnny Walker he smiled and nudged Merrill's cup. "Drink up, mon."

Merrill looked back at Cummings and spared a grin. So radically different in their backgrounds, but like enough in their damned war-imposed loneliness. The Quonset building shuddered as a bolt of lightning thundered overhead. Merrill glanced upward. "Our RAF friends can count their blessings tonight. As can Hitler. No missions in this slop."

"Have you lost many friends in the war, Lieutenant?" asked Cummings, gloomily. The words were slightly slurred, the whiskey he'd consumed before joining Merrill taking its toll.

"Several at Pearl Harbor. And a couple of buddies in the submarine service."

The big Scot's eyebrows knitted. "How about the O.S.S. and G-10?"

"The spy racket is the sour end of the war. Too risky to make friends. Sentiment impairs judgment." Merrill had no sooner said these words than he regretted them. He was thinking of his new companion, Sigi Petersen.

Cummings nodded. "Aye. 'Tis the same with too much Scotch," he added, as a footnote. Climbing to his feet, he headed for the door. "Good luck, Yank. Hope the two of you find what you're goin' after over there."

Shooting Cummings a half-assed salute, Merrill closed the door. The liquor, instead of soothing him, had only vivified his apprehension for what lay ahead. *I'm part of an insane vendetta between Churchill and Hitler*, he mused. Blowing up the U-boat pens on the French coast made crystal-clear sense, but beyond that, going after the German sub ace was part of a damned game. Meaningless, like a fox hunt. Merrill's thoughts came easily now, too easily. The Scotch had done its work. He suddenly took a dislike to Winston Churchill and his ego, wondering if this Dieter Loewen affair was little more than a clever stunt, something the fiery journalist-turned-Prime Minister could write about in his war memoirs.

Merrill tried, unsuccessfully, to fight off his self pity. How had he come by this unlucky assignment? Were there no challenging, one-man, behind-the-scenes demolition jobs left that he might handle? A few bridges, an ammo train, a hydroelectric dam?

As suddenly as Merrill had been overcome with doubt, an overloaded fuse somewhere in his brain shattered, and his rebellion disappeared. Raising his cup, he polished off the rest of his drink. Calmer now, Merrill made an effort to recall what he'd read and heard about the great Dieter Loewen: no man in any navy had matched his record for ships sunk. Loewen the Lion—the sea legend was to Hitler what Baron von Richthofen had been to the Kaiser in World War I. Purportedly, Hitler was going so far as to issue a postage stamp with the sub ace's likeness on it! Heroes are for children to yammer about, Merrill felt, but still he wanted to see the ace and measure him, to find out how he thought, spoke, moved. Was this fellow submarine commander clever and courageous, or just another Nazi myth blessed by luck?

Erika Vermeer pulled her hands away from the warehouse window to find them covered with grime. It hardly mattered, for in her tomboy childhood she'd been accustomed to torn overalls and dirty faces. She turned to Maurice Duval, smiled, and gestured for him to spell her off at the hacksaw. The blade was of the finest Swedish steel, but the iron bars were thicker than they had anticipated.

Les grands boulevards were wrapped in silence, for the Paris curfew had begun. Overhead, the moon was hiding

behind a front of storm clouds. A chill, vagrant breeze made
Erika and the deaf-mute both wish they could have worn one of
the heavy greatcoats popular with German soldiers, but
unfortunately they were too cumbersome for their role as cat
burglars. It took another five minutes, but finally Erika cut
away the last bar and quietly removed it from its frame.
Pausing only briefly to wipe the sweat from her brow and catch
her breath, Erika then pried open the window and wiggled
through the opening. As agile as any man, she dropped to the
floor of the warehouse and took her bearings. Glancing at her
watch, she gestured for her partner to jump down beside her.

Erika nudged her peaked Wehrmacht service cap back on her
head and looked overhead, examining the trussed rafters and
peaked skylight that ran the length of the cavernous structure.
The cap was a size too large, as was the rest of the appropriated
German uniform. Pierre Roger and the others in the resistance
network had scolded Erika to have the jacket tailored or find
another; that despite her big-boned, tough stance and obviously
Nordic features, she didn't look like a disciplined Wehrmacht
soldier.

Tonight wasn't the first time she'd taped her breasts, dressed
and played the part of an enemy serviceman. She'd been clever
enough to get away with it for five days back in Germany at the
U-boat sailors' training facility at Wilhelmshaven. Erika was
good at the masquerade and admitted to emotionally enjoying
the cross-dressing. So much so that she'd fallen naturally into
the male impersonator job at the Left Bank bistro. Whatever
her wardrobe—Erika seemed taken up in one masquerade after
another—she always wore a small silver Roman coin around
her neck for luck. Now, as she waited in the warehouse darkness for her partner to join her, she reached inside the German
tunic and nervously fondled the coin and chain. Her mother
had given her a Star of David necklace before the war, but she
knew displaying that nostalgic gift would only insure her
internment or worse in Germany.

Maurice Duval closed the window, leaped, and drew up
beside her. The mute, too, wore the drab gray uniform of the
Wehrmacht. The Frenchman, in his early thirties, was shorter
than Erika, much shorter, with more fat than muscle on his
slightly stooped frame. His hair was brown, shot with a trace
of gray, the bridge of his nose long and narrow and contrasting
oddly with his pear-shaped face. Though totally deaf, Duval's

deep-set, small brown eyes were alert and keen as any animal's. The mute's disability was often a distinct advantage in dealing with the German occupiers in Paris.

Having earlier rehearsed their mission carefully on paper, they both knew the next move. Straight up. Erika figured there had to be over eighty rungs to the ladder. Climbing swiftly to the top, they crawled out on one of the large trusses supporting the roof. Erika paused to catch her breath and consider the precariously narrow beam that led to the skylight. There was no other way. She'd never liked high places and found the height dizzying. Prodded by the mute, she gathered her courage and inched forward.

At last they reached the skylight. Duval pried open one of the glass frames and they both crawled out onto the flat gravel roof. Erika raised a finger to her lips, signalling for caution as they padded, as softly as possible, to the edge of the warehouse. For a full minute she listened, studying the long brick building next door. The windows were dark except for the guard's quarters on the first level. The warehouse roof where they crouched was connected to the German military headquarters structure by a large vent or heating pipe. The sheet metal tube was at least four feet in diameter, reinforced with ribs and held in place with several cables. Erika hoped it would be strong enough to support them. Gritting her teeth, she began her harrowing crawl.

Erika slipped over the ledge first, Duval following. Cautiously, a foot at a time, they eased across the top of the pipe on their stomachs. A guard stepped out into the passageway far below them. They froze, not daring to breathe, until finally the German wandered back into the office. At the far end of the pipe they found the building cornice lined with barbed wire. Erika had come prepared, but she cut her hand as she hurriedly attacked the barrier with wire cutters.

Under ordinary circumstances, the copper-covered hatch in the center of the roof would be bolted from the inside, but the opening led to a custodian's closet on the top floor, and the mute had earlier bribed one of the French cleaning women to free the hasp.

Erika breathed a sigh of relief. The woman, thankfully, hadn't forgotten. The noise in forcing the hatch would have given them away. Now the difficult part; they had to get from the roof to the basement records center for OB West. Erika knew that there were three SS troopers guarding the building: two outside, poised in readiness on each side of the front stoop, while one duty man inside sat at the first floor desk. She and Duval had to pass within inches of this desk to reach the basement vault. Erika again checked her watch. Ten minutes after one. The guards would be relieved at three, so there was ample time. The German records center was quiet now, but in less than five hours the building would be a hornet's nest of activity.

Erika's nerves twittered like sparrows as they proceeded down the staircase leading to the lower levels. Nearing the first floor, she heard music. Good, she reflected, the creaking wooden steps would have betrayed them. She nodded to the mute, who took off his shoes and unscrewed the top from a small vial he carried. Erika held her gun in readiness.

His back to them, the first floor duty man, an SS staff sergeant, sat at a large table smoking a cigarette in idle concern, listening to an orchestral arrangement of *Tristan and Isolde*. A Schmeisser automatic lay at readiness on the table, inches from his fingers.

Erika suppressed a shiver and covered the duty man with her silenced Luger as Duval crept forward. She didn't want to kill the guard unnecessarily, for Gestapo retribution in the neighborhood might be horrendous. She watched the deaf-mute remove the chloroform-soaked cloth from the vial and stealthily approach the German. The guard's spasmodic struggle was brief, the noise of his toppling chair lost in the loud Wagnerian prelude. Erika rushed up to help Duval. Dragging the unconscious SS sergeant into a nearby office, they quickly bound and gagged him.

Seconds later they reached the bottom of the basement stairwell. Her heart pounding in her chest, Erika had to fight back her feverish impatience, for the task confronting her now required emotional control, and above all, steady fingers. She shook her hands and exhaled sharply in an effort to steady herself. *Safecracker!* That was what many of her Dutch friends called her, but the facts were simply that Erika Vermeer had been a good apprentice and learned her father's locksmith business well.

Finally the latch on the heavy steel door was free. Erika checked the entry from top to bottom for sensors or alarm wires and found it clean. They quickly entered the darkened file room.

The beam of her flashlight probed along row after row of dark green steel files until they at last found a safe marked 1944 Operational Dispatches. Then the word Geheime—Secret. Erika handed her flashlight to Duval, slipped a stethoscope around her neck and fitted the earphones. Perspiring, nerves taut, she studied the three disc combination for several moments, then took a deep breath, exhaled, and set her fingers to work on the tumblers. Her anxiety was costing the operation time, for it took twenty minutes to ring through the final combination. But at last the tumbler fell over and she gently eased the door open.

The file safe was full of buff manila folders, but Erika was interested in only one of the secret sheaves—U-boat sailing orders for the German, Norwegian, and French bases during the first week in June. A folder marked Most Urgent.

Chapter 8

THE U-601, AS usual, had been blessed with incredible luck. Sub duty wasn't bad at all, thought Dieter Loewen. For him, it had been near pleasure. Although his boat stank and was as cramped as a can of herring fillets, the dry quarters and excellent U-boat food were far preferable to the tent accommodations or worse a German officer of comparable rank could expect in the mud and snow of the Eastern front.

Loewen grabbed the wall telephone over his bunk and flipped the switch cutting in the submarine's loudspeaker system. "This is the *Kapitan*," he snapped.

Amidships, the duty crew looked up attentively. Oberleutnant Gunnar Hersch, the executive officer, hastily turned up the gain on the control room speaker as Loewen's metallic voice echoed throughout the hull.

"The patrol has been long and difficult, but considering the unprecedented odds thrown against us, it was highly successful. Still, it was our misfortune to lose three comrades-in-arms." Behind his privacy curtain, the sub ace hesitated, wiping his lips with the back of his hand. Loewen disliked speeches as a matter of course. From the shelf beside him he retrieved a small, leather-bound notebook with a Reichskriegmarine seal embossed on its cover. He quickly thumbed to a soiled, dog-eared page and began to read in an even, expository tone: "Let us remember these seamen whose pledge to the Fuehrer has been paid by the ultimate sacrifice. We shall forever be indebted to these fighting men as we continue our crusade for a more glorious, honorable, and proud Fatherland." Loewen sighed ponderously, wondering how many times he'd read that passage since the Battle of the Atlantic had begun. Committing himself to finish, he added, *"Heil Hitler!"*

In the control room, Gunnar Hersch turned to the diving officer beside him. "The *kaleun* reads well, yes, Mueller?"

In the forward and aft torpedo rooms the crewmen had listened attentively to their commander. All the torpedoes except one were gone, and the case after case of provisions once stacked high in the corridors had been gradually consumed on the long patrol. Gradually, in the opinion of the petty officer concerned with the computing of the ship's ballast. To Rosemeyer, the U-boat's cook, it seemed the crew had gone through the cached food like a hungry Weimaraner at a pan of bratwurst. With the provisions gone, the elbow room, comparatively speaking, was a luxury on the way home. In a matter of minutes the U-601 would surface and the ventilating system would be drawing in clean outside air; the sailors looked forward to it and they were in good spirits. In the control room every man wore a smile of anticipation. The tired crew had accumulated another 90 days of front line service for their records, but most important, and by no means an understatement, they were still *alive*.

Loewen's voice suddenly crackled again on the speaker system. "We sank well over 30,000 tons of enemy shipping on this patrol, despite the harassment from the new American escort carriers. You men are to be commended. Your task, however, will become increasingly difficult in the months to come."

The crew gazed at one another in silent bewilderment, each man wondering how future missions could possibly be more hellish than this last patrol.

"There's more," Loewen announced, after a moment's hesitation. "You've heard enough rumors concerning the command of this boat and you're now entitled to the facts. To my own displeasure, I'll be leaving the U-601 for a position ashore. At morning muster dockside I'll expect to shake hands and say goodbye to each man personally." Another long, expectant silence as the crew waited in anticipation. The speaker system finally cut in again: "Your new commanding officer will be Oberleutnant Gunnar Hersch. Good luck and good hunting, Leutnant Hersch."

In the control room, the diving officer drew a whistling breath through his teeth and turned to the exec beside him.

Dutifully, he said to Hersch, "Congratulations, Herr Leutnant."

"It will not be the same without the Lion," said Hersch, soberly.

Dieter Loewen stepped through the control room hatch, smiled affably, and gave both men a firm handshake and a clout on the back. "So much for speeches," he grumbled.

The captain and Hersch both looked anxiously at their watches. Another fifteen minutes to go before reaching the outer harbor rendezvous point and their minesweeper escort. Crawling homeward submerged, the U-601 was making less than four knots, and they were anxious to surface, where they could engage the diesels and make better time.

Suddenly, as if caught by a stop motion camera, all life aboard the U-boat froze. They all heard it, the rasping, grating noise of a steel cable scraping along the side of the hull.

Gunnar Hersch's mouth fell open like a just-landed fish. He turned to Loewen, expectant. Metal striking metal. The crew knew, instinctively, that it was the sound of death.

Attached to the end of that chafing, anchored cable, Loewen realized, was an enemy contact mine bristling with three-inch glass detonators. The noise had begun behind the bow plane, and now moved stealthily, slowly, along one side of the hull.

Colonel Stuart Foster had retired reasonably satisfied with the day's work. Despite the delay caused by the weather, his two charges were safely ensconced at the Chatham Airfield barracks. They would be briefed and repeatedly tested before leaving on their night flight to France. The preparations were over, the Lion of the Atlantic was reportedly due back in port at any time. Come what may, it was now entirely up to the field operatives, and Foster's work, for the present, was complete. He'd almost drifted off to sleep when the telephone rang. He turned on the lamp beside the bed and picked it up.

"Hello," he said sleepily. "Foster here."

"Colonel, this is Keith Holbrook, Scotland Yard. Sorry to wake you, Stuart old mate."

"I doubt that, Keith. In your business, any inconvenience seems to be cricket. So what the devil do you want at this hour?"

"Odd business that I suspect involves one of your people."

"Go on."

"You want it all over the telephone?"

"Come, come, Keith. You know me better than that. I'll shut you off proper enough if the conversation winds up proprietary."

"Have it your way, Stuart. A disreputable lorry driver from the Covent Garden produce market—an ex-convict at that—was found crushed in a Wolseley saloon car tonight. The blighter was known for being a possible hit man. Hit himself, however, when a building facade struck by a V-1 collapsed on him. Warden in the area said he was speeding through the buzz-bomb target area."

Foster stiffened. He thought for a moment. Finally he prompted, "Keith, I appreciate the news, but I've had a long day. What's this have to do with Admiralty business?"

"Depends on how you interpret what we found in the character's pockets."

Foster sat up rigidly in bed. "I'm listening."

"A bulging envelope filled with 500 pounds, a message, and a photograph. The picture is of a Yank officer. His name is on the back, a Lieutenant Merrill. Ring a bell, Stuart? Following his name there's a reference to G-10, an address that turns out to be the Heathcliffe Hotel, and today's date. Also a note."

"Slow down, Sherlock. The note, what did it say?"

"Not much. *The second 500 pounds when the job is done. Do not fail.* But here's the rub. The money is counterfeit. More of those bad bills printed by the Gestapo in Berlin."

Foster grimaced. "That's enough, Keith. I'm on my way over to your office."

The U-boat quartermaster's face had turned as white as chalk. He'd instantly recognized the sound, and the rudder had already eased a few degrees in nervous anticipation of the next command.

Dieter Loewen could feel the pulse in his neck throbbing like a triphammer. "Right full rudder!" he shouted.

The urgency of his voice brought split-second obedience from the sweating helmsman. Gunnar Hersch and the rest of Loewen's crew needed no further instructions. Bulkhead vent valves were quickly closed and the sounds of slamming watertight doors echoed throughout the submarine.

Loewen grimaced. Perhaps his end, after all, was to be blown to hell, fodder for the fish, and not to retire at a prestigious desk in Berlin. He strained his ears. Somewhere between the motor room and the rear torpedo room the scraping sound stopped. Had the cable—this probing finger of death—not caught on the after diving plane? The only noise Loewen heard now was the steady drone of the electric motors turning the screws; he could almost count the slow ninety revolutions per minute.

Several seconds passed before anyone in the control room dared to breathe. The executive officer broke the silence. "Shall we surface, sir?" asked Gunnar Hersche, anxiously.

Dieter Loewen didn't answer, instead for several long moments continuing to listen. His legs were numbed to nonexistence and his mouth felt as dry as duck feathers. Finally he turned to Hersch and relented. "Take it up to periscope depth." Loewen moved to the plotting table, his moist palms running over the approach charts to their home port of St. Nazaire. He could feel the oppressive silence of the men around him, men who knew as he did that where there was one mine there could be more, and in all probability rigged at varying depths. The fearful tension in the faces around him had mounted like steam in a boiler. Loewen knew that like Jonah, trapped in the whale's maw, they wanted *out*.

The U-601 rose hesitantly, cautiously, barely making its way forward. Loewen heard the familiar sounds of nearing the surface. Mueller, the diving officer, called with apparent relief, "Six-zero meters, Herr Kaleun."

"Up periscope," shouted Loewen, checking his watch. He quickly scanned the horizon. Satisfied, he shouted, "Surface! Let's trust our minesweeper escort is early."

"Three-zero meters, Herr Kaleun. Pressure stabilized," said Mueller. The conning tower had cleared water.

Loewen pulled on his heavy leather jacket and barked at the seaman already halfway up the ladder to the bridge. "Open the hatch!"

The heavy bronze cover heaved open, admitting a trickle of sea water and the sweet, fresh smell of the surface world. Loewen straightened his cap, inhaled deeply of the invigorating night air, and scrambled up the wet rungs of the ladder.

The Luftwaffe weather forecast for the coast of France turned out to be completely correct. Despite the storm raging three hundred miles to the north, the sea was moderate with even swells moving shoreward. Off the starboard quarter Loewen could just make out Brittany and the indented bay which formed the mouth of the Loire. But the port of St. Nazaire was blacked out. Nothing else was visible except one intermittent blue light a thousand meters to port. Loewen focused on the pinpoint of light, studying its flashing interval. Satisfied, he lowered his Zeiss binoculars and spoke into the conning tower intercom. "Lookouts aloft! Exec and radioman to the bridge!"

Hersch bellowed into the intercom and the U-boat's twin 2,170 horsepower, supercharged engines roared back. "All ahead one-third," he said. "Come to three four zero."

Dieter Loewen and Gunnar Hersch abandoned themselves to opposite sides of the conning tower. They stared in silence at the sleek forward section of the U-boat as it knifed through the black water, leaving gleaming waves of phosphorescence to each side. Loewen noted that Hersch's eyes were full of the brooding that often gets in the eyes of sailors. Spitting into the lee of the wind and pulling on heavy sheepskin gloves, Loewen said, "Unseasonably cold for the end of May."

Hersch nodded and smiled back at him.

Loewen gazed back toward the sea. He pulled up his leather collar against the wind, at the same time letting his hand brush over the Iron Cross beneath his neck. Loewen's finger traced over the Oak Leaves and the more recent overlay, an adornment Grand Admiral Doenitz had personally presented to him just six months earlier. The two delicate Crossed Swords of Silver had been accompanied by a commendation from the Fuehrer himself.

Submarine duty suited Loewen. The U-601 seemed to be his creation; he loved his boat with a passion he'd be hard pressed to explain. Possibly it mirrored his need for power by stealth and ingenuity, his love of things mechanical, and his taste for long, brine-smelling weeks at sea.

No other German seaman could match his patience, Loewen was sure of that. They called him the Lion, not for any superhuman ferocity, but for his cleverness and relentless persistence. But a predator needs freedom, he reflected bitterly, not confinement to be admired at the Fuehrer's pleasure. Loewen almost wished the mine had finished him so he wouldn't have to turn this uncomfortable new page in his life.

Loewen turned to Gunnar Hersch, measuring the second in command. "I wish you were going to Berlin instead of me, Gunnar." Removing his soiled white hat and rolling it over in his hands, Loewen held it up before Hersch. The tarnished embroidery on the visor was frayed and part of the Reichs-kriegmarine emblem was missing. In Berlin, among other discomforts, Loewen would be forced to wear a clean, stiffly new hat. Shaving, too, would no longer be optional. He sighed and said remorsefully, "A white commanding cap will be yours tomorrow, Leutnant. As will the U-601." Loewen replaced the tired but comfortable headpiece, tilting it slightly to port as was his custom.

"I am pleased, Kapitan." Gunnar Hersch's tone was noncommittal and placidly cooperative.

Loewen wondered what life would be like not prowling the sea lanes with Hersch, for as a team they had been in and out of hell more times than he could remember. The sharing included danger and boredom as well as a few bottles of schnapps. "They are sending me ashore for good, Gunnar," Loewen grumbled. "High and dry, one more barnacle on the dock." He afforded Hersch an uneasy smile.

"Kaleun, you are going to OKW!" Hersch said emphatically, his eyes sparkling. "To receive an award like the Grand Cross with Diamond Inlays is honor enough, but I doubly envy you being chosen to serve on the Fuehrer's staff with Doenitz."

Loewen shrugged his firm, square shoulders and buried his head in his leather collar. He tried to smile.

"Not only the Reichskriegmarine, but the entire German nation is proud of you, Kaleun," Hersch qualified.

Looking away from the exec, Loewen fixed his gaze on the minesweeper ahead. Such is the fate of so-called heroes like the Lion of the Atlantic, he reasoned. They die supposedly courageous deaths at sea when, given enough time, the odds finally run out, or they are ceremoniously piped ashore for safekeeping before this can happen. Loewen knew the other great U-boat aces, whom even the British acknowledged, were all history. Prien, Schoepke, Kretschner. Only U-boat hero Dieter Loewen remained. And Adolf Hitler had proclaimed him the greatest of them all; his record proved that.

* * *

All night the sleet-swept storm outside bawled at Merrill.
Even with a pillow crammed over his head, he couldn't sleep.
The rain, drumming on the Quonset's metal roof, sounded like
Texas hail. Merrill tossed restlessly on the narrow barracks cot,
cursing the vivid imagination that, as always, was part and
parcel of his insomnia. Even when he slept his dreams were
never dull.

For the first time in weeks Merrill thought about a cigarette.
For several minutes he sweated out the temptation, determined
as he was to keep the resolution he'd made in Honolulu to quit
cold turkey. Merrill wondered if Sigi Petersen, down the
hallway in the women's quarters, was having her own
problems getting to sleep. Again, he thought of his partnership
with her, the slight enmity that had already built between them.
For the present, if it made things easier, he'd let her think he
was her acolyte. Whatever turned her on. It was too early to
speculate on how he'd handle their differences later on.

Outside the wind shook the building. The storm was at least
giving England a respite from German air attack. Still, if they
didn't get off the ground tomorrow night, there would be
timing complications. Perhaps they wouldn't go at all and he
could return to the warmth of Molly Tremayne's bed in
London.

Forget it, Skeet. Sentimentality has no place for the
duration. It was an incident, one more fleeting wartime affair.
Merrill rose, went over to the rain-streaked window, and
glumly stared outside. The storm, instead of abating, seemed
to have intensified.

Chapter 9

_____

COVERED WITH rust and the great cat emblem on its conning tower sorely in want of fresh paint, the 220-foot-long U-601 eased bow first into her slip within the hugh concrete fortress that was the sub base at St. Nazaire.

The change of command ceremony a few hours later was a simple, straightforward affair. Doing without flags and a band, the crew reported on deck in dress uniform while Loewen and Hersch straddled workmen's air hoses and electric lines to take a position in front of them. A boatswain's whistle sounded. Dieter Loewen's farewell address was purposefully brief and to the point. His words were clipped as he thanked the crew for their performance and expressed absolute optimism over their luck for future patrols. When Loewen finished they broke ranks and gave him a spontaneous round of applause. It was now Gunnar Hersch's turn. The men fell back into attention as he read the orders placing him in command of the U-601. He crisply saluted his predecessor.

The cook, Rosemeyer, stepped forward and tendered a gift on behalf of the crew. They hadn't had much time, and the best they'd come up with was a magnum of Bouzy champagne. Loewen smiled, noted that it was an excellent vintage, and thanked them. For the first time since taking command of the U-601, he felt vulnerable. He shook the last crewman's hand, mumbled a few words of encouragement to Hersch and the other officers, then stepped briskly to the concrete dock. The ritual over, the shipyard men hurriedly resumed their work.

The flotilla commander, Korvetten Kapitan Brausdorf, stood waiting to greet Loewen. The two men exchanged salutes, shook hands, and exchanged brief pleasantries. A small girl came forward, the daughter of one of the shipyard supervisors. She smiled shyly, curtsied, and thrust a bouquet of flowers into Loewen's hands. He thanked her and patted her shoulder. Eyes hopeful, she extended a small notebook. Taking a pen the grinning Brausdorf held out in readiness, Loewen shrugged and gave the girl his autograph. She beamed and trotted off.

"You wax lyrical to your crew on their prospects for future patrols, my friend," said Brausdorf, with an indifferent, sphinx-like coolness. "A fine speech, though you're still the incurable romantic, Kapitan."

"Sir, the only romantics are at the bottom of the Atlantic." Loewen abruptly changed the subject. "When do I report to Berlin, Herr Kommandant?"

"In two weeks. The Grand Admiral has insisted you have a well-earned rest leave prior to joining the Fuehrer's staff at OKW."

Loewen nodded without enthusiasm. He paused by the heavy steel door at the end of the sub slip and looked back once more at the U-boat with the rampant lion on its rust-streaked superstructure. If he had to speak then, his voice would have betrayed his emotion. Loewen turned and they climbed a sloping concrete tunnel, Brausdorf rambling on about delays in U-boat overhaul and snorkel conversion. His words didn't register on Loewen, who heard only the echo of his own footsteps taking him farther away from the submarine that for thirty-one months had been his entire life. Halfway up the corridor the senior officer turned to take his leave into a side corridor, one of several honeycombing the massive underground complement of shops, barracks, and storerooms.

Loewen suddenly felt the structure shudder.

"A British blockbuster with a bad fuse. We exploded it ourselves," Brausdorf explained. "Before this spate of bad weather, the RAF was unmerciful with St. Nazaire."

Loewen listened attentively without comment.

Brausdorf gestured to the monolithic cement overhead. "You'll be safe enough under our five meters of concrete."

"I'll be staying in the city just long enough to board a train for Paris, sir," replied Loewen, with a trace of a smile. "I've been at sea a long time."

Brausdorf nodded. "Beware of Parisian women who offer you romance for nothing, my friend." His finger wagged like a metronome. "There is much treachery in Paris, for the French are convinced that they are close to their liberation. For a few Reichsmarks, on the other hand, you can safely take your pleasure with a lovely Swiss fraulein in Montparnasse. An officer friend of mine in the Luftwaffe gave me her address. Would you like it? He tells me her Calvados brandy is excellent, among other pleasures."

Loewen frowned and quickly retorted, "Faust's damnation! Where are your Luftwaffe pilot friends when a U-boat man needs them to fly patrols for us? My compliments to your comrade, Herr Kommandant, but with all respect to his cat house referral, I'm familiar enough with Paris." Loewen clicked his heels and offered a farewell salute.

"As you wish, Kapitan." Brausdorf swallowed his disappointment with an annoyed look, quickly masked. He returned Loewen's salute and strode off down the corridor to his office.

Loewen continued up the main tunnel, but his pace was broken by a hastily flung open door to the base dispensary. A cart of medical linen, propelled into the corridor by an attractive French nurse, crashed into him. The young woman's chocolate eyes, startled as a squirrel's, stared at him.

"*Pardon, Monsieur.* I am very clumsy. A thousand apologies, Kapitan."

Loewen took his bearings on the young French nurse who continued to stare at him as if he were an apparition. "No harm," he replied, smiling. Beneath the tight bodice of her white dress, her breasts were high and round. It had been a long time since he'd seen a woman so lovely and felt the impact of her closeness. Touching two fingers to the brim of his cap, he winked, rubbed his beard, then detoured around the linen cart and stepped slowly away.

Colette Chaban's heart was in her throat. *The U-boat ace,* she thought with alarm. *He is back in port!* Only this morning at breakfast her grandfather, having come off his watchman's shift at the basin bridge, claimed to have seen nothing of the U-601 and the return of the legendary Lion. Yet here was the German submarine hero, as big as life. Poor Grandpapa—old Andre had fallen asleep again, she mused. The undertaker woman would shame him unmercifully when she found out. But Marie Selva must know of these developments, and timing was critical. Abandoning her linen cart, Colette dashed up the corridor.

Outside the Chatham barracks the rain still pelted the airfield. Though the weather forecast was for possible clearing later tonight, it was still touch and go whether they would get off the ground in time.

Merrill's earlier suggestion that they wile away the hours playing chess or cards was finally agreed upon by the others. He and Sigi had a checkerboard spread out on the cot between them and they'd managed to borrow a set of ivory chessmen from one of the base pilots. Before lunch they'd nursed their boredom with a game of Poker until the Scot had run out of money. Now, while Cummings huddled in a chair at the other side of the room reading a tattered copy of *Life* magazine with Betty Grable on the cover, Merrill sweated out defeat at the hands of a far better chess player than himself. Watching Sigi with pained apprehension, Merrill shifted from his lotus position. The barracks cot was cramped and his legs were going to sleep.

Sigi steadied the board with her hand. "Move slowly, please."

"My body or the next play?"

She smiled at him. "Both. I need time to think."

Merrill grinned back at her. She seemed to be doing well enough without heavy thinking.

Sigi looked up and said abruptly, "Do you have contempt for Germans, Skeet?" Her eyes blazed oddly at him.

Merrill again felt the uncomfortable shift of time in transferring from the Pacific theater of operations to the war in the Atlantic.

Cummings glanced up from behind his magazine, but prudently kept out of it.

Merrill finally replied, "Hardly. My great grandmother immigrated from Dusseldorf and purportedly worshipped Frederick the Great. But as for those current hoodlums in Berlin, I'm convinced that the only good Nazi is a dead one. That answer your question?"

Sigi didn't look up. She moved her bishop, taking one of Merrill's pawns and jeopardizing his queen.

Merrill's hands fell to his sides. He'd been set up in the last two plays. So much for distractions. Sigi was fast, very fast. He grinned sheepishly and slowly shook his head.

"Don't *apologize* for inattentiveness," she warned. "It's a sign of weakness. Besides, your daydreams may be important."

Merrill ignored her and concentrated on the chess board. Off to one side he could hear Cummings clucking his tongue. Merrill frowned, determined now to stay more alert, keep the adrenalin pumping, the eyeballs probing. Not only for this battle of wits with chessmen, but for his every wakeful moment in the hours ahead. Again he thought about his brush with death—the escape from the hit and run driver in London. Unwind and relax for one minute, Skeet Merrill, and you'll lose more than a couple of pawns and a queen. *You'll get it in the back.*

A coverall-clad RAF sergeant appeared in the open doorway. He knocked unnecessarily on the wall to get their attention, then dropped a bundle of flight gear on the floor. A parachute and helmet bore tags with Skeet Merrill's name on them.

"Lieutenant, I've brought by your things from Flight Ops." The airman looked at the others. "Yours as well, Miss Petersen. I've put them in your room."

Merrill cursorily examined the parachute, turning it over. He caught the RAF man's arm before he could depart. "A question, Corporal, do you mind?"

"Sir?"

Merrill held his glance. "Where's the folding loft for the chutes?"

"Rear of Hangar B, sir. Is there a problem?"

For a moment, silence lay heavy in the room except for the rain on the roof.

Merrill said shortly, "No offense. I don't fly myself, but like many pilots, I like to take precautions. If it's okay with your superiors, I'll fold my own chute."

Chapter 10

As EVENING CLAIMED the solitude of the Bavarian Alps and the isolated world of Berchtesgaden, the intelligence reports from the coasts of France, Belgium, and Holland grew steadily more confusing. With each scrap of conflicting information on when and where the great invasion might come, Adolf Hitler grew increasingly thin-skinned and querulous. The temperament of his aids had likewise become extremely brittle.

The Fuehrer's waiting chamber was silent, ominously so. Grand Admiral of the Fleet Karl Doenitz, locked leather briefcase in lap, iron gray hair immaculately groomed, sat erect and attentive, patiently waiting for Hitler's summons. Suddenly, shrilly, a small wooden bird bounded from a magnificently carved Black Forest clock on the wall opposite him.

"Kuckuk! Kuckuk! . . . ."

Doenitz counted seven cries. Gratified at any relief from the anteroom's funereal silence, he checked his watch. The Fuehrer's noisy clock, he noted, at least kept accurate time. Doenitz heard raised voices coming from the inner office. He was deeply puzzled over why he'd been summoned so suddenly to the Berghof. A week earlier he'd pleaded with the Fuehrer for a massive acceleration of the U-boat building program and had been unsuccessful. Doenitz wondered if Hitler had had a change of heart on the matter.

Turning his gaze to the tall leaded window extending from the floor to the wooden rafters overhead, Doenitz thought about the old Bavarian folk song of the cuckoo, announcing *Kuckuk! Lasst nacht sein Schrein*—the long winter is past.

Outside, replacing the snow that had melted away earlier, a mantle of edelweiss and buttercups sparkled under the silver moon that filtered through the scrub pines. There was something poignant, ephemeral about the Obersalzberg, but unfortunately, he wasn't visiting this lofty redoubt to sentimentalize on mountain scenery. Doenitz was not a man of fantasies; he knew a good deal about the way the war was going. If he had any misgivings over political strategy or opinions of current Nazi leadership, he prudently kept these opinions to himself. Above all, he was a loyal, obedient German and felt his fatherland was touched by God, and that any drastic steps he or his fellow countrymen might be obliged to take in the difficult months ahead would surely have divine approval.

Doenitz knew that Heinrich Himmler was here at the Berghof with Hitler and he wondered why. He was under no illusions as to the feelings of the SS toward the Reichskriegsmarine. SS leader Himmler was envious, aloof and untrusting. It didn't matter, for Doenitz knew Hitler had confidence in him.

At last the double doors to the Fuehrer's sanctuary flung open. Martin Bormann, quick stepped and confident, strode wordlessly past Doenitz and hurried down the hallway. Adolf Hitler stood somberly into the doorway, waiting. Doenitz edged forward, remembering that this was the same imposing portal that had received Mussolini, the King of Romania, and Neville Chamberlain. Hitler wore an immaculate dark gray uniform and soft leather shoes; his face was expressionless and pallid. Beside him, grim eyes staring out from behind steel-rimmed glasses and bearing his usual waxen smile, stood Reichsfuehrer SS Heinrich Himmler. Himmler raised his hand, anticipating the admiral's salute. Doenitz noted that Himmler's hands were abormally small and delicate, white and transparent with blue veins—inexpressive hands that harmonized with the SS leader's composed, enigmatic face. Doenitz raised his arm and decorously said, "Heil Hitler."

Disappointment coiled deep within Doenitz as he gazed once more into the eyes of the Fuehrer. It had only been a month since their last meeting, but the dull, veiled orbs staring back at him tonight were those of a troubled, angry man. The leader of the Third Reich stepped over to Doenitz, gripped him by the shoulder, and extended a hand. Feeling the uncontrolled tremor in Hitler's fingers, Doenitz had immediate reservations about this visit. Letting out a sharp sigh, he tapped the side of his briefcase. "I'm sorry, Fuehrer, but I bring news of unfavorable odds in the Bay of Biscay. Three more patrols are missing."

The ill-tidings, as chill as the Bavarian mountain air, fell on the morose German leader like the last snowflake of winter. Hitler's eyes were remote, unseeing. Arms folded over his chest, he rocked slightly on his toes. Beyond him, Himmler looked uncomfortable.

Doenitz felt compelled to continue, despite the ominous mood. "Our receiving equipment is not sensitive enough to give ample warning of British attack aircraft with their new radar. Our future must lie with the snorkel. Snorkel equipped U-boats cannot be detected by this enemy long range radar, for their profile above water is too small for a reflection. With accelerated snorkel refitting of the older hulls and fleet deployment of Professor Walter's new Series 21 boats, I promise you we will quickly change the tide of battle."

Hitler's upraised hand ended Doenitz' soliloquy. "The rate of commissioning is still outrunning the rate in which your U-boats are sunk, am I correct?" the Fuehrer asked, irritably.

Doenitz felt intimidated. He slowly nodded.

"Then say no more. And I didn't summon you to Berchtesgaden for a situation report, Herr Grand Admiral." Hitler's oblique glance fell on Himmler. "Inform Doenitz of your intelligence findings immediately. When I next meet with either of you, I'll expect some definitive answers. Gentlemen, I cannot stomach charades."

Doenitz didn't understand. "*Charades*, my Fuehrer?"

"The SS Reichsfuehrer will explain your mission." Abruptly, Hitler spun on his heels and retreated into his private office. The doors closed behind him. Doenitz and Himmler were obviously dismissed.

Nervously fingering his moustache and adjusting his glasses, Himmler pointed to the outer doorway. "Let's walk outside, Admiral. The Berghof's walls have too many ears. Besides, the mountain air is most invigorating." Gesturing for Doenitz to follow him, Himmler proceeded down a brick pathway, finally pausing in an open area behind a run used by Hitler's Alsatian. The SS leader's eyes bore in on Doenitz. "The Fuehrer is proud of your naval leadership, Herr Admiral. You are a credit to Germany."

"Thank you, Reichsfuehrer." His voice slick and alert,

shoulders slight but erect, Doenitz stood like a slab of ice and waited. This was the closest he'd ever come to the schoolmasterish Heinrich Himmler and he felt a distinct discomfort.

The SS leader, apparently feeling Doenitz' veiled animosity, weighed his words carefully. "Remember the enemy spy network Abwehr Intelligence penetrated at the Wilhelmshaven U-boat training facility six months ago? *Garbo? Tricycle?* The young woman posing as a man? Erika Krager?"

"How can I forget? Canaris was fully prepared to spring the trap when the activities abruptly ceased and the operatives disappeared."

Himmler nodded gravely, eyes squinting behind his glasses. "Only to resurface elsewhere, and with more dangerous implications. The invasion." Himmler reached inside his tunic and withdrew a tattered clipping from Berlin's *Voelkischer Beobachter*. He pointed an authoritative finger at a photograph beneath the newspaper's headline. "The Lion of the Atlantic, yes? As usual, Dr. Goebbels' ministry gives much credit to Reichskriegmarine achievements—particularly the exploits of your U-boat hero. I understand Dieter Loewen will soon join you at OKW and be honored by the Fuehrer."

Doenitz smiled for the first time. "An ammunition ship sent to the bottom on his last mission."

Himmler managed a charitable grin. "Indeed. Excellent."

"You try my patience, Reichsfuehrer. Do you imply a connection between the enemy's intelligence apparatus and Kapitan Leutnant Loewen?"

"Precisely why you have been summoned to Berchtesgaden, Doenitz. It is fragmentary information at present, but it appears G-10 in London is undertaking a most diabolical mission. Operation Storm Tide, they've named it. Most important, it involves the Fatherland's popular U-boat ace. The Fuehrer is incensed."

Doenitz looked at Himmler askance.

The Reichsfuehrer again reached inside his tunic, this time withdrawing a folded communication. "You must read this," he said firmly.

Doenitz' eyes grew perceptibly wider as he examined the decoded message. "Most interesting," he said quietly. "This double-agent is reliable?"

"*Viper* is our most valuable operative," Himmler acknowledged.

"Curious, the entire scheme. This name—*Skeet Merrill*. He's an American?"

Himmler nodded, folding his arms across his chest. "The situation is top priority; the Fuehrer is emphatic."

Doenitz gazed in amazement for some time at the long message, then looked up inquiringly. "Priority now? When the Reichskriegmarine has enough challenges? The enemy armada is imminent and——"

Himmler interjected, "We suspect this Churchill-instigated adventure has *everything* to do with the great invasion. Nothing should be more important to the Kriegsmarine. They are probing your snorkel refitting capability at Brittany and there's been radio traffic concerning the whereabouts of Loewen's sub, the U-601. The Paris office of OB West has been penetrated, an SS guard drugged, though nothing appears to be missing. Odd business afoot. And an SS agent we sent to St. Nazaire to reconnoiter the situation has disappeared without a trace. The Devil's at work, Doenitz. And I'm in no position to press our counterspy Viper for more information and jeopardize an important cover."

Himmler took the message back from Doenitz, withdrew a match, and set the document ablaze. The ashes fell to the ground. "I wish to assign my best SD investigator to your staff, Admiral. Colonel Reinhard Schiller. I trust we will have your complete cooperation in this vital matter?"

Doenitz smarted. "I ask the Fuehrer for more submarines and I am given more spies."

Himmler's face was motionless. "The Fuehrer's reasoning is not without precedent. Frederick the Great himself once said: 'When I am in the field, I have one cook and a hundred spies.'"

Karl Doenitz had his own intelligence specialists and wasn't impressed by Himmler's request. He knew the SS had already conspired to eliminate Admiral Canaris, head of Abwehr military intelligence. Canaris was brilliant, powerful, and his organization had now been reduced to an impotent bureau of the SS. There was no question of not cooperating with Himmler, but still, Doenitz was a man of military tradition, protocol, and personal dignity. He turned away, looking out over the mountains toward Salzburg. The night was very still. Finally he turned back to the Reichsfuehrer and forlornly asked, "Adolf Hitler expects me to report directly to the SS on this matter?" Doenitz suspected the question was rhetorical.

"The Fuehrer demands it," replied Himmler.

Doenitz nodded gravely. "Shall I advise our U-boat ace of the situation?"

"Not immediately. I have suggested a plan to the Fuehrer, a clever counter-strategy to foil the Allied intelligence apparatus. And he has approved. Kapitan Leutnant Loewen will be needed to achieve our little surprise."

In his office at 10 Downing Street, the Prime Minister frowned and angrily broke in half the blue pencil he'd been using. The startling, top secret operational dispatch staring him in the face was lacking in details.

In the office doorway, his secretarial aide Pearson asked, "A bit of a squall, sir?"

Churchill swore under his breath, then looked up. "I'm in ill mood for lofty theories and margins for probability. Precisely how I label this gobbet of gore from Foster's G-10."

"Unlike the Royal Navy to botch a job for you, sir."

"Not botching it, Pearson. Merely moving too slowly and out of step." Churchill hesitated; he wasn't about to chastise the Admiralty too harshly. His unsevered tie of loyalty to naval matters still lingered from his own years as First Sea Lord prior to becoming PM. Growling pugnaciously, he tossed the dispatch aside and muttered, "Again, the proverbial fly in the ointment."

As usual, his aide sensed his acute depression and offered a quick fix. "May I bring you a snifter of brandy, sir?"

Churchill shook his head. "Later, later." Digging in a pocket for a fresh cigar, he tore off the wrapper, then sucked it as if it were sour.

Pearson's eyes were still on him, fretting, as usual, over Churchill's spurious change in temperament. As the good-natured aide had done on other ulcer-provoking occasions, he brought in a measure of humorous relief. He placed a copy of the London *Times* before Churchill and drew his attention to a short article on the second page.

The PM leaned forward and quickly read the story. A man of seventy-nine years, it appeared, had been arrested in Hyde Park for making improper advances to a young girl during a drenching rainstorm. Churchill broke into a smile and grunted: "Miserable weather and such ripe vintage! No fear of either the bobbies or pneumonia. Makes you proud to be an Englishman."

Pearson winced.

Stiffening, Churchill turned to the front of the paper and surveyed the war dispatches. He read the story on recent U-boat attacks on shipping, and with it the tonnage sunk records attributed to German ace Dieter Loewen. Having approved the story for release only the day before, he flinched with annoyance as he read the figures again. He pointed a pudgy finger menacingly at Pearson. "In the beginning it was the U-boat wolf packs. Then battleships, mind you. First the costly but successful *Bismarck* affair. Nine months ago the restoration of our naval power was dependent on destroying the *Tirpitz* beast." Churchill closed the newspaper and slapped it down on the desk. "Now the decadent enemy battles us with folk heroes and cunning double agents in our own chain lockers! Snorkels, spies, and counterspies, enough to drive a man to drink."

The aide shot his superior a perplexed look. "Pardon, sir? Shall I bring you a brandy now?"

Silence once more submerged the room as Churchill finally lit his cigar and looked toward the map on the wall opposite. "No," he grumbled, peering over the top of his reading glasses. "Put in a priority call to Admiralty Operations. Never mind the Sea Lord or Ramsey. I want to talk directly to Colonel Foster in G-10."

While waiting, Churchill idly tapped what was left of the broken blue pencil on his desk. "Bog!" he suddenly roared, with a cannibal's grimace. "Forget the call. I'll slip over there myself. Inclement weather or not, I need a constitutional."

His assistant dutifully held out his black overcoat and umbrella. Churchill grabbed them and bolted for the door. Only the width of the Horse Guards parade ground separated the garden door of Number 10 from the Admiralty and in the course of the war it had often been crossed at hot foot.

Stuart Foster glanced up from his desk, startled to see that the Prime Minister himself had entered unannounced. Foster dropped his pipe, clumsily climbed to his feet, and saluted. "Sir!"

Waving him off, Churchill tossed his wet umbrella in the corner and slumped into a chair. He quickly relit his cigar. "Tell me, Colonel," his voice bore the usual bulldog tenacity, "you served in the First War, correct?"

"Yes, sir. A petty officer on the *Royal Sovereign*."

"Fine ship. You were in the thick of it, of course?"

Foster answered in a compressed voice. "I suspect, sir, you know my dossier like the back of your hand."

"Warts and all, you're quite right. A splendid career, Foster. You've not only come up through the ranks dealing with the Germans. I understand you have two uncles in the Fatherland." Churchill puffed his cigar, smiling through the smoke. "Tell me, do you find any truth in the saying 'the Hun is always either at your throat or at your feet'?"

Foster felt perplexed, but nodded in agreement.

Churchill continued: "Well, I believe it. And if that's the makeup of the beast, so be it. But I won't have the rash, infernal Jerry in bed with us, not for a moment. The First Sea Lord suspects a *counterspy* in our midst. Now, of all times, at our most critical moment. After that Halifax takes off from Chatham, God knows what's in store for your people when they hit the silk over France. Foster, I want this turncoat or enemy agent uncovered. Wherever, however. If this rabid Nazi is in London, find him. If there's more than one, uncover them quickly. If there are traitors at Admiralty or if they're pussyfooting about with your field operatives, whatever, I expect you to take measures."

"You have my assurances, sir."

"Get on over to that rat warren yourself if necessary, Foster. The success of D-Day depends on the good fortune of *Operation Storm Tide*. The mission must succeed, at any cost!"

Both men screwed up their eyes in automatic reflex as an attractive Wren warrant officer burst into the room. The pretty, hazel-eyed brunette came to a sudden halt just inside the doorway, her small hand shooting up to her mouth. "Pardon the intrusion, sir," Molly Tremayne said breathlessly.

Churchill cocked his head. "No mind at all, Miss. The visit is quite impromptu and unofficial." He waggled his thick wrist. "Get on with your business, by all means."

Molly blinked and looked inquiringly at the Colonel. "Terribly sorry, sir. I thought you were alone. We've finished with your cover packet." She pushed a thick, large manila envelope across the desk. "Mind the fresh ink on the ration cards."

"Ah, my travel documents," said Foster, turning to the PM. "Just in case I get caught behind enemy lines. Miss Tremayne here and the others upstairs are to be commended for their fast, tidy work."

Churchill's face brightened for the first time. "Then you do intend to go in yourself?"

Foster nodded and tugged at his moustache. "Part way. Farther, if necessary. Let's say I'm going fishing in the Bay of Biscay." He turned to the woman warrant officer who watched him with an expectant, worried look. "That will be all, Molly. Thank you."

Molly Tremayne started to leave, then hesitated. Turning quickly, she blurted out: "Sir, will he be all right?"

Foster's eyebrows knitted, then relaxed. He smiled. "Skeet Merrill? The Yank is the least of my worries." Foster turned to the PM, explaining, "Tenacious enough, that one."

Molly lowered her eyes. She looked embarrassed. Boldly, she ventured, "I've never met Sigi Petersen, but from her security photographs, she's very attractive."

"And unfathomably cunning, from what I hear," interposed Churchill.

Molly nodded wistfully and dug in the pocket of her uniform. Fingers trembling, she withdrew a small blue envelope, hesitated, then placed it on Foster's desk. "Please sir, if conditions permit, I'd appreciate your giving this to Lieutenant Merrill. It's important. I've taken the precaution of writing it in German, of course."

Chapter 11

THE LEFT BANK was strangely subdued. As Dieter Loewen strolled past the church of St. Germain des Pres he felt a distinct awareness of being followed. He stopped and turned quickly, but the darkened street appeared empty and he heard no more footsteps. Loewen shivered as the feathery rain began to fall more rapidly and the wind picked up. The rotten weather made the usually colorful, gay streets of the Left Bank even more foreboding in the Paris blackout. Turning up his collar, he quickened his pace, deciding to chalk up his uneasiness to an overheated imagination and morbid stories he'd heard of waylayed German military men in France. Other officers Loewen had met at the hotel, however, had told him he had nothing to fear, that Parisians had become anaesthetized to enemy occupiers on their streets, that indeed, light-hearted St. Germain was purported to be safer than the Hamburg waterfront. Loewen hoped his advisors were correct.

Retreating into the protection of a *pissoir*, he paused, struck a match, and withdrew from his pocket a scrap of paper. He read the address and message once more and smiled to himself. The cursive scribbling obviously belonged to a woman on the make, probably the unmitigated gall of a local tart. They hung around the German billeting quarters like flies. Although the strange note in his hotel box inviting him to a Rive Gauche bistro had at first only amused him, boredom had taken its measure. Loewen remembered the last leave he'd taken in Paris, some months after his wife's air-raid death; how he'd then nursed his shore leave loneliness with a woman picked up at La Brasserie Louvois. Or had it been La Reine Bleue?

Loewen couldn't remember which. All he did remember was that the harlot had a sympathetic ear and a fat ass.

A gust of wind blew the note from his hands. Loewen shrugged. Once more, despite the blackout, Paris lay before him like a beckoning woman. The city's boulevards and its architecture were unspoiled, untouched by the forces of destruction that had destroyed most of Europe. Loewen liked France and its spirited culture; he wondered how he, the son of a disciplined, hard-nosed Bremerhaven ship's engineer, had become such a romantic and so liberal at heart.

Feeling a pleasant excitement running through him, Loewen crossed the street and walked on past the Cafe de Flore and Aux Deux Magots. He strolled leisurely down Boulevard St. Germain, passing a group of drunken Wehrmacht soldiers. He found the side street he was looking for, Rue de Seine, and turned left. Loewen penetrated the quiet street only a short distance when he heard measured footsteps behind him on the wet cobbles. He turned in time to see a small ferret of a man pause, then nervously dart into a shop entry. Loewen stepped quickly out of the rain into a protective doorway and waited. A street robber or pickpocket? Perhaps his shadow was just a pimp with working ladies on call, like the woman who wrote the note. Loewen could hear the footsteps hesitantly approaching—the man wasn't sure where his quarry had disappeared.

When the lone figure, clad in a oilskin raincoat and dark beret, came opposite him, Loewen stepped boldly out of the shadows. "You follow me for what purpose, Monsieur?" he asked gruffly, in his best French.

The slight individual, his face shielded by darkness, gave out a sharp gasp, dropped his cigarette, and bolted away, moments later disappearing into a bistro halfway up the street.

Loewen shook his head in annoyance and resumed his stroll. Reaching the same point midway up Rue de Seine, he stopped and squinted through the pall of rain to the opposite side of the street. A black Mercedes was parked at the curb, an SS sergeant behind the wheel idly smoking a cigarette. Loewen ignored the car and read the sign hanging over the bistro's doorway. Beneath a carved wooden crown were the words La Reine Bleue in tarnished gold letters. It was the place named in his note, and it was familiar to Loewen. In one of the windows the blackout curtains were askew, causing yellow light to shimmer and dance on the wet cobbles outside. Loewen could hear noise from within—shouting, laughter, and, though the voices were French, the gay polyphony warmed him. As he stood watching and listening, two men, rumpled and perspiring, came stumbling outside and urinated in the gutter. They stood laughing in the rain and when they'd finished their own drizzle, they re-entered the bistro, strutting like Napoleons.

Loewen ambled across the street and followed them inside.

The place was crowded. He saw clusters of men and women sitting at small tables smoking cheap tobacoo, drinking beer, and nursing cheaper grades of Pinot Chardonnay than they might have preferred. The talk was loud, some of it obscene. Loewen's recollection of an earlier visit quickly came back to him. La Reine Bleue, he remembered, was in St. Germain where only it could be. The establishment, before the war, had been famous for its bizarre entertainment and colorful clientele, which ran from pimps and prostitutes to starving artists and writers, as well as social deviates of mixed persuasions. And there were also the curious voyeurs and tourists like himself who came to gape at La Reine Bleue's potpourri stage entertainment, including its talented male and female impersonators.

Caught tonight in its peeling, leprous-green wallpaper, tattered blackout curtains, and sparsely lit interior, Loewen noted that the establishment was but a mocking echo of its prewar gaiety and dash. The attractive single ladies scattered about the audience that he remembered from a previous visit seemed to be missing. Still, he reasoned, the bistro's stage show might be something to see in an otherwise depressing wartime Paris. He'd stay for at least one drink.

Loewen removed his white-visored cap and waded through the noise, smoke, and perspiring bodies to a hatbox-sized table up front by the stage. Seeing no one who remotely resembled his follower on the street, he wondered where the mischief-bent shadow had disappeared. Loewen sat silently, observing the bistro patrons around him with a look of bored aloofness. He knew that back in Hamburg or Ploen a Reichskriegmarine officer would have been greeted by deference upon entering such a low-brow dive or *boui-boui*. Tonight the star and two and a half gold bars on his sleeve went unnoticed. Parisians, he'd heard, had become adept at ignoring Germans, particularly Germans in uniform.

* * *

From behind a large copper bar at one side of the bistro
Pierre Roger, La Reine Bleue's patron, considered the Reichskriegmarine officer who had just entered. Roger had a long,
fleshy face punctuated by an aquiline nose, penetrating brown
eyes, and a circular mouth like a goldfish. His head was
crowned by a soiled navy-blue beret and he wore a tired
gabardine suit but no tie. Of average height, the *patron's* frame
was poorly postured and paunchy around the stomach.

Turning to his wife Dominique, who worked beside him,
Roger nodded gravely, then continued to pour wine for a
waiter. Behind Roger and his wife were several stacks of
empty glasses, a fly-spotted mirror, and a vase of wilted
carnations. Dominique Roger was an amply bosomed woman
with a full face, but the skin of her cheeks had lost its bloom
and despite her makeup there was a faint purplish undertint to
her complexion. Her brown and gray flecked hair was tied back
with a piece of string over which she'd tied a neatly pressed,
spotless white apron.

Roger whispered in his wife's ear. "We are in luck, yes? The
Lion nibbles at our bait." He was satisfied that the German
naval officer matched perfectly the likeness in the photo Marie
Selva had sent Roger from St. Nazaire.

Before he could say another word, the *patronne* had skitted
off to Dieter Loewen's table. Roger overheard the German
order cognac, and by the time Dominique returned to the bar he
was ready with a glass of the bistro's best reserve.

Kapitan Leutnant Loewen, however, wasn't the only guest
to receive Roger's best cognac tonight. Sitting alone at the
opposite end of the room and overlooked by Loewen, sat SS
Sturmbannfuehrer Hermann von Wilme. Von Wilme, whose
inquisitive eyes also took in the sub ace with interest, had
visited the bistro several times before. Roger knew that the
Sturmbannfuehrer—a rank synonymous with major—was the
number two man in the Gestapo headquarters at 74 Avenue
Foch.

Roger heard von Wilme suddenly call out to his wife in
thickly accented French. *"Patronne!"*

Dominique Roger took her time approaching the SS man.
"Yes, Major?" she asked, unenthusiastically.

Hermann von Wilme wrote on a small card from his wallet,

ignoring her presence until he'd finished. "Take this to the Reichskriegmarine officer, Madame."

"Of course, Monsieur." She set off for the other German officer's table. Smiling hospitably, and with considerable emphasis, she placed the note before Loewen, then shifted her eyes back across the room to von Wilme. The SS major nodded his approval.

The U-boat ace glanced up at her, fingered the engraved card, and read the handwriting on the back. Glancing down, Dominique could easily see the message. The query was in German: *Will you join me at my table for a drink?* She watched Loewen glance across the room.

Hermann von Wilme airily lifted his glass. Loewen nodded to his countryman, at the same time taking in the black uniform with the two silver SS flashes on the collar with obvious apprehension. He raised his own glass courteously to return the toast and turned to the *patronne*. "The SS major paid for the cognac?"

"No, no, Monsieur," Dominique said emphatically. "You are a guest of La Reine Bleue."

Loewen looked surprised, but nodded. "Please thank the Gestapo officer for his invitation and inform him I mean no offense, but I prefer to sit alone this evening. I may be joined momentarily." Withdrawing from his wallet a French bank-note, he tucked it in Dominique's hand. "At least I should buy the major a drink."

Dominique nodded and quickly padded over to von Wilme's table to pass on Loewen's reply.

From his place behind the copper bar Roger watched Hermann von Wilme's reaction to his wife's message. The Gestapo man listened intently, then waved the *patronne* away and retreated to his brandy. He appeared affronted, sparing only a thin smile for Loewen. Roger breathed a sigh of relief, pleased the two men had not joined forces. *Mon Dieu!* Why tonight, of all times, had the SS major chosen to visit La Reine Bleue?

Roger knew a good deal about Hermann von Wilme, more than the SS man would ever suspect; the *patron* prided himself in knowing much about many high-ranking members of the enemy occupiers in Paris. Roger was aware that this fair-haired North German with his pink cheeks and firm, flat belly wasn't lacking for vanity. Von Wilme's custom-tailored uniforms were always immaculately pressed and his boots and belt gleamed as bright as polished glass. In the major's handsome face a pair of mouse-gray, intense eyes reflected neither cruelty nor harshness, but rather dedicated persistence. Roger knew that von Wilme, who was thirty-five when he first arrived in Paris, had risen steadily in the Gestapo headquarters hierarchy and was now adjutant to Oberfuehrer Hans Otterling, supreme head of German SS and Police in France. In such a role, Major von Wilme was privileged; he could well afford to be charitable during his off-duty hours and could indulge in bistro slumming under almost any pretext.

Backstage, hovering behind a frayed hole in the curtain, Erika Vermeer gazed balefully out at the night's customers. She noted the usual boisterous clientele nursing beer, wine and brandy as they waited for the floor show to begin. When she recognized the black uniformed SS officer in the corner she let out an uneasy sigh. *Major von Wilme here again?* She wondered if he would repeat his try at picking her up after the performance. He had to be avoided, at all costs.

Erika's mind flashed, once more questioning whether she'd done the right thing returning to La Reine Bleue. She wondered not only how much longer she could masquerade as a Swedish male impersonator on the bistro's stage, but also over her continued ability to function as a safecracker and active member of Pierre Roger's underground resistance cell. Heavy burdens, especially in light of her compulsion to march to a different drummer when it came to sexual preference. Whatever, she reflected, the commitment had been made. Every time she thought about the children back at Izieu it was reinforced.

Beside Erika, water dripping to the stage from his oilskin raincoat, her deaf-mute friend, Maurice Duval, squinted at the audience through his own rent in the curtain. She noted that cherubic-faced Maurice appeared unusually nervous, his small porcupine eyes darting around the bistro as if he were looking for someone in particular. Erika gently nudged the mute on the shoulder. Duval looked up.

"Where have you been, Maurice?" she asked slowly, with

emphasis, so that he might read her lips. "You are soaking wet!"

The little Frenchman ignored her.

Pierre Roger checked his watch and hurried backstage. Seeing Erika and Maurice standing idly behind the curtain, he shouted, "It's nine o'clock!" Roger thrust several centime coins in the deaf-mute's palm. "Why the raincoat? Remove it and go tend your music box, Maurice."

The bistro's floor shows always started on time, Roger was a stickler on that. Each evening was planned down to the last minute, for in wartime Paris the electricity went off promptly at ten, the Metro ceased to run at eleven, and the curfew began at midnight.

Roger pulled a switch and the footlights, what sparse bulbs remained, came up. He signaled to Maurice Duval out front. Prompted by a centime coin and the mute's kick, the ornately carved orchestrion beside the stage stirred to life. When the curtains opened, a miniature white poodle in a red jacket strutted out of the wings and gamboled in circles. A fat man in a tattered tuxedo rolled out a table with a half dozen parakeets. The poodle relieved itself on one of the table legs and the audience laughed.

Roger went up to the young lesbian who still loitered in the wings. "Erika! Your makeup. You'll be late for your act Hurry!" Roger snatched a workman's cap off a nearby clothes tree and flung it at her. Catching it, she scowled at him and sullenly started off for the dressing room.

Roger felt a tug on his sleeve. A primped impersonator sporting a shocking-pink feather boa beckoned to him with a devious smile. It was the fat transsexual, Sebastien.

"Give Erika the night off, Monsieur Roger. She is tired from her *vacation* in the Rhone Alps." Sebastien's mouth was a broad smirk, like the swag of a gaudy festoon. "I'll do a second number in her place, a *good one*, yes?"

Erika whirled, her hands defiantly on her hips. She shot Sebastien a scornful look. "Monsieur Sebastien, there's a show in Pigalle where a fat whore gets reamed by a donkey," she said scathingly. "I hear the woman is worn out and ready for retirement. Why don't you replace her? Your broad ass can provide the donkey with a pleasant diversion!"

Feathers flying, Sebastien hurled himself at Erika, who clenched her fists and stood her ground.

"Enough, enough!" shouted Roger, pulling them apart.

Startled by the outburst, the man on stage gaped into the wings. A confused parakeet missed its cue. Roger waved his arms frantically for the entertainer to get on with the performance, then angrily turned to Erika.

"When you are ready for your act," he admonished, "there is a customer out front we must discuss. The German officer."

"His safe, his billfold, or his brain, Monsieur Roger? Which do I pick this time? Or do I sell my body for the sake of the Resistance?"

"Enough of your insolence." Roger frowned. "It is the Lion himself."

Erika stiffened. Backing off her anger, she nodded to Roger, stole one last hateful glare at Sebastien, then swaggered off the stage.

Roger went back out front to his work station behind the copper bar. Immediately, his wife began to badger him, whispering in his ear.

"To use the transmitter tonight would be suicidal," Dominique admonished.

"But London must be contacted." Roger wasn't in the mood to argue, yet he knew only an hour earlier an enemy truck containing radio direction-finding gear had been seen operating in St. Germain. Now, to make matters worse, a high-ranking SS officer was in the bistro at the same time as Dieter Loewen.

Doffing his beret, Roger untied his apron and dropped it on the bar. Sullenly, he retreated into the back hallway and trudged up the stairs to his cold water apartment. Again he debated whether or not to use the transmitter and jeopardize the bistro's cover. *No. Too much was at stake*. Despite the excellent possibility the long distance exchange would be monitored, he would instead telephone Marie Selva in St. Nazaire, choose his words very carefully, and entrust the woman undertaker to relay his report on to London. But first Roger would dutifully listen to the coded messages that followed the 9 PM news from England.

Throwing the bolt on the apartment door, he hastened to the radio that was sequestered behind a hinged bookshelf. He switched the transceiver to the listening position and waited. Tuning to the BBC was absolutely forbidden by the German occupiers, but flouting the order had become a way of life to Roger and other Frenchmen. The program had another two minutes to run and Roger kept the volume to a whisper. Finally, following the news, the cryptic messages to the French and Dutch underground began. "The donkeys have strayed from the abbey. The porcelain in Orleans needs mending today. Violette has recovered from the measles. Carthage must not be destroyed." There was a pause, then: "The long sobs of the violins of autumn."

Roger's heart skipped a beat. The first line of Verlaine's poem, *Song of Autumn!* The initial warning of the Anglo-American invasion! When the second line of the poem was broadcast, the assault would begin in a matter of hours. The great armada Europe and the rest of the world had waited for!

Roger switched off the radio, replaced the bookcase, and rushed to the wall telephone in the hallway. He found a number scribbled on the soiled flowerprint wallpaper and gave it to the central exchange operator.

Drumming his fingers on the wall, Roger withdrew his pocket watch to check the time. Two minutes went by, then three. In the name of God, he wondered, what was wrong with the circuit to St. Nazaire?

"Hello?" A woman's tired voice crackled at the other end of the line, then became lost in heavy static. The interference, sounding to Roger like a school of snapping shrimp, finally faded away and the voice came through again, much clearer. "Hello? Are you there?"

"Madame Selva?" Roger queried with impatience.

"Yes, yes."

"Please listen carefully."

Chapter 12

MERRILL WAS BESIDE himself at the twenty-four-hour delay. The weather had only improved marginally though the forecasters were counting on improvement within a matter of hours. Even so, it would be too late to get off tonight. The pilots had promised they'd go tomorrow, no matter what.

The parachute loft was a large balcony at the end of a repair hangar. Two smiling RAF men stood by watching Merrill as he unfolded the parachute on a long, plywood-covered table.

His fear was unfounded; the chute appeared to have been packed properly enough and Merrill felt a little paranoid for having raised a ruckus. The two men exchanged brief glances as Merrill carefully refolded the silk and cords. A cockroach darted across the parachute canopy as he worked. Grinning, Merrill buried it in the pack, figuring he'd be generous and give it an opportunity to see the French countryside.

Merrill let out an exasperated sigh. Nothing to do now but go back to the barracks and bury himself in a little reading material, for he'd be damned if he'd let Sigi beat him at chess one more time. Thinking about his close-mouthed companion, Merrill couldn't help fuming again over the way the mission was organized. Eisenhower should have know better than turn the job over to the stuffy stiffs at G-10, but far be it for Merrill to criticize flag staff mentality. Perhaps, instead of knocking his superiors, he should curse John Holland and Simon Lake—or was it some Frenchmen who invented the damned submarine?

As much as Merrill loved pigboats—the principle of submersion, the smooth as glass movement beneath the sea while a typhoon might be raging overhead, and yes, even the stealth—he dreaded the terror a sub could arbitrarily inflict. Merrill was committed to the war as a matter of principle, but like most sane men, he held it in contempt. Were Dieter Loewen's priorities similar or was the Lion motivated by other passions? According to the German's dossier, the ace had not joined the Nazi Party; not so strange for Wehrmacht officers, but the Reichskriegmarine was noted for its roster of NSAP activists.

Merrill stared numbly at the rebundled parachute before him. He felt genuinely confident and optimistic about most things, but not the kettle of *bouillabaise* waiting for him on the other side of the Channel. When Merrill set his bile to work on mysterious fare, he liked to know just a little about the reputation of the people who prepared it. If he was going to work effectively with Sigi, she'd have to be less secretive. The Allies may have mastered secrecy and stealth, but Merrill knew the Germans were good at it too. Very good.

"The pack's satisfactory, sir?" asked one of the airmen goodnaturedly.

Merrill glanced up from his daze and risked a smile. He nodded. Quickly hefting the chute over his shoulder, he grabbed up his rain poncho and headed for the door.

Erika Vermeer thoroughly enjoyed her role. Dressed as a macho Swedish lumberjack, she flicked her suspenders, winked at the audience, and continued her song in a whiskey-baritone. *"Nar kan jag fa traffa Er igen?"* The melancholy Scandinavian lyrics were hardly suited to her uneven, off-key voice, but both French and German taste was unpredictable these days and she felt more secure in a language less readily understood in Paris. *Camouflage*—she'd learned to make the most of it. The Swedish logger act, though it had been difficult to learn, was infinitely safer than openly revealing herself as a Dutch entertainer.

She was halfway through the second verse, enjoying a fleeting flirtation with some pallid-looking women at tables in the middle of the room, when she saw entering the bistro a tall civilian in a gray camel-hair overcoat, billed woolen cap, and black gloves. One more German to contend with, she reasoned, an aristocratic one at that. Erika watched the stranger slip quietly across the room, hover over SS Major von Wilme, and whisper in his ear. She sang without enthusiasm, continuing to observe as the intruder brusquely waved the *patronne* away without ordering a drink. Reaching into his coat and withdrawing a photograph, the man fixed a monocle to one eye and shared the picture with von Wilme. Erika saw them study the likeness carefully, then look up through the bistro's clouds of smoke toward the stage. They were studying her!

"*Ni ar sa——*" Flustered, her heart skipping a beat, Erika missed one of the song's lines. She tried to put her anxiety away, mannishly strutting across the stage and quickly picking up the verse. But from the corner of her eye she noted that von Wilme was now nodding gravely and gesturing for the tall newcomer to take a seat at his table. Erika knew this inturder was not simply a street peddler pushing obscene little postcards; she had a sinking feeling that here was a face from the past, a dangerous face she wanted to forget. Perspiration began forming on the back of her neck as she gulped in a deep breath and finished the song. "*Ni ar sa vacker. Ni ar sa vacker.*"

The audience applauded. Some hooted.

Erika flung aside the workman's cap, let her hair fall to her shoulder, and bowed to the crowd. The women laughed and the men cheered. Several members of the audience tossed centimes on the stage, and there were two coins that had the familiar clunks of francs. When Erika's gaze fell on the apathetic U-boat ace just beyond the footlights, she was disappointed. Dieter Loewen had sat on his hands, apparently unmoved by her performance. No matter, she'd make doubly sure the German naval officer remembered her act. Floating with infinite grace to the edge of the stage in a feminine pose that was very much unlike her, Erika pulled away the single yellow rose from her lumberjack shirt and with exacting aim tossed it to Dieter Loewen's table.

The audience cooed softly and laughed, but at the opposite end of the room, Hermann von Wilme visibly flinched. The SS major was not amused. His lower lip began to nervously twitch sideways, like a person avoiding an annoying gnat. Erika smiled to herself, secretly amused but caring less if von Wilme were jealous. She glanced at Loewen, watching him examine the rose, casually sniff its fragrance, then to the glee of the bistro's clientele around him, tuck it inside his jacket. But she couldn't forget the tall, mysterious civilian seated beside von Wilme. Her eyes nervously darted back to him.

Erika suddenly remembered and was able to place the cold, expressionless face. She recoiled. The man continued to stare at her, and fear began crawling over Erika's arms and shoulders like a hairy centipede. Ignoring the coins tossed out front, she dashed for the wings.

An older woman violinist with pasty makeup gave Erika a bewildered look and shuffled out on the stage, replacing her.

Half running, half tripping, Erika started to unbutton her plaid shirt as she hurried to the dressing room. Pierre Roger, sensing her distress, came up to her. "Trouble?" he asked, studying her intently.

Erika whirled, facing him in the dressing room doorway. "No time, Monsieur Roger. I must go. They will surely interrogate and arrest me!" She watched the *patron's* face turn white except for pink spots above the cheek bones. Grabbing a small duffel, she hurtled for the bistro's rear door. Taking time to change was out of the question. Roger understood.

"You must not return tonight," he said, anxiously.

"Or at any other time," added Erika, her voice trembling.

"Go to my cousin's in Rue Clemont," snapped Roger. "I'll contact you there."

The next instant she was gone.

The *patron* drew in a deep breath and walked calmly up to the two Germans who had just strolled backstage. "Messieurs?"

"The young male impersonator," snapped von Wilme. "Where is *he* or *she*?"

Pierre Roger spread his hands and gave the SS men a perplexed look. "Which one do you wish to meet? We have three, all charming." Roger wondered if he would regret this response.

Hermann von Wilme wasn't amused; he shot Roger a reptilian glare.

Roger was about to apologize for his indiscretion when the tall civilain with the monocle thrust a wrinkled snapshot in front of him. "Do not toy with us, Monsieur proprietor," he warned. "My name is Reinhard Schiller. I'm from Berlin. Your entertainment is decadent, Monsieur, but this photograph resembles a performer on that stage who is of interest to me."

Despite the lack of uniform and his civilian apparel, Roger

suspected from the man's bearing that he, too, was Gestapo. Moreover, by von Wilme's deferential manner, Schiller was apparently in command. The photograph, Roger noted, was an excellent likeness of Erika Vermeer, but she was in a seaman's uniform, her hair hidden under her cap; it was as if the Kriegsmarine enlisted man in the picture were her twin brother.

Roger spoke slowly, trying to buy time. "Erika's probably changing wardrobes in the dressing room, or she's gone to the cellar to her sleeping accommodations." He watched the taller German's eyes shrewdly survey the backstage area.

Reinhard Schiller nodded to von Wilme and both men took off at a clip in different directions.

Brief moments later, rejoining in the stage wing, they once more confronted Roger.

"The photograph," said Roger, baiting them with his own innocence. "The tough young woman is German, then, and not a Swedish neutral as she claims? *Mon Dieu!* Have I employed a deserter?" Roger had made up his mind to say or do anything at this point to keep La Reine Bleue's cover intact. "These young impersonators are nothing but trouble. They come, they go. You must tell me more about Erika, yes?"

Reinhard Schiller had heard him out with a catlike glint in his eye. "Do not concern yourself with Reich intelligence matters, *patron*. Show us your apartment upstairs, immediately!" The German's tone was hard and uncompromising.

Roger nodded. He removed his beret and nervously ran his fingers through his hair. "Certainly, but——"

"You waste your time, *Messieurs*." The nasal, musical voice from behind belonged to the entertainer Sebastien. "The chicken has flown the coop." With a fanatical gaze at the SS men, he smugly gestured toward the rear door.

The menacing vacuum was filled only by the off-key violin music from the stage. The two Germans drew their guns and bolted for the door.

The U-boat ace had better things to do than listen to tonedeaf, blowsy women with violins, difficulties in obtaining wartime entertainment notwithstanding. Loewen polished off the remainder of his cognac and headed for the bistro exit.

As he stepped briskly out into the dark street, rain fell in a light drizzle and hung like a heavy mist, interspersing itself with low nests of fog. Loewen inhaled deeply, refreshed to be away from the heavy smoke and odor of acrid wine within. He wandered down Rue de Seine and let the soft rain, the fog, and the noise of the Left Bank absorb him. St. Germain des Pres had not changed since his last visit to Paris, war or no war. Except for the ladies at La Reine Bleue, who appeared more gross than he had remembered. No matter. If he didn't find a woman to sleep with tonight, tomorrow night he would explore Pigalle, or possibly Montparnasse. The mysterious invitation to Le Reine Bleue, if it could not be called romantically productive, was at least entertaining. And prior to his cognacs at the bistro, the street incident did have a taint of adventure.

Remembering the yellow rose inside his tunic, Loewen withdrew it, allowed the rain to play on its wilted petals, then aimlessly tossed it in the gutter. He suddenly felt an urge to be back on the Right Bank, where there would be fellow Germans in abundance. Once into the Metro it would be a short ride to the other side of the Seine and his hotel on the Rue de Rivoli.

Suddenly the premonition struck again—*was he being followed?* Loewen turned, but the immediate area behind him was empty. Yet when he resumed his stride he again heard measured footsteps. He wasn't alone. Loewen quickened his pace up the dark street, heading for Boulevard St. Germain.

Then he heard running feet gaining on him. Loewen spun around, but before he could react, two shadowy figures were on him, wrestling him to the ground, a scarf held tightly to his mouth. Loewen drove his fist into a fleshy stomach and dodged to one side. He saw the blur of a gun from the corner of his eye, the weapon missing his head by inches. A shrill whistle sounded from down the street and suddenly, as quickly as they had come for him, the two men disappeared.

Loewen slowly climbed to his feet, sucked in a lung full of air, and brushed himself off. The gendarme approached, gestured with his hands, and spoke rapidly in French. Loewen pointed in the direction his accosters had used to escape, then, ignoring the *flic*, straightened his shoulders and hastened up the street. St. Germain des Pres was not safe for Germans in uniform after all, he concluded.

Chapter 13

MERRILL PULLED the poncho over his head as he slogged his way from the parachute loft back to his billet. His route took him past the Base Operations building. Its windows were blacked out as usual, but inside he knew there would be plenty of activity. Activity that Merrill hoped would prepare the way for them to once and for all get into the air.

Some fifty yards away at the far end of the building, Merrill saw parked an olive-drab Morris sedan, its motor and windshield wipers running. Abruptly, from a side door of Operations, two uniformed men emerged and bee-lined through the rain to the waiting car. One of the men was the tall Scot, Cummings, and he now stood at the back door of the Morris, struggling with a broken umbrella. Cummings didn't climb inside with the other individual, an officer who appeared anxious to have his driver get underway.

Curious, Merrill paused in the shadows and watched. A flash of lightning brightened the roadway and for a fleeting moment he saw clearly the serious face conversing with Cummings from the back of the Morris.

Stuart Foster!

Merrill frowned. Why had the Royal Marines colonel suddenly come down to Chatham on a clandestine visit? When Merrill had last seen Cummings an hour earlier, he'd said nothing about this, nor had Sigi Petersen. Did she know?

The car door closed and Foster's driver quickly accelerated. The Morris disappeared through the sleet, heading in the direction of the Chatham base gate. Still fighting his umbrella, Cummings ran back inside the building. Merrill wanted to go

after him, but an odd, tense premonition that told him to wait
and keep his eyes and ears open held him rooted to the spot,
oblivious to the increasing downpour.

Alone in her billet room, Sigi Petersen hummed happily as
she studied her face in the mirror from her compact. For the
past ten minutes she'd been lost in pleasant memories. Placing
the small mirror at a distance on the cot, she examined and
admired—for the first time in several months—her ample, firm
breasts. *Not bad at all,* she reflected. No evidence of slack yet
or a need for cosmetics like tape or uplifting bras.

Sighing, she turned off the overhead light and slipped nude
under the covers. There was a small lamp over her cot and she
directed its beam on the book she'd brought to bed with her. It
was Goethe's last pain of love, *Elegy of Marienbad.* She was
determined to finish the passionate poetry before leaving
England. Sigi smiled to herself, wondering if Skeet Merrill had
any interest in literature. Probably least of all Goethe or other
German authors. She wondered what intellectual ground, if
any, there would be to plow between them.

She read for a good half hour then decided to place the book
aside. It was late and sleep would become precious in the days
ahead; no excuse for not soaking it up while she could. Sigi
turned out the lamp and stared into nothingness.

It was inevitable, she mused, that the Dutch girl would fail
at Wilhelmshaven and Sigi would be sent over to the continent
to pick up the pieces. The assignment couldn't have come at a
better time. Sigi was lucky, as were her superiors, though she
was still puzzled over the American being bundled to England
for the mission. A British demolition man might have been just
as effective, but apparently Eisenhower was determined to
have a hand—or a spy—in the pie.

Basking in confidence, Sigi closed her eyes. She was fully
prepared for this biggest role in her life. Skeet Merrill would
learn some important lessons, among them what it was like
trying to fly in tandem with the queen bee.

In Paris, SS Colonel Reinhard Schiller liberally tipped the
Hotel George V night porter for having rounded up such a fine
bottle of cognac, scarcity of good brandy and the late hour

considered. The porter nodded his thanks, took Schiller's shoes for polishing, and disappeared down the hallway. Schiller closed the door, retreated to a small desk in the corner of the room, and poured the cognac. For a long time he stood there, deep in thought, sipping the fragrant brandy. Finally he sat down, inserted his monocle, and opened his briefcase. Pushing aside the large bundle of counterfeit English and French banknotes, he withdrew several documents and photographs. One at a time he examined them closely, as a stonecutter might study a diamond in the rough before going to work. He began to make notes. Back in Berlin, Himmler and Hitler would insist on a meticulous report when all the dirty work was concluded.

For several minutes the only sound in the room was the steady scratching of Schiller's pen. When Admiral Doenitz and Himmler had seen him off at the Luftwaffe field near Salzburg, Schiller had promised them he would not fail. It was beyond consideration, for Reinhard Schiller had never failed in any intelligence assignment. Though he'd always been impressed with the enemy's espionage apparatus, he now felt complete amazement at G-10's cunning and sheer audacity. For *Operation Storm Tide,* the Allies were extremely well-organized. They'd have to be, to combine personnel from the highly fractured French, Dutch, and Norwegian resistance movements, incorporating them into one cohesive mission.

When he had finished, Schiller removed his monocle and pushed the papers back in the briefcase, carefully arranging them in their original sequence. He was meticulous in his habits and proud of neat files.

Climbing to his feet, Schiller removed his gray, pin-striped suit jacket and hung it carefully over the back of the desk chair. Pulling his six-foot-two frame erect and stretching, he stepped over to the oval mirror above the sink, washed his face with cold water and gave himself a long and satisfying look. Schiller took secret pride in withholding from Nazi collectivization a major fragment of his personality and his expression reflected this.

He smiled at his own reflection. His handsome enough, cleanly-chiseled face, blond crew cut, and dignified, patrician manner were a marked contrast to many SS officers. Indeed, he suspected his mannerisms had more often than not been a source of irritation to others in the ranks. Some of his peers in the SS hierarchy had described his bearing as being too aloof, an enigma; that his private personality and piercing transparent blue eyes made them uncomfortable. He was, in many respects, much like Heinrich Himmler, but far better looking. And Himmler favored him, that was all that really mattered. When in civilian clothing, Schiller could pass for a wealthy banker or landed Baron; few then believed he was involved in one of war's dirtier aspects.

Earlier tonight, at the Rive Gauche bistro, Schiller had deliberately gone in mufti, but tomorrow morning he would put on his cap with the death's head insignia on its peak and the braided black tunic with the cuff titles RFSS picked out in silver thread: *Reichsfuhrer der SS*—the marking of Himmler's personal staff.

The bistro cellar was dim and Maurice Duval had to squint to read his watch. It was just after two in the morning. The deaf-mute opened and examined the small automatic Italian pistol he'd acquired just the week before. Duval had never fired it, and it still had the manufacturer's grease in the barrel. He familiarized himself with the gun one more time, then hid it under his pillow. So the SS was after Erika Vermeer, he thought. The *patron* had warned Duval to watch his step, that he could be next. Duval had only laughed inwardly at Pierre Roger at that.

Taking out his note pad, and despite the dimness and his tired eyes, Duval began to write feverishly. The message took a long time, and when he was finished, he folded and neatly sealed it in a white envelope. The pallet Roger had prepared for him, of straw in a mattress sack, was comfortable enough, but the earthen floor was cold and he kept his stockings on. For the past week Duval had been troubled with rats, so he once more set two traps before retiring. A bare bulb dangled from a frayed ceiling cord, and had there been electricity, he'd have left the light burning all night. Instead Duval would have to make do with the small kerosene lantern, although he doubted it would keep the scurrying rodents at a respectable distance. And the rats were probably too well fed on the bistro's provisions to go for his traps.

A deep melancholy settled over Duval. When the *patron* had explained that both he and Erika would shortly be leaving on a two-day OCM mission to Brittany, his instincts told him complicated things were hidden here—important motives deserving of more clarification. But Roger, predictably, in his usual closed manner, had refused to elaborate.

Stashing his secret envelope beneath the pillow next to the gun, Duval yawned like a cat and pulled the soiled patchwork quilt the *patronne* had given him up over his chin. He was tired. To escape the rats, he'd pin his hope on immediate sleep. He wasn't disappointed.

La Reine Bleue's *patron* tossed fitfully in his bed, a fourposter much more comfortable than the pallet he'd provided Maurice Duval in the cellar. Usually in the solace of sleep Pierre Roger had been able to shrink from his perilous, two-faced responsibilities, but after tonight's appearance of Dieter Loewen and the two SS men at the same time, he suspected his time was running out. Many of the terrors Roger had only imagined were now becoming more real with each passing day. At this very moment, a Gestapo guard lurked across the street in a shadowy storefront. Was he checking on Roger himself or waiting for Erika to return? Roger knew now that he'd made a mistake taking the young, half-Jewish Hollander back in. But where else was she to go? And as long as she was in Paris, he could use her talents for the Operation Storm Tide assignment.

Roger rolled over, pounded his pillow, and again considered his alternatives for the upcoming St. Nazaire mission. He wasn't sure how much assistance Marie Selva needed, and worthy operatives were difficult to find. Unfortunately, *Organization Civile de Militaire*—the French Underground—had often been more disorganized and difficult to deal with than the occupiers themselves. Trust was a fragile commodity these days in Paris. *Maquis*, resistance workers, *collaborateurs*—Roger knew that every Frenchman was actually or potentially one or the other. He himself had strong political beliefs that motivated his actions. And the self-important German occupiers could set no example for solidarity! They had their own individual debts of allegiance: Wehrmacht, SD, SS, Abwehr. The most beautiful city in the world, at this moment to Roger, had become a living nightmare of distrust.

But come what may, he could rely on the mute Duval, and he

was sure he could trust Erika Vermeer. Yes, the young lesbian woman would have to be protected, kept in hiding until they left for St. Nazaire.

Roger's restlessness woke his wife. Sitting bolt upright, Dominique wearily lit the blackout candle beside the bed. "Enough! Enough, Pierre," she grumbled, shaking him like a rag doll. "You thrust around like a wounded tiger!"

Roger rolled to his side and faced her. "Forgive me, Dominique. I have worries."

She looked at him with annoyance. "The rumor of the enemy within our ranks?"

Roger squirmed uncomfortably and shrugged. "I suspect no one but Sebastien."

"The fat one is no agent, only a silly fool," Dominique grunted.

"If there is a counterspy, we will know tomorrow night when help arrives from London."

Dominique frowned. "London! Always, Pierre, you look to the Anglos to answer our problems. I envy them dreaming up the impossible! But it is we field operatives who must soil our hands to make their grandiose schemes work. I suspect if we have a traitor among us, he is not in France but in England at G-10!"

"And supposing he is in *both* places?" he asked her quietly.

She smiled gently and stroked his shoulder. "You're tired, Pierre. But you are as clever as the others, yes? This time your mission will succeed. Marie Selva and the agents from England will need your alertness, so you must now sleep."

Roger met her unsympathetic eyes. "And I need you too, Dominique." He placed his hand in the warm nest between her legs but there was no response. She sighed, slid away from him, and blew out the candle. As the bedroom plunged back into darkness, she whispered, "Tomorrow night, possibly. Go to sleep, Pierre."

The dogs were close at her heels, too close, Erika thought. Staring blankly at the ceiling of the room the *patron* had arranged for her, she tried to grapple with her dangerous predicament. Tonight, in some respects, everything was much clearer to her than it had ever been in her life. The male impersonator routine appeared to be over; the act at La Reine

Bleue had begun to bore her anyway. Perhaps, for the sake of her femininity—if there were enough remaining—Erika Vermeer would be wise to find a new cover. For the duration of the war she might even have to forget pursuing other women if she wanted to stay alive. A steady, inconspicuous companion was what she needed, a pretty, French girl on the passive side.

The sound of a truck halting outside the building shattered Erika's trance. She bolted upright in bed, her body taut. She heard a familiar sound: doors slamming, a tailgate drop, and harsh guttural voices. A replay of the nightmare at the orphanage! Quickly heaving herself out of bed, she slid along the wall to the window. Below her Rue Clemont was full of German soldiers, who moved rapidly to surround the area.

Erika's breath caught in her throat. She was trapped!

Had Pierre Roger betrayed her? Erika searched the street, looking for the tall German with the monocle, the man she had earlier come to know only as Schiller. And where was that even more familiar face, that lecher of Paris, SS Major von Wilme?

She saw a scantily clad woman dash out over the cobbles, cursing loudly in French. One of the Germans brought her struggling back to the truck and pushed her up inside. Erika sighed with relief. The enemy soldiers were raiding a brothel next door apparently operating after the curfew. Pulling the curtain back in place, she clambered back in bed and closed her eyes. But no matter how she tried, she couldn't sleep.

Chapter 14

THEY WERE OVER enemy territory now, almost ready to drop into the lion's den, and Skeet Merrill was as prepared as he'd ever be. He felt better up front in the Halifax cockpit, for the rear of the bomber fuselage was cold and unbearably noisy. Merrill in fact felt invigorated, enjoying an elusive taste of freedom after two months of being cooped up in London. At last he was out in the action again.

Four-engined *Trenchant Tillie* had been twenty minutes late nosing up off the macadam at Chatham Airfield. Merrill glanced at his watch. Despite Flying Officer Clinton's efforts to pick up time over the channel, the mission was still behind schedule. Long minutes had been lost when Clinton revised his course to avoid flak over the coast of France, and after that they'd been forced to jog southwest to avoid a Luftwaffe fighter concentration at Amiens. Finally, in a determined effort to stay as far away from metropolitan Paris as possible, the plane made a wide sweep east and was now approaching the parachute drop point from the direction of the German border. Merrill suspected that if enemy plotting tables locked on to *Trenchant Tillie* this night, the Germans would think the Halifax pilot hopelessly lost or unforgiveably drunk.

Pilot Clinton pointed to a small pinpoint on his map of France. Merrill looked over his shoulder and nodded. The RAF flying officer appeared to be a proficient old hand at sneaking across the backyards of France, making his rapid references to photographs, compass, and air speed indicator with all the confidence of a fox in a blind man's hen house.

"How much longer?" Merrill put a distinctly impatient ring to the question.

"Fifteen minutes at best." Clinton peered out the side of the windscreen at the checkerboard farms and winding streams of the pastoral countryside below. "Beautiful country," he called.

"Yeah. Idyllic," Merrill acknowledged, without enthusiasm.

"Looks too innocently peaceful! From where I sit, too often dodging flak over Germany, the spy racket appears damned comfortable! You're lucky, Yank."

Merrill nodded.

Clinton shouted again. "Not every bloke in this war gets to work shoulder to shoulder with enticing females like the cross-channel fare I'm carrying tonight!" He gestured toward the rear of the Halifax. "A definite knockout you have there, you don't mind me saying."

Merrill grinned, patted the pilot on the shoulder, and headed for the rear of the plane.

Pierre Roger slowly backed the appropriated Wehrmacht supply truck off the highway.

"Why are we stopping?" asked Erika, uneasily.

Roger looked at her with impatience. "Only a fool would directly approach Levec's farm without first scouting the area."

Concealing the tarpaulin-covered *kraftswagen* in a nest of willow trees, Roger killed the engine and checked his watch. It was twenty minutes past nine. He knew there was little chance of traffic on the road between Meaux and Nanteuil-Le Haudouin except for a possible north-south German freight convoy or a stray farmer on a bicycle. Still, Roger would play it cautious, for another OCM team had been caught red-handed at an earlier Allied airdrop. Tonight, not only might the cunning enemy have staked out the drop area, but it could even be disguised Germans themselves who would drift in under the big silk canopies.

Twenty minutes passed. Roger had sent Maurice Duval up ahead on bicycle, reasoning it would take the mute all of fifteen minutes to properly reconnoiter the produce farm. Roger turned to the silent young woman sitting beside him in the cab.

Erika ignored him, continuing to stare pensively out into the moonlit night.

"Your thoughts are elsewhere," said Roger quietly.

"I am wondering how SS Colonel Schiller knew I was in France. How do we know whom to trust any longer?" Erika looked sharply at Roger, lowering her voice. "The men in the back, for example. Those are new faces."

"They come recommended." Roger shrugged and glanced over his shoulder. Gervais and Roland sat in the darkness, their presence revealed only by the intermittent glow of cigarettes and heavy breathing. Despite Erika's concern, Roger was thankful he'd been able to recruit these additional operatives in nearby Meaux. Now, together with the farmer Levec, Erika, Duval, and himself, there would be six tin-sleeved flashlights to properly mark the drop area perimeter. Roger saw the man nearest the tailgate, Gervais, lift the canvas flap, push his head out and gaze through the willows at the patchy gray clouds and werewolf moon.

Gervais hunched his shoulders and turned back toward Roger and Erika at the front of the truck. "The moon shows both cheeks," he said gruffly. "I say it is too bright!" Gervais, like the others, was aware that the Allies always made drops to the Resistance when the moon was full or nearly full, and that the Germans knew this also. "Damned stupid in my book," he ranted. "If I were handling things, the drops would be made only in total darkness."

Pierre Roger shook his head and snorted, "If you were handling things! You make me laugh, Gervais."

Erika promptly added, "I can see you parachuting on an ink-black night with no moon, landing with a weathervane up your ass!"

"*Merde!*" Gervais retorted. He dropped the canvas roll and returned to his seat.

During the pregnant silence that followed Roger caught a pungent whiff of smoke from the rear of the truck. "That's exactly what your tobacco smoke smells like, Monsieur," he grumbled, "*Crap!*"

"I smoke the same brand, Pierre." It was the first time Roland, the second man in back, had spoken, and the voice was unfriendly. "It is the best available in Meaux."

Erika fired off another salvo. "Roger is right, Roland. It smells like you smoke dried camel dung from Algeria."

Gervais sneered, "Bring us better cigarettes from Paris and we'll pay for them. If not, curb your tongue."

Roger couldn't care less about tobacco shortages in France. He listened to Gervais, Roland, and Erika drone on about the black market in hard-to-find items, sometimes following what they were saying; sometimes his mind was a thousand miles away. Leaning out the cab window, Roger cocked his ear toward the roadway. Above the cricket chorus and croak of the bullfrogs he heard a squeaking bicycle. Only the mute Duval would have neglected oiling noisy wheels.

Maurice Duval turned the bicycle off the hard-surface road and walked with it until he reached the truck hidden in the willows. Hurrying up to the vehicle, he thrust a scrap of paper through the cab window to Roger, who conscientiously studied it for several seconds without comment. Duval didn't wait for Roger's reaction to his scribbling. He hastened to the back of the *kraftswagen*, where two figures emerged from beneath the drop canvas and hauled in his bicycle. The mute scrambled inside himself and huddled in the corner, away from the others.

Roger brooded over Duval's message for several minutes. Finally, he turned to Erika and said somberly, "Maurice tells us there is a German sidecar motorcycle with a flat tire one kilometer past the junction leading to Levec's farm." Roger slowly rubbed his chin, weighing the possibility of a trap. *Was the enemy expecting them?*

"How many *boche*?" Erika queried, "two, three?"

Roger handed her the mute's note. "According to Maurice, only a driver and a footsoldier passenger."

Erika smiled at him. "Two of them and five of us. Six, including the farmer Levec!"

"He is old and infirm," admonished a gruff voice from the back of the truck.

Shrugging, Roger started the engine and put the vehicle in gear. He said to the others, "The mute has seen Monsieur Levec, who claims his farm itself is safe. Speed will be in our favor, and our escape route toward Meaux and Paris takes us in the opposite direction from the Germans."

No argument came from Erika or the men in the back. They were fully resigned, when it came down to it, to let Roger make the difficult decisions.

Wheeling the *kraftswagen* out onto the hard-surface road, Roger drove north to the Levec farm turnoff, a dirt road sorely in need of repair. The truck bounced over the ruts several minutes until it finally rolled to a stop beside an old stone barn. Roger anxiously checked his watch. It was 9:45. The British bomber bearing the man and woman was due at ten. Just enough time to dispatch his torchbearers to the drop zone.

Levec, the old farmer, hobbled out from inside the barn. Roger conferred in hushed tones with him, then promptly sent the entire group into the freshly plowed field. Each team member knew his precise task, for the farm had been used once before for an airdrop of OCM supplies.

Roger was still concerned over the nearby Germans. He hoped their flat tire was fixed and that they'd moved on. Signaling the RAF plane to return to England with its passengers would be simple enough, but Roger knew there wasn't time to get off another flight or arrange a second drop area. The two operatives would have to land at Levec's farm tonight, within the hour.

Ten o'clock came and passed. Roger sat on the rise of a tilled furrow, eyes straining toward the northern horizon. He watched the moon dip behind a bank of low clouds, then emerge again, bathing the field with gray light. Roger knew the Levec property was ideally suited for its assignment tonight. The soft, freshly-plowed vegetable field, flanked between gently sloping hills, measured 400 meters long by 300 wide. The grass-covered knolls to the sides were neither steep nor rocky, and a slight deviation in the drop could be made with safety. There was less margin for error on the north side of the farm because of the large stone barn, but if and when the plane arrived, Roger and the others were not anticipating mistakes, for they knew the RAF pilots and stagers were highly proficient and took fierce pride in their jobs.

Skeet Merrill played *Besame Mucho* one more time on his harmonica, then tucked the instrument away. The aircraft fuselage was so noisy no one else could have heard his rendition if they'd wanted. He watched with amusement as Sigi lifted her tin cup and emptied the last of its rum-spiked coffee. Beside her, a freckle-faced, gangly RAF corporal grinned, took away the cup, and shouted to make himself heard above the roar of the Rolls-Merlin engines. "Time you were getting set up for the drop, Miss!"

Merrill wondered if the corporal's proffered brace of toddy would do its work on time, for Sigi's face was still pale, her blue eyes apprehensive and frightened. All the stager could do now was give her the usual grin for good luck and a reassuring clout on the shoulder, which he did.

"Nothing to worry about, Miss, except the bloody Jerries down below. I'll get you down on top of a shilling piece if you'll mind the green light and my gentle push!" Leaving her, the youth came over to double-check Merrill's gear.

Merrill removed the four giant wads of cotton from his ears and took the jump helmet from the stager. He'd avoided conversation in the rear of the fuselage mainly because of the ridiculousness of screaming to make himself heard. Merrill rose, went up to Sigi, gave her a reassuring nod, and broke his self-imposed solitude. "Your lipstick is smeared, *Fraulein Schramm*," he shouted.

She looked back at him quizzically.

Merrill smiled. Just as well she didn't hear, he mused. Something about this attractive partner bewildered him—the feeling that she moved easily without him, an aloofness, a self-sufficiency that he'd never known in other women. Merrill looked at her, considering her weaknesses and her strengths. It seemed he'd already summed her up a dozen times, but now that they were about to jump into the inferno together, it was well to refresh his memory. Again he wondered how she'd bear up under enemy fire when the going got rough, really rough. Were her basic instincts in proper order? Self-preservation, sex, and instinct of the herd? Or by some fluke of temperament, physical condition, or upbringing, were the priorities bungled?

Not much he could do about it now. Eisenhower, the PM and Colonel Foster had crammed her down his throat, those impeccable credentials and all, and it was his job to protect her. And God willing, protect her he would. Still, the sexist that he was, he'd be a fool to completely ignore the biological imperatives. Considering the fact that Sigi was a tantalizing woman, he resolved to himself that any sudden intrusion of the sexual element in their partnership shouldn't come as a surprise.

Merrill handed Sigi her helmet, waited patiently until she managed to carefully tuck each strand of her pale blonde hair inside it, then helped secure the chin strap. Cute as a button, he mused. Too damned pretty for the grimy job at hand. He watched her unzip the calf pocket in her coveralls and withdraw her last package of Lucky Strikes. She shook it, offering a smoke to the RAF stager. The youth's eyes lit up perceptibly, but he kept his ears glued to the intercom.

"No time, Miss!" he shouted, handing the earphones to Merrill and pointing to the red warning light above.

Almost immediately the aircraft started losing altitude and went into a slow banking turn. Sigi shrugged and slid the American cigarettes into the stager's pocket. The flaps of the Halifax dropped and the bomber began to buffet and shudder at the slower air speed. The four propellers were feathered to take smaller bites of air and seconds later the drop speed of 130 knots was reached and maintained.

Merrill watched the stager open the floor hatch. In all, four parachute ripcords had been attached to the fuselage static wire. The first two he'd joined to the heavy, felt-wrapped supply containers bearing plastic explosives, wardrobe, and weapons.

The red light went out, the one below it burned green. With two forceful kicks, the stager dislodged both containers through the hatch. Almost immediately, the Halifax climbed slightly, banked, and prepared for a second approach over the drop area.

Merrill heard Flying Officer Clinton's voice rasp into the intercom: "Lieutenant Merrill, you alive back there?"

"Ready as I'll ever be."

"I'm beginning our last pass over that artichoke patch. It's all yours this time. Send me one of those French postcards for the barracks wall at Chatham."

Merrill retorted, "I'll do that. Thanks for the lift, old boy." He handed the intercom back to the stager and nodded to Sigi.

The plane finished its tight bank and leveled out. Once more the Halifax was lined up for a direct run across the produce farm below.

"Ladies first!" the stager bellowed.

Merrill watched Sigi bite her lip and fight back the panic. With the hatch open the roar of the engines was deafening and a fierce blast of wind screamed through the bomb bay. The red warning light blinked on again and Sigi looked back at him briefly, her teeth clenched. The light turned green.

"Go!" yelled the dispatcher, giving her a firm slap on the shoulder.

She disappeared through the hatch. Four seconds later, Merrill leaped after her.

The slipstream caught their bodies, flipping them back horizontally under the tail of the aircraft, carrying them along like feathers in the wind until quick jerks in the canvas webbing caught them and held. The bomber, its four engines belching blue flames as they increased in power, began to climb into the night and was quickly lost to sight. Almost as rapidly the drone of its engines dwindled to nothing and the moonlit night fell strangely silent. Merrill looked down. Sigi's parachute swung in an easy pendulum beneath him and off to the right. They were both making perfectly normal descents. But down below dark shadows folded over the drop area as a cloud wisp began to obscure the moon. Merrill cursed the timing.

Considering the drift, Merrill brought his legs together, knees bent. The ground was soft, freshly furrowed. His hands caught the lines, gathering them in as he deftly spilled the wind out of the silks. A good landing. He struck the release clasp, pulled in the rest of the chute, and looked for Sigi, who had landed a considerable distance downfield from him.

Merrill whistled softly, surprised to be greeted, not by his partner, but by a sudden flash and sharp metallic click. Off in the darkness, a gun being fired! There was an ominous hiss of air as a bullet just missed his ear.

Merrill wanted to shout, but his heart was in his throat. Cursing silently instead, he crouched, trying to focus into the darkness. Another shot. This time the bullet glanced off a harness buckle, leaving a long tear in his tunic. Luckily, it drew no blood. Merrill crouched and gritted his teeth in fury. "Sigi! You okay?" he shouted.

"Yes! I'm over here."

Merrill wiped the sweat from his face. Someone wanted him dead. He whistled softly again and he heard Sigi approach, but there were other footsteps as well.

"What happened? That noise?" she asked breathlessly, coming up beside him.

"Silencer. Appears we're being set up for target practice. What's more——." Merrill didn't bother to complete the sentence. He heard jackboots pounding through the dirt, coming from several directions. Instinctively, he flattened, pulled Sigi down beside him, and quickly withdrew the Luger from his pocket. Swearing again at the playful cloud that obscured the moon, he stared fixedly into the blackness, determined to wait for the welcoming committee—or whoever was out there—to make the first move. There were no shouts, no exchange of conversation, only the footfalls of the approaching men. Merrill was finally able to count six shadowy figures. The tallest in the group halted and flickered a flashlight.

The signal was friendly, as prearranged.

Breathing a sigh of relief but still wary, Merrill released his sweating trigger finger from the Luger and helped Sigi off the ground. Suddenly the cloud slid away from the moon and the field was bathed in cold gray light. The approaching individuals were closer now, within twenty feet, but they wore uniforms—the uniforms of the Wehrmacht!

Merrill's jaw dropped; he felt a sinking feeling in his stomach. Fouled luck so soon. Clocking the opposition like a low-hurdle track man at the starting line, he let out a low, forlorn moan. "Rotten deck of cards, Sigi," he whispered, eyeballing the bevy of Schmeisser machine carbines his opponents held in readiness.

Merrill's decision to choose discretion over suicidal valor was both immediate and automatic. He dropped his pistol into the dirt.

Chapter 15

MERRILL NUMBLY WAITED as one man came forward from the group. "I am Pierre Roger. The name is familiar to you, I trust?" Speaking in English with a thick French accent, he extended a hand. "Forgive our appearance, but the *boche* uniforms make movement about the Paris *arrondissements* easier for us."

"The name's familiar enough," Merrill said guardedly, gripping Roger's hand.

Sigi stepped forward to be introduced. Merrill remained totally wound and watchful; he was determined, for the present, to say nothing about the silenced gun moments earlier. Instead, he'd keep his eyes wide open, his back to no one, and see where that route took him.

Roger introduced the others using first names only, then admonished, "Do not concern yourself with the parachutes. The farmer Levec will promptly bury them."

Merrill watched Levec smile sagely and begin gathering up the silks. Sigi stepped quickly out of her jumpsuit and tossed it to the farmer. Under it she was wearing a brown finely-tailored deerskin jacket, a khaki blouse, and a dark green wool skirt that clung to her hips with a wet look. It was the typical uniform of a female Nazi party worker or government employee. When Sigi removed her parachute helmet and long golden locks fell to frame her face, the farmer beamed. She smiled back at Levec.

Merrill pulled his own things together, brushed off his Wehrmacht uniform and straightened his gray field cap. He winked at Sigi. They were both as ready as they'd ever be.

"We must move quickly," urged Roger. "Follow me." As the Frenchman led the way, stumbling through the furrows toward the farm buildings, Roger warned of the disabled enemy motorcycle patrol that had been spotted a half-hour earlier. Merrill exchanged a brief worried glance with Sigi but made no comment. Leaving the plowed field and following a path of worn stones patched together in the grassy slope, Roger led the group behind the barn where the *kraftswagen* was hidden. Gervais and Roland were already loading their personal belongings and the munitions from the supply parachutes.

Merrill briefly examined the truck, then conferred in hushed tones with Roger. Borrowing a flashlight from Gervais, Merrill examined the faces of the other members of the team one by one. No one moved. They were waiting to be told what to do and expecting Merrill to tell them, not Roger or the newly arrived woman. Merrill felt his confidence soar, despite the distinct probability that one of these characters had surreptitiously taken a bad aim at him. He'd be careful, damned careful; there was something fishy about the entire set-up.

"Hurry, please," Sigi said coldly.

"Any special instuctions?" asked Merrill.

She shot him a perplexed look. "None. As I explained earlier, this part of it is all your show. Just deliver me to our Paris hotel in one piece."

He bowed slightly. "Consider the job done."

"Skeet——" She came up to him and whispered, "I sense something is bothering you, other than that silencer incident back in the field."

"It's your imagination." Merrill turned, once more studying the others with his flashlight. "You're chauffeuring, Roger?"

The Frenchman nodded.

Merrill examined Maurice Duval.

"Duval cannot speak or hear, Lieutenant," apologized Roger.

"Not Lieutenant, Roger. It's *Herr Sergeant*; the name's Schmidt. Please get used to that and don't forget." Merrill looked back at Duval. "The mute will do fine if he has civilian clothing."

"Duval has a change of clothes in the truck," Erika explained.

"We all do, as a precaution," added Roger. He turned and

signed for Duval to change wardrobes. The mute nodded and instantly bound inside the vehicle.

"For God's sake, stop wasting time," said Sigi, suddenly. "Tell him to hurry."

Merrill looked at her and smiled. *Fear? Coming from the tough Sigi Petersen?* The cold, calculating blonde might be human after all, he mused.

When Duval was ready, Merrill double-checked the loading of the suitcases and explosives, then nodded to the others. He instucted Gervais and Roland to climb in the back, followed by Sigi and the mute, who were to take a place directly across from them. They all gave him a bewildered look. Sigi's eyes especially widened with curiosity over his fussing with a specific seating arrangement, but she cooperated without comment.

Merrill smiled to reassure her, dropped the rear canvas, and scrambled around to the cab. "Let's make time!" he shouted, jumping in and letting Erika straddle the shift. Merrill gave Roger's Wehrmacht uniform a shrewd look of appraisal as the Frenchman slammed the truck into gear. "Unfortunately, you don't look or sound the part of a German, Roger," he said sharply.

"Don't worry, *Herr Schmidt*. I never speak. Erika here always rides up front with me. She has had much experience at the bistro as a male impersonator. And her German is flawless, like your own." Roger turned, making a quick, thumbs-up gesture to Erika. "The American here also passes very well for one of the *boche*, yes?" He grinned. "Too well perhaps?"

Merrill should have smiled, but didn't. He speculatively eyed Erika in the rear-view mirror. "You're obviously not French. English or Norwegian?"

She stiffened. "Dutch. They didn't tell you about me in London?" Her eyes zeroed back at him with the force of javelins.

"They didn't tell me a lot of things. You're also young. A little wet behind the ears for the espionage racket, aren't you?" He let his eyes zero in on her with the force of javelins.

"No," she replied coldly, gazing back at Merrill in the rear-view mirror, continuing to size him up.

By the way she held his stare Merrill guessed he was rapidly losing points with Erika. It didn't matter; he wasn't about to back down now. Whatever it took, he was determined to know more about every member of the team. "How old are you, partner?" he asked. Ever since leaving school in Texas, he'd tried, not too successfully, to break himself of the habit of using *partner* in a condescending, offhand way. In London it had caused more than one Englishman to raise an eyebrow.

"Old enough for the job," she replied, again with a tone of soft contempt. Abruptly, she switched from German to careful, precise English. "And you can play cowboy on someone else's time."

Surprised by the English, Merrill shrugged. "You have a grudge against cowpoke types? Or Americans in general?"

Erika Vermeer chose her words carefully. "You seem to enjoy mining fool's gold, *Herr Sergeant Schmidt*. Irrelevant questions. What is next? Unasked-for, bad advice?"

"If you're going to play on my team I expect facts, not riddles, when I ask a question," said Merrill, sourly.

"I'm twenty."

"Much better, a start. Now then, my tag reads explosives and submarines. What's your specialty, young lady?"

She shrugged and thought for a moment. "Breaking and entering. And I'm learning to pick pockets." Erika's eye ignored Merrill, looking straight ahead at the road as she spoke. "My real name is Erika Krager, not Vermeer. My father was a skilled locksmith who taught me his trade; he was also Jewish and over a year ago the Germans took him away and I haven't heard from him since. You need to know more about me?"

Merrill looked the other way, biting back both his curiosity and urge to continue the conversation. The silence grew oppressive.

Roger changed the subject. To Merrill, he quipped, "Your partner in back. Captivating! An attractive Norwegian miss, yes? You're lucky indeed."

"Unfortunately, she's as cold as a reindeer's tit in January." Merrill smiled at Roger. The *kraftswagen* hit a pothole and Merrill's head slammed into the roof of the cab. "God almighty, this road's a kidney buster. How did you come by this Nazi bucket of bolts, Roger?"

The Frenchman gripped the wheel tighter and grinned.

Erika answered for him. "The Resistance has two operatives who run a laundry for the Germans in Montparnasse. Each night the Wehrmacht drivers leave two *kraftswagens* for unloading and loading. They retrieve them in the morning."

Pierre Roger added, "Very convenient for us, yes?"

Merrill shook his head. "Don't they check the kilometers?"

"The odometer in this truck is broken," Roger replied. "Our only difficulty is replacing petrol. We take great risks stealing it from other vehicles."

As they rounded a bend in the rutted road, Roger suddenly hit the brakes.

"Rotten, rotten luck," growled Merrill as he stared at the three-wheel enemy motorcycle just ahead that blocked their passage.

Erika turned with alarm to Roger. "They've repaired the tire."

Merrill watched with dismay as the two Wehrmacht soldiers climbed off their BMW motorbike. The driver carried only a holstered pistol, but the sidecar's occupant, a corporal, bore a more persuasive machine carbine that he held in readiness. Both Germans appeared vigilant but uncomfortable as they stood in the road blinded by Roger's headlights. Slowly, Merrill reached for the Schmeisser Erika had placed on the floor of the cab. Grasping the weapon, he thought how simple it would be to make Swiss cheese of these would-be heroes now while they were still blinded by the truck's headlamps.

Merrill tensed as the corporal swaggered up to the *krafts-wagen*, duly noted the black cross insignia on the door, then glanced in the driver's window. After scanning their uniforms and taking in Merrill's sergeant's stripes, the German saluted clumsily.

Merrill pulled himself together. For the moment every inch *Burger Schmidt*, he leaned across Erika and Roger and in wooden rigidity confronted the corporal eye-to-eye. "Move that pregnant iron pony of yours out of the way, soldier!" Merrill paused, having startled even himself; for a first go, his blunt, idiomatic German was unmercifully abusive. "Fool! This is urgent Abwehr business and you delay us!"

The Wehrmacht enlisted man's sense of self-importance, whatever it might have been, was shattered. He obediently stepped back, lowered his machine pistol, and snapped his heels. "Herr Sergeant, I regret delaying you. We are only Supply Corps soldiers, but nevertheless felt it our duty to investigate."

Merrill sprang back like an adder. "Investigate what?"

"An airplane and parachutists. A man and woman. We were about to go up the farm road." The corporal was defensive, a trifle unsure of himself, but nonetheless probing. Back at the motorcycle, his companion shifted his feet uneasily. Both men, though disconcerted by Merrill's authority, stood their ground.

Merrill smiled wryly. "You'd do better to give more credit to the intelligence arm, Corporal." His voice tightened. "You waste our valuable time, but look in the rear if you like. Quickly now! Under the tarpaulin!"

The soldier hesitated.

"You deaf, soldier?" Merrill's tone became even more menacing. "Go look for yourself. We haven't all night!"

The German, deflated as he appeared, was intensely curious. Merrill watched him wander back to the truck's tailgate and nervously push the canvas drop aside with his gun barrel. *Cretin*, Merrill thought to himself. But for the safety of the Levec farm, they might have eliminated this meddlesome pair and been on their way by now. Merrill impatiently grabbed Erika's flashlight and stabbed the darkness in the back of the truck, allowing the light beam to move slowly across the benches.

"*Mein Gott*," the corporal stuttered. He took in the scenario that Merrill had carefully set up—two men in Wehrmacht uniforms pointing weapons at a pair of civilians opposite them. One of the captives, the German soldier noted with consuming interest, was an alluring blonde woman. His curiosity apparently satisfied, he dropped the canvas, hastened up to the passenger side of the cab, and smiled at Merrill. "Congratulations. You've made a good haul, Herr Sergeant." Again, he snapped his heels.

"Good night, Corporal."

"Heil Hitler!"

No one in the *kraftswagen* spoke until the motorbike was out of sight. It was Pierre Roger who broke the long silence. "Well done, Herr Schmidt. Prospects are looking up for us."

Merrill wasn't listening to Roger at all. A sixth or seventh sense stirred in his brain. Not good at all. Something was bothering him and he couldn't get a bridle on it! He looked in the rear view mirror. From the concerned look on Erika Vermeer's face, he knew the Dutch girl's radar-like instincts were also in high range.

She suddenly turned to him. "Lieutenant!" she blurted out, her mannish voice quavering. Their eyes met in immediate alarmed awareness.

Merrill shouted, "Get this truck turned around, Roger! *Now*. Find that motorcycle patrol again, and fast." Merrill felt an involuntary shudder as if Gestapo jackboots were already stomping on his grave. *Stupid, Skeet,* he reflected. *Your first damned mistake*. Where in hell had his brain been?

"Forget something?" Roger asked, with genuine surprise. Bewildered, but sensing the American's urgency, he tore through the gears and quickly had the truck moving back toward the farm.

"The corporal. *He knew!*" Erika said to him through taut lips.

"Yeah. I should have caught it," added Merrill. "He said a woman and man came in by parachute, all this *before* he looked in the truck. Too dark and distant for him to spot our gender in the air. The bastards were tipped off and expecting us."

Chapter 16

ACCELERATING, PIERRE ROGER leaned forward over the wheel, his eyes following the forward thrust of the headlights, alert for the first sign of the Germans. His face looked pained.

An instant later they caught sight of the motorcycle. It was still parked in the roadway leading to the produce farm, but the soldiers weren't in it. Kneeling on the ground a short distance away they were hurrying to set up a portable field radio. The corporal was struggling with a collapsible antenna.

A look of unfathomable cunning came into Roger's eyes as he accelerated again. "No time to stop," he mumbled.

Merrill looked back over his shoulder. Sigi Peterson was staring through the opening in the truck's cab, her face a mask of bewilderment. Her eyes darted first to Roger, then, frightened by what she saw, shot over to Merrill. "You're going to run them down!"

"That seems to be the plan, partner," Merrill retorted, bracing himself against the dash.

The two surprised soldiers looked up, eyes blinking against the stabbing glare of Roger's headlights. Their gaunt faces paralyzed with terror, the corporal barely managed to lift his machine pistol and point it at the onrushing vehicle. The *kraftswagen* crashed over them as the gun barked, but the brief burst of bullets roared skyward, straight up, spending themselves harmlessly in a low gray cloud.

Roger stopped the truck and backed up. Merrill hurriedly climbed out and went over to the victims. Erika ran to the radio. Both men were dead.

"The radio is cold," Erika said. "They didn't have time to get off a message."

Merrill heaved a sigh of relief. The others climbed out of the truck. Erika went over to the crushed bodies, turned them over without so much as wincing. Merrill was impressed by her calmness. She brought the bloodied corporal's identity papers up to Merrill.

Sigi, testing her authority for the first time, took the documents away from him and read them herself. "Hard to believe you ran them down in cold blood," she said icily.

Annoyed, Merrill arched an eyebrow. "Forgive Roger's zeal and my crude, locker-room manners. Where did you pick up your spy training, Miss Petersen? In a convent? Damn it, whose side you on?"

"There's a specific time and place for everything. Have you paused to consider the complications?"

"Sure. Tell me about them. It was their jugular or ours. Another minute and they'd have sent off a message." Merrill watched Sigi study the ID papers and purse her lips.

"Interesting. Hardly supply soldiers as they indicated," she said. "Abwehr Intelligence under SS orders. The corporal, it appears, is in fact a junior lieutenant!"

Merrill winced. Just what he wanted to hear. He went back to the victims. Still mulling over his own body being used for target practice just minutes earlier at the airdrop, he removed the pistol from the dead German's belt and sniffed the barrel. It hadn't been fired recently and the weapon bore no silencer.

"*Merde!*" moaned Roger. Glumly, he stared down at the dead men and shook his head. "Unfortunate complications indeed."

Merrill nodded, continuing to mull over the scene. *Deadly complications*, Roger should have said. Complications that could easily compound themselves in vicious momentum, interlock in subtle combinations until the enemy closed its net around the entire operation. All before they even reached first base! Merrill looked back at the others—Sigi, Erika, the mute Duval. Gervais and Roland stood far off to one side, confused, still waiting for instructions. Roger appeared the most disturbed of all.

Sigi calmly went up to him. "Don't fret, Monsieur Roger," she admonished. "I suspect the enemy knows far less than you imagine."

Merrill looked at her. "You positive about that?"

"A woman's intuition, Skeet. Nothing more, but trust me."

He replied dryly, "You're either a foolish optimist or downright heroic." Merrill slowly shook his head as Sigi came up to him. He felt her smooth fingers touching him, closing around his wrist like a Venus Flytrap.

"I understand you and the German sub ace have something in common beyond torpedoes and salt water in your veins," she said, moving even closer.

Merrill stood his ground and looked at her sharply. "Meaning what?"

"Meaning medals of valor."

He lowered his eyes. "I see. Colonel Foster still talks too much. Earned and forgotten, Sigi. Gathering dust in the attic, as they should be."

The others were watching them. Sigi smiled sagely. "Ah yes, misplaced heroics. As for tonight then, does the hero propose we now back out or take our lumps and get on with the mission? Are we all together or not?"

"We're together," replied Merrill, irritably. "But I don't like playing with one hand tied behind my back. I like to win, I like winning teams, and lopsided scores are the safest kind. I'm sorry Sigi, failure leaves a rotten taste in my mouth." *Together, teamwork*. Merrill repeated the words to himself as if they were a broken record. More like *Panhandle bullshit*. The way things were already falling apart, even this charming blonde— despite her enviable record—might stab him in the back. Doubtful, but not impossible.

Erika had scornfully watched Sigi confront Merrill, and now she coughed lightly and beckoned Pierre Roger off to one side. "*Patron*, perhaps we waste valuable time with these newcomers."

Though her voice was meant to be a whisper, Merrill heard every word.

Roger gave the Dutch girl an incredulous look. "So?"

Erika glanced at Merrill and Sigi, spat on the ground, then turned back to Roger. "They will complicate our movements. Our first plan was better. Will you and Marie Selva please reconsider? You must trust me to work alone for a few days."

Merrill interrupted, "Mind if I ask what this is all about?"

Ignoring him, Roger grinned at Erika in abject amazement. "Alone?"

"Yes, or with the mute, if you insist."

Roger said quickly, "*Mon Dieu!* Erika, we are now under orders from London and cannot act independently. As a lockpicker, you have two talented hands, yes. But this mission will require strong hands. Too many. I fear that we will not be enough." Roger forced his frown away, turned to Sigi and Merrill, and apologized. "She is young, impetuous, and filled with foolhardy bravery." He turned back to Erika. "Forget this divisiveness and help me load these dead soldiers in their motorcycle. There is a bridge down the road where we can simulate an accident."

Five minutes later they were at Roger's proposed accident site.

When the termite-infested railing had been properly demolished to Roger's satisfaction, the others gathered behind the motorcycle and pushed. The three-wheel BMW with its inanimate passengers shot over the side, tumbling until there was an appalling crash as it hit the rocks and water twenty feet below.

Merrill hurried over to the guard rail and looked down. The motorbike was on its side, the front wheel pointed straight up, its headlight burning dimly, an eerie beacon of light aimed skyward to mark the grave. A few rocks and stones shifted, the shallow stream continued to trickle past, but all else was peaceful, moonlit silence. "Let's get out of here," Merrill shouted.

Less than ten minutes later the *kraftswagen* skirted the town of Meaux where they halted to let off Gervais and Roland. The two men jumped down from the truck and silently hurried off in the darkness. Roger waited while Sigi, at Merrill's request, came up front, changing places with Erika. As Roger drove westbound toward Paris on Route Three, a gray night mist crept over the road. Merrill was silent, totally uncommunicative, and Sigi only stared sleepily at the monotonous straight road before them. A long string of headlights approached; a German convoy passed quickly without incident and the road was deserted again. Roger accelerated. Merrill pulled out his harmonica and began playing "I Walk Alone."

Beneath the wind-whipped canvas in the rear of the vehicle, Erika and the mute huddled in opposite corners trying to sleep.

Erika listened to Merrill's harmonica music and smiled. Her
father had been good with the instrument too. Removing her
regulation Wehrmacht helmet and placing a folded greatcoat
under her head, Erika closed her eyes. If things went well
tonight, she'd be back in her borrowed Rue Clemont room,
comfortably in bed within an hour's time. If not, she and the
others could be in German custody or dead sooner than that.
Giving the latter possibility a slight edge for the moment, Erika
would doze while possible. She and Duval slept just thirty
minutes before they were jolted awake by the truck's brakes
just outside the Porte de la Pantin.

"*Zut, alors!*" groaned Roger, glancing sideways at Merrill.
"It is a spot check."

The Pantin traffic circle before them was quiet, the steel
shutters drooping on the stucco buildings that surrounded it all
snapped shut. But just ahead, at the entrance to Avenue Jean
Jaures, a German military vehicle straddled the center of the
roadway. The open-top, armored car contained a lone soldier,
but beside it stood two alert French gendarmes. A striped
barricade was in place beside them.

Merrill turned to Erika and Duval in the rear. "Look alive
back there! Unfriendly visitors coming up."

The SD sergeant sitting in the gray *panzerkraftswagen*
glanced up at the approaching Wehrmacht supply truck. Apparently accepting its presence without question, he returned to a
Signal magazine he was reading under a portable lantern and
let the two *flics* do his legwork for him.

"Your papers, Monsieur," requested the taller and more
vigilant of the gendarmes.

Roger drew in a deep breath, first handed over the yellow
permit for the laundry truck, then his own forged identity
papers. The gendarme scrutinized the German documents with
bored contempt, for like most Frenchmen, he was stung in his
pride at doing this routine work for the enemy occupiers. The
second gendarme looked inside the cab, gave a cursory glance
to the woman and man seated beside the driver, then went back
and leaned against the duty sergeant's armored car. Merrill
smiled and handed over his own and Sigi's identity cards to the
remaining *flic*, but he ignored them and waved the truck
through.

"Damn," said Merrill, "a note from Marie Antoinette
would have gotten us past the *flics* tonight."

Roger silently nodded, turned down the blacked-out Boulevard de Sebastopol, and drove toward the Seine.

Merrill followed Sigi's disappointed stare out the cab window. *Les grand boulevards* had obviously lost their sparkle for her and she was disappointed. Indeed, the supposed city of light was now a place of minatory blackness and desolation. The streets of Paris were completely empty.

"There are no people, Monsieur!" Sigi said somberly to Roger.

"Gloomsville," Merrill added.

For a long time it seemed the Frenchman behind the wheel didn't hear them. Pierre Roger's strong Gallic profile stared through the windshield as the truck hurtled forward over the cobbles. "Sorry, my mind was on intelligence leaks and double agents. I now even wonder about Gervais and Roland back in Meaux. And there is the old farmer Levec's safety to be considered." Roger rubbed his cheek and looked at Sigi askance. "The streets are empty because the curfew begins in ten minutes. Another reason we wear *boche* clothing, yes? We can move about after midnight without being stopped."

Roger drove across the Île de la Cité and turned north, following the cobblestoned quay along the Seine's left bank. The street was deserted when he pulled up in front of the Hotel Clarice-Almont.

Merrill quickly eyeballed the five-story structure with its dirty granite facade, black shutters, and copper regency roof. "Good. Not too fancy, and not a flea bag," he said to Roger. "Inconspicuous, if nothing else. A good choice, Pierre."

"Do we have one room or two?" Sigi asked, smiling impudently.

Merrill smiled. The question was obviously for his benefit.

"But of course, *two rooms*, Mademoiselle!" replied the Frenchman with great dignity.

Merrill would have no objection at all to letting her cuddle in his arms all night, protected. Again he remembered Sigi's fleeting flirtation with him at the London embassy reception; how, in her fickle manner, she'd eventually snubbed him in favor of a handsomely moustached Australian air force major. She'd said something about rangy, rowdy Texans being too aggressive for her. The incident rolled off in Merrill's brain like an old news film. He wondered if Sigi too, had a good memory. He watched her skittishly fidget with her skirt and brush back her hair. Merrill crammed the rememberings back into his dead business file where they belonged; the mission was fraught with enough problems without mawkish thoughts like these.

Merrill leaped down from the truck cab, turned, and waited, his arms outstretched. Sigi hesitated, then jumped. He touched her hair, very lightly, then withdrew his hand almost immediately; but he looked her up, down and sideways with eyes that studied, weighed, and judged her without the slightest pretense. Sigi flushed only slightly under his candid scrutiny.

"Anyone ever tell you your self-composure is an art in itself?" he asked.

"I'm flattered," she replied calmly, staring back at him as if satisfied that he was at a loss for words.

On the contrary, Merrill felt more sure of himself than ever. She could manage the mission's ground rules, fine, but no way would he let her control his emotions. The awkward silence between them was broken by Erika Vermeer's drowsy but emphatic voice from behind the canvas in the back of the truck. "Good night, Fraulein Schramm and Sergeant Schmidt."

Erika's insistent farewell brought Merrill out of his trance. "Yeah. Good night," he retorted, ceremoniously. Merrill still found the Dutch girl's tone uncomfortably bullish, but he'd get used to it. Her sexual orientation hadn't occurred to him before, but now he wondered about it. Merrill dismissed the thought. It didn't matter; what really mattered was her ability to cover third base with a Schmeisser automatic.

Roger handed over their personal luggage and said to them, "You'll trust us to hide the explosives, of course?" He gestured toward the rear of the truck.

Merrill nodded, then turned to Sigi and offered his arm. She surprised him by taking it with a faint purr of approval.

Roger climbed back in the cab, waved, and drove off. Merrill and Sigi headed for the hotel lobby.

He felt at home with her now, but then Merrill no longer felt any woman was a stranger. After the divorce and years of military service, any reserve had been shattered. What remained was desire and taste, both seemingly endless. War did strange things to a man's priorities and sense of timing. A woman's too, for that matter. There was something very special about Sigi Petersen and Merrill felt challenged to find out what it was. If she'd allow him.

Chapter 17

SIGI PAUSED IN the hotel entry, considering the darkened lobby, the soiled rococo wallpaper, and hard-faced night clerk in a plum-colored coat who waited behind the front desk. Merrill was halfway across the dismal chamber before he realized she had hesitated. He turned, beckoning to her. "What are you waiting for?"

"All the warmth and coziness of a mausoleum on All Soul's Day," she replied, her voice betraying her qualm.

The only illumination in the lobby came from a smoking kerosene lantern on the registration counter. Awakened from his nap in a side closet, an elderly stooped porter wordlessly brought in their luggage, then waited as they signed the register.

"Welcome, Fraulein and Sergeant. Your reservations are in order." The emollient voice belonged to the night clerk behind the desk.

Sigi took a prompt dislike to the hotelman. The balding Frenchman had suspicious, sea-green malevolent eyes, a long scar under his left eye, and an adam's apple that shook when he spoke. His German, she noted, was far better than the occasion demanded. From the expression on Skeet's face, Sigi knew an alarm had gone off with him as well.

Rooms 417 and 416 conveniently faced each other across the narrow, close-carpeted hallway. The old porter opened both doors, abandoned their luggage, and silently shuffled off without thanking them for his gratuity.

"So much for wartime hotel service," Sigi said softly. She stood framed in her doorway, smiling as if in a trance.

Merrill grinned and boldly asked, "Bother you sleeping alone? Lonely traveler in a strange town, strange bed?"

"Is that a proposition to share my mattress with a *strange* person?" She moved across the hall toward him.

Merrill's eyes widened.

Sigi brought the candle the porter had given her up between them, for several seconds studying Skeet Merrill's hard-lined but pleasant features. Despite his alien appearance in the Wehrmacht field cap and notwithstanding a few more crow's feet than she remembered from when they'd first met, his was a handsome face. Firm, strong. Merrill's inquiring, possessive gaze was the kind that on other occasions with other men had melted her like striped candy in hot water. There were complications, however, that beat back such a temptation now. Merrill held her gaze, and she was the first to look away, pretending to examine her watch.

Finally she picked up on his invitation. "I've learned to do without my Teddy bear," she whispered softly in English, with her faint Scandinavian accent. She offered him a dreamy smile as if it were a consolation prize.

"I doubt that." Merrill propped an elbow against the wall and leaned his entire body forward, close to her, his clear brown eyes studying her intently. Pulling out his harmonica, he gently tapped it on her shoulder. Smiling, he cajoled, "You have a choice. Take me in or I play 'I Walk Alone' again, right here in the hallway."

All Sigi offered in return were a pair of coolly amused eyes and silence. Finally aware of the lengthening silence and afraid he really might begin to sound off with the instrument, she indulged him with a grin. "Look, cowboy," she blurted out, thawing more than she'd intended, "get me in and out of St. Nazaire, *alive and kicking*—as you loosely say in the States— and we'll pursue social overtures then. Fair enough?"

Skeet Merrill's spirits had obviously risen only to fall. "In the meantime?" he asked dully.

"A desperately needed night's sleep. *Alone*." Behind the smiling mask she offered him, Sigi let her voice cool a few degrees more. "And in the morning, if you don't object, strictly business." She gestured toward the harmonica. "Now if you want to wake the entire hotel, be my guest." The lies had rolled off her tongue effortlessly. She was curious and really wanted him, provided he played his cards right. But definitely not tonight; later down the road. She'd have to pick the time and place very carefully.

Shrugging, Merrill backed off and returned the harmonica to his pocket. "So much for another intellectual affair, or is it the older sister act?"

Sigi held back her laughter. Her chauvinist companion had obviously worked himself into a lather, hot to trot, only to discover that he had a first class pricktease on his hands. Merrill's expression had turned sullen, like a pouting small boy's.

Bristling, he asked her, "You take your work damned seriously, don't you?"

"Have you known many Norwegians, Skeet?" Her tone was deliberately glacial. She watched his excitement ebb.

"Matter of fact, no. Why?"

She sighed with impatience. "The Germans call our Resistance work fanatical. Cold, calculating, but nonetheless fanatical."

Merrill's expectant eyes were on her, fixed in an almost blank stare.

Sigi slowly continued, "My brother was a dock worker by day, a proficient anti-Nazi terrorist by night. Until he was caught. The Gestapo hung him by a meat hook in the public square at Stavanger. I have a sixteen-year-old cousin who was brutally raped by two drunken Luftwaffe fighter pilots. When I disappeared from my teaching post, my father's bookstore in Oslo was burned by the occupiers in retribution. My passion, what's left, is with my relatives and fellow countrymen who still live under the enemy boot. Yes, we Norwegians take our work seriously. Very seriously." She hesitated, lowering her eyes. Then she asked, "And you, Skeet?"

"Sorry." Merrill shrugged and said impatiently, "So much for the cruelties and ironies of war. Each of us has our own motivation to fight. I do my job, leaving the histrionics and philosophy of this war to another generation."

Sigi smiled and shook her head. "Then perhaps it's futile for your kind to fight. History only repeats itself. Let a generation pass, twenty years, a quarter of a century—and even the so-called democratic nations will rally behind their flags and seize the sword again."

Merrill said quickly, "Wars come, wars go, but the important things survive."

Sigi smiled. "Like the indomitable wildflowers at Carthage? I'm going to sleep," she whispered, with a smile. "I suggest you do the same or try a cold *douche*!" On this chill note, with a decisive click, Sigi Petersen closed the door to room 416.

Left standing alone, Merrill felt clumsy. Sigi's ill-tidings had been delivered in a lugubrious monotone, rationed out deliberately, one sour tidbit at a time, as if watchful for his every reaction. Why was she toying with him? And there was something about her impassioned, trilled soliloquy—especially the grim events in Norway—that mildly bothered him. Had it sounded a trifle rehearsed? And why was she so nervous and anxious to dismiss him, despite the tell-tale desire in her eyes? He not only hated himself, but he hated Sigi for having switched her ass at him. He felt guilty and suddenly wished he were back in the happy-go-lucky Wren's flat in England. Just possibly Molly Tremayne was more than a port in a storm. Merrill went into his own room, closed and locked the door.

He smiled to himself as he reflected on the affair back in London. Molly did her damndest, but to the cheerful English brunette, Babe Ruth was merely a chocolate bar in a red and white wrapper and a Texas longhorn was an instrument in the Houston Symphony. But then Merrill too, had often come up with short change. He'd never grasped the difference between Hamlet and King Lear, ghost or no ghost, and popular or not, English bangers for breakfast gave him heartburn. In spite of the gaps, Molly was a good cook, fun to be with, and no slouch in the sack. If it were in fact just a wartime affair, Merrill might do well prolonging the damned conflict. Unlike Sigi Petersen, not once had Molly belabored him with speeches, let alone brilliant conversation. He liked it that way. Nor had she ever sent him to the showers without first playing a little cricket. The more he thought about her, the more his conscience ate away at him. Merrill made himself a mental note to buy Molly some Paris perfume and take it with him back to London—provided he came out of this mission alive.

* * *

At 10 Downing Street the household knew that when Winston Churchill admitted a visitor before eight in the morning it had to be a matter of crisis proportions. The raised voices coming from the closed-off dining room reinforced their suspicions.

Pacing the floor in his blue silk dressing robe, Churchill looked at the First Sea Lord narrowly. "You're absolutely sure of your information? Colonel Foster made no mention of it to you whatsoever? Official or otherwise?"

Admiral Cunningham held his gaze without flinching. "Stuart is usually thorough on these matters. Completely unlike him not to bring it to staff attention. Particularly as it concerns his own relatives in Germany. What else can we assume but that he's hiding something?"

Churchill shook his head. "Estranged kin he hasn't seen in over a dozen years? Perhaps these individuals went to Stockholm to escape the Nazi terror, the inevitability of Germany's collapse."

"Sir, they were in Sweden only a week, then returned to Berlin. Purportedly on business, but appearing in many strange places in Stockholm. Our agents lost track of them for a full forty-eight hours. God knows they had the opportunity to make contact with one of ours." Cunningham lowered his eyes and exhaled sharply. "Or one of Foster's."

Churchill sat down at the end of the dining table and glowered, ignoring the glass of orange juice an aide had placed there earlier. "No. I won't believe it. The Colonel's character is beyond reproach. It doesn't wash, Admiral. Examine his record."

"I have, Prime Minister. More than once. But dire times require extreme measures. And I know your own feelings about going to the core if necessary to remove the worm from the apple. Perhaps we should warn the American now, tell him what we're really after."

"No, not yet." Churchill put both hands on the table before him. "As for Foster, if you insist, we'll have a proper chat with him. But you'd damned well better find him quickly. In our last exchange he indicated that he was about to leave for France to reconnoiter the Storm Tide matter himself."

"That's the problem, sir. I'm afraid the colonel's already gone, headed down to Southampton or Portsmouth."

Churchill grinned elfishly. "Then there's precious little we can do about questioning him until he gets back to London, is there? I say we gamble on the man's veracity."

"If he comes back, sir," admonished Cunningham.

Chapter 18

WHEN SIGI OPENED the hotel room shutters the morning was flat, gray and wet. Caught for a moment in puckish fantasy, she saw before her—on the surface at least—the Paris she remembered from prewar visits. Beneath the overcast sky the picture-postcard copper rooftops shimmered from the light rain. She watched a coal barge, the owner's laundry flying despite the drizzle, emerge from under the Pont Royale and chug slowly up the muddy river. Across the Seine the trees lining the opposite quay ruffled in the slight breeze. If no one else were cheerful this drab second day of June, 1944, Sigi couldn't tell from the animated birds; they were everywhere, filling the sky with flight. She stood at the window a long time, comparing the peaceful city skyline to the V-bomb destruction she'd seen in London.

From the street below she heard several motorcycles roar by. Looking down, she saw a German patrol speeding along the quay, the men shouting at one another. If Sigi had any spectacular or profound beliefs about war, she recognized the inferno simply for the insensate folly it was. She was convinced that inevitably, repeatedly, it was provoked by the male of the species. *Sexists*, she reflected, *like Skeet Merrill.* Her intellect made her wonder if war proved anything, except, perhaps, that God was on the side bearing the biggest club. Battles definitely made fence-straddling or any kind of wavering impractical; one had to choose sides.

Sigi smiled to herself. Rational thinking no longer really mattered, for there were things Sigi felt compelled to do in this struggle. Her rigid background, the long months of training, her political indoctrination necessitated this, and she'd thus stashed kindness and understanding away for the duration. If Sigi Petersen were motivated by patriotism or retribution, she'd keep that part of it to herself. The spy business was tolerant of silence and a woman's normal instinct for charity was completely expendable.

"Will there be anything else, Mademoiselle?" The ebullient room waiter placed the rose bud vase in the center of the rollaway breakfast table and bowed slightly.

"No, that will be all." She watched him leave, then winked at Skeet Merrill who had just entered.

To her surprise her untalkative companion immediately began exploring the draperies, moldings, and pictures for hidden wires and microphones.

Sigi observed him briefly with disinterest, then seated herself at the table and began nibbling a croissant. "Your breakfast is getting cold, *Sergeant*," she called, idly stirring her tea.

Merrill bristled at Sigi's tone. Ignoring her, he continued his methodical examination of the radiator and chandelier, then probed under the bed. Finding nothing and a trifle disappointed, he took his place opposite her at the table.

"Content?" she asked, flippantly.

Merrill smiled and snatched a croissant. "For the moment."

Sigi took a sip from her tea, eased back in her chair, and dreamily began humming. Merrill looked at her and drew a blank.

"Solveig's song from *Peer Gynt*," she offered, buoyantly. "Have you seen the play in America? I understand our Grieg and Ibsen are popular there." She bit into her croissant.

"No," Merrill apologized. "I read the work in college."

"Oh. Then you know Ibsen is Norway's most famous playwright and influenced many social reforms—even in your country, I understand."

Merrill stirred his black coffee and smiled back at her. "As I remember, this Peer was a scoundrel."

"But lovable. And typically Norwegian in character."

"You're nostalgic this morning, to say the least. Why?"

Sigi reached across the table and teasingly drew her fingernail across his wrist and hand. "Progress, dear Skeet. I'm always happy when I accomplish things."

Merrill nodded but felt genuinely confused. Observing her probing finger all he could think of was a phrase out of the past: *God gave woman her finger, but the devil gave her a nail.*

Sigi smiled indulgently. "Favorable news. I made a phone call before you came in. The first step."

"I'm listening," he said quietly, sipping at the atrocious ersatz coffee.

She studied him. "I sometimes wonder."

Merrill ignored her, instead watching a fly struggle to untangle itself from the orange marmalade.

"Skeet?"

He finally suffered her a raised eyebrow.

"You're a nice guy," she said abruptly. "I like your style, most of the time. But please pay attention."

Merrill looked up. He found her light, flirtatious manner a sharp, annoying contrast to her frigidity of the night before. "Okay. I'm impatient and morbidly curious, then. Phone call *where*?"

Sigi eyed him a moment, then explained, "A half hour ago I talked with Kapitan Leutnant Loewen himself. At the Ritz Hotel. And he's agreed to meet with us."

Merrill gulped down his bite of croissant without chewing and glared at her. "A phone call to the ace, *before* I checked for bugging? I'd like to pound some sense into that pretty but obviously foggy brain of yours."

Sigi's blank expression indicated no hint of apology. Digging into her purse, she pulled out her compact.

Merrill slowly shook his head. *Why had she made the call without his presence?* He had either an empty-headed blonde on his hands or a very clever one hiding something. "I'm waiting, charming lady. So what did he say?"

Sigi looked into the compact, putting on her lipstick. "Regarding the possibility of hidden microphones, I checked the room last night before retiring." She hesitated, then glanced up at Merrill. "As for Loewen, he's a suspicious devil, and hardly the publicity-minded type."

"Submariners could care less about publicity. We do our work silently, without fanfare."

Sigi looked at him over the top of her compact. "I forgot. You two have so much in common. One hero against the other—or as Colonel Foster so aptly put it, *employ a thief to catch a thief.*"

Merrill beat the palm of his hand on his forehead. "Maybe I'll do that if you'll cooperate. Continue, please."

"No interest in an interview at all until I did some appropriate name dropping."

Merrill tried to swill down some of his coffee, wincing in the process. "That's Java?"

Sigi put her lipstick and compact away. "Add some milk," she said flatly.

"Whose name did you use? Dr. Goebbels?"

"No. The Fuehrer himself."

Merrill again shook his head. "Our quarry was motivated, I assume?"

She nodded. "The Lion will be joining us here within the hour."

Merrill was stunned by the escalating events, but was determined not to let it show, He leaned back, precariously balancing his chair on two legs. "Tell me, Sigi. What makes you think you can handle a tough, egotistical naval officer of Loewen's caliber and grit?"

She softly laughed. "With poise, power, and a measure of telepathy, I can handle any man."

Merrill wasn't impressed. "Seduce, you mean."

"If it comes to that. Whatever it takes to accomplish the job, Skeet." A smile sliced across her fine-boned face. "My innocence and virginity were jettisoned quite early in life. What do you suggest, that I wear thick underwear?"

Merrill scowled in annoyance. The telephone rang before he could open his mouth to respond. He picked it up, answering in his best German. "Hello. Yes, this is Anna Schramm's room. Sergeant Schmidt speaking."

"Listen chum," he heard, "you can relax a mite." Merrill's eyebrows knitted and his face slowly paled. The terse voice at the other end of the line was speaking in fluent English, and a Cockney accent at that! "The telephone's all right and both your rooms are clean enough. No electronic bugs here. Hold it, pal, don't say a thing. Not necessary for us to have a chat at all. Just want to warn you the Jerries have partially caught on and have a wild card or two up their sleeve. Heinrich Himmler's bloody SS is even working with the Reichskriegmarine, so beware. And it appears that you, personally, *Sergeant Schmidt*, are being set up to be knocked down by a double agent named

Viper. In my opinion, Guvner, you've been set up in the wrong hotel at the wrong time, so the sooner you get your wrong business ticked off and out of Paris, the better. One more point. We may be on the same rugby team, but I'm in no position to help out if you get your nose bloodied. Beware, chum. There's a rotten apple in the box." With an abrupt click, the voice was gone.

Dieter Loewen, clad in his calf-length leather coat, walked the several blocks to the address on Quai Anatole France that the presswoman Anna Schramm had given him. Annoyed as he was by this unexpected interruption in his rest leave, he could think of no way to dismiss or postpone a meeting with an Information Ministry emissary apparently having the blessing of the Fuehrer himself. Of small consolation, Goebbels had sent a woman whose telephone voice and manner, at least, were warm and inviting. But why, Loewen wondered, hadn't the request filtered down through the usual channels, like Grand Admiral Doenitz or his flotilla commander in St. Nazaire?

More vulgar hero propaganda for the home front, he presumed; additional inspiration for the mothers, sisters, grandmothers, and whoever else back in Leipzig, Ulm, and Frankfurt. Loewen was determined to get the bothersome interview over with quickly and go on to Versailles tomorrow, there to continue his role as a tourist.

Arriving at the Clarice-Almont Hotel, Loewen hastened up the front steps with his habitual air of ownership. He found the lobby empty except for a tall, crewcut blond SS colonel who held his hat in his arms as he chatted in hushed tones with the clerk at the reception desk. Their conversation was abruptly terminated as Loewen approached, nodded to the fellow German, and inquired of the hotelman in thickly accented French for the room of Anna Schramm.

Eyes flashing, the bald clerk smiled, and without checking the register, replied in fluent German, "Four sixteen."

Loewen strode over to the brass-barred lift, climbed inside, and pushed the ivory button with the faded numeral four on it. The cage shook, then noisily, as if in protest, began its ascent. Gazing back across the lobby, Loewen saw the imperious

looking SS officer continue to gaze his way. Loewen suddenly
remembered he'd seen that face before, at the Left Bank bistro,
the previous night. But the man had been wearing a monocle
and civilian clothing then. The elevator passed the first level
and the SS colonel was lost from view.

The three-way handshaking dispensed with, Sigi presented
her credentials from *Deutsches Nachtrichten Buro*, hopeful the
forged letters of recommendation were as impeccable as
Colonel Foster and G-10 claimed. It didn't matter, for Dieter
Loewen sighed impatiently and gave the counterfeit document
from Berlin only the most cursory of glances. He took a seat in
a straightback chair and placed his white command cap
squarely in the center of his lap, the visor pointed forward. The
U-boat ace appeared plainly anxious to get on with the
interview and be done with it.

Admiring Loewen's prematurely gray temples, Sigi—as
Anna Schramm—took a deep breath, smiled, and went to work
in earnest. "Kapitan, the question of prestige, of maintaining
confidence in the U-boat arm, is urgent. You must understand
that we can't generate enough publicity about our Reichskriegmarine heroes and their exploits."

Loewen's eyes twitched, his face reflecting an amalgam of
despair. He sighed wearily and said to her, "When a U-boat
crewman comes off a patrol, Fraulein, he seeks little more than
a long bath, a change of clothes, and a sympathetic woman.
Least of all does he hunger for the platitudes of the public."
There was a strong note of irritation in the German's voice.
"Speaking for myself, I feed only on self respect and quiet
efficiency. If you have connections in Berlin or the ear of the
Fuehrer, I wish little more than to be restored to command of a
U-boat. Nothing would be more rewarding."

"I'm only a journalist, Kapitan," she replied. "You're not
pleased with your imminent promotion and upcoming honor?"

Loewen didn't respond; he gazed back at her for a long time,
his face reddening slightly. Though he obviously liked what he
saw, he shifted uneasily.

Sigi smiled, aware that she'd have to work harder to make a
breach in the ace's calm reserve. As if in some delayed reaction
to her smile, Loewen's eyes focused on her legs, the softly

rounded calves; he traced them up past the green wool skirt above her knees and took in the full contours of her hips.

Sigi remembered her adversary had been at sea for a long time. She caught Loewen's gaze and looked down at her hemline reflexively. Cocking her head to one side, she smiled. "The medal with precious stones you are to receive in Berlin— is it true that it is equivalent to the Blue Max given to Richthofen in the first war?"

Loewen grumbled, "Women are always interested in diamonds."

Sigi backed away precipitately, anxious to put more distance between herself and Loewen's chill, penetrating stare. She had expected him to be more friendly. Gathering herself, she admonished, "Folk heroes are an important thread in our cultural fabric, Kapitan. You should be more cooperative."

Loewen straightened his shoulders, hissing, "I'm not here to sabotage your mission for Dr. Goebbels and I do not wish to be quoted, but I'm fatigued of all this talk of heroes." He paused, looking away from her and out the window. "Sorry, but there seems to be no end of it. Frederick the Great, Hindenburg, Tanenberg, Schlieffen, and in the air, Richthofen! Idolized. Each of them schooled in the theory that war is the ultimate adventure, yes?" Loewen's eyelids appeared heavy, his face suddenly gone tired. Impassively, he added, "That adventure has become one long, costly, gruesome nightmare for the Fatherland, Fraulein. We must end it soon."

"Victorious, of course," added Sigi, properly.

"Of course," he snapped, turning his hat over in his hands. "But at the front we need more support, and immediately. Yes, as a journalist you must write that. It is not U-boat ace notoriety or hero propaganda that is imperative, but more *belt tightening*! This war is more than machine gun politics, Fraulein. It's a technological battle. Our factory people must work longer hours and harder. You must shorten the training time for sub crews and deliver the 21C U-boats to us with no further delay. Give us all snorkels, and quickly. Then we will annihilate the combined enemy fleet. Roosevelt can build as many victory ships as he chooses, and we will sink them all. Churchill will soon realize that Britannia will never again rule the seas. Then, Fraulein, we so-called military heroes will have spectacular stories for you! It is time that we—"

Overwhelmed by his own zeal, Loewen broke off the speech, his voice oddly trailing into silence.

Sitting quietly in the corner, Skeet Merrill had politely listened to Loewen's outlook on the future of the sea war and discarded it—in the Texas vernacular—as pure bullshit. Merrill began shuffling his feet noisily but Sigi ignored him.

World record for tonnage sunk, brilliant tactician, lucky SOB, or whatever, to Merrill the German U-boat ace came off as a pious flea on the back of a cur. Did Loewen really believe the Third Reich, after the loss at Stalingrad, had the slightest chance to turn the tide of war? God! The man's brain was constipated. What level had blind stubbornness come to? Still, Merrill realized that in a curious way he was indebted to Dieter Loewen. By the ace's high-handed manner and lofty prognosis, he'd unwittingly fired Merrill's hatred of the enemy, any compassion for fellow submariners be damned. Now, more than ever, Merrill was committed to seeing the German war hero back in England alive or, if need be, otherwise.

Merrill loudly cleared his throat.

The sound failed to ruffle Sigi, but she did finally come to the point. "Herr Kapitan," she said, "we plan a story on your U-boat and the new snorkel. In St. Nazaire, not Paris. We need you back in Britanny."

"I no longer command the U-601."

"We're aware of that, Kapitan. Precisely why we were sent to intercept you before you reached Berlin to report to OKW. You will accompany us?"

Willingly, Merrill hoped. Much easier that way.

Loewen frowned at them. "Why return to the coast? I'm here today, at your service."

Merrill had been dutifully silent too long. He figured it was time for Sergeant Schmidt to toss in a Reichsmark or two. Merrill drew himself up to his six foot two and interjected, "Herr *Kaluen*, sir. With your permission. I'm a photographer, and DNB requests pictures, many of them for *Signal* magazine. Of your former crew, the U-601, the snorkels, and the sub pen itself."

Loewen measured him with an expert eye.

Merrill had briefed himself on the U-boat ace's personal life, habits, and naval career, but wasn't quite prepared for the collected and completely controlled power of the man whose cool eyes surveyed him now. Still, he went on: "And you're needed in the pictures, sir."

Sigi quickly chimed in, "What form of publicity could we devise of a rugged U-boat sailor in an elegant Paris hotel room?" She sent Loewen a smile that could melt ice.

Loewen grinned back, as if aware that her statement admitted of no argument. Teeth clenched, he slowly climbed to his feet. He weighed her request thoughtfully as long as it took him to reach the tall window facing out on the river, then said quietly, "In Paris only two days and I am being asked, unofficially, to return to duty."

Sigi pressed him again. "It's only temporary, Kapitan. Endure us a day, two at the most, at the U-boat base, then you may continue your rest leave in Paris."

Returning from the window, Loewen suffered her a smile of defeat. He sat again in the straightback chair. "I planned to visit Versailles and the Chateau at Fontainebleau." Loewen's smile widened fractionally. "The trip to St. Nazaire does not appeal to me, but I must admit your charm is irresistible."

Sigi smiled back. "I understand your reluctance. In war, so much must wait." Revoking her small measure of tolerance, she added, in a businesslike tone, "The Fuehrer and Dr. Goebbels will both be pleased."

Loewen sighed. "When will I be needed in St. Nazaire?"

Pleased that he'd done his homework, Merrill rose to his feet. "Trains this afternoon at three and six, sir."

Loewen looked at him stonily. "Impossible. A dinner engagement this evening. I can't leave until tomorrow."

Sigi couldn't hide her disappointment. She hastily lit a German cigarette and exhaled the smoke. Turning to Merrill, whose Hamlet-like scrutiny seemed to agitate her even more, she asked, "Well, Sergeant?"

"I didn't check the A.M. departures." Merrill cursed his lack of foresight. His disappointment, too, was undisguised. The prospect of spending another night in Paris with an unknown counterspy in their midst was hardly encouraging.

"Obtain the schedules," Sigi instructed. "Let's not inconvenience our Reichskriegmarine officer friend more than is necessary."

Merrill gave Sigi a proper nod, at the same time covertly studying her. Somewhere behind all this officious veneer there's a hot-blooded woman, he mused. He'd watched Loewen's slow seduction with mixed envy and amusement. Sigi Petersen was apparently one of those women who could rebound quickly, wiping off whomever the man with last night's lipstick and setting off on a new fling or conquest. Merrill smiled at her once more, gave Loewen the proper salute, and hastily left the room.

Chapter 19

THE GRAY CITROEN parked along the quay across from the Clarice-Almont contained two occupants. SS Colonel Reinhard Schiller impatiently tapped his gloved hand on the wheel of the car, glanced up at the fourth floor window of the hotel, then sighed as he picked at the lint on his black SS uniform. "There is too much waiting in the espionage business," he grumbled. "Most fatiguing." His eyes focused again on the hotel's entrance. He saw a covey of doves take off from the steps as the lobby door swung open. Schiller fully expected Dieter Loewen to come back outside and it was his intention to follow the U-boat ace. Instead, it was the pretending Wehrmacht photographer who had emerged and come down the steps; the American spy who had complicated matters was leaving the hotel alone.

Schiller's mind raced, weighing the alternatives. Off in the distance, the brass bells of Notre Dame musically chimed ten in the morning. Schiller had to quickly make up his mind. He would remain here and keep track of the U-boat commander.

Turning to the passenger in the Citroen's rear seat, Schiller said, "You've been paid well for your information and I'm pleased. Will you now take on a more difficult assignment? One worth five thousand francs?"

"What is your request, Colonel?"

Schiller pointed across the street. "Follow that man and eliminate him."

"But murder?" The voice in the rear quavered. "I am not an assassin, Colonel."

"The man is not a German soldier, but an American spy.

145

Extremely dangerous, an assassin himself. You will be doing a great service to both France and Germany."

"I would like to consider the matter."

"There's no time! Think about it as you follow him. Go now, quickly. Complete the job before nightfall."

"My price is ten thousand francs."

Schiller didn't have time to bargain. "Agreed. Don't lose him. And you should make it appear to be an accident. Most important, you must not be apprehended, under any circumstances."

Skeet Merrill sprinted down the steps into the sooty, white-tile, cavernous world of the Paris *Metro*. He bought a first class ticket, then consulted the map on the wall. He would go to Gare Montparnasse and not only obtain the train schedules to St. Nazaire, but book passage as well. Valuable time would be saved in the morning.

The Metro station was humid and smelled of scented bodies. Merrill waited at the end of the platform where it was less crowded. Next to him, propped precariously against one of the steel uprights, a ragged *clochard* with an empty wine bottle puffed on a dirty cigarette. A fat woman nearby, gloating over an old romance magazine, suddenly reached down and snatched it from his lips. Merrill smiled in amusement. War had its odd priorities. He watched the drunk curse and stumble away.

From the far end of the platform came the high-pitched roar of an approaching train, its hard white light cannonading the tunnel. Feeling the surge of the others, Merrill stepped forward, closer to the edge of the platform. German soldiers, he knew, would be expected to ride in one of the first class coaches. The train was some fifty yards away and slowing.

Suddenly, someone from behind pushed him. In his split second horror there was only one instinct. Keenly honed reflex was all that mattered. The scream of air brakes abruptly applied shattered Merrill's ears as one foot struck the center of the track. His other leg bending beneath him, Merrill rolled like a tossed cat, allowing his momentum to carry his body sideways. The tucked position carried his feet out of reach of the oncoming train wheels by scant inches. The sound of skidding wheels was terrifying. Stunned, Merrill sat frozen in the adjoining tracks, carefully avoiding touching the electrified rail. His bladder involuntarily began to empty and it took a determined effort to stop it. Shaking his head numbly and sucking in a long breath of air that smelled of burnt copper, Merrill tried to shut out the Metro's heavy-pitched roar. His thigh ached where it had struck the rails, but nothing was broken.

The train had stopped and a cacophony of agitated voices descended on him from all sides. A wave of nausea hit Merrill. He wanted to get up, run to the other side of the train, but he didn't trust his legs. *Just sit still,* he told himself. *It'll pass.*

Pressed against the windows of the car above him were a score of wide-eyed faces—faces he remembered from seconds earlier on the platform. Aside from the drunk who had wandered off before the train arrived, Merrill remembered that the half-dozen or so passengers in his immediate vicinity on the platform had *all been women!*

Alone with the attractive journalist, Loewen felt a distinct uneasiness sweep over him, strangely disconcerting but at the same time pleasant. He felt a new electricity in Anna Schramm's movements as she said softly, "I look forward to our little journey." Then she hesitated. "How long have you been a widower, Kapitan?"

"Call me Dieter, please. Two years." Loewen suddenly found himself swallowing with difficulty. "How did you know?"

"Research is imperative to journalists. I'm sorry for your loss. The residential bombing of Dusseldorf, like other cities, was merciless."

"Have you visited Paris before?" Loewen asked, anxious to change the subject.

Smiling provocatively, she lied. "No, Dieter."

"Fraulein, tonight I must meet with an admiral friend for an early dinner. Afterward, may I suggest the two of us rendezvous for a drink?" He leaned toward her, this time his eyes consuming her without embarrassment. "What is your taste? *Le célebré cancan? Le jazz hot?*"

She met his gaze with a pleased look. "A diversion from war business would be satisfying. Providing you remember to call me *Anna.*"

He looked at her narrowly. Suddenly, she seemed strangely uneasy. Loewen heard a slight shuffling sound in the corridor just outside that had apparently distracted her. Ignoring the noise, Loewen said uncertainly, "I know of several bistros that are definite diversions. Le Crazy Horse? Fifis? La Reine Bleue? Petite Maison?"

"I've heard about the notorious La Reine Bleue," she admitted with a slight frown.

Loewen didn't understand what was troubling her, but he lightly continued, "A bizarre stage show, but the Calvados and Napoleon are excellent. A rough neighborhood, however, and I speak from experience. I must escort you. Is nine o'clock satisfactory?"

She nodded, but her attention was still riveted to the entry. Loewen watched curiously as she smashed out her cigarette and edged toward the door. "The hour is fine," she finally replied in a voice betrayed by agitation. "May I meet you at the bistro? The sergeant will see me safely there."

She startled Loewen by suddenly throwing the door open. In the corridor an embarrassed balding man in a plum-colored coat stood awkwardly; it was the hotel reception clerk. He smiled conspiratorially. "*Pardon, Fraulein.* I was just about to knock, but I see now I have the wrong room." The hotelman gave them an unctuous bow, wiped his perspiring face, then padded off.

Loewen wasn't sure what to think. Anna Schramm slowly closed the door, turned back to him, and nervously straightened her skirt. "Merely carelessness or eavesdropping? What's your opinion, Dieter?"

"Spies, spies, spies," he shrugged. "I'm told one cannot escape them in France. Perhaps, for your safety, Anna, we should contact the Paris SD or SS."

"Hardly necessary. I can take care of myself, I assure you."

Loewen heard the rim of coldness in her voice and admired it. "You aren't afraid?"

She slowly shook her head, all the while studying him.

Loewen looked back at her curiously, measuring the significance of her stare. It was Anna Schramm's eyes that rattled him; they were blue, glacial blue, but at the same time inquiring and filled with desire. Loewen shifted uneasily. Never before had he come across such an intriguing, aggressive woman.

"Do I make you uncomfortable, Dieter?" she asked.

"Your charm is absolutely ruthless," he stammered, feeling his last shred of resistance being ripped away.

"Heroes of the Reich deserve the best hospitality a woman can offer," she whispered, moving closer.

Loewen smiled back. Leaning forward, he gently kissed both her cheeks, hesitated, then tossed his white cap to a nearby chair. He took her face in his hands. Loewen gazed at her hypnotically for almost a full minute, and when he saw there wasn't the slightest resistance to his advances, he feverishly kissed her lips.

She moaned softly. The firmness of her body against his own excited Loewen. Anna Schramm was a passionate, tantalizing surprise indeed. A flash went through Loewen's mind. Would this experience, like others since his wife's passing, reach an exciting high point, collapse, and then she would be gone? Whatever, he suspected he'd be powerless to alter the escalating course of events. Loewen saw the goosebumps shoot up her arms as she felt his masculinity stir—masculinity that had been denied pleasure for so many months while he'd been at sea on patrol.

She pushed his leather topcoat aside and gently rested her hand on his trousers and the taut muscle underneath. Slowly, very slowly and purposefully, she undid the buttons between his legs. As quick as a Hamburg whore, Loewen thought; unusually aggressive for a woman of her class and intelligence. In impassioned response, Loewen gently slipped his hand inside her blouse and firmly cupped her breast, fondled it, then tenderly took the tip between his thumb and forefinger. He felt the nipple swell and distend as he softly plied it back and forth between his fingers. They kissed again.

Their lips finally parted. Breathless, Anna Schramm looked down between them. *"Mein Gott!"* she whispered.

Loewen smiled sagely; he knew that for her to say that it was substantial would be an understatement.

"What else could I properly expect from a military legend larger than life?" she said softly. Quivering with anticipation and bending to her knees, Anna Schramm closed her eyes and moistened her bright red lips.

* * *

In Rosenheim, Germany, the civic leaders felt honored beyond measure. They had reason to celebrate this last week in May. The town, situated near the foot of the Bavarian Alps, was far removed from the metropolitan centers of Germany and had not been ravaged by Allied bomber attack. Secondly, being the birthplace of one Kapitan Leutnant Dieter Loewen, the Fuehrer had declared Rosenheim the place of issue for a postage stamp bearing the U-boat hero's likeness. And now the townspeople were honored to have Adolf Hitler himself take time out from his busy schedule and drive down from nearby Berchtesgaden to participate in the stamp dedication, a ceremony which coincided with a gathering of Hitler youth.

The town was gayly decorated with Nazi banners and flowers, and propaganda ministry motion picture cameras captured the event for Dr. Goebbels. Adolf Hitler did not intend to stay long. Since the major setbacks on the Eastern front, he'd become a virtual recluse and no longer took readily to crowds. His face had become increasingly pallid, for seldom did he venture outdoors, except at the Berghof. Today he was also pressed for time, as his plane was waiting at the nearby Salzburg Airport to carry him back to Berlin.

The Fuehrer spoke informally, without a public address system. He praised U-boat commander Dieter Loewen, explaining that when the ace returned to Germany he would be specially honored in Berlin. Hitler turned his attention to the adults present, who seemed to be far outnumbered by children. Overhead, a banner fluttered in the wind, reminding him of his prewar rise to power. It read: *Ein Volk, Ein Reich, Ein Fuehrer.*

Standing in the back of his 12 cylinder black Dusenberg, Hitler raised his voice as he concluded his speech: "In 1940 we drove them away from the European continent at Dunkirk. Afterward, you will remember I convened the Reichstag and Germany urged the world to make peace. But the Allies ignored us. Now they stubbornly come again. This time we will brook no compromise! It will be a fight to the last American and British soldier on the beaches."

The gathered crowd raised their arms. *"Sieg heil!"*

Hitler bore a look of smug, dogmatic certainty as he stepped out of the car and ventured forward among the children. His personal photographer, Hoffman, was at his heels.

"These children of the Hitler Youth are the depository for all I have worked for. For the Fatherland!"

A young boy in lederhosen blew a prearranged tattoo on his trumpet, this followed by a quartet of shiny-faced, pigtailed girls who recited a poem from memory:

"We shall always obey you, like father and mother.
And when we grow up, we'll help you like father and mother.
And you'll be proud of us, like father and mother."

The girls curtsied and Hitler smiled, just in time to have the folksy, paternal scene immortalized by Hoffman and the cinematographers. An aide brought up a basket of candies.

Hitler, weaving his sorcerer's spell on the children, gave them a choice of lemon lollipops wrapped in cellophane or foil-wrapped chocolate in the shape of miniature submarines. All the children eagerly chose the submarines.

Out of the Fuehrer's earshot and standing alone on the other side of the Dusenberg, Heinrich Himmler paced and checked his watch. He looked up at Martin Bormann who stood nearby. "We must be leaving soon if we are to reach Berlin by dark. It is curious the Fuehrer spends so much time honoring the Reichskriegmarine when in fact he hates the sea so much."

Bormann smiled thinly. "Perhaps our leader is prone to seasickness and fears embarrassment. This hydrophobia may have been one of the underlying reasons he did not push earlier for an invasion of Britain."

Himmler frowned and exhaled sharply. "Save some of that hard-to-come-by chocolate for the children of our staff, Herr Bormann." Slowly shaking his head, Himmler added, "Indeed. Foil wrapped submarines, when there are food and metal shortages!"

Bormann smiled again. "From Switzerland. There, anything is possible."

Chapter 20

"FALLING IN love again, what am I to do? Can't help it."
Sebastien's clumsy *Blue Angel* parody drew only mixed applause. The overweight female impersonator bowed unctuously, gathered up his coins, and retreated into the wings.

Skeet Merrill sat silently, oblivious to the shabby entertainment on stage and sucked up by a double glass of brandy he continually sipped, not only to forget his brush with death in the Paris Metro, but also to make his visit to Pierre Roger's *boui-boui* less miserable. Merrill's mind began to aimlessly drift over the miles and years. He thought of Rita Hayworth, Glenn Miller's *Moonlight Serenade*, the high school prom, college holidays at Panama City and Fort Lauderdale, and his first car—a Plymouth coupe. Somehow, the sum total of all these formative years, all these memories, had come oddly to this? A curious *ménage à trois*, of sorts—a night out on the town with Sigi Petersen and Dieter Loewen where Merrill was definitely odd man out.

La Reine Bleue, to Merrill, was no Tuxedo Junction. By no stretch of the imagination was it a Texan's kind of place to live it up on Saturday night. Some mission they'd given him, he mused. Hullabaloo over U-boat aces; a scheming, frosty female for a partner—or boss; strange Cockney voices out of the blue; a mysterious, dastardly double-agent on the prowl who apparently wanted Merrill dead; and now, the frosting on the cake, frilly female impersonators. What had war come to? Merrill's mind felt boggled. Thank God for the cognac, he reflected, taking another swig and feeling its immediate warmth. It had been one hell of a lot simpler, *yes, safer,* in the

Pacific war, where he'd been his own man on his own submarine.

On top of everything else, Merrill was sure he'd detected a glimmer of genuine interest in Sigi's eyes as she animatedly chatted with the German sub commander seated next to her. Merrill watched with annoyance as Sigi plucked a cigarette from her lips and blew a stream of smoke toward the sub ace to once more capture his attention. Dieter Loewen didn't applaud the performance on the stage.

Merrill continued to observe Loewen as the German repeatedly drank in with his eyes the woman he knew as Anna Schramm. The ace made it obvious that he was enjoying her lush contours, shiny flaxen hair, and smiling red lips. Merrill sensed Loewen's excitement, but he also noted that Sigi's reaction was changing; her smile became tight and nervous.

Loewen glanced briefly at Merrill as if resenting his presence. Then the German's eyes again lingered on Sigi, at the same time his hand slipping beneath the table in search of hers.

Pierre Roger approached, interrupting the ace's mesmerized stare. The *patron* nodded discreetly to Merrill, then winked at Sigi as he placed another glass of his best Napoleon before the German. The cognac remained on the table for only a fraction of a second.

"To your health, Fraulein," said Loewen, obviously in a drinking mood.

"You forget to call me Anna," she replied, raising her own glass of Pernod. Her pleasant, lingering gaze at Loewen was cut short by a clipped, boisterous voice from behind them.

"You are a long way from your man-of-war, Herr Kapitan!"

Loewen pivoted slowly and looked up.

"We meet again," gloated SS Major von Wilme, gazing icily down at them. "Surely this time you won't object if a fellow countryman joins your table? The three of you appear to be new to Paris, am I correct?"

Merrill exchanged an alarmed look with Sigi, but kept his silence.

The SS officer ceremoniously clicked his heels. "May I offer you a drink? My welcome to the city." He signaled to Dominique Roger behind the bar.

Merrill, as a Wehrmacht sergeant, was badly outranked.

Climbing to his feet, he offered his chair to von Wilme. The German wasted no time requisitioning it.

"I'm Major von Wilme. Hermann von Wilme."

"Kapitan Leutnant Loewen here," the sub ace said gruffly.

"The name is familiar, *Kaleun*," the SS man replied. His eyes counted the stripes on Loewen's sleeve then darted to the Iron Cross around his neck. "Of course, forgive me. Our illustrious U-boat ace? I am honored." Brusquely dismissing Loewen, he turned to Sigi. "And who might you be, Fraulein?"

"Anna Schramm, associate editor for the D.N.B. in Berlin." She gestured toward Merrill. "My photographer assistant, Sergeant Schmidt, from *Signal* magazine."

Von Wilme ignored Merrill. "Interesting," he said, searching her eyes. "Your first visit to Occupied France, Fraulein Schramm?"

"Yes," she replied quietly.

Merrill grimaced, suspecting his partner had already said too much. The SS major was obviously confronting her. Edging away from the table and leaning against the wall, Merrill's expressionless face belied him. He felt lit by a spark—the spark struck by the collision of opposing teams. Wary, saliva drying in his mouth, Merrill readied himself for the slightest sign of trouble. He watched von Wilme survey Sigi carefully, as if trying to place her in his memory. From his own lengthy study of German, Merrill knew Sigi's accent lacked regional exactitude and definition. It wasn't Bavarian, or Prussian, or Austrian—or Hanoverian—like von Wilme's. And it seemed to be this absence of character that now bothered the SS major.

Confirming Merrill's suspicion, von Wilme asked abruptly, "Where is your home town, Fraulein Schramm?"

Sigi hesitated. "I expected you to ask what I am doing in Paris." She smiled enigmatically. "I forget, you SS men are too adroit to ask the obvious. You delight in working with the most difficult parts of the puzzle first."

Von Wilme smiled back, but repeated the question.

She hastily replied, "I have lived in Berlin for six years. Before that, Heidelberg. But I was raised as a child and schooled in Norway, where my parents were assigned on consular business."

Clever, thought Merrill. The Gestapoman should buy that. Loewen waved his hand in objection and turned to von

Wilme. "Tell me, Herr Major, do you join us to socialize or to interrogate? Must you poke at Fraulein Schramm's credentials like a hungry woodpecker?"

Surprise softened the hardness of the moment. Von Wilme grinned at Loewen passively. Dominique Roger approached, placed a round of drinks on the table and the SS major paid. He tipped her generously, but held her wrist so she couldn't depart. "Wait, *patronne*. The other young impersonator—Erika Vermeer. She has not, by chance, returned?"

"No, Major."

Von Wilme dismissed her with an impatient wriggle of his hand and turned back to Sigi. "To your stay in Paris," he prompted, lifting his glass and trying a new subject. "A decadent, dying metropolis. But when long-range German reorganization and new order are accomplished, you'll then find it one of Europe's most delightful cities."

Merrill looked away to hide his expression of contempt.

"And I disagree," groaned Loewen, apparently irritated by the new direction the conversation was taking. "You officers of the SS are forever dreamers," he said boldly. "I don't argue with German destiny to occupy France, Major, but I question our ability to change its culture. Impossible!" Loewen took a long, thoughtful sip from his cognac. "Order and precision are instruments contrary to French temperament, even though this mechanization may be what gives the Fatherland invincible superiority."

"At sea, also?" queried von Wilme, his eyes narrowing.

"Our setbacks are temporary," retorted Loewen, not about to be manipulated. "The Kriegsmarine will have command of the sea again, and very soon." Lifting his glass, the ace snapped, "To invincible superiority!"

They drank, this time, von Wilme without enthusiasm. Merrill polished off his round and placed the empty snifter on the table. Loewen signaled for refills.

Sigi glanced at von Wilme without impatience. The solemn SS major apparently wasn't about to be dismissed by the awkward silence. Again, he stubbornly pressed his argument: "Paris is a frivolous city, hopelessly corrupt."

Sigi seized the initiative. "Gentlemen, the fate of both France and our dear Germany is in good hands in Berlin. I propose a toast to the Fuehrer."

Von Wilme sent her a glaring frown. "Adolf Hitler is a

teetotaler. Personally, I consider it a mockery to toast a man who looks with strong disfavor on liquor," he said piously.

Red-faced with annoyance, Loewen gazed up from his cognac. "Nonsense. *Prosit!* I say." The drinks had slowly taken hold and the ace's eyes looked vague. His speech was wooly. Loewen rose unsteadily to his feet. "I agree with the Fraulein. *To the Fuehrer!*"

Sigi prudently raised her glass, but only sipped at the pernod. Merrill too, drank, but this time only sparingly. The cognac was potent and he was feeling the lightness in his legs. He shifted and leaned against the wall for support.

Hermann von Wilme sluggishly climbed to his feet with the others and brought up his glass. He drank, showing considerable displeasure at the obligatory gesture. His gray eyes surveyed Loewen with active dislike.

"Another drink, Major?" asked the sub ace, expansively.

Merrill watched in satisfaction as von Wilme's pained look deepened. Apparently to the SS major, compulsive swilling of Napoleon brandy was totally inappropriate and unbecoming to a military officer. Merrill doubted that von Wilme was much of a drinker, certainly not by the consumptive standards of the Reichskriegmarine officer beside him. The SS, with the intense fervor of its faith in the Nazi ideal, would be highly intolerant of drunken behavior in its ranks.

Von Wilme glowered at Loewen then turned to Sigi. "The Kapitan imbibes too much, and you, Fraulein, think too much."

She smiled coyly.

Treating von Wilme to a smoldering glare of his own, Loewen retired into his drink. The increasing warmth of the cognac continued to dull his speech as he slowly said, "It's obvious, Herr Major, that you have more nerve than a jawful of bad teeth. And it's also apparent that you enjoy pulling rank on me. Kindly remember, I am *not* of the SS." He looked away from von Wilme and shouted, "*Patronne!* Another round here!" Ignoring the Gestapoman, Loewen's eyes went back to Sigi, ravishing her without reservation.

"We have all had enough, *Kaleun.*" Von Wilme placed a hand firmly on Loewen's arm.

The U-boat ace wrenched away. "I'll be standing long after they measure your length on the bistro floor, my friend. A pity the men of the SS cannot hold their drink as well, eh?"

Glowering, von Wilme jackknifed to his feet. His chair crashed down behind him, the clatter charging the bistro with electricity. Conversations ended and all eyes looked their way.

"Your toasts and your swilling bore me, Kapitan. My apologies for an impetuous departure, Fraulein. Possibly we'll meet again under more pleasurable circumstances."

"Possibly, Herr Major," Sigi replied, politely.

"Good evening, then." Von Wilme's voice was sharp-edged. Ignoring Loewen and Merrill and clicking Junker heels, he bowed slightly to Sigi and strutted out of the bistro.

Untightening, Merrill watched von Wilme depart with a loathing that did his stomach good. Checking off the new dangers facing them, Merrill wondered if this Gestapo interloper would confront them again before they could get out of Paris. Too easily von Wilme could put the screws to the mission. If worse came to worse, Sigi might turn on the sex tap for the black uniformed beast, but Merrill had a premonition such a gesture would be futile. In fact, he wondered if the SS major had any consuming interest in women. Thus far von Wilme hadn't shown the slightest interest in either Sigi's face or figure, which seemed to be working so unfailingly well with other males coming under her spell.

Merrill saw that Sigi was beckoning to him. She needed help, for Loewen was getting plonked. So this was the salty pin-up hero of the Third Reich, he thought. The legendary U-boat ace so universally admired, whose very name stirred the hearts of German women and children and gave lesser men vicarious visions of grandeur! This was the awesome Lion of the Atlantic. And he was drunk.

Merrill went back to the table. With a third cognac soothing his senses, he felt less of the annoyance at having been brought to La Reine Bleue and more of his usual nonchalant attitude toward danger. A perilous mission was nothing new to him, and toughness and cleverness toward violence was, after all, what he was being paid for. He was supposedly a profession-al—slick, shrewd, acutely aware. Sigi had her way of doing things, he had his. The edges were now a little blurred, but he was sure of one thing: the past hour had been a complete waste of time. Damn this woman; had *he* been running the show, the German U-boat commander would have been neatly bound, gagged, and hidden in the back of Roger's appropriated *kraftswagen*. They would have made a decent dash for it and been half way to St. Nazaire by now.

* * *

From behind the copper bar, Pierre Roger watched Merrill as he helped Sigi guide Dieter Loewen out of the bistro. When they were gone from sight, Roger grabbed his coat, nodded to his wife, and hurriedly left by the back door. In his haste he forgot to remove his apron.

Across the street from La Reine Bleue, the tall, quiet figure of the SS colonel—straight, hard, and as cold as a butcher's knife—waited in a darkened storefront. Reinhard Schiller once more adjusted his monocle and squinted toward the bistro. Standing watch for the last forty-five minutes, he'd been surprised by Major von Wilme's hasty and apparently angry departure. Schiller had deliberately avoided being seen by von Wilme, for the Paris Gestapo officer—beyond their common pursuit of the Dutch girl Erika Krager, had still not been taken completely into his confidence regarding Operation Storm Tide. Nor had von Wilme been informed of their double agent, Viper. Heinrich Himmler and Hitler had intrusted Schiller, praising his closed manner and knack for utmost secrecy. Accordingly, he'd shared the real purpose of his mission with absolutely no one in the Paris SS office.

Schiller lit a Soldaten cigarette. His intuition had quickly transformed itself to a sudden, sick certainty. He was sure there were curious developments going on inside La Reine Bleue. Viper's leads, at least, turned out to be accurate. Unfortunately, there were still a few missing pieces to the charade, but the elements seemed to be coming together, more quickly than Schiller had expected. The American, unfortunately, was still very much alive, the cat with too many lives. The Allied invasion was obviously gathering itself. *How many enemies*, Schiller wondered, confronted him?

Schiller took a long drag on his cigarette, savoring the smoke. Despite the frivolous, gay climate of the bistro, there was a terrible threat to Germany here. The enemy was ruthless, extremely dangerous. Working alone had its disadvantages. He would have to be doubly careful. Schiller knew that hardly a day went by without an SS investigator being killed in the field. Himmler had reminded him that their current losses suffered were greater in proportion than those of army officers. Everywhere, SS casualties were increasing at a tragic rate. A bomb had destroyed a staff car and its passengers in Belgium only this morning; in Amsterdam, two Gestapo officers were ambushed just the day before; and the situation in Norway was becoming more intolerable by the week, despite accelerated reprisals. Thus far on this immediate operation alone, Klieber was missing in St. Nazaire and Richter and Wiedmann had been killed the night of the enemy parachute drop.

Schiller stepped quickly back into the shadows as the woman, her assistant, and the sub ace left La Reine Bleue and straggled up the street in search of a taxi. Gazing at the unsteady Loewen, Schiller considered briefly the advantages of alerting the fellow German to his imminent danger. *No.* Himmler's instructions—despite Admiral Doenitz' misgivings—were to use Loewen as bait for as long as possible for the most important facet of their plan. Diabolical as the enemy plot appeared, Schiller knew the fate of the Reichskriegmarine and the course of the great Allied invasion hung in its balance.

Schiller's instructions were clear enough, but what if the American, in the meantime, should prove trigger-happy? The sub ace was in too much danger. Schiller cursed to himself. Possibly he'd need a measure of help after all. Out of necessity he would consult Major von Wilme in the morning. Schiller would seek assistance, but only a small measure of it, from the local SS detachment. In the meantime, the tall American posing as a Wehrmacht photographer was still alive and a bone in the throat. Schiller had to move quickly.

Chapter 21

MERRILL PAUSED in the hotel hallway and turned to Sigi. "I'm telling you it was a woman who pushed me in the subway."

She gave him an incredulous look.

Merrill had discussed the incident with her all the way back to the hotel but evidently she still found it hard to believe. Quickly, he added, "It had to be. Either a woman or someone dressed like one." Merrill began fumbling for his room key.

Sigi held up the candle the desk clerk had given her. "So anyone particular in mind?"

He shook his head. "Whole thing's crazy. If the Germans were on to us they could pick me up with a snap of the fingers. Why try to knock me off without a thorough grilling? And on the sly? It doesn't make sense."

"But my suggestion that it was a coincidence does."

Merrill opened the door to his room and looked over at her.

Sigi continued: "You were in a German uniform, standing at the edge of the Metro platform in front of several French women, among whom——"

He looked at her impatiently. "Come now."

"The opportunity may have been too much to resist for one of the *boche* haters."

"The Metro's full of Germans every hour, every day. Why me?" Merrill slowly shook his head. "And there's more trouble. When I went to the can at the bistro, Roger told me the young lesbian was forced into hiding."

"I know." Sigi thought for a moment. "Erika Vermeer doesn't look Jewish," she said calmly.

160

"Nor do I look half-Irish," replied Merrill. "What's the point?"

She thought for a moment, then said, "None. I'm sorry." Standing in the dim hallway, she eyed Merrill speculatively for several seconds, then finally broke her self-imposed silence. "You admire Loewen, don't you?"

Merrill answered sourly, "Maybe half-ass envious of his skills. But he's still on the wrong team, and his ideology smells."

"Why are you so fascinated with submarines, Skeet?"

He shrugged with impatience. "There's a little brine in every man's blood. Mine a smack or two more. Down under it's another world, hard to explain. Some folks get their rocks off flying—for them euphoria is up in the clouds. I prefer the depths."

"And the danger?" she asked quickly.

Merrill shot her a look of appraisal. "Beyond your patriotism, what keeps you in Special Services?"

Sigi grinned. "Men like you." She watched him laugh, then added: "You have a steady flame back home?"

"I like to play the field; call it my weakness. But there's a favorite."

Sigi's eyebrows shot up marginally. "Where is she? Texas?"

Merrill shook his head. "Back in London. Bright little naval reserve warrant that gives back rubs better than any masseur. She also brings me breakfast in bed."

"Pretty?"

"Very."

"And no doubt as mindless as a marsh hen?"

"I like her chattering." Merrill felt challenged and threatened. He stiffened slightly as Sigi came closer and brushed her hand against his cheek, then just as quickly withdrew it. *Was she planting the hook?* He grinned and said to himself, *Relax, Skeet. Play with the bait.* She started to back away, but Merrill's outstretched hand blocked her retreat. "Coming in?" he asked, at the same time gently nudging her inside the room.

"No, Skeet," she said firmly.

He kept his hand across the doorway. For the moment Merrill's spy instincts were alert to all the wrong things, like admiring Sigi's lithe contours, inhaling her intoxicating perfume, and trying to determine which direction their relationship was taking them. Having succumbed to her charm, he was

now determined to push a little. Merrill squeezed his hands
gently, slowly around her arms. Trying to be as casual as
possible, he eased her up against the wall. Sigi's blonde hair
glistened in the candlelight; her blue eyes sparkled, halfway
intrigued with his advances and not the slightest afraid. Merrill
kissed her softly on the forehead, then ran his fingertips across
her cheeks, carefully tracing the shape of her pretty lips.

"No, Skeet," she repeated. "I mean it. I told you last
night——"

Merrill was undecided whether to seize the moment and kiss
Sigi full on the mouth, or comfort her with more smooth,
deliberate conversation. While his brain flirted briefly with
both ideas, his lightly moving fingers started to probe. She
quivered and gave up a little sigh as he deftly opened the collar
to her blouse and reached inside her brassiere for her breasts.
They were exactly how Merrill had imagined them—well
contoured with peaked nipples that firmed instantly under the
stroke of his fingertips.

"Please, I said no," she whispered, this time pushing him
away forcefully. Abruptly, she swung at his face and Merrill
reeled, his red cheek mirroring his stunned disbelief.

Sigi's knuckles shot up to her mouth.

Merrill felt both irritated and confused. He instinctively
knew she was being drawn to him like a magnet, but there was
something poisoning her mind, fighting off the compelling
force. What? Her sharp reaction made Merrill feel strangely
alien. Once more he studied her face.

Sigi suddenly looked transparent and vulnerable. The candle
in her hand dripped a pool of wax on the carpet. Hesitantly, she
looked up at him across the flickering light. "I'm sorry,
Skeet." Her eyes were soft now and repentant.

Merrill slowly shook his head and pointed a menacing finger
toward her nose, teasing. "Lady, you're one intense pain in the
ass."

"Good night," she whispered.

Closing Skeet Merrill's door and treading softly across the
hall to her own room, Sigi thought to herself, *God, woman,
you're becoming one first-class bitch*. She knew something
important had been left unsaid, the night itself not properly
consummated. And why? Two men in one day was nothing

new for her record book; she'd done it before. Her impulsive
fury had been spent in one of those moments that are suddenly
over before they really begin. Never before had she behaved so
ambiguously; did she want Skeet Merrill or not? Her mind
went back to Dieter Loewen and she felt uncertain, confused,
and irritated.

Sigi reached for the latch, but her hand paused. The door
was slightly ajar and by no means had she left it that way. She
regarded the entry, suddenly alert to danger. There was only
silence. She thought about summoning Merrill before entering,
then decided against it. She'd relied enough on him, and there
was probably no cause for alarm; more than one French
chambermaid had been known to be careless. Easing the door
open and extending her solitary candle, she cautiously proceeded inside.

Halfway across the room her measured footsteps struck a
soft, pliable form. "Oooohh!" Her sharp intake of breath was
like a child's balloon suddenly deflated.

As still as the floor it lay on, the body at her feet was face
down, arms grotesquely bent sideways. Seeing the bald head
and the plum-colored coat with brass buttons, Sigi knew at
once it was the officious desk clerk. *Was he dead?* Heart
pounding, she backed slowly away one step at a time, toward
the door. But she drew back into two strong arms that
immediately coiled around her, hoisting her as easily as a child
picks up a kitten. From out of the shadows a second figure
appeared, hastily extinguished her candle, and forced a wad of
cloth in her mouth. Squirming desperately, Sigi tried to kick
her assailants, but a short arm jab that rattled her teeth
dampened her enthusiasm. She quit struggling.

They quickly bound her ankles and wrists with long rayon
stockings. The beam of their flashlight blinded her until a
pillowcase could be dropped over her head. Whoever the
intruders, they were in a hurry. Sigi could feel the lashings
around her wrists were clumsily tied; the ankle job, likewise,
had been blotched. *A chance!* Suddenly she was lifted and
wrestled inside what she assumed was the tall wooden armoire.
The door closed, clicked, and a darkness closed around her that
smelled faintly of mothballs.

For an interminable time, relaxing as much as her bindings
would allow, she just listened as they rummaged through the
room. Neither of her assailants spoke. Finally there was silence

outside the wardrobe. Given a little time and no interference, she knew getting out of her predicament was no particular trick, but had her assailants left the room?

Sigi gave herself three minutes more to be sure, then started wriggling. Bending forward and straining, she finally worked her arms under her hips until her bound hands were in front, just below the knees. Despite the blackness, the rest was easy. Peeling off the pillowcase and removing the gag, she tried the armoire door. It was locked, with no handle inside. Not even a keyhole. Mustering all her strength and kicking, the thin veneer shattered.

Sigi struggled out of the wardrobe and fumbled at the night table for her lighter. Striking it, she quickly surveyed the room, once more eyeing with considerable displeasure the body on the floor. The aura of death hung like heavy smoke in the disarray and she could feel little beads of sweat starting to form on her spine. Sigi went to the door and tugged on the handle, but it wouldn't budge. Locked and the key was missing.

Kneeling, she squinted through the keyhole. The passage outside was ink-black. She wanted to scream, shout, and pound fiercely on the door. No, arousing the entire hotel would be counterproductive and dangerous. The lock was the ordinary type found in European hotels. Spotting a wall fixture, Sigi quickly detached the parchment shade and removed the wire stiffener from the rim, straightening it into a single length about ten inches long. Bending the wire into a shape resembling an oversize crochet hook, she attacked the lock. After several attempts the hasp snapped free. Alert and listening, she eased open the door. The hallway was empty.

Hurling herself across the corridor, Sigi rapped softly on Merrill's door. Interminably long seconds dragged by with no response. She rattled the knob repeatedly.

Merrill rolled over and slowly opened his eyes. He'd slept no more than ten minutes, fitfully at that. He sat up, pulled on his pants, and padded to the door. Through heavy eyes he looked at the disheveled Sigi inquiringly. "What the hell is going on?" He waited patiently for her to recover her equanimity.

Finally catching her breath, she blurted out, "I've got company in my room, and he's not very talkative."

She led him back across the hall. Merrill's eyes roamed over her scattered belongings then focused on the body sprawled in the center of the floor.

Sigi examined her baggage. "It's been searched. Every inch of it." Her frightened eyes flashed back to Merrill as she wearily slumped down on the edge of the bed.

Merrill rolled the hotel clerk's body over, checking for wounds. He found none. "Not a trace of blood. Looks like a nasty chop to the back of the neck."

"Why here? In my room?" Sigi asked anxiously.

Merrill let out a deep breath. "Doesn't make sense. Seriously doubt if he's on our side. But either he or his friends who locked you in the closet rifled through your belongings." Merrill glanced inside the splintered armoire then went to examine the window, noting the shutters were all locked securely from the inside.

"I don't understand," she said in a trembling voice.

"Nor do I. Inexcusably sloppy snooping. Amateurish espionage work, to say the least." Merrill flashed on the Cockney voice that had warned him about the hotel. "Anything missing?"

Sigi was already picking up her belongings. "Nothing."

Merrill slowly shook his head. "We won't be here after tomorrow morning to worry about it. Whoever, you can bet they're putting considerable distance between themselves and this warm, incriminating body. We're probably safe enough for the night here . . ." The absurdity of his words struck Merrill as he'd said them. *Bilgewater. The desk clerk would be missed!* They might already be looking for him. To report the incident would mean an immediate investigation they couldn't afford. And if they bailed out of the hotel now and departed for St. Nazaire early, an all points Prefecture of Police bulletin would be issued within hours and they'd have Abwehr, SD, Gestapo, the local gendarmes, and perhaps a dedicated Doberman or two on their trail.

Merrill glumly gazed down at their unwelcome, still guest, then over to Sigi who sat stiffly on the edge of her bed dragging on a cigarette. Her usual benign calm was missing now. The room fell into a sickened, appalled silence as Merrill considered their options. The attempts on his life and the odd, warning phone call had put a curious distance between himself and the other participants of the team, Sigi Petersen included.

With this latest incident, the gulf would widen. His mind whirred with alternatives like fruit on a one-armed bandit, but nothing fell into place.

"Now what?" Sigi asked, despairingly. She didn't look up, her eyes still fixed on the body on the floor. "Are there no open wounds at all?"

Merrill replied, "No." Remembering the terrible bruise at the back of the victim's head, an idea came to him and he snapped his fingers. "Remember that torn carpet at the head of the stairwell?"

Sigi understood. She gave her swift stamp of approval.

Merrill lifted the incriminating corpse by the feet and began dragging it to the door. "They'll find him soon enough. Just start praying it'll appear he took a fatal nose dive."

"Let me help."

"No, you stay here." He tossed his Luger pistol on the bed. "In case you need it."

Enclosed by an ornamental iron banister, the hotel's stairwell had a small kerosene lamp burning at each of the landings. Merrill looked over the rail at the dizzying, five-level drop to the marble floor of the lobby below. Too spectacular. He turned to examine the stairs. A tumble there would at least appear as a believable accident, not a go-for-broke suicide.

Merrill gave the dead porter a firm shove off the top step. The body rolled like a rag doll, crumbling head over heels with a series of hard thuds until it lay sprawled on the landing below. Merrill went back over to the iron rail to check the central shaft. He leaned over and listened, but saw no apparent movement and heard no sound from the lobby below. Taking his hands off the balustrade, he was about to turn away when it happened.

All too quickly, he was being *pushed*! Caught completely off balance, Merrill's body careened over the rail. Terror gripped him as he convulsively flung out his arms. One hand struck the floor beneath the balustrade and his fingers clawed for a grip. He managed to catch hold, but only tenuously.

There had been no time to see who shoved him. Heart pounding, Merrill looked up, away from the vertiginous view of the lobby beneath him. Frantically spinning his body, he planted his free hand firmly around a railing upright. His left arm was in agony from the sudden shock of catching himself, his shoulder sinews feeling like they had been torn apart.

Trembling, his hands damp with sweat, Merrill scuttled, crab-like, toward the staircase. But suddenly feet began stomping at his hands!

Merrill's gaze shot frantically upward, but through his haze of frozen terror he could see nothing in the darkness. The kerosene lantern on the landing had been extinguished. The trampling feet tore a nail from his finger and he grimaced with pain.

Merrill swiftly calculated the distance to the lower end of the stair rail. No choice, he'd have to leap! As his left hand was kicked away from its tenuous purchase, he gulped in a deep breath and launched himself out and downward. Merrill's body slammed into the creaking, protesting handrail, where he managed a firm grip. Struggling, he clambered over the railing and crouched low. In panicky reflex he grabbed for his gun, only to remember that it was back in Sigi's room. Terror finally gave way to anger and determination, and he slowly edged up the steps only to discover he was now alone. The landing was empty.

That's all I needed, he said to himself, followed by a swift recital of every swear word in his vocabulary.

Merrill wearily explored the landing and hallway in both directions but saw nothing. The fire escape door at the end of the hall, however, was open and gently swinging in a draught. Merrill edged up to it and cautiously checked outside. It was too dark to see, but he heard no sound of footsteps on the metal stairs.

Someone's still determined to see me dead, out of the way. The harsh thoughts once more plucked at Merrill's brain like angry blackbirds. Finally regaining his composure, he staggered slowly back to Sigi's room, quietly closed the door, and bolted it securely. Both the woman and his Luger were safe, on the bed, exactly where he'd left them.

Sigi looked up impassively. "How did the tumble go?"

"*Which one?*"

She sent him a perplexed look. "You're white as a ghost. Are you all right?"

Merrill exhaled slowly. He was about to elaborate, but changed his mind. He studied her. No, not now. This wasn't the time to provoke panic or knee-jerk decisions. For the night, at least, he'd keep his near-demise to himself and barricade the door. "I'm fine," he grunted. "The body was heavy. You still frightened?"

Sigi shivered. "A little, yes."

Merrill stared at her, marshaling his thoughts. "You want to remain here or set up housekeeping in my room?"

Sigi met his expectant gaze coldly. "Bedding down at the scene of the crime is hardly appealing. Let's go, please."

Merrill led her across the corridor.

Chapter 22

At Falmouth, Sub Lieutenant Nigel Smythe of the Royal Naval Volunteer Reserve completed his conversation on the shore telephone, then hung up, disappointed. Once more he silently cursed the busy port commander. The young naval officer turned to the motor gunboat's waiting crewmen and grumbled, "Sorry gentlemen, there's still no word." He paused, looking around him. "Fastest steed in the stable and they keep us bridled like a bloody buffalo in a rice paddy."

Smythe examined his watch in the light from the binnacle. It was going on one in the morning and their boat was still on official stand-by. Since late afternoon a long parade of troops had tramped across the temporary gangways extending from both sides of the MGB's mahogany hull and he had grown impatient and irritable. The paint on the deck was becoming badly marred and littered with cigarette wrappers and other debris. There were six torpedo boats and four motor gunboats moored next to the huge troop carrier transport, all placed there for lack of dock space elsewhere in the crammed harbor. Falmouth was a virtual hornet's nest of pre-invasion preparations. Around the clock, ships of every kind were taking on cargo and personnel, and the larger vessels all flew anti-aircraft barrage balloons at the end of stout cables.

Nigel Smythe had never seen so many ships gathered in one place, and he knew this same scene was being repeated in other English seaports. He wondered about the upcoming convoy and the behemoth transports like the one hovering over him, how it would carry thousands of American 4th Division troops across the Channel. Despite the V-formation minesweepers and sleek, destroyer shepherds, Smythe knew these unwieldy, lumbering vessels would be sitting ducks for U-boats. He, like many other Naval officers, was concerned over how many men might die even before the chance to set foot on the beachhead.

The other 112-foot Fairmiles had already received their deployment orders for the great armada, but his boat and one other MGB still waited for specific sailing instructions. The crews were restless and expectant. Smythe knew both MGB's engines were tuned to perfection, that these were the fastest boats in the flotilla by several knots. The gunnery crews were experienced and had honed themselves to razor-sharp accuracy. Why had they been placed on immediate standby alert when the convoy assembling in the harbor wasn't yet in an imminent state of departure? None of the vessels were making steam, and there were still thousands of troops funneling into the city with tons of cargo still waiting on the dock to be processed. There was something else about his boat and the other MGB tied alongside that differed from the rest of the fast patrol fleet. Both hulls had been fitted, only forty-eight hours earlier, with auxiliary fuel tanks on deck, boosting their range from 600 to 1,000 miles.

Suddenly the shore telephone on the bridge buzzed. The quartermaster, sitting idly nearby reading a magazine, was closer, but Smythe leaped across the cockpit for the receiver.

"MGB 307. Sub Lieutenant Smythe," he said in a clipped voice. Listening for several seconds, his eyes lit up excitedly. "You bet, sir. We're alert, ready to move out." Smythe listened for several seconds longer, then said, "We'll make good time, sir. You can count on it, just as soon as the Colonel arrives. I'll keep an eye popped for him." Smythe hung up and looked toward the dock. He didn't have to look far for his priority passenger.

Colonel Stuart Foster, an aide in tow with a canvas duffel, was already hastening up the gangway. Exchanging salutes, he thrust a folded navigation chart in the MGB commander's hands. "You're Smythe, I understand?"

"Yes, sir. I have a message before we get under way, Colonel. Admiral Cunningham called an hour ago from London. He asked that you get in touch at your convenience."

Foster frowned and looked at his watch. He paused, considering. "The hour is late. I'll send him a radio message in the morning. Pull in the lines, Lieutenant. Let's see just how fast this oyster scow of yours can make it to France!"

Sigi rubbed the goosebumps on her arms as she examined Merrill's double bed with its ornate brass filigree headboard. For the past half hour her blood had been freezing her body, but now she could feel it begin to thaw and pulsate again. She was unharmed, very much alive, and conscious of it as never before. She watched Merrill bolt the door, shove a tall wardrobe closet against it, then stroll over to the bed. He checked his Luger and crammed it under his pillow. Merrill was half undressed, standing in his underwear at the foot of the bed. He turned, suddenly aware that she was staring at him.

"If you think I'm going to play the nineteenth century gentleman and sleep on the floor, you're crazy," he said in a nonchalant, off-hand manner. Smiling with smugness, he went over to the basin to wash and brush his teeth. When he was finished, he sized her up again.

"Relax, Sigi. Unwind. Who you trying to kid with the performance?"

"No one. Just trying to decide whether it's your vanity or lack of class that I find abrasive."

Merrill laughed at that. "The sexpot turns out to be a fusspot."

Sigi looked at Merrill scornfully, waiting for his next parry.

He said quickly, "You'd rather spend the night with our infamous U-boat ace, maybe even get it on with the bastard? All in the line of duty, of course."

"I already have."

Merrill chortled, "I don't believe it. You're fast, but not that fast."

Sigi frowned at him. "The ace was faster. Believe what you will."

Merrill started to say something, but bit the words back. His mouth remained partially open.

Sigi grinned. "Well? What's it going to be? A puritanical tongue lashing or one of those Texas smiles?"

"Congratulations," Merrill said finally, slowly shaking his head. "I still can't decide whether to be properly jealous, angry or confused."

Unfastening the buttons of her blouse, Sigi quickly slipped it off and tossed it aside. "You're in for several surprises when you get to know me better," she said. "I'm calculating, spoiled, and selfish. And who knows? Maybe I'm also a little oversexed." Falling silent and studiously ignoring Merrill, she kicked off her shoes and unzipped her skirt. The room's silence was shattering. She knew her little confession was like a needle stabbing at Skeet Merrill's already bruised feelings.

"Mahoola!" he suddenly grunted, giving her a sideways, appraising glance as he dried his face. "In colloquial English, *Fraulein Schramm*, that's *baloney*."

Sigi regarded him. Skeet Merrill fitted the boots of the perfect cowboy, she mused. He was a total, uncurable, male egotist, replete with all the swash of the old west. One of those sexist military types who had slowly built up in America since Indian-fighting times and by their ego alone guaranteed the preservation of the species. Such annoying men, she reasoned, needed to be put in their place. Before the mission was over— if they both lived that long—she'd definitely teach this headstrong Texan a thing or two. Catching Merrill's attention, she smiled enigmatically. "Like other Yanks I've met, Lieutenant Merrill, your precious ego seems to be all in your joy stick."

Merrill felt pissed, no longer in the mood for cute conversation from Sigi or anyone else. The term joy stick had been hurled in his direction before, and again it galled him. For too many years back—more than he cared to recount—he'd been of the unwavering conviction that women were preoccupied with three emotions: anger, laughter, and tears. Now, from knowing this outspoken Scandinavian siren, he was learning that they could also think and scheme, and this new awareness strangled him. Merrill had always worked well with men of his own stamp in the Navy and the OSS; they were tough, resourceful, resilient, and always easy to understand. This sultry female operative was an all-new ballgame with different ground rules. The nervous tension of waiting in the outfield while Sigi ruled the mound, the sense of powerlessness in a crucial situation, was drying up Merrill's vital juices. He let out a sharp sigh, figuring the hell with it. For the next few moments, at least, he appeared to be at bat.

* * *

Sigi didn't have to look up. She could feel Merrill's eyes licking like a snake's tongue over her bare shoulders and breasts. Half-nude in the barricaded room, she suddenly felt trapped, helpless, stripped of any defense. She hated it and she loved it. Perhaps it didn't matter, it was at best a rhetorical question—a matter of lust, not love. Sigi knew it could never be a question of love and fulfillment, for that ancient conflict had yet to enter her life. She turned to find Merrill standing before her, his hand extended. In it was a small silver grand piano. She was pleasantly surprised, but eyed it warily.

He said to her, "Take it. Open the lid."

"For me? A gift?" She followed his instructions. It was a music box, and it began to play. It sounded like the romanza theme from *Aida*, but Sigi wasn't sure. Under the lid was a tiny bottle of perfume—Chanel Number 5.

Merrill smiled. "I went for a walk to ease my nerves after the subway incident. Did a little shopping."

She gave him a quick peck on the cheek. "You're a dear. But this after my cursed hand slap in the hall? I deserve a paddling instead."

He winked at her and crawled into bed.

Sigi sighed. Folding her skirt over a chair, she looked at him nervously. What she wanted to say now was: *If we must do it, for God's sake, let's do it right and get on with it*. But instead her eyes flicked away from him and she slid into bed, her back facing him like a cold, impenetrable wall.

Again, her ambiguous nature surfaced. Anguish pierced her; it was not a new pain, but one from memory. She'd have to delve deep in the past to unearth a similar uneasiness. Sigi remembered her fickle pursuit of Skeet Merrill two years earlier all too well. Now things were much different. *No emotional involvement*, her superiors had repeatedly warned. Though her stubborn, calculating mind wouldn't give itself away, her hungry, demanding body turned her over. She offered her lips to Merrill feverishly.

Merrill's mind flashed. The decision in the French boutique to purchase two musical pianos, two bottles of perfume. The second for Molly, back in London. Would she be waiting when it was over?

Suddenly, Sigi's passion spilled over him and any tinge of guilt he felt was smothered, buried, flooded away by an undeniable force—a raw instinct that needed no explanation, an instinct that cancelled all others. She whispered something in Norwegian he didn't understand, then quickly sowed a deep kiss in his mouth. His body throbbed with pleasure. Merrill had suspected Sigi was wild and fast, but hardly this fast.

He could feel the pressure of her fingers as they sunk deeper, repeatedly into his skin, sending little tremors and thrills through his muscular frame. She was everywhere at once, demanding, consuming, insatiably draining his passion and energy. He grabbed her writhing buttocks and pulled her closer. Merrill grew larger inside her, exploring her piquant depths with relish. She responded by arching her back to let him thrust deeper. For several minutes her legs contracted violently, then she gasped and whimpered softly. For both of them, it was over too quickly, almost as quickly as it had begun. But it had been good. Very good.

Merrill did not withdraw immediately, but remained with her, exhausted, his cheek buried deep in her thick blonde hair, now damp with sweat. His breath still came quickly, and there was a sweet, fragrant smell about her that he liked. Good God, what a Teutonic tigress, he reflected. His back stung from her clawing nails and his earlobe ached where she had lustfully bitten him. Minutes passed and Merrill felt awkwardly alone. He raised his head. Sigi slept, purring softly; not the tigress, but a kitten.

Noiselessly, Merrill rose, put on a robe, and walked to the window. Quietly opening the shutters, he gazed out into the blackness of the city. It was the still hour of the morning when street sounds had totally subsided, when Paris had come to its stillest hour. Though for brief moments Merrill had enjoyed the supine form curled on the bed, even taking turns at being in command, he knew that in the morning this Norwegian Mata Hari would reclaim her right of independence and with it the absolute authority Colonel Foster had bestowed on her in London. The fleeting moments of heated excitement they'd just experienced would be added to his war memories and Sigi's diary. Merrill exhaled slowly. He had at least tallied, and it had been a wild scene. He was hooked and determined to try again, if he lived that long. Something about this unusual boss lady obsessed him.

Inhaling the invigorating night air, Merrill's breath suddenly caught in his throat. There was a movement across the cobble-stoned street below.

The hotel was being watched. Merrill saw a shadowy figure quickly extinguish a cigarette and retreat into the darkness behind a pissoir.

"Do you plan to stand at the window all night, or get some rest?" The voice from the bed behind him was sleepy but insistent.

Merrill continued to stare into the trees along the river quay for a full minute. Then he closed the metal shutters, slowly shook his head, and said to Sigi, "You awake enough to digest some sobering information?" He padded back to bed.

Sigi nodded, her now wide-open eyes consuming him with apprehension.

Merrill exhaled sharply. "I'm sure whoever wants me dead is waiting outside, just across the street."

Chapter 23

THE ORNATE PLASTER flowers on the hotel room's wall traceries
had been committed to memory, for Merrill had been staring at
the wall paneling since dawn. Sigi lay beside him, sleeping
peacefully, but he'd been unable to coax his own body back to
sleep. For the first time, Merrill's apprehension had turned to
genuine fear, a fear of something he couldn't swing a bridle on,
no matter how hard he tried. He felt he was a pawn on a roomy
chessboard, that he'd been allowed certain moves because they
didn't interfere with the enemy game. Other moves meant sure
death. Merrill admitted to himself that he had the insane desire
to guardedly play the game out, unravel the mystery, then take
the enemy on, play by his rules, and defeat him accordingly.

The telephone suddenly shrilled. Startled, Merrill shook the
gritty thoughts from his head and picked it up.

"Morning, chum." It was the same Cockney voice Merrill
had heard earlier. "Time for another health tip, Yank. If you're
taking your smart pills this morning, you'll bail out of the hotel
an hour *earlier* than planned. Got it, chum? You're on
someone's hit list, I'm afraid. Your shadow outside is gone, but
he'll be back soon enough." The line went dead.

Merrill hung up the phone, lay back on the bed, and blew
out a long breath like a boxer clearing his lungs. Again the
voice had all the inside information, but who was it? He turned
to Sigi, closed his eyes and inhaled the fragrance of her hair,
lightly kissed her cheek, and opened his eyes again. She was
real and he was awake; no dream, the phone call had been
genuine enough. Their situation was becoming more grotesque
by the hour. The Cockney voice had been right before, that

176

alone was significant. Merrill would heed the advice and entice
Sigi to leave earlier than planned.

She stretched and smiled. "Who was it?"

"Only a wake-up call," he said quietly.

At five past eight they checked out of the Clarice Almont
without incident. Merrill noted the calm new face behind the
desk; the lobby was quiet with no evidence whatever of any
accident the night before. Had the *flics* already been here and
left? Merrill hurriedly paid their tab and led Sigi out of the
hotel.

The morning sky bore gloom, with storm clouds threatening
each other as if to do battle. It was a short distance to Gare
Montparnasse, but Merrill and Sigi were wary of followers
and, having an extra hour to kill, chose a circuitous route to the
subway entrance, twice doubling back to check their trail. No
one, thankfully, had followed them. To burn time, they stopped
at a *patisserie* for cinnamon rolls and a leisurely *café aux lait*.

Precisely as planned, they entered Gare Montparnasse ten
minutes before train time. Merrill gently nudged Sigi and
pointed to a pair of familiar faces by the second class ticket
window. Together, they approached the waiting Frenchmen.
Pierre Roger remained silent, merely nodding and laconically
pointing to a nearby hallway. Picking up his luggage, he strode
toward it, the deaf-mute Duval in tow.

Merrill hesitated. He gestured for Sigi to stay put and stand
watch, then followed them. When they were alone in the back
corridor, he asked, "Where's the Dutch girl?"

Roger shrugged. "Erika has taken her ticket and gone ahead
to the platform."

Merrill nodded. "Stay out of sight until Loewen boards the
train. And I suggest you settle in several cars away just in case
he goes for a stroll. Let's do this job right."

"*Comme il faut,* Monsieur," replied Roger, irritably.

"Come what?"

The Frenchman translated into English. "As it should be,
Lieutenant Merrill."

Merrill winced. The French had clever phrases for everything. "Look, Roger, how many times do I tell you it's *Herr
Sergeant Schmidt*? No more Lieutenants or Monsieur Merrills,
understand? You'll hang us all."

Maurice Duval, apparently uninterested in Merrill's chiding of Roger, had seated himself on his suitcase. He gazed up at them with a bored look.

"The *plastique*?" asked Merrill, impatiently. "Where is it?"

Roger pointed to his valise.

Merrill's acute eyes noted Roger's bag, then darted over to Duval's. The brown, fake leatherette luggage was spanking new and conspicuously identical. Merrill scowled and shook his head.

Shrugging, Roger tried to explain in fractured German, "The *plastique* is divided equally between the three of us. Erika Vermeer has the remainder."

Merrill cursed under his breath. "Don't tell me, please. You just bought her luggage as well. All *three* bags are alike?"

Roger's eyebrows arched. "So?"

Merrill tightened. He was maddened by Roger's calmness. "What are you, an imbecile? Roger, you disappoint me."

The Frenchman's face reddened in stunned disbelief as he glared hatefully at Merrill. "The luggage was all that was available. Your arrogance, quite frankly, Monsieur, is suffocating. You are the American cowboy with his six-shooter. But without it, you are cut down to your own miserable size. *Merde!* Or as you would say in Texas, bullshit." Roger had reverted to English.

Sigi, who had been loitering just outside the corridor, heard the agitated voices and came up to them. "Why the graveyard expressions?"

"Slight disagreement." Merrill scowled once more at Roger then turned to Sigi. "The explosives are in three identical bags. Too conspicuous. Look, we've got to get that plastic through, at least part of it." Merrill thought long and hard, then turned back to Roger and Duval. "You two set off alone, travel second class. We'll take Erika up front with us and keep an eye on her—I'll carry her bag myself if necessary. If any low-rank Jerry inspectors make a luggage check, they'll probably bypass me in this Wehrmacht uniform."

They set off for the gate. Merrill, still wary of followers and alert as ever, took close notice of the people milling around them. The passengers in Gare Montparnasse, he noted, walked with a much lighter-than-to-be-expected step. He guessed that although travelers were subject to difficult pressures, these French citizens were expectant, waiting on the eve of their deliverance. A few of them were elegant, but most were anemic-looking; many had unhealthy circles under their eyes. But they all moved quickly, without hesitation. Some, he suspected, were undoubtedly black marketeers, arriving from the country with luggage stuffed with sausages, pâtés, butter and cream.

From their London briefing, Merrill knew the distance to St. Nazaire was minimal, but he was also aware the journey was fraught with peril, for the vast French rail network ringing Paris was under attack almost daily. Pierre Roger, too, had warned him that the trains were seldom on schedule and the German inspectors tired, the strain having made them thin-skinned and irritable.

Merrill suddenly pulled Sigi to a halt. A young boy approached, all of sixteen. He had dirty unkempt hair and wore a tattered green oilskin raincoat, but what first caught Merrill's eye was the large needlepoint carpetbag the youth gripped as if it were his entire world. The youth appeared to be leaving Paris, not arriving, so the bag wasn't likely to contain contraband. Sigi looked on in surprise as Merrill caught the boy by the arm, spinning him on his heels.

"Monsieur?" he said, with an expression of flurried astonishment. The blemished face looked vacuous and pale and his voice bore undisguised fatigue. Merrill wondered if the French youth were heading for a country convalescence.

The boy was frightened by Merrill's uniform. "I don't understand," he said repeatedly, in a squeaky, uneven voice. Merrill's proposal, translated into French by Sigi, apparently made no sense to him.

"You want my soiled old carpetbag, Monsieur? The one my mother needlepointed five years ago? Strange nonsense!" He smiled and quickly shook his head. "No, no, Monsieur."

Merrill stood his ground, aware that the young man was fascinated by the French banknotes enticingly fanned out before him. Before the boy's bewildered eyes could blink twice at them, Merrill calmly added another five hundred Francs.

Sigi continued to look on with bewilderment.

Merrill wondered what was going on in the French youth's mind—obviously thoughts of how peculiar it was for Germans to be begging him. Too fatigued to protest and too jealous of the treasure Merrill held in his hand, the transaction proved too brief for words. The boy reluctantly handed over the carpetbag, then, without a murmur, he snatched up the money and ran off into the crowd.

"So far, so good," Merrill said to Sigi. "Fetch some cheese, whatever, and some wine for lunch later. I'll find Erika."

A large group of Wehrmacht soldiers lined the concrete platform, ready to climb aboard the trains bound for the coast, there to man Rommel's purported great wall along the Channel. Merrill quickly spotted the Dutch girl; she was beyond the soldiers, standing off to one side of the noisy platform. Beside her was another conspicuously new, brown leatherette suitcase. Merrill clenched his teeth.

The ramp became more congested as passengers hurried toward the front of the train. Merrill came up beside Erika. Though aware of the American's presence, she said nothing, obeying the instructions she'd received earlier. Merrill was about to take her aside when he glanced off in the distance and saw a familiar navy blue uniform approach. Even before he could make out the face in the crowd he knew those gold-striped cuffs, white hat, and impetuous stride belonged to Dieter Loewen.

Merrill broke his self-imposed silence, whispering to Erika, "Our friend the Lion arrives. Listen carefully. You see this pretty blue carpetbag I've dropped beside you? Erika, when you board the train, take it. I want your luggage."

She looked at him. "But Monsieur Roger said—"

"Forget him," Merrill commanded. "I'll handle it."

"What's in the carpetbag?" she asked, curious.

"Don't have the foggiest idea." Merrill ended his terse instructions, picked up the controversial brown valise, and walked quickly away from her. He very nearly collided with the U-boat ace.

"Sergeant Schmidt, good morning," snapped Loewen.

Merrill promptly saluted. "Fraulein Schramm will join us on board in a moment, Kapitan." He pointed to the first class coach beside them.

Loewen nodded and climbed aboard the train like a man who intended to take possession of it.

Chapter 24

THE TRAIN TRUNDLED out of Montparnasse Bienvenue as though beginning its journey in anguish. It stopped five hundred yards out of the station, then started again, then stopped. At last, after twenty minutes, there was the steady click-clack rhythm of wheels on steel track.

Loewen had appropriated two seatbenches in the crowded first class compartment. Sigi settled in next to the sub ace while Merrill had slid into the seat opposite them.

Merrill looked up, surprised to see Erika Vermeer standing in the aisle. She approached warily.

"Good morning, *Herr Kapitan*," she said, in her best German.

Startled and curious, Loewen looked up at the young woman hovering over them. He appeared not to recognize her.

Merrill glowered at Erika. This wasn't how they'd carefully planned the journey. Sigi too, looked up at her askance, but said nothing.

Erika blushed, but continued to hold Loewen's unfriendly gaze. "You've surely not forgotten already, Kapitan? The yellow rose at La Reine Bleue. I threw it to your table." She waited as the German glared back at her for what seemed an eternity. When he finally managed a thin smile, she continued, "My name is Erika Vermeer."

Loewen replied without ceremony, "You are German?"

"No, Kapitan." She calmly lied, "I'm Swedish." Ignoring Skeet Merrill's eye signal for her to get lost, Erika now turned to Sigi. "Good day, Fraulein. May I sit here?"

181

Sigi shrugged and gestured for her to take the place next to Merrill.

"I remember your song," Loewen admitted, his voice quiet and curiously restrained as his eyes slowly measured the boyish figure confronting him. At last he found words for what appeared to be going on in his mind. "Do you ever dress like a woman? Or is that another of your stage costumes?" Loewen shook his head. *"Theatre people! Bah!"*

Erika tensed. "It is only a living, Kapitan. Until I return to Amsterdam." She hesitated. "The bistro's *patron* is sending me to Brittany to visit his sister." Grinning, she added with a whimper, "To bring back butter and pâté."

Merrill stifled a smile. The young lesbian was a pokerfaced natural with the lies. He kept his silence and continued to listen to her dialogue with the German.

"Where is your home in Sweden?" Loewen asked her.

Erika smiled "Gothenburg."

The ace thought for a moment, then flinched.

Sigi leaned forward. "Is something wrong, Dieter?"

"Curious," Loewen replied. "This young woman stabs at my memory. Some bitter, arrow-swift echo of the past, an incident with my own daughter, perhaps. It is unimportant." He turned to Erika. "Why are you in Paris?"

She eyed Loewen warily. "The theater, Kapitan."

"La Reine Bleue? Hardly the theater! You belong in school, or better yet, in a factory, learning a useful trade. There are good jobs in Sweden."

She shrugged. "My parents have disowned me there. And I have a trade," Erika said defensively, staring out the train window.

Loewen blew an exasperated breath of air. "An outrage! A male impersonator? Parading oneself about in a Rive Gauche *boui-boui* is no trade."

Merrill shifted uncomfortably. Erika was baiting the sub commander, but why?

There was an uncomfortable silence as Loewen looked at each of them in turn. Sigi smiled enigmatically, while Merrill nodded without enthusiasm. He really didn't give a hoot. In his book, male or female impersonators, dancing poodles, and lady violinists had nothing to do with winning the war one way or the other.

Loewen thought for a moment, then his eyes narrowed on

Erika. "How much do you earn at La Reine Bleue dressed as a man? How many francs a day?"

"Five hundred, but there are coins on stage."

"Great God. St. Nazaire shipyard pays over eight hundred francs a day for an ambitious woman apprentice! And the V-weapon assembly factories back in Peenemunde need intelligent, able workers."

Merrill watched Erika Vermeer swallow hard and give herself the firm shove show people always use to propel themselves from the wings to stage center. She was obviously acting again, and enjoying it—not in her familiar role at the bistro, but nonetheless acting. The Dutch girl seemed to have some intricate scheme up her sleeve. What was it?

When Loewen glanced out the window, Erika gave Merrill a waggish grin. Abruptly, she turned back to the ace, grabbing his attention again. "You have proper connections then, in St. Nazaire, Kapitan Loewen?"

In the dirty, second-class coach toward the rear of the train, Pierre Roger glanced down at the mute beside him. Duval was asleep. Roger resolved to pinch himself, if necessary, to stay awake. One of them had to remain alert. They had heaved their incriminating luggage above an empty seatrow, close enough for Roger's watchful eye, but conveniently enough removed to disclaim ownership should a German inspection team suddenly board the train.

Roger glanced idly around him. Up front a baby was crying, a mother without milk. An old man across the aisle was losing himself in the stupor of wine. Voices were being raised behind Roger and Duval; two shabbily-dressed women angrily debated the impending fate of France. Second-class travel, as usual, was a tangle of sad humanity. Roger had never, in his lifetime, travelled *Wagons Lits* or deluxe. If things went well in St. Nazaire, he was determined to celebrate and treat himself on the return trip to the comfort of a first-class red mohair seat.

Roger could not rid himself of the gnawing uneasiness he still felt over the operation. Thank God, Skeet Merrill appeared confident enough; it was easier to follow instructions than to give them, Roger reflected. He'd let the Norwegian woman and the American lead the way, let them do all the worrying.

Merrill sat silent while for over an hour Sigi Petersen carried
on an animated conversation with the U-boat ace. She
continued to pour on the charm, managing to hit all the right
notes, and though Merrill would have liked to sleep, he didn't
want to miss any of the conversation. But as the miles wore on,
Loewen grew increasingly uneasy, a discomfort apparently
brought on in part by Merrill's watchdog, stony silence.

Now Loewen too, was silent. Merrill and Sigi both watched
the German puff on his thin cigar and gaze vacantly out at the
fleeting French countryside. Merrill followed his gaze. The
monotonous nettles beside the track, the flattened grass
embankment, the patchwork farms all began to merge into one
tedious canvas, interrupted only by an occasional overgrade
where a crossing keeper stood duty. Merrill wondered what
was going on behind Loewen's cold, level blue eyes—eyes that
he'd seen in a different light back at the Paris hotel. Then they
had flickered softly, openly appraising and admiring Sigi. Now
these same orbs appeared veiled in deep thought, miles away.
What was the bastard thinking?

As if to tease Merrill, or perhaps to amuse herself, Sigi
brought out the piano-shaped, silver music box. She opened
the lid and let it play. Loewen only looked at her with mild
amusement, but Merrill saw no humor in the gesture. *She was
teasing again.* When Sigi surreptitiously looked his way and
winked Merrill forced himself to smile. He turned to Erika.
Ignoring them all, she was intently buried in a newspaper.

Sigi closed the lid to the miniature piano and sat quietly. The
silent scene was suddenly disrupted by the banging open of the
steel door at the front of the car. Two uniformed Germans
strode into the aisle. One bore a sub-machine gun slung over
his back; the second, a somber-faced sergeant, bore the chain
and silver breastplate of the military police.

Erika dropped her paper and looked up, her eyes widening.
Sigi watched with concern as the Germans examined the
identity cards the passengers in the first row routinely held up
for them. Their luggage was checked next. The tattered valise
of the first Frenchman was given only a cursory examination,
but his seat partner, a prosperous-looking businessman, wasn't
so lucky; the German inspectors probed through every corner

of his bag like hungry weasels. Merrill suspected they had time only for spot checks.

A gray pallor came over Erika's face and she fidgeted in her seat.

Now, thought Merrill. Perhaps he'd find out how well Erika Vermeer held up under pressure. He watched the Dutch girl hand over her passport, then sink back into her seat, ignoring the duty-bound German who studied first her passport, then the description beneath it. The inspector-sergeant then asked for Erika's luggage. Merrill was thankful he'd exchanged bags with her, but he was still wary.

The soldier opened the carpetbag, shook his head, and frowned. *Men's attire!* The surprised German withdrew a pair of coveralls, shirts, and men's underwear from the carpetbag. Erika's face reddened slightly. "The clothing is mine," she said, retreating even deeper into her seat.

The two military policemen in the aisle chortled. Merrill made a point of exchanging smiles with them and the sub ace.

The gloating sergeant showed his assistant Erika's identity card and pointed to the entry after OCCUPATION. "She, or he, is a *dancing entertainer,*" mocked the sergeant, pushing the clothing back in the bag. He turned to Sigi. "And your *ausweis,* please."

A swift, sliding movement of Merrill's hand under the folded greatcoat in his lap and the silenced Luger was there, cocked and ready to go. Gripping the gun, his finger tendons crawling slightly, Merrill hoped he wouldn't have to use it now, prematurely. He watched Sigi smile indulgently and hand their papers over to the Germans. When they saw the green identity cards they eyed Sigi, then himself, with much deference.

Merrill knew the inspectors did not see many *green cards* with the signature of the Armed Forces Kommandant and the Chief of the Political Police, the card that paved the way for the bearer to accomplish his or her mission without hindrance. The prized green cards were definitely at the top of the hierarchy of German travel documents, and the two men in the aisle were aware that no one had the right to detain its bearers, certainly no right to inspect their luggage.

"Thank you, Fraulein and Sergeant."

As Merrill expected, the two Germans glanced cursorily at the luggage above them and moved quickly on. The heavy brown valise, containing enough plastic explosive to blow the railroad car and everyone in it to Paris and back, remained untouched, swinging innocently in the baggage net.

Merrill wasn't ready to unwind just yet. Although the explosives had escaped detection, the cold sweat on his spine had increased perceptibly, for he knew a similar spot check conducted in one of the second-class coaches three cars back could put the screws to their mission. He had to get to the rear of the train before these military policemen, warn Roger and Duval, and either find a place to stash the remaining luggage or heave it off the coach. If they couldn't outwit the prying Germans the other alternative was to eliminate them.

When the sergeant and his assistant had finished interrogating the last of the first-class passengers and sauntered out of the car, Merrill quickly rose and put on his greatcoat, at the same time unobtrusively shoving the Luger in his pocket. He whispered in Sigi's ear, "If I'm not back in fifteen minutes, you and Erika are on your own."

The train bore on, its hypnotic steel stride grinding out the minutes and kilometers. Merrill edged cautiously down the corridor, figuring to hurry past the Germans in the next car. While they were occupied there, he hoped to have ample time to take precautionary measures in Roger and Duval's coach. Merrill opened the vestibule door and froze. The following car was filled with Wehrmacht soldiers. There wasn't a civilian among them and the military policemen strode rapidly through without stopping. *Snafu!*

It was the same for the next compartment. More troops and the Germans pressed on again! To Merrill's chagrin, the two inspectors entered the second-class coach he suspected was occupied by Roger and Duval. Cautiously, Merrill peered through the grimy glass of the vestibule door.

Merrill bit down hard on his lip. There, above the empty second row of seats, were the two perversely familiar suitcases. Merrill suddenly thought of his mother, who had always wanted him to become a dentist; he should have taken her advice. Too late now. Merrill desperately needed time to think and there was little of it.

By any standard, the Germans were accomplished ferrets. They broke the locks to the mysterious unclaimed bags and noted the English labels on the plasticine. Merrill knew that the most illiterate of German footsoldiers would never mistake the suitcase contents for Yorkshire pudding. Staring into the coach, he saw the passengers grow white-faced with alarm; all were aware of their heinous predicament and fearful of the consequences that would arise. A pandemonium of heated denials broke loose.

Eyes round and hot, the sergeant strode the length of the car, angry as a wasp at the masks of innocence facing him. His companion lingered at the far end of the aisle, submachine gun wavering nervously over the passengers. Merrill saw Pierre Roger's eyes dart frantically from one German to the other. Maurice Duval appeared calmer. Under the circumstances, there was nothing the two Frenchmen could do but remain alert, cautiously bide their time. Merrill watched helplessly as the sergeant—his coarse voice reflecting undisguised contempt—continued to castigate the passengers. The German's eyes took in Roger and the mute uncertainly, just as he had the others one by one.

Merrill quickly realized the two military policeman were too hopelessly outnumbered to conduct an immediate and effective interrogation. There were ample military reinforcements on the train, but Merrill guessed infantry men weren't the kind of support the German topkick required. For an important discovery like this he needed an SS superior and a few assistants, and without a doubt they'd be available at the next station. Merrill looked outside. The train gave a moan and hurtled over a long overpass. He had to move now while they were still in the countryside.

The distraught German sergeant, pacing like a nervous bear, at last approached the near end of the coach. Abruptly, pretending shortness of breath, Merrill flung open the vestibule door and shouted, "*Herr Sergeant!* Come quickly! There is trouble in the next car!"

Two emergencies at once were too much for the wary but highly motivated German. Rattled to the core, he turned to his assistant and said sternly, "Shoot the first one who leaves his seat." Then he plunged forward into the dim vestibule.

Merrill, quickly stepping back to let him pass, slipped his hand into his pocket. The metal was cold and hard as his fingers tightened around the spring cosh. *Timing was the answer*, and with this realization came a quick surge of power. The weapon didn't miss. There wasn't a sound, not a gasp or any sign of any kind to indicate the sergeant knew what hit him. Out for the count, he lay crumbled over the expansion plate between the cars. Merrill struggled with the bottom half of the vestibule outer door, finally flinging it open. Wind, coal smoke, and the sound of steel chafing against steel engulfed him. The train had been pounding along at a fast clip, but now it had slowed for a sharp bend. The German would pick up a bundle of bruises, but he'd survive.

Struggling, Merrill was at last able to heave the limp form out the opening. It caught briefly on the upper step, then rolled off and disappeared along the grassy bank beside the track.

One away, one more to go. Merrill suddenly remembered that the second man carried a very persuasive scatter gun. *Bad odds.* Okay, Skeet old pal, you've graduated to bigger stuff! He could use the silenced Luger, make it final, but the spring cosh was neater. No blood and less chance the man might cry out. But first things first; the corporal had to be drawn out of the coach.

Roger and Duval watched the second German with trepidation. The young corporal's curiosity over what had happened up forward had obviously been stirred. The wind banged the door at the end of the aisle, the clatter of the couplings outside was making a considerable racket, and choking smoke filled the car. Most disturbing, his superior had not immediately returned as expected.

Filled with misgivings, but hardly anxious to turn his back on his passenger prisoners, the corporal's movement up the aisle was slow and guarded. Reaching the swinging vestibule door, he halted, apparently reluctant to explore further without instructions.

Roger sat restively, weighing the chances of helping Merrill. Could they rush the German from behind? Risky, considering the menacing machine carbine swinging all too nervously and indecisively back and forth over the passengers. Roger would play it safe and wait.

Edging forward a foot at a time, the sweating corporal shouted, his tone a trifle pathetic: "Sergeant Puhlmann?" He kicked the banging vestibule door wide open and held it there with his jackboot.

* * *

Merrill crouched behind the leather folds of the baggage alcove, waiting, but all he could see was the German's protruding foot. Merrill silently cursed. His quarry was as reluctant to venture out of the coach as a fat cat in an aviary. Merrill felt a gnawing urgency as he waited. Almost a full minute elapsed. *Krauts*, he reflected, *damn their Teutonic sense of discipline!*

Finally, almost hypnotically, morbid curiosity seized the duty-bound corporal. Inch by inch, he edged out of the coach, his gun muzzle pointing the way. Merrill, in a bad position, quickly pocketed the cosh, grabbing for the gun barrel instead.

"Mein Gott!" The short plea was all the surprised corporal had time to spit out as Merrill ground the Schmeisser butt savagely into his stomach. Gasping for breath, the corporal doubled over. The weapon dropped, hit the vestibule wall, and slid out the open doorway. Merrill made no effort to reach for it, but the split second he helplessly watched the gun fall away should have been spent bringing the spring cosh or his Luger to bear. The cursing corporal, still fighting for air, dove desperately for Merrill's legs, knocking him off balance and sending him reeling against the steel wall.

His head hit hard. Merrill felt muddy, as if some great mailed fist had slammed into his brain. *The danger signal.* Shaking his head, both feet braced against the baggage rack for leverage, he brought up the cosh and aimed for his opponent's head. No slouch at self defense, the alert corporal parried, catching the blackjack with his raised forearm. Wincing at the painful blow and baring his teeth in anger, he made a desperate lunge for the emergency fire axe on the vestibule wall.

Merrill's well-aimed karate kick met him halfway. The German corporal's head snapped backward, only to hit with equal force against the bulkhead wall. He slumped to the floor, out cold.

Merrill repeated his little housekeeping act, shoving hard and watching the corporal's body tumble along the side of the tracks. It was over, but Merrill's breath still came fast and labored. *You're getting sloppy, old man*, he thought, considering the untidy trail of banged-up Germans left behind along the right-of-way. Removing a handkerchief from his pocket, Merrill mopped the sweat from his brow.

"You've very efficient, Sergeant Schmidt." The staid voice from behind him was Pierre Roger's. The Frenchman's eyes sparkled as he gave a Gallic shrug and smile. Maurice Duval peered curiously around Roger's shoulder and shook his head in amazement.

"And the first man, the sergeant?" asked Roger.

Merrill gestured outside the train. "Said goodbye the same way."

Roger looked away from Merrill, his eyes staring out the open door at the rushing landscape. The train rolled on under increasingly gray skies heavy with the threat of rain, through rich Loire Atlantique farmlands green with spring crops.

Kicking the outer door to the vestibule shut, Merrill turned to his accomplices. "You two. Get off the train at the next stop and take the hot suitcases with you. We need some lead time before they find our unconscious friends back there along the tracks. What's the next station, Roger?"

"St. Nazaire, Herr Sergeant," Roger said stoutly, grinning in self satisfaction. "Your suggestion is unnecessary. We have made it."

The train gave a long, moaning whistle and began to slacken speed.

Merrill slowly shook his head. "You French are too damned confident for me."

Roger, with a sense of showmanship and a prideful expression that seemed to say he had more stored away beneath his beret than any other member of the team would ever require, somberly replied, "We have to be, Sergeant Schmidt. We haven't much left. When the resurrection comes, you must never forget this. The world must know of the sufferings of France during the enemy occupation."

Chapter 25

IN PARIS, it had been an unusually quiet and dull morning for Hermann von Wilme. At 74 Avenue Foch, even the seven-by-nine foot flag of the Third Reich hung motionless from its staff outside his second-story office. It was an inviting chamber with its large windows, high-paneled wainscoting of stained oak, ceiling of gilded traceries, and deep red Persian carpet. The SS major's inlaid mahogany desk was scrupulously neat, bearing only a few file folders, a bronze letter opener, an ink well, and a Louis Quinze marble clock. From above his leather chair a portrait of the Fuehrer, taken in 1938, gazed benevolently across the room. The antique timepiece on the desk chimed, then gently tapped out the hour. It was one o'clock.

Von Wilme, when dining inside alone, usually sat at his desk with a little wine, some bread, sausage, and perhaps a bit of cheese or fruit. But today, as was his custom the second Tuesday of every month, he was entertaining Chief Inspector Phillipe Leclusier of the Paris Prefecture of Police. Aides had carefully laid the spacious conference table by the window with a snow-white tablecloth, neatly ironed damask napkins, the best Bavarian china, and von Wilme's own cut crystal glasses he'd carried with him wherever he was stationed. Completing the pleasant luncheon setting, the Paris songbird, Edith Piaf, importuned *Il pleut dans ma chambre* from von Wilme's table radio.

The visits of the portly chief inspector were all alike. After lunch the Frenchman would routinely offer von Wilme a cigar and routinely be refused. Then Leclusier would light his own smoke, unbutton his pinstriped vest, and give a little sigh of

satisfaction, visibly pleased by the monthly opportunity to dine
on far better food than to which he was accustomed. From their
beginning von Wilme had hated these monthly luncheons, for
he found the Paris police official to be a boring table
companion. But his SS superiors had insisted on the ritual, and
over the past year, from the standpoint of loose bits of
information, the sessions had not been entirely unproductive.

The benefits, however, had not fallen exclusively to the
Gestapo. Von Wilme knew Chief Inspector Leclusier was no
fool. The Frenchman was good at bargaining for intelligence
information and had an uncanny talent for playing both sides of
the fence.

An orderly refilled Leclusier's goblet with wine. When the
waiter was finished, von Wilme, with a quick gesture of his
hand, dismissed him from the room.

"It is very good," the inspector said, putting down the glass
and patting his lips with the damask napkin.

"I am pleased. It's Lafite Rothschild. I have only a few
bottles left." By no stretch of the imagination was von Wilme
pleased with the inspector's compliments. He was as coldly
indifferent to what his guest thought of his wine as he was to
everything else in France. Von Wilme had even come to be
indifferent to the elegance and easy comfort of his surroundings, which were far more sumptuous than SS officers of like
rank might occupy at other Reich assignments. Paris, after all,
was Paris. Von Wilme accepted his life in this requisitioned
luxury much like a land-beast in a cave, insulated and alone.
His friends were few, and as a loner he feared men known only
to himself. Even when venturing outside into the streets, he
buried himself behind his fearsome black SS uniform, the
hermit carrying the cave along with him.

Leclusier was thoughtfully silent for a long time, chewing
his cigar and puffing out little clouds of smoke. Von Wilme
refused to be disconcerted by the Frenchman's withdrawal, for
well-timed silence was a technique he himself often employed
to rattle an adversary. But the forced conviviality of the past
hour, from the Gestapo viewpoint, had been totally unproductive of security information and as such a wasted effort. Von
Wilme was determined to conclude the luncheon and return to
more important Gestapo business at hand.

"*Monsieur l'Inspecteur*, I fear it has been a quiet month for both of us," von Wilme said dully, offering the guest a smile that might as easily have come from an automaton.

"Quiet? For you?" Leclusier paused to sip his wine. "The camps at Chateaubriand and Compiegne have never been so taxed with activity."

"Your French terrorists, Leclusier, have intensified their activities. The Resistance is under the peculiar misbelief that France is on the verge of liberation. The relentless countermeasures we're now forced to employ against these troublemakers are, in fact, a pity. If they were true patriots concerned over the welfare of France they should know their true liberation occurred in 1940! There are no patriots at Compiegne or Chateaubriand, Monsieur. Only communists, anarchists, and terrorists."

Leclusier settled back, gazing through his cigar smoke at von Wilme. His hands patted his paunch. "I'm sorry, Major, but your blunt remarks are not nearly as easy to digest as the fine lunch. I am stuffed like a Strasbourg goose for, as usual, you are a generous host."

Von Wilme didn't smile. He knew what Leclusier really thought; some men could veil their hostility, others couldn't. The Frenchman probably believed von Wilme and other SS officers belonged on the roof of Notre Dame with all the other monsters.

The radio voice of the little Parisian songbird suddenly had a disturbing effect on Leclusier. Von Wilme watched him rise uneasily from his chair, rebutton his vest, and saunter over to the radio.

"Do you mind?" the Frenchman asked, not waiting for a response before turning the knob. The room was awkwardly silent and suddenly cold.

"Ah, *politics*," von Wilme said, modifying his tone. "I apologize, Leclusier. I forgot our agreement. More of the good wine before you leave."

The chief inspector quickly waved his hand. "No," he sighed. "I have a long afternoon, an interesting case, and a staff of incompetent detectives. My head must be clear."

"I envy you, *Inspecteur*. The petty crimes of the street— child molesters, pickpockets, arsonists, pimps, and not-so-clever thieves. Exciting, interesting, challenging. You deal with the fate of individuals. With me, it's the fate of hundreds, often thousands." Von Wilme smiled and casually gestured

with his thumb to the nearby benign portrait of Adolf Hitler.
"With our Fuehrer, it is the fate of nations, of the world!" The
wry smile von Wilme sent Leclusier was a judgment of that
world.

The Frenchman, unimpressed, shook his shoulders stoutly
and headed for the door. "Right now, Major von Wilme, I'm
concerned only with the fate of one hotel night clerk, very
dead, who is about to undergo autopsy."

Von Wilme stood stiffly and followed his guest to the door.
"Your attention to detail impresses me, Leclusier. It is as if the
fate of Paris is hinged on one man."

Leclusier smiled as he put on his threadbare overcoat. "In
your list of street crimes, you failed to mention *homicide*, Herr
Major. In civilized France, murder is still taken quite seriously."

Von Wilme opened the door, clicked his heels, and extended
his hand. "Good hunting, *Monsieur l'Inspecteur*."

"Good day," Leclusier said.

After the Frenchman departed the orderlies silently entered
and cleaned the dishes and linen from the conference table. As
the last man hastened out of the office he was nearly knocked
down by the agitated entry of an SS officer. Lieutenant Karl
Angermeyer's square face and hard eyes were flushed with
excitement as he gave the customary salute. "Heil Hitler."

Von Wilme cursorily returned the gesture then sat, coiling
himself serpentlike in his tall, brown leather chair. He snapped
his fingers authoritatively. "Proceed, please."

The SS lieutenant appeared strangely shrunken and apprehensive. "I have curious news, Major."

"Well? Stop trying my patience."

"An incident last night across the Seine. There is still
considerable confusion." The starch seemed to seep out of
Angermeyer's voice. "It appears one of our men was making a
routine undercover investigation at the Hotel Clarice-Almont.
The *concierge* there and one of the porters have been on our
observation list for some time."

"Yes, I recall. We have a collaborator employed there to
observe them?"

"The desk clerk, a fellow named Chabrier. He's a
Cagoulard," added the junior SS officer.

Von Wilme's face betrayed no emotion. As a meaningful
source of intelligence information, he'd never been impressed

with the *Cagoulards*, more properly the *Comité Secret d'Action Revolutionnaire*. Though the French political group was of the extreme right wing and had often cheered the German cause as anti-red and heroic, their cooperation with the SS was sporadic and could not always be depended upon.

"The hotel clerk is dead, sir. But before his accident, he gave me some interesting observations on two of the hotel's guests—a minor thing, missing railway checkpoint stamps on their travel papers."

With bored indifference, von Wilme opened one of the manila folders on his desk. Examining it routinely, he didn't look up. "A hundred times a day, somewhere in this city, some Frenchman's papers are not in order. Why do you bother me with such trivial details?"

"The travelers in question are not French, Herr Major. They are fellow Germans."

Von Wilme abruptly closed the folder before him and looked up.

The SS lieutenant shifted on his feet. "Early this morning, what should have been properly reported by the hotel as a homicide, was, in fact, described by the investigating gendarmes as an accidental fall. Very odd indeed."

Von Wilme frowned and drummed his fingers on the big mahogany desk. Something the French chief inspector had said earlier rankled his memory. In France, Leclusier had insisted, murder is still taken quite seriously. Von Wilme thought for a moment, then caught himself up. The junior investigator before him was repeating a question.

"What?" asked von Wilme.

"I said, are you aware of the incident, sir?"

"Only vaguely. Leclusier touched on it," he replied with a wan smile.

"Yes. We know his men are investigating."

Von Wilme reflected again before looking up from his desk. "And our staff is doing the same?"

"Of course, Major."

"Who are the Germans in question? Businessmen?"

"That is where we have made a mistake. They are a very important party from Berlin." Angermeyer quickly unfolded a notation and read from it. "A Fraulein Anna Schramm of Dr. Goebbels' staff and a Wehrmacht photographer for *Signal* magazine."

The names pierced von Wilme like a bayonet, reviving unpleasant memories of the night before. *The pretty blonde woman from DNB!* He stared out the window for several moments, then turned his gaze back to Angermeyer. "I wish to see these visitors from the Fatherland immediately. Where are they now?"

The young SS officer shrugged and spread his hands. "We do not know. They hurriedly checked out of the hotel and left no forwarding address."

Von Wilme was instantly on his feet. "Find them!"

Angermeyer sighed in abject resignation. "We'll try, sir."

Fury consumed von Wilme. "You'll do better than try. You will succeed."

The SS lieutenant drew back as if he'd been belted across the face. He saluted quickly, turned on his heels, and was about to leave the room when a cold, calm voice from the doorway froze him in his tracks.

"One moment, please. The individuals you seek are en route to Brittany." The sharp statement of authority belonged to SS Colonel Reinhard Schiller. Von Wilme and Angermeyer both came to attention as the tall, monocled officer strode steadfastly into the room, saluted, and stood framed in the window. Schiller ran a hand over his crewcut and looked at von Wilme with the dispassionate regard of a hangman measuring his subject for a rope. Dryly, he said, "The other evening at the St. Germain bistro, Major von Wilme, you were surprised by my information on the female entertainer—the young Dutch girl Erika Krager—whose trail we lost. Again you are caught unaware, this time by the developments at the Clarice-Almont Hotel. I might awaken you further. An enemy airdrop was made in your sector in the last forty-eight hours. Indeed, the efficiency of the Paris SS office seems questionable, Major von Wilme. Perhaps you missed the point of our earlier discussion? I am here at SS Reichsfuehrer Himmler's personal request. Sit down, Major. And your assistant can leave the room."

Von Wilme promptly dismissed Angermeyer, but gazed numbly at Schiller for several seconds before taking a seat. Reinhard Schiller calmly adjusted his monocle and exhaled. "As a Gestapo officer, you supposedly have a highly-trained, resourceful mind, and you're paid to use it. Locate Kapitan Leutnant Loewen and you'll find the woman and the photographer! And also, if I suspect correctly, the Dutch girl Erika

Krager. You must remember, no harm must come to her until I have made a personal interrogation."

Von Wilme felt an uncomfortable spasm of guilt. "The U-boat ace," he said soberly. "And this Left Bank entertainer. What is the connection with our friends from the DNB?" Von Wilme was thinking about how close he'd come to forcing his affection on the tomboy Erika.

Reinhard Schiller smiled thinly. "Soon enough you'll find out what is happening. Suffice it to say time, Major von Wilme, is of great consequence."

Von Wilme frowned. "I'm getting the distinct impression, Herr Colonel, that the people who work for me report to you first."

Schiller smiled.

"Whatever," acknowledged Von Wilme. He sat on the edge of his desk and cracked his knuckles. Von Wilme had a few inflexible beliefs—most important, he believed in ruthless power and its exercise by a select group who had prepared themselves to assume it. Now Schiller had sharply, rudely reminded him the SS must now use this power to the fullest. "Your methods are like a corkscrew, Colonel Schiller. If you will permit me, I wish to be more direct." Von Wilme picked up the telephone and demanded an immediate, priority line to *Deutsches Nachtrichten Buro* in Berlin.

Schiller came over and replaced the phone on the hook. "Unnecessary, Major," he said. "You do not need to talk with Dr. Goebbels. He and the Fuehrer are both aware. The journalist and photographer are not only frauds, but spies of the most dangerous order. What we need now is a very fast command car and a capable driver."

Chapter 26

MERRILL LOOKED up at the sky. Intermittent, dirty gray clouds boiled over St. Nazaire and the air was filled with the stench of cordite and smoldering fire. Cocking an ear, he listened as the angry drone of B-17 bombers grew louder. The American Flying Fortresses were making another pass, and Merrill could see at least a dozen approaching. Again, from every quarter came the staccato roar of anti-aircraft fire.

Merrill prodded the others to make a run for it. He wondered who the beset citizens of St. Nazaire had come to hate more, the German occupiers or the American aviators. Blockbusters dropped futilely on the thick concrete roof of the U-boat pen had too often missed their mark and fallen on the town itself. Merrill looked around him and shook his head. The rubble was everywhere, the fortunate buildings that remained seeming to embrace each other as if to give themselves strength.

A series of bombs fell close by. A German sentry blew his whistle, frantically waving for Sigi, Roger, and Merrill to get off the street and take cover. The ground beneath them suddenly heaved and the sentry disappeared, buried by smoke and debris.

"Run! Quickly, this way!" Roger shouted authoritatively. "I'm familiar enough with this neighborhood." He took off at a run.

More bombs shrieked downward and fountains of rubble erupted nearby. Several cobblestones came toward them like projectiles. Cringing, Merrill took off at a gallop, following Sigi and Roger across a landscape of craters. Sigi stumbled and briefly fell; ignoring Merrill's outstretched hand, she picked herself up, wiped the debris from her face, and ran faster. A bomb struck in the middle of the street less than a block away. It dug a deep shellhole, and a rolling cloud of smoke engulfed them.

Merrill saw Pierre Roger race into a side street and huddle in a narrow walkway between two buildings. The plaster on the house above the Frenchman suddenly fell away in a large section. Merrill shouted a warning and Roger leaped aside. Roger, his hands on his knees, coughed violently from the dust as the others stumbled up beside him.

Merrill held Roger upright. "You okay?"

The other man nodded and Merrill quickly asked, "How much farther?"

Roger rubbed his eyes and pointed. "Over there, the side street off Rue d'Anjou."

Sigi stepped forward, her body and hair covered with dirt and dust. She looked like a ghostly apparition. She said unhappily, "So much for Colonel Foster's thoroughness. You'd think he would have taken St. Nazaire off the bombing list for the duration of our mission."

Merrill half-smiled, half-grimaced. Before he could answer her another bomb came down, howling like a malicious, scornful animal. There was a deafening explosion around the corner, followed by the cloying smell of destruction. Then a strange silence fell on the street as the air raid ended as abruptly as it had begun, the sounds of the planes finally fading off in the distance. Merrill hoped Loewen, Erika and Duval were safe back at the station, where he'd last seen them.

It was obvious Pierre Roger had been to St. Nazaire before; he knew his way around the city. He now led them into a dead-end street no more than a hundred yards long. It went up slightly between several three-story structures and a high-walled court, then ended in a cluster of small houses. From somewhere behind the wall came the sound of a bell around a goat's neck. Roger pointed to the drab, gray brick building with the number nine on its blue ceramic address tile. An orange cat stood next to the front stoop glaring at them with baleful amber eyes.

Merrill went up to the door without hesitating and rang the bell. Sigi glanced uneasily in both directions as they waited, but the only person in sight was a stooped streetcleaner near the corner who ignored them. The door was opened halfway by a cadaverous old man dressed in white. His lizard-like eyes considered them one by one, then lingered on Merrill's Wehrmacht uniform.

"Good day," he said, without a trace of emotion.

"Good day, Monsieur," Roger swiftly replied. "We are from Paris, friends of Madame Selva. I believe she is expecting us."

Roger whispered to Merrill in English, "The old timer must be a new assistant. I don't remember him from my previous visits."

Frowning, the old man opened the door the rest of the way. "Very well. You will please come in," he said stiffly.

They all shuffled inside. Merrill checked the street again as he brought up the rear. The man in the white uniform secured the door, then gestured with a liver-spotted hand for them to follow along as he shuffled down a dim hallway. The long corridor, with several mysterious doors like those of a sacristy, was lined with shoulder-high green tiles, and there were several missing and loose ones. The odors of formaldehyde and carbolic were distinct.

"You will please wait in here," he said, flinging open two double doors at the end of the hall. When they were all inside the room he rationed out a smile and tottered off.

"Hardly the guest parlor," quipped Merrill, sniffing the air and contemplating the facilities around him like a new dog at the pound. He saw the same sickly green tiles, but now they covered the floor and extended to the ceiling. The sterile-looking chamber had no windows; illumination came from a peaked glass skylight. Three wooden caskets, several stools, a metal cabinet, an embalming rack, and some antiquated pumping apparatus were the only furnishings. A door at one end of the room, half ajar, led to a lavatory.

Marie Selva strode in almost at once. She wore a starched white jacket, frayed at the sleeves but otherwise neatly pressed and clean, save one blood stain on the lapel. "Good day," she said cordially.

Merrill flashed: *Marie Selva*—her quick, short name suited her well. He watched with curiosity as the short, animated woman nervously sniffed both her palms.

Marie immediately turned to Sigi and extended her hand. "Ah! The charming maiden from Norway that they promised us. Sigi Petersen." Marie hastily shook her head and corrected herself, "Or should I say *Fraulein Schramm? Enchanté*, my dear. Welcome to what remains of our coastal city."

Sigi smiled back at her.

Merrill studied Marie Selva at length. He'd never met a mortician before, let alone a woman mortician. The energetic Brittany operative, however, appeared exactly as Colonel Foster had described her. She had an intelligent face, a decisive manner, and gestured rapidly with her hands to make her point. Marie Selva had a quick, light manner that Merrill liked. He smiled back as she came up to him with heavy bonhomie.

"Lieutenant Merrill. London tells me you've been to St. Nazaire before."

"The dockyard area. A very short visit, Madame."

When Marie embraced Pierre Roger, she waved a scolding finger. "And you, Pierre. You must be more cautious with our friends, yes? The three of you wandering about the streets attract too much attention. During the daylight hours you must travel individually." Her eyes swept across the room like probing beacons. "Several elements of the upcoming operation seem to be missing, my friends. There is trouble? Where is the young woman Erika—our talented locksmith? And the quiet one, Duval? Your supplies?"

Roger shrugged. "Erika Vermeer may get inside the submarine pens before any of us. She went with Loewen, who is determined to find her a job at the facility—or so he foolishly believes."

Sigi added, "Erika will join us later. And the mute is still at the *gare*. If it survived the bombing."

"The *plastique*?" Marie asked quickly, her eyes shifting to Merrill.

"We got it through," he told her. "Checked the lot in the station baggage room. Duval's keeping an eye on it. Roger here insisted we could use your hearse to pick it up."

Marie nodded and turned to the Parisian. "Good. Pierre, the two of us will go, for there is other business we must also attend. But first there is something the American must see." She turned to Merrill.

He had seated himself on one of the empty caskets, wondering if it were empty. Merrill watched with amusement as she studied him from head to toe.

She finally finished sizing him up and said, "So, Lieutenant, you're the *plastique* genius they promised us?"

"He also knows submarines," Roger pointed out. "An enviable command record."

Marie smiled and said quietly, "One submarine hero against the other. A trifle diabolical, but interesting."

Sigi stepped forward, pre-empting whatever moment of glory Merrill might have felt. "We expected to be met by another operative. An RAF sergeant was to have parachuted in last night. Were you alerted?"

Marie's eyes lost their sparkle. "The Scot. I'm sorry." Sighing, she looked around the ring of watchful faces. "The Germans were waiting for him."

Merrill silently ground his teeth. "He's dead?"

"No, Monsieur. But he soon may be. They took him alive."

Sigi frowned. "If Cummings is in the hands of the SS, he might talk."

"He'll stand up to them," grunted Merrill, squaring his shoulders. "If not, according to Foster, he knows nothing about the purpose and thrust of the operation."

Sigi warned, "He knows a good deal about us. Too much."

Merrill looked around him, taking in the glum faces. "Cummings was not only our ticket out of here, but he was also a skilled diver. I was counting on him. I hadn't planned on getting my own feet wet."

Marie spread her hands. "We may all wind up swimming."

Sigi stared at the Frenchwoman forlornly. "But our escape route? What now?"

The woman undertaker shrugged. "I regret I was unable to contact this Cummings before the *boche* interfered. In such situations, Resistance regulations are explicit and I must wait for the next scheduled time to attempt to radio contact with London. Only then can I make alternate arrangements."

Merrill irritably looked at the French woman. "And when is your next *scheduled* radio contact with London?"

She shrugged. "In twenty-four hours. You'll have to wait until then for procedural information."

Unable to contain his impatience, Merrill bore in on their hostess. "Twenty-four hours? Procedural information? *Negative*, Madame Selva. I'm sorry, but you'll have to do better. And you'll have to expect one thing from me. Frankness. Excuse my manners, but I'm an ex-sailor off a grubby submarine; we don't call them pigboats for nothing."

Sigi started to interrupt. "Skeet, please—"

"Let me finish. I believe in getting things done the simple way, okay? So don't confuse me with some tailored-blues, paper-shuffling dilettante from a desk job at the Pentagon or British Admiralty. I like plain language, forthright action. I'm sorry, Madame Selva, but this tight-ass gobbledigook and blind obedience to regulations may impress the Limeys, but it leaves this field operative cold. Flat-out cold."

Marie Selva appeared visibly shaken. "I'm afraid I don't understand."

Merrill tightened but kept his voice calm. "It's my job to get the lady out of here within twenty-four hours outside, and preferably less. On top of everything else—just for the record—it appears I'm a man marked for death. I want out of Brittany the second the job is finished. Enough said? You'll kindly break radio silence and make contact with G-10 tonight, or Sigi and I will do it ourselves."

Pierre Roger's and Marie Selva's eyes met and like puppets they frowned in unison. "I'll consider your request," Marie said sullenly.

The embalming chamber fell into hushed silence. Merrill turned to Sigi and saw her nose crinkle in displeasure. She strolled around the room, taking in its Spartan furnishings. Abruptly, she said with a rueful tone, "Haven't you a more pleasant place, Madame Selva, where we can discuss the mission? This room is cold and reeks of death. It's morbid and uncomfortable."

The tile walls, Merrill noted, seemed to echo her words.

The woman undertaker stiffened, her dignity now twice offended. "A cheeky woman," she grumbled, to Roger. With considerable effort, Marie smiled at Sigi. "Espionage can't always cater to feminine sensitivity, my dear," she importuned, her small mouth wrinkled in displeasure. "Beyond embalming the dead, the chamber is well-suited for Resistance work. The long hallway provides ample warning of intruders. The radio is hidden behind a cabinet in the lavatory, and the important records and our weapons are kept beneath several loose floor tiles."

Pierre Roger swiftly added, "And should the need arise, the room is wired with explosives for instantaneous destruction."

Merrill asked, "No alternate exit? What about escape, should the need arise?"

Marie and Roger smiled knowingly and accorded Merrill the
practiced politeness properly due an outsider. Roger interposed, "We understand your concern. Alas, two years ago
Marie's late husband planned well."

Sigi shot Merrill a puzzled look.

The woman undertaker smiled, flung open the lavatory door
and gestured toward an old galvanized bathtub. Merrill
watched, fascinated, as with surprisingly little effort, Marie
rolled the rusty metal tub away from the wall. "Beneath the
loose linoleum is a trap leading to the *egouts anciens*, the
labyrinth underground sewage system of St. Nazaire," she
explained. "Our supplies for an emergency escape are cached
below, as well as the triggering mechanism for destroying what
might hurriedly have to be left behind up here."

Skeet Merrill's wonderment, like Sigi's, was genuine. He
nodded his approval.

Marie pushed the bathtub back in place, her dark eyes
dancing as if amused by the whole affair. "Now is the time for
the real surprise," she said buoyantly, heaving her breasts and
beckoning Merrill over to the old embalming table at the center
of the room. She deftly removed four wingnuts and raised the
six-foot steel pan that formed its tóp, revealing the most
intricate wood and cardboard model Merrill had ever laid his
eyes on. Before him now, in amazing detail and apparently in
exacting scale, was a *maquette* of not only the underground
U-boat base, but the entire Penhouet Basin, including the locks
and shipyard drydock.

Merrill whistled sharply.

"A masterpiece, Madame," said Sigi. "It must have taken
you months to complete."

"A bizarre hobby of my husband, before his passing."

Pierre Roger had obviously seen the model before. He stood
silently off to one side as they examined the elaborate
recreation that by itself could hang them all. For a long time
Merrill subjected the *maquette* to the same feverish scrutiny a
curator might lavish upon an ancient artifact. Finally he looked
up at Marie Selva and began a barrage of questions.

It was clear that the Frenchwoman had properly done her
homework. She listened carefully, then replied, "If my information is accurate, there are ten U-boats in port at this time;
two undergoing snorkel outfitting, seven refitted and ready to
leave on patrol, and the new arrival, Kapitan Loewen's boat,

the U-601. *No*, the eighteen-inch diameter roof ventilators are not large enough to accommodate a man. *Yes*, guards patrol the tall fence near the supply yard, and it is charged with electricity. At night they use Dobermans as well. *No*, a boat cannot be launched in the adjoining water basin. *Yes*, a man could possibly swim underwater. *Yes*, the power supply for the base is heavily guarded."

Merrill remembered Marie's earlier comment on the old St. Nazaire sewer system. "What's the tunnel pattern around the sub pen?" he asked.

Marie was head of him. "*Impossible*. They are not connected to the U-boat base," she said authoritatively. "The Todt Organization, when building the facility, was precautious. They sealed off the city's one connecting sewage tunnel and installed a separate piped system."

As she indicated on the model exactly where the old sewer gallery had been bricked across, Merrill's brain clicked on an idea. "The discarded tunnel," he asked. "Is it dry and where does it lead?"

Marie indicated the place on the model. "It is above water and not *tidal*, Monsieur. But there are heavy, very thick iron bars that preclude any access from the only opening into the ship basin."

Merrill hovered over the *maquette* and began whistling softly.

Beside him, Sigi seemed lost in brooding silence. Finally she asked, "The chances?"

"Next to impossible!" grumbled Roger, surprising them all. "Despite Anna Schramm's charm, and your camera, Sergeant Schmidt, the walls will be impregnable for the rest of us." He pointed to the intricate model. "Mines, electrified fences, pill boxes. Guards every hundred feet, on the roof and around the perimeter. And in the water, two heavily armed patrol boats. In all of France, there is no enemy fortress as formidable or heavily protected. On our last attempt to penetrate the base we lost six men. Six valuable men, Monsieur!"

Merrill gave the Frenchman a hard look. "Failure hasn't entered my mind, Roger. When I sign on for a job, I finish it." He turned to Sigi. "Okay, you're purportedly the sparkplug on this operation, love," he said softly, as though he were still fighting a battle within himself. "Electrify us."

"There are two sparkplugs, Monsieur," interjected Marie. "You've forgotten Erika, our clever locksmith."

Merrill frowned. "Sorry. I stand corrected." He turned back to Sigi and winked. "I'll place my money on the Norwegian lady. Sex appeal, cover story double-talk, whatever. Her job is to get me inside the gate the first time. Do that, Sigi, and I promise our German friends inside more trouble than a bear in a Bavarian *gasthaus*." Ignoring Roger, who appeared ready to say something, Merrill resumed his whistling, settling on the tune *Harbor Lights*.

The doorbell rang loudly. The notalgic love ballad died on Merrill's lips, replaced by an all-too-familiar knot in his stomach.

Chapter 27

DEEP BELOW GROUND level in the concrete-buttressed vitals of the Admiralty, Commander Peter Warrington paused at the bottom of the stairway to catch his breath. Straightening his tunic, the G-10 intelligence adjutant approached the steel door to the operations center. Warrington checked his watch, discovering he was a half hour late in reporting to the First Sea Lord. Despite Colonel Foster having instructed the intelligence officer to mind his punctiliousness, Warrington had not properly allowed for contingencies; the prolonged blitz on the streets above had delayed him. Hastily exchanging greetings with a Royal Marines sergeant guarding the entry, he signed the operations log and stepped into the War Room. The naval operations center was humming with purposeful activity, just as it did twenty-four hours every day of the war.

Before him a thirty-foot-long plotting table stretched out diagonally across the large chamber. Several high-ranking British flag officers, an American brigadier general, a Canadian admiral, and a French liaison general were drawn up to it. Warrington knew that the nerve center was normally used for updating and plotting of naval activities—friendly and hostile—indicating the current position of all known ships in the English Channel, the North Sea, and the Atlantic. But tonight the operations center table was pre-empted for a full scale planning session for Operation Overlord—the D-Day invasion fleet. The Channel area of the table was covered with ship models of every description.

Peter Warrington drew up beside the First Sea Lord and was about to salute, but the green telephone between them buzzed sharply. Ignoring Warrington, Admiral Cunningham picked up the receiver and carried on a hushed conversation for several minutes. His pencil scribbled aimlessly on a pad of paper before him but he took no meaningful notes.

A polite, careful murmur came from the other high-ranking officers around the table. They knew, instinctively, that there were just two men who could be talking to the First Sea Lord from the other end of the priority line; Churchill or Eisenhower. From Cunningham's deferential manner, Warrington suspected it had to be the PM. Every eye in the room was on Cunningham, patiently waiting.

The admiral at last put down the receiver and hastily pushed one of several buttons on the table before him. Almost immediately, the head of cryptography, Section 8-S, a Captain Tibbets, hurried into the room.

Cunningham shrugged. "The gentleman upstairs hasn't been so feisty since his *Burn and Bleed* speech to Commons in February." Ignoring the waiting Warrington, he said to Tibbets, "The PM wants to know if you've made any progress on the bloody code."

"No, sir. We're still working around the clock. And I might say the crew's a trifle exhausted," Tibbets gloomily replied.

"And so am I. Churchill's chomping on more than cigars tonight. Get back there and tell them to keep at it, fatigue or not. The new ciphers for the Enigma machine must be broken."

"Hear, hear," added Air Chief Marshal Tedder. "I'll second that. *Before* the fleet sails to France." The three rows of ribbons heaved on his chest as he let out a sigh of discouragement. Tedder swiftly added, "Eisenhower, too, is emphatic."

Cryptographic specialist Tibbets nodded and quickly left the room.

Admiral Cunningham finally turned to the waiting adjutant from G-10. "You come on your superior's behalf, Warrington? Where the devil is Colonel Foster? I asked him to return my call."

"I'm to give you his regrets. He's en route to Brittany. Still after that sour note in the Operation Storm Tide orchestration."

"He left without my authorization?"

"Sorry, Admiral. He claimed to be under the PM's direct orders. I suspect he'll fill you in when he returns."

Cunningham frowned. "He leaves before Eisenhower's briefing tomorrow!"

"I believe General Eisenhower's been apprised of the situation. G-10 has a traitor on the line, sir."

The First Sea Lord scowled. "I'm aware of that, thank you."

Warrington continued, "The colonel has given me complete responsibility for any intelligence update you may require."

"Then I trust you bring favorable news. Weather's one element of uncertainty—hardly need another with the U-boats. Ike's aides are on their way up from Southwick. In an hour they're due for the pre-invasion Naval Operations Stats, and there's still too much perverted silence and unknowns—*status four blighters,* as you G-10 people call them."

"Sorry, sir. Not much to supplement Colonel Foster's report yesterday. Hitler's retired the capital ships. Your enemy will be solely an undersea one, aside from the shore batteries and the Luftwaffe. Intelligence from our Norwegian sources indicates a large force of U-boats left Stavanger and Bergen, bound for St. Nazaire and snorkel outfitting. Two new 21C hydrogen peroxide boats have finished their sea trials and are bound for the Channel."

Warrington hesitated. Moistening his lips, he looked nervously around the large table. "Without the code, we can't determine whether Doenitz will employ U-boat wolf packs or try to outflank the fleet by sneaking individual subs into the Channel. In France, the U-boat bases at Brest and Lorient are empty; all operational vessels are at sea in the North Atlantic. They'll be waiting for us, well enough. The veritable fortress at St. Nazaire is still the key. They're working round-the-clock on snorkel conversions and the pen there is full of submarines preparing to sail."

There was a slight commotion at the end of the table as Winston Churchill himself burst into the room, his maple cane clearing the way. He wore no jacket and his white shirt with its banker's stripes was open at the collar, tieless, and rumpled. Eyes flaring, his face pinched in anger, he swaggered up to Warrington and the First Sea Lord.

"Toad-spotted traitors underfoot or clever infiltrators!" he snapped, waving his cigar over the assembled brass like a bishop aspersing his flock with holy water. "When you've got a case of gangrene, you amputate, and quickly!"

The PM seemed to be shouting at no one in particular, yet every man in the room felt his fury.

"And this confounded new German code! We broke the first Enigma; we can surely do it again!" Churchill's eyes tightened on the adjutant from G-10. "Any word—anything at all from the Norwegian woman?"

Warrington shook his head. He suddenly felt numb.

Churchill frowned. "She may be cunning, but it's the Yank who'll keep her out of trouble."

"Lieutenant Merrill is not superhuman, sir," said Warrington, bravely.

"True enough. But Eisenhower's people claim he's known to pull off what others thought impossible." The frustrated Prime Minister gently nudged the First Sea Lord aside and grabbed a long wooden rake from one of the Wren attendants. He pulled it across the plotting grid, gathering up some two dozen U-boat models that had been scattered across the North Atlantic. He pushed them all before the startled Warrington, then paused to allow the significance of the next few words to sink in. "Intelligence, Commander. We're hurting badly for it! The largest fleet since the Persians sailed into Salamis—the greatest armada the world has ever known—is preparing to embark. God knows the millions of tons. Over five thousand ships, almost a million men."

The room became very still as Churchill paused, lowering his head. "My memory is still soured by the Atlantic U-boat attack on Convoy HX 229. Out of one hundred and sixty ships, thirty-two were sent to the bottom."

Admiral Cunningham sighed and added, "One destroyer. The rest were freighters."

Looking back at him, Churchill winced. "But in the D-Day armada we will be dealing with crowded troopships! If our naval intelligence predictions are accurate and Operation Storm Tide is not successful, I will carry to my grave an unbearable burden of conscience justly accusing me of stupid, blind sacrifice. Thousands of the flower of American, British, Canadian, and Australian youth." The PM dropped a firm hand on Warrington's shoulder. "Tell me, Commander, would you want to remain and explain Foster's curious silence and the continued U-boat threat to Eisenhower?"

"Sir, I'd gladly make a stab at it, but considering the gravity of the G-10 crisis, I suggest my time is better spent monitoring the radio for messages from Brittany. There's still that ugly worm in the apple, sir."

Churchill's face reddened and his eyes narrowed. "Indeed, then brace yourself to your duty. Cut it out, for God's sake! Get word to Foster to bloody those parchment Groton hands of his if necessary. Whatever, cut the vermin out!"

Chapter 28

Marie Selva pulled down the lid of the embalming table as a precaution and gestured for silence. There was a moment's stillness, then her cadaverous assistant could be heard treading down the hall to the entry. They heard muted conversation, then approaching footsteps. A moment later, the old man admitted Erika Vermeer.

Reveling in self-satisfaction, she immediately went up to Pierre Roger. *"Patron!"* she blurted out with a mischievous urchin's tone, "my plan is working!"

Roger smiled, spread both hands, and turned to Merrill. "You see, my American friend? We do have alternatives."

Merrill looked speculatively at Erika, then ignoring her, reopened the embalming table lid and went back to studying the model.

Sigi asked the girl, "Why are you so confident?"

Erika smiled. "I need at least four hours. Then you'll see that the Kapitan will——" her voice broke off abruptly. Eyes widening, she took in the intricate model in the center of the room.

Merrill turned, gazing at her with impatience.."Well, Erika? We're all waiting. I'm not opposed to miracle workers if they're legitimate, but so far your ideas have bordered on the bizarre. So what's your secret for bribing Loewen? I doubt you're peddling your body, like Sigi, or even pretending to peddle it."

Beneath the skylight, the gray day fell livid over Erika's pained face. She threw him a look white with hate. Sigi, too, had a sudden look of contempt.

212

Merrill wished he'd kept his mouth shut.

Sigi said to him, "Okay, Skeet, come off it. Once and for all, spill it out. Whatever's poisoning your mind is hurting the mission, so let's all hear it."

Merrill slowly shook his head, reflecting that all this was a fuck-a-duck waste of time. *Didn't they understand they were slowing him down?* He looked at her and grumbled, "Sorry, Sigi. This hanky-panky tries my patience. I just want to roll up my sleeves and get to work."

Erika's face reddened. She turned to Sigi. "I have a plan; your partner doesn't. You're both winging it, yes? If I'm being set up to be knocked down, you can count me out at the beginning."

All eyes turned to Merrill, waiting for an explanation of his blunt manner. He kept his silence.

Erika cleared her throat, her eyes misting over with anger and frustration. "So? Let's have it. What's wrong, *Sergeant Schmidt*?" Her inquiry bit of sarcasm.

Merrill backtracked. "Forget it. I'm sorry," he said quietly, not looking up.

"You disagree with my methods?" asked Erika, swaggering closer and becoming more insistent.

Her tone was a trifle too hard and aggressive for Merrill. The bistro entertainer was definitely a fly ball, but ignoring her wasn't going to work. "Maybe I do disagree," he complained. "Matter-of-fact, absolutely yes. It's the wrong image, wrong place. And this mission is the wrong place to march to a different drum."

Erika held his gaze. "While you still grope in the dark and play with your toy model there, or depend on Sigi, I at least have a plan."

Merrill groaned. "You said that in Paris. What else is new?"

Her lips twisted in annoyance. "Kiss my ass."

Merrill's jaw dropped. "Same to you. You're really the bitch, aren't you?"

Interlocking her fist, Erika swung her hand in an uncoordinated arc. Grinning, Merrill had plenty of time to dodge his head and turn to one side, watching the would-be impact of the young lesbian's fury dissipate in thin air. Carried forward by her own momentum, the infuriated Erika tripped over Merrill's hastily extended foot and wound up sprawled awkwardly on the floor, face down. Merrill's foot went instantly to her elbow, pinning her to the tiles.

"Woman or no woman, while there's a war on I get nervous when someone comes at me," Merrill said calmly. "Don't ever try that again." He made a mental note to remember that Erika Vermeer was not only tough, she also had a short fuse.

Erika's breath came unevenly as she spat out, "Let me up, you arrogant bastard!"

Merrill pulled her to her feet, offering a mock bow of apology. The Dutch girl was smaller than Merrill, much smaller, and he had no reason to be wary. But the instant Erika had caught her breath, she brought her left heel down like a pile driver on Merrill's arch, at the same time ramming an elbow into his solar plexus.

Gasping for air, Merrill reeled back into Sigi's arms. Erika grinned and bounced away, but Roger and Marie held her.

"Enough! Enough!" shouted Marie Selva, angrily.

"Some hellcat," Merrill said under his breath. He wasn't eager to tackle her again.

The air was full of conflict. Sigi broke in half the cigarette she'd been smoking and dropped it on the floor. Testily, she said to Merrill, "Leave her alone, Skeet. A bad performance from both of you."

With a perplexed look, Erika searched the other faces in the room. "Pansies all of you. I can and will do this job alone!"

"You'll follow orders, like the rest of us," Merrill said quietly. For long seconds, he studied the Dutch girl's narrow, anger-sparked eyes, her trembling shoulders. Merrill then turned to Sigi, started to open his mouth, but changed his mind. It hadn't been often he'd been called upon to think so hard about the rightness of what he was saying and how the hell he should say it. Finally he said to her, "Sorry, boss-lady. I'm a little edgy. But you'll have to take my word for it. I know pigboats, and I understand the mentality and gut instincts of the men who crew them. Once we're inside that fortress, matching either Erika or yourself off against Loewen on a one-to-one basis, however you work it, is playing the wrong card. And we don't have time to wait for any interview Erika may or may not get inside the base."

Erika stood as squarely as she could, her expression mirroring some sudden understanding of Skeet Merrill. Speechless but still angry, she continued to glare hatefully at him.

Merrill wasn't about to be put off by her menacing stare. "Look, Erika. It wasn't my idea to ship you along. Obviously, you enjoy a good fight, but how many Nazis have you put on ice? That's *kill*, understand?"

She stared at Merrill, lips thin and pressed against clenched teeth.

Pierre Roger broke the extended silence, answering for her. "Erika has proven her competence to us, Monsieur. More than once." His tone was final, as menacing as Marie Selva's had been moments before. "It is now your turn."

Merrill felt outnumbered.

Sigi managed a smile of apprehensive amusement. Abruptly, she said to him, "Forget it, Skeet. That's your first irrevocable order."

"Sigi, listen to me——" The sentence died in mid-air as he stared back at her, remembering she was a woman, not a man, and she was skilled, very skilled, at blurring the differences between the sexes. Sigi would probably never understand him. The revelation was bittersweet, like drinking wine on an empty stomach.

Merrill glanced over at Erika—a trapped, wounded animal—and felt a token of compassion for her. He now wondered if he'd overreacted, feeding on some unrealized paranoia. Turning back to Sigi, Merrill sent her one of his roguish, Texas smiles. He could afford to put on the charm, but something still gnawed away at his conscience, tormenting him. Unable to resist just one small, final parry, he said quietly to her, "Thin ice is still thin ice."

Overhearing Merrill, Marie Selva's face flushed with anger. She was about to shout at him, but dignity calmed her. Folding her arms over her breasts, she said emphatically, "I have a suggestion. We either function as a team, or forget the operation." The hint of contempt in her voice had been overlaid with a thin air of diplomacy. "Without skillful, precisely timed teamwork, we stand no chance against the enemy."

Merrill nodded in agreement, but still he wondered. He was less worried by men of the Master Race who guarded their submarine base than he was by careening automobiles, potshots at parachutists, and strange hands that pushed him off balconies and subway platforms—all unknown entities that had struck without warning and would probably strike again when he least expected it.

The mood in the room was still oppressive.

Marie spoke up again. "This divisiveness is counterproductive." She turned to Erika Vermeer. "Mademoiselle, you will please come with me." Then, to the others, "You must excuse us. I have private advice for our young friend."

Avoiding the lingering resentment in Merrill's eyes, Erika followed the woman undertaker out of the chamber.

Marie Selva closed the double doors to the embalming room behind her and gave a quick sigh. "Now, then."

"We don't need the American," snapped Erika, still pouting.

Marie looked at her. "We need every hand we can get. He can be trusted. Now, it is not advice, but important information I have for you." Withdrawing a folded envelope from her pocket, Marie thrust it into Erika's hands. She waited, looking on benignly, as the Dutch girl tore it open and withdrew a black and white enlargement.

Erika examined it and smiled. "How long ago was the photograph taken?"

"Only last week. You've seen such a Kriegsmarine ship's locker and strong box before?"

Erika nodded. "This lock is of different manufacture, but the trip mechanism is far from foolproof. I can open it easily." Pocketing the photograph, Erika thanked Marie, then swaggered down the hallway, quickly disappearing out the front door.

Marie Selva watched her depart, then went back inside the embalming room and beckoned to Roger. "Come, Pierre," she called. "We will go for the mute and the explosives, as well as run another special errand." She paused to check her watch. "There are some guests en route from Paris we must welcome." She turned back to Sigi and Merrill. "Please make yourselves comfortable. We will return in two hours."

After all the conflict they'd just been through, Merrill didn't feel like questioning the lady mortician any further. He watched her exit with Roger, then turned to Sigi and shrugged. She avoided conversation by calmly lighting a cigarette.

Merrill went back to examining the model on the embalming

table, but he felt a peculiar discomfort. Sigi came up behind him and leaned over his shoulder. Without looking up, Merrill sensed she was studying him, and not the *maquette*. Ignoring her, his hands moved purposefully over the miniature buildings, one by one, committing them as best he could to memory.

Sigi's hand caressed the nape of his neck and he shivered. Merrill could feel her breasts, her hard nipples brushing along his shoulder blades.

"We may have a long wait on our hands," she said in a soft voice.

Merrill exhaled but didn't look up. Never in his life had he come across a woman who ran so alternately hot and cold. Her flip-flop manner both infuriated and intrigued him. Now he felt her hands on his ears; they touched his face and gently grasped his chin, slowly turning his head to face her.

"You really are a stubborn hunk, Skeet. Sorry to be such a tease before."

Merrill grinned and gripped her wrists. "From that look in your eye, I'd guess you're not wearing your thick underwear today." He stared at her for several seconds, then without another word, brazenly pulled her blouse over her head and tossed it to the floor. Surprised, Sigi looked at him for a moment, then boldly responded by pushing her skirt down, revealing a strip of pale white skin.

Moments later they both stood nude, embracing under the skylight. Merrill's pants were at his ankles as he pulled her to his chest and lips. He kissed her so hard she moaned. Abruptly detaching herself from him, Sigi scampered to the door of the chamber and turned the deadbolt. "The old man," she warned. "We hardly need unexpected company."

Merrill grinned. "I thought the room turned you off," he whispered. Feeling foolish and vulnerable, Merrill stepped clumsily out of his pants.

From the corner of the room Sigi's intense eyes consumed him unashamedly. Hips rolling, she strolled over to one of the wooden caskets, raised the hinged lid, and ran her hands over the smooth, padded satin. "Purple," she said whimsically. "It's not my favorite color."

She's crazy, Merrill thought. His erection started to wither.

She beckoned to him with a swift movement of her head. "Take off your shoes or you'll tear the lining. The fabric's delicate."

Merrill swallowed hard. *Weird,* he mused. And *sleazy.* No, there wasn't anything cheap about Sigi, far from it. Long ago Merrill had recognized the difference between a honey pot and a cesspool. But a mortuary coffin? Bizarre, to say the least, if not downright perverted. "A little on the obscene side, don't you think?" he asked with genuine innocence. The imagination of European women still never failed to amaze him.

She quipped, "Perversity is just one of life's little adventures. And you, my dear, look the adventurous type." She patted the edge of the coffin and said seriously, "Don't be silly. I'm being practical. It's cleaner and more comfortable than the floor and not as cold as the metal embalming table."

"Still looks like a pornographic hallucination to me." Merrill laughed, but finally gave in. Scrambling into the padded pine box with her, he again quickly became aroused.

"Cozy, isn't it?" she whispered, reaching for him. "And comfortable."

Merrill didn't answer, kissing her instead. He wasn't about to break the spell by complaining over bruised elbows or the lack of leg room.

Chapter 29

THE OKW OFFICE in Berlin was so quiet both men could have heard a feather drop.

It was Heinrich Himmler who finally broke the silence. "If England's warlord Churchill chooses to be blatant, in counterpoint we must be subtle."

Staring fixedly through the smoke curling up from the tip of his pencil-thin Danish cigar, Grand Admiral Karl Doenitz considered the words of the SS Reichsfuehrer seated across from him. "You are sure the Fuehrer has approved all this? Your plan still leaves me with reservations," he said irritably. "And considerable distaste."

Himmler stiffened in his seat, adjusted the glasses on the bridge of his nose, and glared back at Doenitz. "Do you have a better suggestion, Herr Admiral?"

"No. But military heroes of the Reich should not be treated as pawns."

Himmler said dully, "Castles, horses, even bishops are routinely sacrificed in the game of chess."

Doenitz frowned and flicked the ash from his cigar. "I am unaccustomed to playing team chess with your *Schutzstaffel*, Herr Reichsfuehrer. And I'll remind you, the slightest miscalculation in this game of yours could be deadly. Perhaps you've forgotten that I myself was captured off a U-boat in the Mediterranean during World War I? From personal experience I know what it is like to be taken to England as a prisoner!"

Himmler nodded gravely. "I may not understand the subtleties of dealing with military heroes, but I do as the Fuehrer commands."

"We all do," replied Doenitz, unimpressed. "Some of us blindly."

Himmler stared at him, unsmiling. The room took on a slight chill.

With a blue pencil Doenitz idly traced over a swastika on an official letterhead before him. "I find it curious, Himmler," Doenitz deliberately subdued his voice, nearly muffling it, as though he were speaking to Himmler through a piece of linen, "in fact, a pity. Men like Loewen are shadows from which thousands of German fighting men cannot escape. A hero's name is known to all, but the common sailor—or soldier—is known to none."

Himmler shrugged with impatience. "I suspect you are correct. Loewen's likeness will find its way into the history books, while the unknown soldier's tribute at best will be an eternal flame or a pylon covered with pigeon droppings."

Doenitz exhaled a long column of cigar smoke toward the ceiling. "Whatever the outcome, Reichsfuehrer, I still say it is a mistake for our lion to be used as a pawn."

Heinrich Himmler gave a grunt of annoyance and climbed to his feet. "Good luck has been with the U-boat ace until now. Let's trust he'll be blessed with it for one more day. I'll leave you now so you can complete your report to the Fuehrer. Good luck, Herr Gross Admiral."

Doenitz nodded gravely as Himmler left the office. Neither man bothered with the Nazi salute. Doenitz returned to his notes. The Fuehrer had summoned him for a meeting within the hour and Doenitz wanted to be ready. Unfortunately, there had been no further reports from SS Colonel Schiller in St. Nazaire, and Doenitz was concerned. Feeling a sudden twinge of uneasiness, he bit down on his cigar and nervously rubbed his moist palms together. There was now nothing more he could do; as Himmler had admonished, what happened, happened. Dieter Loewen's fate was now in the hands of the SS field man and the double agent.

Doenitz turned and surveyed the chart behind him with its ominous red flags. Unfortunately, there was also little he could do to save the rising percentage of U-boat sailors not returning from their patrols. The grim statistics were staggering. Only this morning he'd issued strict orders that no U-boats were to venture into the North Atlantic or Bay of Biscay unless first equipped with the new underwater breathing device. The

Fuehrer had disagreed. Calling the precaution an act of cowardice, he had flown into one of his usual tirades. To accommodate Hitler, Doenitz was forced to prepare new, uncompromising invasion alert instructions to be sent to all submarine commanders.

Doenitz now signed the orders, then read once more the harsh words he'd written:

1. EVERY VESSEL IN THE ENEMY LANDING FLEET, EVEN IF IT HAS ONLY A HANDFUL OF MEN OR A SOLITARY TANK ABOARD, IS A TARGET OF UTMOST IMPORTANCE AND MUST BE ATTACKED REGARDLESS OF RISK.

2. ALL U-BOATS MUST CLOSE WITH THE INVASION FLEET REGARDLESS OF THE DANGER FROM SHALLOW WATER, POSSIBLE MINEFIELDS, OR WHATEVER THE SURFACE THREAT, FOR EVERY MAN AND WEAPON DESTROYED BEFORE REACHING THE BEACHES LESSENS THE ENEMY'S CHANCE OF SUCCESS.

3. EVERY U-BOAT THAT INFLICTS LOSSES ON THE ENEMY HAS FULFILLED ITS FUNCTION EVEN THOUGH IT PERISHES IN SO DOING.

The desperate, near-suicidal orders would now be taken to the Fuehrer for final approval, then sent by the new code to all U-boat commands. Doenitz puffed on the stub of his cigar and turned to the calendar on the wall opposite him. He studied the dates for the week ahead for extreme high and low tides. Military intelligence was one thing, he thought, his own instinct another. Relying on the latter, he'd place the German fleet on stand-by alert and put his battle plan for the Channel into operation. Doenitz was fortunate. He had ten snorkel-equipped U-boats at St. Nazaire ready to sail immediately. Forming the nucleus of a wolf pack, they would be ready, on station off the Isle of Wight, to ambush and sink a good part of the enemy invasion force.

The OKW command telephone behind him rang shrilly. Doenitz looked at it morosely, then picked it up. It was Martin Bormann, and he sounded agitated: "The Fuehrer has post-poned your appointment until tomorrow, Herr Admiral. But in the meantime, he has asked that I convey some special instructions."

"Tomorrow?" Doenitz started to protest, but thought better of it. "Yes, I am listening," he said dully.

There was an uncomfortable series of clicks at the other end of the line, then Hitler himself could be heard berating Bormann in the background. Suddenly, the Fuehrer began venting his rage into the telephone mouthpiece itself. "Doenitz! I have lost faith in your scheme to use our illustrious submarine ace as spy bait."

The admiral's stomach muscles knotted. "My Fuehrer, the plan was *not mine*, but Heinrich Himmler's."

"You both assume too much risk. Where is Loewen now?"

"St. Nazaire, my Fuehrer."

"I want him here, as soon as possible. In Berlin!"

"May I suggest that, considering the imminent invasion, there are other alternatives?"

"Speak up, Admiral. You dare to bait my patience?"

"No U-boat commander is more skillful, daring, and experienced than Dieter Loewen. His record speaks for itself. The war's outcome, my Fuehrer, could well be determined by the success or failure of the great enemy armada. Under the unusually dire circumstances at hand, I suggest we send our hungry and talented lion back to sea. He could lead the packs. Both he and the course of the war will be far better for it."

Hitler's voice rose several decibels in the receiver. "For Loewen, however, a risky and unnecessary gamble. You would chance depriving the German people of their last living folk hero?"

Doenitz paused, then cautiously said, "The Fatherland does not need a more paternal, steel-willed folk hero than you, my Fuehrer."

"Your flattery is kind but ill-timed, Grand Admiral. Cancel our lion's leave. Immediately! You are to contact General Kruger at Luftwaffe Divisional Headquarters at Nantes. I expect Kapitan Leutnant Loewen to be taken out of the fire immediately."

"As you wish, but there are complications that may take time—" Doenitz was trying desperately to put some order to his thoughts.

"Do not contradict me! Have Loewen flown to Berlin by the

fastest available plane. One more thing. Himmler tells me the American agent is still alive. You must find Colonel Schiller."

Doenitz could almost see Hitler's eyes glittering with rage and the trembling hands barely able to grasp the receiver at the other end of the line. He wondered if Martin Bormann was listening on an extension wire.

Doenitz said to Hitler, "Certainly, sir. I will try—"

"Find Colonel Schiller!" the Fuehrer shouted. "Do you hear?"

"Of course, my Fuehrer. And his instructions?"

"Have him contact me immediately. Tell him to bypass Himmler."

Continuing their performance as Anna Schramm and Burger Schmidt, Sigi and Merrill decided to walk through the city to the U-boat base. Most of the journey had been made in silence. Crossing the Place Marceau, Sigi hesitated and looked squarely at Merrill. "Why so tight-lipped?"

Merrill kept walking. "The gears in my brain—not quite meshing on our traitor problem. I'm not sure of the motivation, but I suspect the double-duty man is our bistro operator friend, Pierre Roger."

Sigi had to hurry to catch up with him. She pulled his sleeve and he stopped. "A bottle of Scotch says you're wrong," she insisted. "More likely the callous Dutch girl Erika. My guess is that she's a graduate of the Hitler Jugend movement serving an apprenticeship of sorts in the SS. And *not* the Dutch kid with her finger in the dike."

Merrill laughed. "Right folklore, wrong gender." He gave Sigi a doubtful look. "I say impossible. As for SS membership, we could check that out easy enough; she'd have a serial number tattooed beneath the armpit."

They started walking again, Sigi insisting, "I said *apprentice*. If I'm right, they're too clever to mark her up just yet. She'll have to prove herself before taking the oath."

Merrill shook his head. "Sorry to be so stubborn. I still say Roger. If I lose, I'll throw in a dozen red ones, long stems, in addition to the Scotch."

"Save it for when we get back to London," she quipped, squeezing his hand.

Merrill smiled; glancing sidelong at her, he couldn't resist seducing her again with his eyes. "Speaking of making it back to England—if and when—how about the two of us, a week down at Brighton?"

She edged closer to him as they turned the corner. "Sounds exciting. I'll think about it and let you know."

Merrill wondered whatever happened to plaintive-voiced, submissive females. "You're a challenge, boss-lady. One hell of a challenge."

"There's your *challenge* for the moment," she prompted, pointing to the fortress-like submarine base looming ahead. The ominous concrete structure at the end of Rue A. Courbet looked anything but receptive to their visit. The sheer scale of the U-boat facility threw them both into a depressed silence.

As they approached it, Merrill thought about the explosives. Earlier, he'd figured he had up to twelve hours to pull off his demolition work—unless granted a full day's extension from London. Now, as he neared the foreboding walls and felt dwarfed by their immensity, Merrill felt an irresistible challenge to level the entire edifice. Saturated blockbusting, however, wasn't the reason they'd picked him. Hardly his specialty. To reduce this monolithic structure—twice the length of a football field—to rubble would require several truckloads of dynamite, perhaps as much as four tons. Four tons of cordite they didn't have. Besides, hauling a load of munitions that size inside the wall would be like slipping one of the Pyramids past Rommel.

"Losing confidence?" Sigi asked smartly.

"Never. It'll be a piece of cake." Not that easy, Merrill reflected, but someone had to sound confident. He knew that infinite skill, a bit of engineering, and old-fashioned luck would all be in order when it came time to place the plastic as well as the kegs of dynamite; it would all be a matter of selective vulnerability. The more Merrill gaped at the bomb-pocked, concrete fortress, the more the challenge of penetrating inside intrigued him.

A crowd of townspeople milled restively in front of the base entrance as they approached. A twelve-foot high gate topped with barbed wire was closed and padlocked. Behind the barrier, spread out like an apron from the bomb-proof central structure, was a broad, brick-paved yard, and in it, straddling the recent bomb craters, stood well over two hundred civilian workers. They appeared curiously idle as if waiting for the start of a political rally. Merrill noted that the two black-and-white-striped sentry boxes, one on each side of the shackled gate, were manned by both garrison sailors and the green-uniformed men of the SS police. Merrill let Sigi squeeze her way through the agitated crowd first, but followed closely at her heels.

The SS duty man at the sentry box ignored their credentials. "I'm sorry, Fraulein," he said diffidently. "No one is permitted to pass."

Sigi frowned and pleaded, "But we have the proper papers and an appointment."

"I have my orders," he snapped. "The gate remains closed until after the SS Captain's speech."

Merrill expected an explanation, but the guard continued to ignore them and looked toward the courtyard where a stir of activity was taking place. Following the German's gaze, Merrill saw a wooden gallows that dominated an empty space before the massed workers. Standing at attention in front of the structure was the largest group of Waffen SS men he'd ever seen—two long rows of them bearing submachine guns, enough firepower to cut in half most of the crowd in a matter of seconds. To one side of this vigilant group was a quartet of grim-faced sailors with parade snare drums. On the gallows platform itself stood an immaculately uniformed naval officer accompanied by a short, glowering SS captain.

The SS officer held up his baton as if it were a command instrument of witchcraft and the crowd reluctantly hushed. Seagulls circled overhead, watchful and expectant.

Sigi's hand suddenly went up to her mouth. "Oh God," she gasped.

The guard at the gate turned and looked at her curiously.

Merrill quickly discovered what had alarmed her. One of the three faces being led up the gallows steps was familiar. The busy red sideburns! It was the Scot, Sergeant Cummings. Merrill's spirits plummeted. The other two men appeared French, probably local citizens or shipyard workers. Under the circumstances, his hands were tied and they were helpless to do anything. Merrill felt the bile rise in his throat. He knew Cummings was doomed.

Sigi looked over to Merrill, her brows furrowed.

He whispered in her ear, "Look the other way if you have to. I'm sorry. There's *nothing*, absolutely nothing we can do. Understand?"

The SS officer on the platform, a youngish, thick-set Schwab, lowered his head and pushed it out at the glowering crowd like a bull in a ring. He shouted: "This is the fate of enemy parachutists! A spy from England. And one of your St. Nazaire citizens who attempted to assist him! Also, there is this third man, a fellow shipyard worker who committed sabotage!" The SS captain gloated, intensely satisfied with his haul. He continued: "This subversion is not only against German seamen who risk their lives beneath the sea, but against you fellow French workers as well." He raised a plump fist and shook it at the pipefitters, welders, painters, electricians, and mechanics before him. "You have been betrayed by these enemies of the state!"

The high ranking Reichskriegmarine officer beside him was quickly introduced as the flotilla commander, Korvetten Kapitan Brausdorf. A small brown sack with a drawstring exchanged hands.

"Sugar!" the red-faced SS captain rasped, turning the bag upside down and permitting the white granules to trickle to the gallows floor. "Sugar in the lubricating oil! And the others here—an Anglo spy and a *collaborateur*!" Pausing, his cruel eyes surveyed the sea of downcast worker faces before him. With much finality, he pointed to the gibbet and shouted, "These men are fortunate! Death by hanging is too kind a penalty." Waving his baton at the drummers, he turned and strode down the gallows steps. The flotilla commander followed, leaving the captives to the hangmen. The drums began a long, dismal roll.

The gibbet being a mere twenty yards from the gate, Merrill could see the gallant faces of the two Frenchmen being led to the ropes. The Scot's face looked bruised and beaten, but he showed no sign of fear, only fatigue. The hangmen, Merrill noted, went about their grim tasks with amazing alacrity.

Gripping his arm, Sigi looked away from the grisly tableau.

"Bastards," Merrill whispered, biting out the words. His stomach muscles knotted as his fingers tightened around the bars of the gate. The impulse to do something, anything, to intercede, was irresistible. He had to struggle to remain motionless; to do anything else in their German disguise would be idiotic. Merrill suddenly hated his job and hated himself more.

* * *

The scopolamine had barely worn off Sergeant Cummings' tortured body. The Gestapo butchers had beaten him unmercifully, but it didn't matter; they'd learned nothing. The sea of faces in the courtyard was little more than a dim blur, and the roll of the snare drums meant nothing to Cummings. Like the two men beside him, he was drained, too tired to be afraid, even when the reality of the situation was brought into sharper focus by the rough hemp noose being slipped around his neck. "God save Scotland," he muttered groggily to no one in particular. Then the only halfway eloquent thing that came to him was a childhood poem, *Shropshire Lad*. As loud as he could, he choked out the words:

"And naked to the hangman's noose
    The mornin' clocks will ring
A neck God made for other use
    Than stranglin' in a string."

Suspecting that with typical German efficiency the levers for all the gallows would be pulled at the same moment, the two accused Frenchmen beside him had prepared themselves accordingly. They started to sing the *Marseillaise*. Their voices could barely be heard above the thunder of the drums, but volume wasn't necessary. Every person in the courtyard knew the words

Al-lons en-fants de la Pa-tri-e,
    Le jour de gloire est ar-ri-vé.
Con-tre nous, de la ty-ranni-e
    L'é-ten-dard sang-lant est le-vé. . . .

Skeet Merrill suspected the proficient SS hangmen had better things to do than wait while their victims recited poetry and finished patriotic anthems. He was right. The gibbets were sprung. The drums and singing stopped, leaving an unsettling, empty silence as the bodies played out their individual dances of death. At last, the only movement was a gentle afternoon breeze that swept in from the river Loire.

Several women in the crowd around Sigi and Merrill wept

openly. Angry murmurs swept over the yard as the quailed workers shuffled back to work inside the concrete structure. The gate creaked open and the crowd outside dispersed, urged on by the departing SS troops. Merrill breathed a sigh of relief as the sentry belatedly came up and offered to take them to the base security office. When Merrill saw that their passage took them directly beneath the gallows, he held Sigi's arm tightly. Her face turned pale.

"Gruesome," she whispered, biting her lip.

Their young SS escort sensed her displeasure. "You visit our facility on the wrong day, Fraulein." His voice seemed to hang in the air like the nearby bodies.

Merrill did his best to stifle the fury creeping over him, for never before had he observed a man hanging by the neck. But he knew Hugh Cummings' suffering had terminated quickly; the tough Scot was, by curious measure, fortunate. Instead of rope, the SS often used piano wire or meat hooks on saboteurs and spies with excruciatingly painful results.

The base security officer immediately dismissed their escort. "You two are together?" he asked sullenly.

Merrill pulled their credentials from Sigi's hand and thrust them on the duty man's desk. "Our papers, sir."

"We are to see Kapitan Leutnant Loewen," added Sigi, firmly. "He's expecting us."

The German nodded. He took his time perusing the documents, eyes gradually widening behind his steel-framed glasses.

Merrill knew the identity papers, down to the photostatic facsimile of Joseph Goebbels' signature, were perfect to the last detail. Their fabrication was all in the day's work for Colonel Foster's talented staff in London. Merrill watched, impatiently, as the balding warrant officer before them withdrew two yellow cards from his desk and briskly pounded them with an oval stamp.

The duty man said, "We regret the delay at the gate, Fraulein Schramm. Kapitan Leutnant Loewen is upstairs, the wardroom at the end of the corridor."

Almost too easy, Merrill thought, drawing back into himself and preparing for the ordeal ahead. Colonel Foster's admonition that female charm was the answer had thus far rung true. Sigi's siren's song appeared to be working. The Germans loved her. They were swallowing the bait, lure, line, and sinker.

Chapter 30

ON THE PRIMARY road ten kilometers east of St. Nazaire, the gray Horch slowed for a sharp curve. SS Colonel Reinhard Schiller checked his watch. Beside him in the rear seat, Hermann von Wilme looked up and said anxiously, "Forgive me, Colonel, but supposing we arrive too late?"

Schiller smiled and calmly replied, "I seriously doubt if our opponents will strike before dark. Tonight, Major von Wilme, you are in for some surprises."

"You sound extremely confident, Herr Colonel." Von Wilme paused. "But I could be more resourceful if you would confide in me to a greater degree."

"All in good time. A matter of Reich security, my friend," replied Schiller. Leaning forward, he stretched his cramped body. The seat was uncomfortable and they'd been on the road for several hours, making excellent time by not stopping.

The heavy-footed driver braked the Horch as it approached another curve. On the passenger side, their armed SS escort steadied himself, one hand on the dashboard.

Suddenly, machine gun bullets ripped across the front of the car. A tire blew and the top of the windshield shattered. The vehicle swerved violently. All four occupants ducked, barely managing to avoid the bullets. Swaying from side to side, tires screaming, the Horch tilted crazily on two wheels, then came to a grinding halt on its side. Perched like a coin on edge, it hovered briefly, then fell back on its four wheels with a crash.

Slumped against the door, Schiller shook himself and staggered out of the car. Von Wilme, too, was dazed and took his time crawling from the back seat. The SS trooper and driver accompanying them had already taken refuge behind the Horch's hood and begun firing across the roadway. On the opposite side of the pavement was a small forest and several brush-covered hills. Ideal terrain for a hit-and-run ambush.

A shout came from the retreating assailants. "*A chacun son boche!* Let everybody kill his own German." It sounded like a woman's voice. The SS trooper and driver leveled the muzzles of their guns and repeatedly fired into a distant cluster of trees.

Contained anger flashed in Schiller's eyes. "Too convenient and neat. They were waiting for us, von Wilme." In the silence that followed, Schiller held his pistol in readiness, but the agitated voices in the woods became more distant.

"They will live to dearly regret this," von Wilme snarled.

On the highway a German army truck approached. The vehicle came to an abrupt halt beside the bullet-ridden Horch and three Germans jumped out to join them. A wide-eyed Wehrmacht lieutenant came up and saluted Schiller.

"The terrorists are escaping through the woods!" Schiller shouted, pointing across the road. "Lieutenant, I'll need your truck until I can obtain another command car in St. Nazaire. I'll leave my guard and his Schmeisser automatic with you. Take him, along with your own men and go after those responsible for this ambush." Schiller nodded to his driver and wordlessly, they crawled into the *kraftswagen* cab. Von Wilme looked bitterly across the roadway one more time, then jumped in beside Schiller.

"I know you would prefer to stay and pursue this, von Wilme," Schiller said calmly, "but we're after bigger fish in St. Nazaire."

As the truck drove off, Schiller stared in the side mirror. Behind them the flustered Wehrmacht lieutenant withdrew his pistol while his two assistants checked their carbines and fixed bayonets. Accompanied by the SS sergeant and his machine gun, the duty-bound group reluctantly set off across the highway.

Sigi and Merrill hesitated in the doorway to the officers' lounge. The room's only occupants were three men seated at a long oak table. Before them was a bottle of schnapps. Hanging prominently on the wall was the popular color poster of a clear-eyed blond youth on the bridge of a U-boat, staring vigilantly seaward; beside him perched a keen-eyed eagle with a swastika medallion around its neck.

Eyes widening perceptibly as they took in Sigi's opulence, the three men at the table scrambled to their feet with much decorum.

"Heil Hitler," Sigi said sprightly, to Dieter Loewen. "I'm sorry we're late." Her eyes rested briefly on each of the others in turn.

Merrill saluted his superiors and properly stood off to one side.

The U-boat ace stepped forward, handed Sigi a small bouquet of carnations, then immediately introduced his associates. First to click his heels was Kurt Brausdorf.

Sigi and Merrill both recognized the base commander from the scene at the gallows minutes earlier. *My God*, Merrill flashed, *was Brausdorf sitting here drinking to the grisly event?* Gunnar Hersch was introduced next. His was a new face, but Merrill took him for a man of the line. A submariner like himself or Loewen, a spark from the same fire.

When they had finished shaking hands all around, Loewen asked, "Your camera, Sergeant?"

Merrill's hands were conspicuously empty. Before he could reply Sigi's voice calmly interposed, "It's our intent to first reconnoiter the facility. There's time enough for pictures later."

Loewen shrugged. "You see, Herr Kommandant? The beguiling lady journalist has me wrapped neatly around her thumb." Loewen waved a finger menacingly in Sigi's direction and winked. "But I still have over a fortnight of leave coming, Fraulein. When we finish I wish to return to Paris. Tomorrow night, I trust. So you will make haste, agreed?"

"Of course, Kapitan."

Merrill smiled inwardly. The situation and the company, he reasoned, at least precluded Sigi from calling the German *Dieter*. Merrill knew that this being a military base, in proper Reichskriegmarine protocol, Loewen should properly be called *Kaleun*. She was obviously flattering him by calling him *kapitan*.

"Schnapps, Fraulein Schramm?" asked Brausdorf, thumping his heels and raising a glass. "A Luftwaffe colonel, a friend of mine, brought back a case from Yugoslavia."

"With pleasure, sir," she replied graciously.

Merrill suspected she was cozying up to Brausdorf. Sigi's tone alone indicated she enjoyed his lingering stare as much as she did Loewen's. Merrill continued to observe both men carefully. Was Brausdorf suspicious? No, those staring eyes were intense with feeling, but they had little, if any, insight.

"The korvetten kapitan has many well-placed friends in the Luftwaffe," said Loewen, sarcastically, as he brought up two more glasses and poured the fragrant gold liqueur.

"It's real *Slivovitz!*" added Gunnar Hersch, proposing a toast.

They lifted their glasses and drank to one another in the German fashion.

Merrill smiled to himself, noting that Loewen couldn't seem to take his eyes off Sigi. Again, from all appearances, the mere sight of her excited him profoundly.

Merrill was basically a Jack Daniels and soda man. He detested schnapps, but dutifully joined the group, surmising it would be un-Germanlike for him to do otherwise. He felt the drink ignite a small flame in his throat and a moment later in his stomach.

"Fraulein, my office is at your disposal," offered Brausdorf.

Loewen looked at him sharply. "I'm sorry, sir. Berlin wants action! Submarines, crewmen, outfitting in progress—not pictures at a desk."

"A little of all, in good measure," added Sigi, precisely. Capturing a strand of hair that had escaped from her braid, she tucked it back in place and smiled.

Loewen smiled back. "A suggestion, *Anna.* I have matters to discuss with the Kommandant here—among them, an employment referral for the young Swedish woman. And you need time to get your bearing here at the facility."

Amen, mused Merrill. *No truer words.* He sipped unenthusiastically at his schnapps. Time was running short and he was eager to keep his fireworks show on schedule.

Loewen said to her, "I give you for a guide Oberleutnant Hersch, my capable replacement on the U-601. He will provide you an engrossing tour of the most modern base of its kind in the world. When you decide where and when you want me, I'll be available for photography."

"Aboard the U-601, of course," said Sigi, seductively.

"It is impossible to board the vessel until after the day

shift." The voice of authority belonged to Gunnar Hersch. "Much painting and refitting are in progress."

Brausdorf nodded, adding, "There are fewer riveters at night. Return then when you will be able to hear each other speak." He polished off his drink, beckoned to Loewen, and rose to leave. "And Fraulein Schramm, since you will be spending ample time later tonight with our Fuehrer's submarine hero, I propose you permit me the honor of *diner à deux* earlier?" Two clefts of a smile appeared on Brausdorf's cheeks as though cut there by a scalpel.

Sigi thought for a moment. "How can I refuse, Herr Kommandant?"

Ebullient from the liqueur, Brausdorf turned to Loewen and asked in his squashy, Saxonian voice, "Do you object, Kaleun?"

Masking his disappointment, the ace replied, "No, sir, I expect base protocol demands it."

Merrill watched as Loewen turned to Sigi and smiled thickly. The ace raised his glass, again consuming her with his eyes. "After dinner, then. We meet at eight aboard the U-601."

The ace sounded a trifle oily, mused Merrill. It didn't matter; at least they were making progress.

The last drops of schnapps were emptied and a chorus of *Auf Wiedersehens* filled the room. Tour guide Gunnar Hersch led Sigi and Merrill away.

When their visitors were gone, Brausdorf gestured to Loewen, but the ace was still caught up in Anna Schramm's trance.

"Shall we adjourn to my office, Kaluen?" Brausdorf had to ask the question twice.

Loewen waved his hand. "Go on ahead. I'll join you shortly."

The senior officer left the room.

As Loewen sat alone, staring into his empty glass, he once more felt the pangs of sexual hunger. And he felt something else that mildly bothered him. Beyond Anna Schramm's apparent professional capability, aside from her intense, passionate nature, he wondered vaguely if inside this sensuous enigma from Berlin there was a woman of any domestic substance and potential. Did she have any *hausfrau* sensitivity whatever? Or was her disarming smile and air of innocence merely a facade of a very clever paramour?

Loewen swore softly to himself. Damn this flirtatious woman. What did she want? Was Anna Schramm hiding a price tag? Loewen sighed, at once hating and loving the challenge she presented. Why had he allowed her to mesmerize him so? Loewen was determined to pursue Anna Schramm again and find out. But later, after all this unpleasant propaganda business was concluded. There would be plenty of time. He was fortunate, for, after all, they would both be employed in Berlin!

Gunnar Hersch's excursion was more than U.S. Navy submariner and explosives expert Skeet Merrill would have dreamed of asking for. Under the immense concrete roof, a virtual shipyard had been assembled. Two by two the U-boats lay moored in their pens. There was pounding, sawing, and rattling everywhere; the furious sounds of riveting deafened them with its thunderous uproar. During the grand tour, Merrill remained conspicuously silent, his brain preoccupied, trying to assess the challenge.

Sigi did most of the talking. With consummate skill she had posed her questions to Hersch and nodded her head at precisely the right moments, and Merrill was impressed. The oberleutnant was not only cooperative, but he'd gone beyond the call of duty, suggesting that Merrill climb ladders to out-of-the-way places where he might find more dramatic camera angles. Photographer Schmidt discovered all the special angles and more.

They went everywhere except beyond the closed steel door marked *Radio Raum*. The U-boat communications center, its entry guarded by two heavily armed and attentive SS men, was off limits to even Gunnar Hersch. But Merrill remembered its location, as well as the layout of the snorkel assembly facility, the generator room, and the guard quarters. Impressive, he concluded; damned impressive. Merrill suddenly realized why the impregnable underground fortress was such a high priority target. He knew that Sigi, too, was fascinated. She had strolled along catwalks over the submarines, passed through enormous automated steel doors, observed cranes moving snorkel assemblies, and stood at the end of a concrete slip as a U-boat went out for a sea trial. The workers looked up and gaped, as men invariably do when a pretty woman appears in an unlikely place. A few admiring hoots came from the German sailors far enough away to escape Hersch's stern eye, but the French workers only stared in silence.

Merrill buried a chuckle. He knew it would never occur to any of these rubberneckers that this innocent-appearing blonde and her photographer assistant posed a far more dangerous and immediate threat to the St. Nazaire U-boat pens than the fearsome blockbusters the Allies dropped overhead.

From the catwalk at the end of the structure, Merrill once more surveyed the assemblage of U-boats in their slips. He now had a decent plan and felt confident. While Sigi was dining with the base commander he'd return alone with the photographic accessory cases loaded with plastic explosive. He remembered that the U-boat battery storage room next to the last sub slip was dark and unattended. It would be a perfect location to launch himself into the water for a little swim.

Chapter 31

THE AUSTERITY OF life in the concrete bunkers in Berlin or East Prussia was a striking contrast to the Obersalzburg and to what the Fuehrer had experienced in earlier years in the spacious Reich Chancellory. The contrast was startling to everyone except Hitler himself, who had become oblivious to the inconvenience and discomfort. The V-bomb terror imposed on London was not without its sweet revenge, and to avoid the RAF and American bombers, Hitler had become a hard-shelled, underground recluse.

The news that made its way to his subterranean quarters was not good. In the East, the Red Army had paused for the Spring thaw, but now it was gathering itself to renew its attacks. In Italy, General Kesselring was in retreat, at this very hour the Allied forces were marching on Rome. Despite his growing bitterness, Hitler was grandly confident that the sixty German divisions he held in readiness would be able to hold a Western front that extended from Holland to the south of France.

Gone now from Hitler's bunker were the phonograph records and the easy moments of relaxation that he might experience at the Berghof with Eva. For some time she had been banned from this place of command. War, he reasoned, was a serious, twenty-four-hour-a-day business. Goebbels had suggested that Hitler had become too much of a hermit and needed more pleasant diversions. Weakmindedness, a waste of time, Hitler had retorted in no uncertain terms.

Nonetheless, Goebbels had persisted, concerned over Hitler's health and welfare. Giving in, Hitler permitted a projectionist to bring in a feature film as well as the latest newsreel, and would now make an effort to sit through them. He'd seen the classic picture twelve years earlier—*Maedchen in Uniform*. The aide threaded up the projector, respecting Hitler's silent, brooding manner. Goebbels entered the concrete-walled apartment in the company of Professor Morrell. Hitler nervously checked his watch, noting that it was time for his sedative. Goebbels' face bore its usual scornful expression, for he and Bormann both considered Morrell more of a superstitious quack than a medical doctor.

The professor packed away his syringe kit and silently left the chamber. Goebbels joined Hitler to watch the film, sitting attentively at the other end of the green brocade divan. "There is fascinating footage in the newsreel, my Fuehrer. Scenes of the English gathering their ships at Falmouth and Southampton, as well as large scale minesweeping practice off Dover."

The projectionist ran the film. Hitler shifted uncomfortably, arms folding and unfolding across his chest. He kept up his own monologue, ignoring the newsreel's narration, which the projectionist prudently kept tuned down. Hitler admonished, "The Allied landings will not succeed, Goebbels. Their armada must be destroyed in mid-channel. You will see. It's all a matter of time until we can deploy the bigger V-2 rockets and the new technology U-boats. And Goering must get his revolutionary jet fighters into the air; with them we'll shatter, once and for all, the myth of Allied air superiority."

Hitler continued to stare at the newsreel, which had been considerably edited to show German forces in the best light possible. Still, the over-all picture, especially from the Eastern front, was far from encouraging and he grew impatient and increasingly hostile. Abruptly, he tore off his glasses and shouted to the projectionist, "Enough! I'm not in the mood for films tonight." Turning back to Goebbels, he ranted, "Have Heinrich Himmler report to me immediately. I want an immediate updated report on this espionage affair involving our U-boat ace."

Goebbels started out of the room to find Bormann, who arranged all the Fuehrer's appointments.

"Wait, Goebbels," Hitler said in a more subdued voice. He kept his hands folded in his lap to keep them from noticeably trembling. "I understand that Himmler and Colonel Schiller are concerned over the American's role in this diabolical *Operation Storm Tide*. Is it true the Ami is a submarine commander—purportedly some kind of hero himself, like Loewen?''

Goebbels nodded.

Hitler thought for a moment. "Instead of eliminating this man, I would like to meet him. Have this individual brought to Berlin with Dieter Loewen. Alive.''

"I'll see what can be done, my Fuehrer.''

"What is the American's name?''

Goebbels grinned. "According to Himmler, this bogus photographer who has the audacity to represent my staff is in fact a Lieutenant Skeet Merrill.''

"A peculiar name." Hitler sat back on the divan and smiled for the first time in days. "Who knows, Dr. Goebbels? Perhaps, after his visit with us, I'll let you decide whether he winds up in the stalags or on a meat hook.''

Merrill swam slowly, conserving his strength. The U-boat's propellers, once polished brass, were now green with algae. The chill water was murky, obscuring his vision through the face mask, and Merrill had to rely partially on touch. Though Marie Selva's contacts had gone to great pains to appropriate the black rubber diving suit, it was a poor fit. The tunic was tight enough, but the legs were loose, making his underwater movements clumsy, despite the flippers. Swimming along with several waterproof packets of plastic explosive and a coil of wire, Merrill had no need of diver's lead weights; if anything, he needed some additional buoyancy. But his primary enemy now was water temperature. The cold was drastically reducing his concentration, draining his energy, and pushing his endurance. Diving of this nature was definitely a two-man job. Merrill again cursed the fate that had come to Hugh Cummings.

Already Merrill had twice swum the forty yards from the iron grate of the sewer outlet to the first U-boat slip. Under cover of darkness, he'd kept to the mouth of the overhanging structure, staying underwater as long as his breath would permit, paying out the waterproof fusing to each of the nine U-boats in the slips. The fusing wire led to the abandoned sewer opening where he'd later connect it to a timer mechanism.

There were currently ten boats in the St. Nazaire pens, two to a slip, but Merrill had no intention of placing a charge outside the hull of the U-601, the sub that they would all be working within in a couple of hours. The parcel of plastic explosive destined for Loewen's former boat Merrill would somehow carry aboard. The other nine U-boats, thanks to the instantaneous fusing and a single timer, would be blown up later, at a predetermined hour.

Merrill reached for the wire cutters on his shock cord and tied down a packet of plastic to another U-boat hull. He attached the explosives to the stuffing box, the point where the propeller shaft entered the engine room. If the U-boats didn't sink from a flooded compartment before help arrived, at least their drive mechanisms would be out of commission and, at a minimum, a lengthy drydocking would be in order. Either way, Merrill calculated, the entire lot of subs would be out of the war, useless to the Germans while France was being liberated.

Again, he was hurting for air. Struggling with the cutter, he finished securing the plastic, but dropped his waterproof flashlight in the process. It jerked up short on the line attached to his wrist. Merrill grabbed the light, turned it off, and pushed himself to the surface, breaking water under cover of the U-boat's stern. Spitting out cold salty water, he gasped, removed his goggles, and worked hard to control himself.

Merrill heard a cough. One of the French welders, squatting in the shadows at the end of the slip, was sneaking a cigarette; he was less than twenty feet away. The worker turned lazily in Merrill's direction, but he seemed to be staring at nothing. The cigarette brightened, then arched before Merrill as the butt hit the water just inches from his face. As the dockworker stood and stretched, his eyes followed the cigarette's trajectory. Merrill held his breath as the Frenchman paused in the middle of his yawn and squinted toward the water. *At the light reflection from Merrill's goggles?* The bastard, obviously, had spotted him! Merrill's heart thudded.

Drawing in a deep breath, Merrill dove deep, kicking hard and scrambling for the other side of the U-boat. He followed the wire fuse he'd laid earlier. *Wait, no Skeet!* For safe measure, *swim on past* the next boat in the slip! But how far was it?

Losing sight of the yellow fusing line, an alarm sounded in Merrill's head. His arms and legs became stiff from the relentless cold, his movements more awkward, as if he were struggling in molasses. The water grew darker. Merrill's brain was fogged; losing his sense of direction, he felt confused and panicky. Then he again spotted the fusing line and swam along it, but his lungs were empty and aching. Merrill finally struggled to the surface, gasped in a lungful of air and listened carefully.

He heard no commotion from the dock area he'd just abandoned. The night shift workers were continuing at their normal pace, with no shouts, no evidence of alarm. Could the Frenchman who had spotted him be trusted? Merrill knew there weren't any options. Exhausted, he wondered about the time, for his task was consuming too much of it. He had to meet the others shortly in the abandoned sewer and there were still charges to be attached to two more U-boat hulls. Merrill rested for as long as he dared, then inhaled vigorously and once more lowered himself into the murky water.

Following Merrill's instructions, Erika Vermeer and Maurice Duval grabbed hand picks and started swinging at the wall. Roger stood by, waiting to spell them off.

"Pure speculation," Erika whispered to the Frenchman as she and the mute chipped away at the dead-end brick barrier the Germans had installed across the sewer three years earlier. "Tearing down walls is not my *forte*, Monsieur Roger. I'm better at breaking and entering with a degree of finesse."

"You're doing just fine," Merrill urged her on. "Save your breath and keep digging."

Erika looked back at him hatefully, then resumed handpicking at the wall. Merrill was glad to get back into warm, dry clothing, for his underwater odyssey had chilled his bones to the marrow. Again, he checked his computations on the scrap of paper before him.

They took turns, and after a half-hour's sweating, the two-foot thick wall was penetrated by a hole the size of a pizza plate. Erika Vermeer was ready to burrow through when Merrill grabbed her by the shoulder and gently pulled her back. "Wait here," he instructed. "I intend to check this out myself." Merrill squeezed through the hole, climbed to his feet on the opposite side, and scanned the abandoned tunnel with his flashlight. Overhead, as he suspected, were the snorkel assembly facility floor drains. *Perfect*, he said to himself. Phase one of the demolition would come off easily enough.

Scuttling down the tunnel, Merrill passed around two bends

and finally found the tall iron grate that led to the turning basin outside the submarine pen. His eyes were momentarily blinded by the brightness. Beside the opening was the coil of waterproof fusing he had shoved through the bars a short time earlier. Satisfied with the layout, Merrill ventured back up the abandoned sewer shaft. He intended to keep the others occupied at the inside end of the tunnel, for demolition of the U-boats—until it actually came off—would be his secret alone.

Returning to the hole in the brick wall, Merrill shouted through it to the others: "We're on the button. Keep at this opening, make it bigger, okay? Then shake a leg and pass those dynamite kegs through and stack them in a pile—ten feet inside the hole. Wake up, Roger, and hand me that truck battery and timer box."

While the others busied themselves with widening the hole and transferring and stacking the explosives, Merrill again crept off alone, carrying the battery and small metal box back to the waterfront end of the tunnel. Curious as he knew the others had been, they didn't follow or ask questions. They trusted him, fully aware of their ignorance when it came to this highly specialized, delicate, and dangerous work.

Merrill was pleased the abandoned tunnel had a couple of bends in it and a deep niche in one wall where he could safely place the timer and battery. He intended for the kegs of dynamite cached under the snorkel facility to go off first, and he didn't want that blast to destroy or activate the delicate timer and circuits for the delayed explosions under the U-boats. *Sympathetic detonations* could be a ticklish situation. Timing too, was critical; Merrill knew the French laborers on the swing shift would go off duty at midnight.

Attaching the copper clips to the battery, Merrill opened the black metal box and set the timer dial to twelve-fifteen—plenty of time for the workers to depart and make good his own escape. Then he flipped two switches and pushed the test button. The small green light glimmered. Pleased with himself, Merrill secured the fusing wires to the box, closed the lid, and backed away.

Rejoining the others at the opposite end of the tunnel, Merrill counted the small kegs stacked neatly against the wall. Roger, Duval, and Erika were nearly finished. Merrill beckoned to Roger. "That's enough. Take the others and clear out. I'll wrap it up here myself."

Chapter 32

An HOUR AND twenty minutes later, Erika Vermeer lingered on the waterfront in front of the Bon Ami Cafe. The nauseating smell of the sewer scrubbed away and wearing fresh clothing, she waited patiently, as instructed, for Dieter Loewen to join her. This wasn't what she had in mind at all, meeting the German *outside* the U-boat base, but it was better than nothing. A beginning at least.

The overcast Brittany sky was threatening and there was little traffic on the street when she first saw the long Mercedes sedan, its black, white, and red swastika flying but its lights out. The SS command car drove past rapidly, slowed at the next intersection, circled around and crept by one more time. It then disappeared around the corner. In the darkness Erika couldn't see the faces of the car's occupants, but still an uneasiness crept up her spine. She had the distinct feeling either she or the Bon Ami cafe was under observation. Did the local SS know she was in St. Nazaire?

Erika shifted uncomfortably. Though no one had emerged from the SS command vehicle and it had finally driven off, it still made no sense standing on the street inviting trouble. Besides, the wind had picked up and a light rain began to fall. She decided to go inside and wait for Loewen.

Erika sauntered through the crowded, smoke-filled cafe and squeezed into a *banquette*. Several German sailors looked up, ogling her and whistling. The blue haze in the room that passed for air was heavily scented with freshly cooked cabbage.

Almost immediately Dieter Loewen appeared in the doorway and made his way to her booth. The seamen at the other tables ceased staring at her.

Worrying over her next move, Erika felt uncomfortable. Thoughout the dinner the U-boat ace seemed friendly enough to her though not very talkative. Neither of them could pick an argument with their bratwurst and spatzle; the meal was excellent, for the French *patron* who owned the cafe was skilled at catering to the needs of the St. Nazaire occupation forces.

Erika observed the boisterous sailors around them, probably U-boat men resting between patrols. Many were her own age and younger. She looked at Loewen. "These men, Kapitan. From their appearance, their life's philosophy seems simple, yes?"

Loewen didn't look up from his plate. "I don't understand."

She shrugged. "Eat, drink, and make love while you can, for tomorrow you may be no more than fodder for fish?" Once more she scanned the room, noting that some of the sailors were sullen and contemplative, others were relaxed, easygoing, and filled with laughter. It was not difficult, even without Loewen's prompting, for her to tell who had just returned from a mission and who was about to sail. Erika watched four laughing seamen shuffle noisily into the cafe and settle at the last empty table; two were drunk and intent on losing themselves in still more beer. A plump, middle-aged French waitress served them each a frothing steinbecher, then wandered back to the *banquette* occupied by Loewen and Erika.

"More beer, Monsieur Admiral?" she asked Loewen flippantly, her hands in the place where her hips should have been. She smelled of onions, rum, and musty clothes.

Looking up and frowning, the ace slid his own and Erika's empty steinbechers toward her, then went on eating.

When the beers were delivered, Erika took a long, less-than-feminine swig and glanced toward the cafe's front door. She glanced nervously at her watch, still worried about the SS staff car she'd seen outside minutes earlier. Thankfully, the occupants of the black Mercedes still had not come nosing inside the Bon Ami. Focusing on the U-boat ace, she said cautiously, "Kapitan, after our dinner you meet the journalists from Berlin aboard the U-601. I would like very much to join you."

Loewen looked surprised. He gave her a speculative look.

"Impossible. It is official business, not a visitor's tour. Perhaps you'll some day have an opportunity to go aboard a submarine as a base employee." Stony-faced, Loewen continued to fork at his bratwurst.

Disappointed, Erika lowered her eyes.

Gazing at her, Loewen finally said, "You're too much like my own daughter. Forever asking about submarines and wanting to go aboard them. U-boats, unfortunately, are not designed to accommodate women."

"To the discredit of German ship designers. Some day all this will change." Erika smiled. "Where is your daughter now?"

Loewen stiffened and lowered his eyes. "Dead. Killed along with my wife in an Allied bombing raid."

"I'm sorry, Kapitan."

Loewen retreated into meditative silence.

There were other things Erika wanted to say to Loewen, but obviously this wasn't the time for it. "When shall I apply for the job?" she asked, shattering the oppressive silence between them.

"Tomorrow at two. It's arranged. And I suggest for once you wear a skirt, instead of men's pants."

Erika was tempted to reply caustically, but decided against it. There was an uneasy silence. She knew tomorrow afternoon would be too late. Skeet Merrill's taunting face came into her unfocused gaze once more. Despite the American's insistence that she remain outside the U-boat pen, she was determined, and her yeasty brain was working on another plan of action. A plan she needed to put into effect tonight, not tomorrow.

"The dour expression. You don't appear pleased," said Loewen.

"So much destruction here." Erika sighed. "In Paris, the only visible signs of war are the soldiers' uniforms and the curfew."

Loewen put down his fork, leaned both elbows on the table and stared at her over joined, pointed fingers. "In Paris there are people wearing rags, wooden shoes, and starving to death." He hesitated, then his sepulchral warning continued, "And you'll be among them, Fraulein, if you go back."

Grinding her teeth, Erika looked away, relishing some inaudible imprecations at Loewen and all the other paternal advice givers she'd known. The ace was talking to her as if she

were a child. She watched the German frown, look across the
room, and signal the waitress for the check.

"Patronne!" he called.

Once more Erika studied at length the hard lines on
Loewen's face. Hours earlier she had not known their detail; it
was amazing how familiar the U-boat commander had become
in such a brief period of time, but his sudden ill-humor came as
a surprise. Now Erika would worry whether she had pushed
her tenacity and scheming, purposely petulant as it had been, a
trifle too far.

"You'll make the interview tomorrow with no further
arguments?" Loewen asked, harshly.

"Yes, Herr Kapitan," she dishonestly replied, forcing
herself to remain painfully humble and alert, as though she
were listening to some rich, crochety old uncle.

Loewen paid the tab, climbed to his feet, and briskly walked
to the entry. He made no gesture that she should follow.

Erika sat where she was, thinking. She took her time
finishing her beer, then pushed the steinbecher away. Walking
to the front of the cafe, she pulled the door open part way to
check the street.

Erika froze, not daring to venture outside. Across the way
the Mercedes was back; two SS officers had climbed out of the
rear seat and were headed toward the cafe! Loewen had already
disappeared up the street. Erika spun around and scurried
through the crowded tables, smoke, laughter, and admiring
stares to the Bon Ami's rear exit.

She bolted outside, discovering the weather had taken a turn
for the worse. Rain fell steadily as she ran through the dark
back street. She cursed her civilian clothing. In a garrison town
it was too conspicuous. As soon as possible she had to bind her
breasts and find a sailor's uniform.

Chapter 33

MERRILL CAUTIOUSLY poked his head out the undertaking parlor door and examined the dark street. There was no one in sight, but still, he felt edgy. Quietly, he helped Marie Selva carry the empty wooden coffin down the front stoop. It was made of pine and light enough, and it slid easily into the back of the hearse alongside the brown suitcases filled with plasticine. Merrill closed and secured the doors and they drove off, the Frenchwoman sitting on a pillow behind the wheel.

Across from the undertaking parlor, two shadows detached themselves from a building alcove. Reinhard Schiller and Hermann von Wilme watched the old hearse rattle off in the distance, confident that they knew where it was going. It had been a long drive from Paris and a dangerous brush with death and both men were still edgy.

Schiller had been up most of the night before and needed sleep, but rest would have to come later. The continued vigilance had paid off handsomely, and he was satisfied. Thanks to their informer, whose cover still appeared neatly intact, the final pieces of the Operation Storm Tide puzzle were rapidly falling into place. Schiller knew that both Himmler and Hitler would be pleased with his efforts. He wasn't so sure about Grand Admiral Doenitz.

Checking his watch, Schiller said to von Wilme, "We'll move in now, before it is too late. Find Loewen and take him into our confidence while I report back to OKW in Berlin on these developments." Schiller knew the Fuehrer and his entourage, including Doenitz and Himmler, had left Berchtesgaden and returned to the Berlin bunker, where they impatiently waited for an update. Unfortunately for Schiller, the industrious, alert American—out of practical necessity—remained on the enemy team, a definite bone in the throat. It would have been easy enough to have captured or shot him as he descended the steps of the undertaking parlor moments ago, but the little Frenchwoman would have been a witness, not to mention prying neighbors. Witnesses that Schiller, under the present secret circumstances, couldn't afford. And the longer he allowed Marie Selva to live, the wider the snare to trap other Resistance operatives. Perhaps Berlin would have new instructions for him on the matter of the American.

Von Wilme looked at him skeptically. "How much should I tell the Kapitan?"

"It is time for everything," Schiller said grimly. "But first you'll have to find him. And we must also locate the young lesbian woman. I understand she is one of your former Paris playmates, Major."

Von Wilme stiffened with embarrassment.

Schiller put away his smile. "Go now, and I'll meet you in one hour at the designated place."

Both men pulled up their collars against the increasing rain, separated, and hastened off to separate vehicles.

As Schiller quickened his pace over the cobbles, he once more weighed his options. Churchill was mad, absolutely mad; the Fuehrer was right about that. What wild scheming for the English leader to attempt to capture alive a man of Dieter Loewen's importance. And worse, the vulgar audacity of the Ami and the woman undertaker to plan on sequestering him in a casket!

Erika breathed a sigh of relief and smiled to herself. Once again she could be thankful that she had small breasts and walked like a truck driver. The sailor's uniform fitted perfectly, for she'd taken her time about selecting the victim. A well-placed tap on the head was all it took to incapacitate the young, slightly tipsy German seaman. It was almost too easy, she reflected. Erika was glad the refuse container lid didn't fit securely, for the bound and gagged sailor would need air when he came around.

Knotting the navy blue tie over her striped shirt and

straightening her cap so the ribbon fell precisely where it belonged, Erika examined the seaman's wallet. Carefully noting the rank, name and identification number, she committed them to memory. Not a seaman, but a *hospital corpsman*! Her victim had apparently consumed his last few Reichsmarks in Calvados or beer; there was no folding money. Erika was as ready as she'd ever be. Now she would show the American and the Norwegian woman a thing or two. She'd surprise them with some valuable, unplayed cards, and since Dieter Loewen would be of no significant help to her—at least tonight—he, too, would be in for a surprise.

Entering the U-boat base behind several other sailors, the duty guards at the gate gave her stolen identity card only the most cursory of glances. Erika smiled to herself, feeling a sudden increase in stature and a surge of power. She was inside! Quickening her step, she headed for the U-boat berths.

Skeet Merrill glanced up at the brass clock in the U-601's control room. It read 20:10. He watched Dieter Loewen pull a record out of its sleeve and place it on the ship's gramophone. Merrill fully expected to hear a rousing chorus of *Horst Wessel Lied,* but instead was surprised by the sparkling voice of Vera Lynn, sweetheart of the British armed forces. Eyebrows knitting, Merrill glanced down at the turntable. The record, as he suspected, had been manufactured in England, not Germany.

Loewen smiled cautiously as he read Merrill's look of amazement. "Have you heard Vera Lynn before, Sergeant?" the ace asked.

"No, Herr *Kaleun,*" Merrill lied.

The German gestured toward the recording. "The spoils of war. The *war song* was taken from a captured British destroyer. Fraulein Lynn is well received by the crew as an amusing diversion. I must admit, this scratched record is one of my favorites. My only un-Germanlike vice."

Vera Lynn's voice on the ceiling speaker unfolded with sentimental urgency:

"There'll be bluebirds over
  The white cliffs of Dover,
Tomorrow, just you wait and see . . ."

Sigi exchanged swift glances with Merrill, then smiled back at Loewen.

"There are few pleasures in submarine life, Anna," he explained, gently squeezing her arm as he escorted her past the U-boat's cramped electric galley. "Of course there is our superior food, but even that luxury soon becomes tedious."

Vera Lynn's voice continued to echo hauntingly through the corridor.

"Jimmy will go to sleep,
    The valley will bloom again.
There'll be bluebirds over,
    The white cliffs of Dover——"

Merrill, his camera suspended limply from one hand, grew increasingly impatient. There were several intricate phases to his plan of attack and proper timing was imperative. Roger and the mute were still holding out in the sewer below the sub pen, waiting for his signal. Just after midnight, the other nine U-boats—too nearby for comfort—would blow. Each passing minute of Loewen's monologue was a painful eternity to Merrill.

"Locate, engage, eliminate——" lectured the sub ace, "the classic mission of any warship. To accomplish this with speed and dispatch, the U-601 is superbly equipped, the finest fighting machine German ingenuity and craftsmanship can provide. Until our fantastic new models, of course, come into service in the months ahead."

Sigi appeared genuinely fascinated.

To Merrill, Loewen's words were caught in a draft; they went in one ear and out the other. Merrill was thinking only of explosives, like the plastic charge he intended to place just a few yards away in the U-601's engine room. Following this, he'd go to the sub base's generator room where he'd mold cordite rings of plastic around the power transformers and emergency alternators. Not too difficult there. Pencil fuse igniters would set off these delayed explosions. His final target, the important U-boat communications center, would be his most dangerous challenge. Merrill was counting on stealth, speed, a diversionary explosion or fire, and his silenced Luger for that ticklish phase of the operation.

As they listened to Loewen winding down his monologue,

Merrill surreptitiously counted the pencil igniters in his pocket. Everything was set for him to go to work, provided the duty man on the U-boat's gangway didn't go snooping inside the baggage Merrill had passed off as a photographic accessory case when he'd left it on the deck.

Topside the only evidence of the U-601's crew was the armed seaman at the gangway plus the officer standing the duty.

Leutnant Mueller had already interrupted the sub ace to inform him there was an urgent telephone message at the base security office, but Loewen had shrugged it off and insisted on not being disturbed. Now Mueller heard music coming up from below——*the English vocalist!* He shrugged and went up forward, where he divided his attention between two French pipefitters laboring over a faulty torpedo loading hatch and a night shift painter working on the sub's conning tower. Already, on the starboard side, Dieter Loewen's cat emblem was half-obliterated by fresh primer. Mueller wondered what mascot or emblem the new commander, Gunnar Hersch, might have chosen for the boat.

When the touring trio below deck at last re-entered the corridor opposite the Kapitan's compartment—what there was of it—Loewen turned and smiled. The record music ended, as if on cue. Switching off the turntable, Loewen said, "There you have it, the U-601. Built at Deutsche Werft Shipyard in Hamburg, launched in January, 1942. Now you know almost as much about her as I do." His easy smile vanished. No longer able to contain his boredom, Loewen's voice took on a deferential tone. "Time for business, yes? My debut in *Signal* magazine. Where do you want me for your first photograph?"

Sigi thought for several moments, or pretended to, before replying. "Yes," she said defensively, "Let's begin."

She and Merrill exchanged glances, not thoughtful glances, but the quick exchange of partners in crime who knew exactly what they had to do and were merely recommitting themselves to getting on with it. With considerable authority Sigi first directed Merrill to photograph the sub ace at the plotting table. *Click.* Next she asked the German to stand in the galley with a coffee cup. *Click*. Another angle, with more of a smile. *Click*. They went back to the control room. The Leica's flash caught the ace before several brass gauges. *Click*.

Merrill was unhappy with the pose and needed more depth of field. *Wasn't he supposed to come off as a halfass professional?* He said with authority, "Back a little more, *Kaleun*. Fine. Now move to the left and place your hand on the aft ballast control."

Loewen suddenly frowned.

Merrill's heart skipped a beat as he remembered that the ace had said nothing about these complicated controls during their earlier indoctrination.

Loewen's periscope eyes, with their knack of instant orientation, focused on him. "For a soldier in the Wehrmacht, you seem to know a great deal about submarines."

Sigi looked at both of them with concern.

Merrill kept his slightly red face behind the camera and snapped another picture. "My brother, *Herr Kaleun*," he quickly fabricated, "serves on a U-boat out of Brest."

Running interference, Sigi turned on the charm. "Dieter, come over here, please."

Merrill breathed a sigh of relief as she guided Loewen, one arm around his waist, to the cramped commander's compartment. Gesturing for him to sit at the fold-down desk, she removed his white cap and stood back, considering him like a thoughtful artist. "The vessel's log, we'll need it," she said softly. "Very important. You should be writing in it."

Loewen glanced up at the gray metal strongbox and its combination lock. With weary consternation his eyes roamed back to the attractive woman beside him. Smiling, he said, "I'm beginning to feel like a responsive marionette at the end of your expertly manipulated strings, Fraulein." He gave her a withering glance, then said firmly, "The log is unimportant."

"Definitely it is. And call me Anna, please."

Impatient, Merrill once more checked the brass clock on the wall. Why was she wasting precious time with the locker? He tried to read some clue in her expression, but saw only resolute determination. Something else? A faint glimmer of cunning? Damn it all, this clever woman was hiding something!

Chapter 34

DIETER LOEWEN DIDN'T consider a publicity photograph of himself writing his final entry in the U-601's log book to be important at all, but he wasn't up to telling the Fuehrer or Dr. Goebbels their business. Exhaling sharply and grumbling to himself, he turned to the combination lock. He knew the combination wouldn't be changed until just before Gunnar Hersch took his new command out on a patrol. Still, he didn't belong here. Reichskriegmarine regulations to the contrary, this was a stubborn, assertive female and she seemed to have all the D.N.B. credentials from Berlin to back up her determination. Loewen flipped the dial four times until he heard the familiar metallic thud. Swinging open the steel door to the locker, he groped inside.

It happened then. It happened so fast Loewen reeled in amazement and total disbelief. First he felt the soft feminine hand on his wrist, then came the uncomfortable nudge of a gun muzzle against his rib cage.

"You needn't bother with the log, Dieter. Just back away from the locker very slowly and sit down, please," the woman said without a trace of emotion.

Stung with shock, Loewen did as he was told, at the same time turning to face her.

"Not at your desk. Sit over there, on the bunk." She indicated the place with an abrupt wave of a Lilliput .21 automatic.

Loewen stared at the gun in amazement, his breath catching in his throat. Then he looked back at her eyes. Anna Schramm's geniality and warmth were gone now, replaced by a tough, insistent manner. It was obvious that she was determined to eliminate even the slightest resistance from him. Turning to the Wehrmacht photographer, Loewen saw only caterpillar eyebrows arching in bewilderment. Sergeant Schmidt appeared equally thunderstruck. The photographer's eyes were strangely fixed on the Lilliput as though he'd never seen it before.

"Sorry to deceive you so, Dieter," she said coldly. "War is replete with unpleasant little surprises."

Loewen studied her with eyes as cold and as hard as ball bearings, then turned his focus back to her assistant. But now he saw that the blank, dazed expression on the sergeant's face had disappeared, replaced by a conspiratorial, determined look that left little doubt in Loewen's mind that whatever the plot, it was a team effort. The cameraman Schmidt—or whoever he was—definitely appeared to be on the opposing team.

With all the gallantry he could muster under the crisis curcumstances, Loewen announced, "Whatever your intent, be warned. I've been under fire too often in battle to stand down now in fear of a miniature revolver." Settling back against the bunk, he folded his arms and smiled stoically, deliberately keeping his voice modulated and under control. "Your pistol of glory, Fraulein Schramm, despite its lilliputian size, makes noise. Considerable noise that will galvanize every man in the U-boat pen into action."

"We plan ahead, *Ace*." The equally calm voice had come from the photographer, who now brought to bear a Luger with a long, perforated silencer screwed to its muzzle.

Loewen frowned and let out an audible gasp. His brain seemed to shrink back into itself, for what was happening to him was incredible. Sitting back in the bunk he tried to determine by what wrong turning he'd arrived at his agonizing predicament. For the first time in his life, he'd been led gullibly, helplessly, by strange elements and forces beyond himself.

Merrill stared at Loewen, realizing that here was a man who would never crack. The Lion's monolithic calm appeared impenetrable. Merrill couldn't help being impressed.

"British?" the German asked in an even voice.

For the first time in days Merrill spoke English again.

"Wrong guess. I'm an American; the name's Skeet Merrill, Lieutenant, U.S. Navy. Your lady friend is a Norwegian school teacher, so you can forget the Anna bullshit and call her Sigi. We're all going to get to know each other well enough in the next forty-eight hours."

Loewen looked puzzled. He was thoughtful for a long time. Finally he said, "I should have known. You knew too much about submarines."

Merrill shrugged. "Should know a little. Skippered one for 18 months."

Loewen's eyebrows furrowed. "You were a submarine commander?" he asked dully.

Merrill nodded, but didn't elaborate.

The German's seething anger gave way to curiosity. "In the Atlantic or the Pacific?"

Aware that he'd whetted the ace's appetite, Merrill made up his mind to slip Loewen the full course at once and get the meal over with. "Scored a Japanese carrier, the *Kuru*. And four oil tankers. Hardly compares with your record, *Ace*, but if and when I get back behind a periscope there's still time to improve the statistics." Merrill turned to Sigi. "He knows enough. Now can we move out as planned, boss-lady?"

Fixing Merrill with a predatory eye, Sigi said firmly, "Not yet." She stepped over to the bulkhead door leading forward and swung it closed, then quickly dogged the bolts. "I don't want Loewen's shipmates up on the bow to come wandering down the corridor interrupting me."

"Interrupting what?" Annoyed and puzzled, Merrill looked on as she started to probe through the open ship's locker.

Sigi ignored the cipher machine and the small metal box of cash and valuables. Even after all the dialogue expended on its behalf, the U-601's log was tossed aside without a moment's glance.

Merrill looked at his watch. "Sigi, what the hell are you doing? Let's go." There was measured sarcasm and impatience in his query.

Red-faced with hate, Loewen glared at him.

Sigi smiled at Merrill. "Mind your job, *Schnuki*. Keep your eyes on our U-boat hero. If he moves or shouts, *shoot him*."

The sudden chilly mandate that Merrill should confine himself to that one task was unmistakable. He steadied his Luger and waited, watchful for signs of weakness, a hint of panic in Loewen's cold steady eyes, any attempt to escape. Any moment, Merrill thought, the romantic brave image of his imagination, the image of the daring, proud hero he'd secretly envied, longed to become—would be shattered. The U-boat ace would start to sweat like any other man. But Dieter Loewen didn't move or show even a small sign of fright. He sat rock steady, unflinching, his eyes seeking no mercy, not even a trace of sick reluctance.

Instinctively, Loewen knew that the worst thing he could do would be to show fear. Yet if the truth were known, his insides were a clenched mass of anger, a cinched knot that couldn't be picked. Loewen sat impassively, considering his options, which so far appeared nil. Looking up at the American, Loewen's eyes encountered an annoying, sticky smile.

"It would be an ignominious way to die, Kapitan," declared Merrill. "Shot in the belly by a pair of safe robbers? Better to eat the bottom while fighting off a fleet of corvettes, right?"

Loewen glared first at Merrill, then to the Luger. He said bluntly, "A master understatement." Loewen turned to Sigi and narrowed his eyes. Suddenly his dry lips opened in alarm, then closed.

Probing inside the locker, the Norwegian woman spy had obviously found what she'd been seeking; the new operational codes that had come from OKW just ten days earlier! What was happening to the German Reich was now agonizingly clear to Loewen.

Fighting back his malaise, Loewen again focused on Merrill's gun hand. Despite the terrible humiliation fate was causing him, Loewen knew going for the Luger now would be a suicidal gesture. He watched the woman he'd earlier known far too intimately flip open the lead and clothbound cover to the code book, read a few of the dispatches inside, then turn to the highly classified conversion pages.

Sigi, the American had called his partner. Loewen eyed her again, closely. Not with lust, but queryingly, with a terrible penetration that made her glance up.

"Everything as it should be," she said with an icy calm. Withdrawing a piece of clean, white paper from her purse, she ignored Loewen and began to write.

Loewen glanced at Merrill and heard him say, "We've both been hoodwinked, Kapitan."

"Geneva, gentlemen," Sigi said without looking up. "Ten months of studying cryptography. Section 8-S needs this quite badly since Admiral Doenitz changed the earlier Enigma cipher."

Loewen slowly shook his head. Glancing around the compartment, he caught sight of Gunnar Hersch's silver letter opener with the embossed black swastika on its hilt. But it was three feet away, beside Sigi where the U-601's new commander had left it on the shelf of the folding desk. Somehow, Loewen had to get his hands on the shiny sharp stiletto.

Chapter 35

ERIKA STOOD ON the concrete slip beside the U-601. She gazed in wonderment at the other subs in the pen, breathing in the faint aromas of red primer, diesel oil, and battery acid—odors that were as much a part of a U-boat as the keel that held it together.

Stepping across the U-601's gangway, Erika's alert eyes took in, from bow to stern, every detail of the Lion of the Atlantic's infamous warship. She warily noted the man standing the deck watch. The armed seaman looked the type who might give short shrift to an unfamiliar pharmacist's mate attempting to board the submarine.

"Visitors are not permitted," the duty man said gruffly, confirming her suspicions.

Erika showed her identification and quickly fabricated, "Kapitan Leutnant Loewen has requested me to meet him below with the journalists." There was a slight ring of impatience to her voice.

The sailor examined her credentials and stepped aside.

Stepping off the gangway, she smiled to herself and breathed easier. Dieter Loewen might not be a high-ranking admiral, but he was an important Kriegsmarine personality. Apparently, instructions from a man who was a legend in his time were not to be taken lightly.

Erika saw an officer huddled with workmen on the bow. To avoid confronting them, she passed behind the conning tower and headed for the U-boat's stern entry. Now came the choice: approaching Loewen and her companions and giving away her male disguise, praying that the American and the Norwegian would assist her, or hiding below in another compartment until the others had left. The U-boat's strongbox and its precious code was close, tantalizingly close. Erika made up her mind to go below and try and stay hidden.

At the gangway the suspicious duty man had contrived to watch the pharmacist's mate take the long way about entering the U-boat. The young sailor as not only unfamiliar, the duty man thought, but there was something odd and nervous about his behavior. The deck guard made up his mind to go forward and discuss the matter with the diving officer, Leutnant Mueller, who commanded the watch.

Dropping as quietly as she could down the aft hatch, Erika was about to duck behind the engine room generator, when from far up the narrow passageway Sigi spotted her. Erika cursed to herself, shrugged in resignation, then stepped through the bulkhead and headed forward in the boat.

Seated before a fold-down desk, Sigi Petersen waited for her with a look of annoyance. As Erika approached, the Norwegian woman put aside the pencil in hand and reached for the Lilliput on the desk before her. Erika gazed at Sigi and the strong box with veiled speculation. *Too late!* They had the code. Her first reaction was one of disappointment, then, regarding Sigi's gun uncertainly, she grinned. When Erika's eyes found Loewen guarded by the gloating American, she whistled softly through her teeth. Safecracker Erika Vermeer, she now realized, as of this moment was a Johnny come lately. Erika saw Dieter Loewen staring at her sailor's uniform, his face a mask of disbelief. Beads of sweat gleamed like glycerin on the German's forehead as they looked at one another for a long, taut moment. There was no doubt that he recognized her.

"Good evening, Kapitan," she began. Sucking in her breath, Erika wasn't quite sure what to say next. She saw that Sigi—still staring at her in stunned perplexity—had tightened her grip on the gun. Erika started to ask, "I'm sorry, I tried—"

"Say absolutely nothing!" Sigi abruptly called out, severing Erika's intentions as neatly as a meat cleaver. "Move over by the Kapitan and sit quietly."

Confused, Erika felt a flattening, panicky feeling in the pit of her stomach. Something was wrong here, very wrong. The Lilliput automatic not only continued to bear down on her, but Sigi Petersen wore a strangely hostile expression as though she'd never laid eyes on Erika before! What madness was this? Staring down the barrel of the miniature revolver, Erika wallowed in woozy emotion. "I don't understand," she suddenly exclaimed.

"Must I repeat myself? I said *silence*."

Erika slowly shook her head. Finally divining that Sigi apparently had some special performance she was fretting over, Erika would remain quiet; for lack of a better part, she'd continue the role of the German sailor.

When Skeet Merrill had recognized their intruder as Erika Vermeer, once more dressed as a man, he'd drawn a blank. And he felt more confused than ever when Sigi had confronted the Dutch girl with a gun. When Sigi finally managed to dispatch a private wink his way he felt a genuine relief, so deep it was almost a spasm. Merrill decided he'd just have to wait; she was testing his patience again. Nothing, Merrill reflected, made any sense any more; it griped him that he was losing control again. From the corner of his eye Merrill watched Sigi place the Lilliput back on the desk and return to copying the code. Merrill's main concern, however, was keeping track of Loewen, and he wasn't about to drop his guard there for even a fraction of a second. He could tell Dieter Loewen was dumbfounded by the Dutch girl's arrival and infuriated by her appearing in a German naval uniform. The ace's eyes remained riveted to Erika as if he were restraining himself from spitting out an obscenity.

Loewen finally asked, "Young lady, who are you trying to deceive in that costume, and why?" For the first time there was a hint of despair in the German's voice. Loewen ran his worried hands over his knees, wiping off moist palms.

Erika rewarded the ace with a sideways grin but kept her silence as instructed.

Merrill waved his Luger menacingly at Loewen. "No talking. The lady wants to concentrate on the code."

It took Sigi Petersen four minutes to finish copying what she needed. Merrill watched her fold the completed document, tuck it carefully inside her brassiere, then replace the code book, log, cipher machine, and cash box back in the locker exactly as she'd found them. Closing the steel door, she flipped the combination lock. "So far, so good," she said eagerly. "Now the next challenge: getting the code and the Lion here out of St. Nazaire and back to England."

Merrill looked over at her, trying to make it all fit together in his fogged-up mind. "I'm impressed, Miss Petersen. Damned impressed." With just a hint of derisiveness, he added, "But what about my own little assignment—the big bang, remember? Guy Fawke's Day, Shanghai New Year's, the Fourth of July, *whatever*. Or did I just come along to help paddle your canoe?"

"Sorry, Skeet. You did come in for the *last half* of Colonel Foster's briefing, remember? There was a reason then for not telling you everything and there still is. I'll explain it all later. Getting these documents out of France is now top priority. Your demolition work, though still important if you can pull it off, is last in order." Smiling, she thought for a moment. "You can forget placing plastic *inside* the base; your target should be whatever damage you can inflict from outside. According to your own calculations, the dynamite in the sewer below should more than take care of the snorkel facility."

A passion of resentment seized Merrill. "You're suggesting I now forget the generator room and communications center, not to mention this sub?"

Loewen's hawk-like eyes were on them both.

Sigi replied, "We have the code. From an intelligence standpoint, the St. Nazaire base must not appear to have been penetrated from *within*. Now that we've broken the new ciphers, we don't want them changing them. Especially before D-Day."

Merrill grew angry. He was determined not to tell her that he'd been successful in his underwater swim two hours earlier; that nine U-boats would sink by the stern and render themselves as well as the sub berths useless. Nine less threats to the Allied armada! Whether sabotaged from *inside* or outside the pen, the technicality, at this point, was moot. The evidence was already there; removing the charges was unthinkable. Not enough time. He'd blow them to hell as planned and explain all after the fact.

"Do we understand each other?" she asked, tartly.

Merrill nodded, though he still yearned to leave a mold of

plastic inside the hull of the U-601. Of all the subs in the base, the Lion's boat deserved to die first. A rotten turn of events, Merrill thought. And why had he been kept in the dark until now? *Damn Sigi. Damn Colonel Foster.* Fury continued to sweep over him, and if not for the more immediate threat of Loewen, sitting vigilantly just inches away, he could easily strangle his partner's pretty throat. Hearing Erika cough, Merrill looked at her. She appeared agitated and ready to complain.

A sharp, disarming glare from Sigi made it unmistakably clear that the Dutch girl was to remain silent.

"Let's move, Dieter," Sigi instructed with a smile and a wink. "You too, are needed in England."

Odd, Merrill reflected. After all this she was still flirting with Loewen.

For the first time the U-boat ace laughed. It wasn't loud laughter, but to Merrill it was contemptuous and unsettling. Loewen, from all appearances, had no more amazement left in him. Ignoring Merrill, his amused gaze remained on Sigi. "The moment we leave this submarine, you'll be outnumbered and outgunned," he said with bravado. "And are you so foolish to expect me to remain silent?"

Sigi replied, "Like most men, Dieter, you underestimate my strength as a woman."

Merrill watched with interest as she went up to Loewen, in her eyes a strong hint of future intimate occasions. The German looked back at her surreptitiously with small red sparks in his eyes; it was obvious that he'd come to hate her with a passion. Merrill suspected she could strip in front of Loewen right now and he wouldn't bat an eyebrow.

The ace warned her, "We'll soon discover how weak or strong you are."

Sigi replied, "In any event, Herr Kapitan, my associate is more ruthless than I could ever be." Gesturing with her shoulder toward Merrill, she icily added, "He'll stop at nothing, I assure you."

Merrill nodded in swift agreement. *Clever vixen*, he thought. Belittles one minute, butters up the next. Whatever her game, he'd cooperate for the time being by doing a little persuading of his own. Merrill waved his Luger at Loewen. "Get on your feet and let's move."

The ace's battle banner was still flying. "You waste your

time threatening me. Far more important Germans than I have died for the Fatherland." He remained motionless, as if nailed to the bunk. "And I would not be the first U-boat ace to be sacrificed."

Merrill looked at him. "Quite correct, my friend. Prien, Schultze, Schepke—the elite of the *unterseeboot* guard—all eliminated. The famous as well as the infamous, like Werner Henke, who sunk the *Ceramic*. A passenger ship with women and children, correct? One survivor returned to tell the story after thousands were dumped at night into a stormy sea."

Loewen's calm remained impenetrable. "Your bombers leveled residential Dresden, including two crowded hospitals."

Merrill had a method for casting off any periodic tentacles of guilt from the terrors of war purportedly committed by Americans. He handled the problem of retribution by simply focusing back on the ugly, canted bridge and charred masthead of the *Arizona* protruding above the fiery waters of Pearl Harbor, and the 1,200 men who went down with her. Remembering the sights and smells he'd personally experienced on that fateful Sunday in Hawaii and the close friends lost in the sneak attack, Merrill's resolve for the task ahead hardened.

Merrill slowly shook his head and asked Loewen, "How many U-boats will you lose before waking up?"

"If it takes hardships and sacrifices to turn the tide of battle, the Reichskriegmarine is resolute. Grand Admiral Doenitz is a brillant tactician."

"He's about to become a tragic loser. As for this passion of yours—so big on sacrifice. For whom? Superiors swelling with superiority and fanaticism with medals?"

"A matter of duty. Undisciplined Americans will never understand."

Merrill again shook his head. "Your Nazi friends have never learned to change the bill of fare at their theater."

"Say what you mean," said Loewen, irritably.

"The world's had a toilet full of grand tragedy, that's what. Same old chips on the shoulder, same unhealed sores, the need to dramatize and romanticize."

Loewen glared at him. "I have no interest in Grand Opera. Nor am I a philosopher. I am a professional seaman."

"So am I. But I know a rotten cause when I see one. This

boat's a technological masterpiece, I'll hand you that. Better in many respects than our own. But the nation that built it has sold its soul to the devil."

Sigi said to Merrill, "Skeet, save it please."

"No. Let the worm squirm a little before it's confined."

Loewen's shell had not been penetrated. Staring holes in the air, he said coldly, "A good sailor must cut his sail to the new wind. You know very little of complicated German temperament."

"I know your pompous Nazi leaders are the ham actors of the century, and that's enough." Merrill thought for a moment. He needed to find a way to get Loewen to move out peacefully. "Already figured, Ace, you wouldn't mind suffering for the cause. But it's also a matter of your watching a few other innocent faces die needlessly if you don't cooperate." Merrill glanced at Erika and decided to do a little fabricating. "I can start, if you like, with the young tar—the *actress* in the sailor's uniform. You might be convinced she's a neutral Swede, but my partner here is convinced she's German, caught up in a counterespionage masquerade."

Loewen looked at Erika, then over to Sigi. Both of them avoided his eyes.

Merrill continued: "We're hiking out of this U-boat pen with the two of you in front of me. I'll be carrying a coat, under it this silenced Luger. One wrong word, one step out of line, and the young woman there dies first, then whoever else happens to be close by. You'll watch them fall and go last. Needless, unreasonable deaths. And you strike me as a reasonable man. I'm sorry, Kapitan. Confronted with our current odds, I'm not."

The ace fell silent, his face contracting slightly. He looked angry but at the moment defeated, helpless as a fly caught in a web. Suddenly there was the sound of squeaking gears, a wheel turning. Merrill's eyes darted to the round bulkhead door leading forward, the one Sigi had closed and dogged earlier. It was being cranked open from the far side! Merrill saw a perceptible spark of hope flit across Loewen's face as the bronze door slowly hinged open.

Body frozen and mouth agape, the diving officer, Leutnant Mueller, stared in disbelief at the situation confronting him. His eyes flashed with uncertainty.

Merrill knew their opponent was calculating the odds.

Abruptly, Mueller tried to heave closed the heavy hatch before him, but he was nowhere near as fast as Skeet Merrill's angry Luger. Mueller gasped as the hot lead seared his forearm.

Dieter Loewen's exclamation, whatever it might have been, caught in his throat like a cold ice cube. He swallowed hard and shook his head.

Merrill said to the wounded duty officer, "Step in here quietly. Very quietly if you want to live."

Mueller cursed. "Bastard!" Blood trickling from his arm, he hoisted himself through the bulkhead. He stood there, his body wavering and breath labored. Mueller's eyes glanced briefly above him, then he raised both hands slowly as if to surrender. But his one arm seemed to be reaching for something.

Merrill glanced upward, instantly recognizing the diving alarm. *The klaxon!* His Luger spat again, this time zeroing in on Mueller's hand. The diving officer winced in pain but wasn't about to give up. Madly, his other hand went for his holstered automatic. He managed to get it halfway brought up to aim at Merrill, but he was too late.

No choice now. Merrill fired for keeps.

Sigi stepped forward. "No!" she shouted.

Dieter Loewen flinched, sucked in a deep breath, and glared hatefully at Merrill.

"You see, Ace? I'm as desperate as your deck officer was foolishly stubborn. Don't try me."

Sigi stared incredulously at the crumpled body and blood spilling on the deck. "Fine work, Skeet. Just excellent. So what do we do with the incriminating evidence? Brazenly carry him out with us on a stretcher?"

Merrill ignored her, his brain clicking through the possibilities. He turned to Loewen, who sat impassively. "How much water outside the sub pen?"

"Drops off to at least fifteen meters," Loewen replied with a numb voice.

"That'll have to suffice. Any air in the tanks?" Catching Merrill's drift, the ace turned away, retiring into firm-lipped silence.

Merrill suspected the odds were excellent there would be plenty of pressure. He turned to Sigi. "Trust me, okay? We're all heading for the stern torpedo room." He gestured to Erika.

"You'll help me wrestle our dead friend through the passage-way. The two of us go first, then the Kapitan. Sigi, you'll follow with *this*." He handed her the Luger. "Don't think twice before using it on either Loewen or Erika."

"What then?" Sigi demanded.

"We wrap our incriminating corpse in bedding from one of the bunks and weight him down." Merrill turned to Erika. "It's your job, *sailor*, to round-up some heavy chain. You'll find enough of it overhead in the torpedo block and tackle. If there's a monkey wrench or sledge hammer nearby, throw them in the package for good measure. And don't either of you get any funny ideas with them. Sigi's as good a shot as I am."

"It won't work," Loewen grated. "There will be noise, air bubbles, and the hull will lurch. There are men topside."

"Yeah, I know. *Up forward*. You forget, the ass-end of this U-boat is facing out toward the basin. We fire a stern tube and propel the body out thirty feet where it drops off into deeper water. If the workers or the duty sailor above get nosy, tell them you were merely demonstrating to the journalists how a pickle is fired."

"Supposing I won't?"

Merrill smiled. "Simple enough. *Three* bodies go out through the tubes and the Fraulein and I take our chances. None of us, Kaleun, has any options left. Understand? Let's travel."

Up until this moment Merrill thought Erika looked tough. Now, as they pulled the body through the confining corridor, he discovered she was even stronger than he'd imagined.

Less than ten minutes later, the sub ace closed the breach, opened the outer doors, and fed a charge of air into the number-six torpedo tube. The U-601 shook slightly. The grisly chore over, Merrill led them back to the control room and waited while he had Erika wipe up the last traces of blood.

Without asking permission, Loewen sat on the bunk beside the fold-down desk. Nursing his misery, he rubbed the sides of his face with his palms. The woman he'd made passionate love with in a Paris hotel room just a day earlier was staring at him almost apologetically.

"Your pique is understandable, Dieter," she said quietly. "You also strike me as perceptive. We now have to move. Are you satisfied that my companion's silenced Luger means business?"

Masking his inner rage, Loewen nodded. Through narrow eyes he again considered Sigi, then Merrill and his Luger. Unseen by either of his captors, he managed to slide the silver letter opener off the desk and into his rear pocket.

Chapter 36

THE WOMAN UNDERTAKER was worried. Once more Marie Selva impatiently checked her watch. Forty-five minutes had passed since the agreed meeting time and still not a sign of the blonde woman and the impulsive American! Though they'd asked her to wait in the hearse, Marie had grown increasingly apprehensive. Had there been trouble? Curiosity finally got the better of her and she decided to check out the main gate. Leaving the hearse unattended in the side street, Marie walked rapidly toward the sub base entrance. The fitful offshore wind picked up and the rain, until now only a drizzle, began to fall harder.

SS Colonel Schiller smiled in relief, pleased to see the feisty little woman abandon the hearse. Eager to get out of the driving rain, Schiller left his vantage point across the street, hurried over to the vehicle and calmly climbed into the passenger side of the cab. Wiping the water from his face, he withdrew his service pistol, sat back, and slowly exhaled. At last he was ready to spring the trap.

Somewhere overhead a bolt of lightning tore across the sky; the deserted street grew more brilliant, then even darker than before. Reinhard Schiller considered the immediacy of his predicament. He wondered if von Wilme had reached Loewen in time to warn him. And would the enemy spies strike tonight, as Schiller suspected? If he ever wanted action in this war, he had it now, more than he could handle. Up until the present, Schiller's involvement in the conflict had been a matter of intelligence statistics assisting Heinrich Himmler—the mathematics of feasibility, probability, and inevitability; administrative decisions on who would walk away from an interrogation, who would go to a concentration camp for safekeeping, and who might be immediately eliminated. Gazing out into the dismal night, Schiller once more recalled his training, accomplishments, and promotions to date—uneventful, when compared to the daring exploits of other German officers he'd known in the field. Schiller still had no Iron Cross, only the lesser decorations. Still, he had been fortunate enough to be assigned to SS Supreme Command in Berlin. Schiller had earned the personal confidence of Heinrich Himmler, and he had several times shaken the hand of the Fuehrer.

Schiller pulled himself together, opened a slim silver case, and withdrew a cigarette. He lit it, inhaled the smoke, and felt deeply reconciled with himself and his place within this espionage battle. It was much better being the hunter than the hunted. Himmler had even hinted that there might even be an Iron Cross out of this dangerous assignment. *Provided Schiller's luck held.* Checking the cartridge of his Walther pistol, Schiller settled back in the shadow of the hearse cab and patiently waited.

Merrill had assigned Loewen and Erika the job of carrying the plastic-filled suitcases out of the base. Keenly aware that the U-boat ace's first hope of escape would be while passing by the tough security sentries, Merrill hovered close behind the German as they approached the gate. He kept his Luger ready, hidden beneath his folded greatcoat. With typical German rigidity and devotion to the rulebooks, the sentry demanded that Erika—still posing as the young sailor—surrender a leave permit.

"The pharmacist's mate is assisting us," Merrill said quickly. He held his breath as Sigi presented their own credentials and the permit for the photographic equipment.

Loewen bit his teeth as Merrill nudged him firmly with the concealed gun. Then, purely for the ace's consideration, he jabbed Erika as well with the weapon, causing her to flinch and rock forward. There was a warm, dancing malice in her eyes as she glared back at Merrill. The sub ace looked desperate, as if he wanted to signal the guard. Merrill's eyes remained on Loewen like a hungry hawk and the German backed down.

The duty man was still considering what to do. "The regulations are explicit, Fraulein," he said.

Merrill stared at Loewen. "Herr Kaleun, *tell him.*" He waited. The sub ace was apparently calculating his chances.

Loewen finally nodded to the guard. "It's all right, Sergeant," he said wearily. "I'll assume all responsibility."

"Sir!" replied the sentry, saluting and stepping back.

Immediately they were beyond the dogs and high electric fence, out into the rainy night. The weather, Merrill noted, appeared to be worsening.

Marie Selva came breathlessly up to them when they were a few yards from the gate. "*Mon Dieu!* We are running behind schedule!" she cried.

Sigi frowned. "Madame, your instructions were to stay with the transportation."

They hastened down the street without further dialogue. A short distance from the hearse, Merrill beckoned the group under the protection of a storefront awning. The street was deserted. "You can drop the bags and rest," he indicated to Loewen and Erika.

Water coursed down Marie Selva's face as she came out of the rain and hovered under the awning. Her expectant eyes darted from the two suitcases to the U-boat officer and Erika in the sailor's uniform. Now they focused on Merrill. "You brought the *plastique* back out? I don't understand."

He replied, "Neither do I. The lady made a change of plans."

"I don't understand," Marie repeated, nervously sniffing her palms.

"You will soon enough, Madame Selva," Sigi said flatly.

Dieter Loewen stood away from the others, withdrawing into himself in his own special way. His past, like a moth long corked up in a bottle and suddenly released, was flying at him, fluttering in his brain. What was he doing in this damning predicament? His fights, until now, had always been waged through a periscope eyepiece, win or lose situations involving tonnage sunk, firepower extended, and chances of escape. Technological odds that challenged and exhilarated him. The

Battle of the Atlantic had become a major driving-force in Loewen's life, and death as part of that lifestyle was regrettable. He had learned to accept its possibilities without fear, but the crisis confronting him now was totally new, personal, and immediate.

Loewen's eyes went back to the American's silenced Luger, and he bit his lip. He knew the moment deserved total alertness, not daydreaming.

Merrill could see that Marie Selva was becoming increasingly agitated.

"*Allons!*" she warned, "the sewer! If the heavy rain continues, the galleries will flood and be dangerous for us. We must hurry!"

Merrill turned to Sigi. "My cue, at last, boss-lady? Do we now proceed with the last act, or has it too, been subjected to rewrite?"

Sigi smiled, but she seemed caught up in a trance of thought.

Merrill stared back at her in chill silence. The rain didn't increase in its intensity, but the water falling on the pavement seemed to grow louder in Merrill's ears. She still stirred him to the core; while he waited for her to make up her mind, he suddenly felt cold. Vestigial signals were again going off in Merrill's proximity system.

Marie Selva's small eyes flashed in the dim light, not at Sigi, but toward Merrill. Impatiently, she said, "Roger and the mute are waiting, Monsieur." She seemed pleased to be the icebreaker.

Sigi gazed steadily at him. "Explosives expertise, Skeet," she said slowly.

Merrill winced. Now, suddenly, she was pushing. His mind raced with accumulating impressions of the contemporary Mata Hari before him. Here was a female spy who, he was forced to admit, had almost everything—except readability. He studied her one more time. As a woman she was completely unlike Merrill's former wife Diane, who had been inhibited by an uppity Southern social background that challenged his financial fitness and his Texas prairie manners. Nor could Sigi be compared to his devoted, dependable Molly back in her London nest. They were both birds of a different feather.

Once more Merrill felt a twinge of guilt. Sigi was fast, a

runaway express train to adventure if nothing else. She had everything a soldier-of-fortune type like himself might want or expect in a woman. *Almost*, but not quite. And it was this minuscule, fuzzy reservation that kept Merrill from making a complete ass of himself.

He handed Sigi the silenced Luger to cover the German, then bent over one of the suitcases and struggled with the clasp. Determined to take a packet or two of plastic with him, he shot her a pre-emptory glance. "There's a Tiger tank farther up the road. Some diversionary fireworks will take the heat off the base and the sewer below. Any objections, *Fraulein Schramm?*"

Sigi didn't answer. Her eyes, like those of the others, were glued to the contents of the luggage Merrill had just opened.

He stared, then ran his hand swiftly over the folded newspapers and bags of flour. "What the hell?" Merrill's voice was an enraged roar.

Hands on her hips, Marie Selva gave Merrill a swift, significant look. *"Egouts anciens!"* she shouted, her voice trembling. "Are the explosives down below safe?"

Merrill quickly opened and dumped the contents of the second suitcase. More of the same! Stunned, he looked at the others in turn. Sigi frowned; Erika gazed blankly at the useless bags of flour on the wet cobbles; Marie looked helplessly back at him; Loewen smiled thinly.

Merrill's temperature soared as he sent the German a clipped, derisive salute. "It appears, Kapitan, that you've got a bastard friend among us." Merrill's words were uttered with optimum contempt and sarcasm that was completely lost on the sub ace.

Loewen mockingly spread his hands in apology.

Merrill's mind raced back over his earlier brushes with death, clicking through the possibilities—Erika Vermeer, Marie Selva, Pierre Roger, the mute Duval, or someone he'd yet to meet? There wasn't time for detective work, not now. He and Sigi would somehow have to go it alone, trust only each other. He went up to her, whispered that fact in her ear, then whirled and headed out into the storm. The wind picked up and rattled in his ears as he ran. *They're raising the hurdles*, he thought, as he pounded along in the darkness toward the sewer entrance.

* * *

Held captive by three women! Or was it two? Loewen still wasn't sure whose side Erika was on. He sighed, then managed to smile in satisfaction as his opponents stared at one another in varying degrees of suspicion. The French woman, more than the others, seemed genuinely numbed by the complications confronting the enemy team.

Sigi turned her gaze on him.

Loewen smiled thinly in return, drew in a long breath of the night air, and slowly shook his head. "Your mission appears to have been penetrated, Fraulein." There wasn't a way in the world he could now call her by her real first name, for now he felt nothing but contempt for her. "What is more, has it occurred to any of you that when I am missed my superiors will immediately change the code?"

She slowly came up to him. Her eyes danced as she traced her fingers over his Iron Cross, admiring it. "Dieter, you disappoint me. You believe I'm so simple-minded and naive!" Aware that Marie and Erika were watching her, she hesitated, her easy smile fading. "You've over two weeks remaining of your leave, Kapitan. It's unlikely you will be missed until then and that is long enough for London's needs. It's entirely possible after the Admiralty is finished with your complicated new ciphers, that you'll be returned to your Fatherland at a later date."

Loewen grimaced. His retort was bald and brief: "In an English casket, no doubt?" Gazing out into the rain, Loewen felt a sudden, keyed-up, manic feeling of being unwittingly caught up in a losing poker game. He could very nearly still taste her lipstick, but now he hated her passionately. And the girl in the uniform—why had she suddenly become so silent and withdrawn?

"You are but one phase of the mission, Dieter. I'm sorry. The reasons——"

The French woman broke in, *"Entendu!* It is enough. I suspect he knows too much already. We should leave, yes?" She pointed to the hearse parked a short distance away.

Sigi waved her gun.

Walking slowly, Loewen looked back at Marie Selva. "It does not matter, Madame. Your daring plan has no chance of success. I'm a man of infinite patience and I'll wait. Whenever, I'll strike when the opportunity presents itself. You would be wise to kill me now, for I promise you neither the German code nor this many-lived cat will ever reach England!"

Sigi again menaced him with the Luger. "*Herr Lion,* if that name pleases you, kindly crawl in the back of the hearse." She turned to Marie. "You, Madame, will drive while I guard our friends in the back."

Finding his spine still menaced by the silencer-equipped weapon, Loewen reluctantly heaved himself into the rear of the vehicle. As silent as ever, Erika followed him, while Sigi, prudently measuring her distance, slid inside last. Sigi pulled the door closed and took a place opposite them, across the wooden casket. Loewen watched her carefully, but they all sat in silence.

Chapter 37

MARIE SELVA cursed both the change in plans and the rain as she dashed to the front of the hearse. She was halfway into the driver's seat before she saw the shadowy figure in the passenger side of the cab and the gun leveled steadily in her direction. A flash of lightning brightened the street, and she saw that her adversary wore a German officer's hat with the familiar skull and bones insignia of the SS. From beneath the visor a pair of cold, unfriendly eyes bore in on her with intense concentration.

"Come, come, Madame. Close the door and start the engine," the intruder instructed. "Stay away from the glass slider and do not look in the back of the hearse. Not a whimper, if you value your life!" The SS officer's warning was no more than a whisper, almost lost in the sound of pouring rain.

Her heart thumping like a captured bird's, Marie obediently closed the door, rested both hands on the steering wheel, and gave up an audible sigh. She felt helpless. If she were younger and prettier, she flashed, there might be other options. So much for fate.

"Now we go," her captor demanded. "It is near the hour for your radio contact with London, agreed, Madame Selva?"

Marie tried, unsuccessfully, to conceal the expression of amazement flickering across her face.

"My name is Schiller. Colonel Reinhard Schiller, SS Amt 4-E, Berlin."

Marie put aside her surprise and stared with scorn at him. The name Schiller meant nothing to her, but the uniform and important rank said enough.

He quickly instructed, "You'll proceed with your journey precisely as planned."

Marie remained stubbornly immobile.

"Come now, must I navigate?" Schiller leveled his 9mm Walther directly at her head and snapped, "Drive to the mortuary on Rue d'Anjou, and quickly!"

Grimly, she put the hearse into gear. *Que signifie?* The German knew more than she'd have guessed. The hearse's headlights cut feebly through the rain that shrouded everything as Marie reluctantly drove back to her house. She knew the cab's rear window was too small for those in back to see the intruder who menaced them. How was she going to warn Sigi and Erika?

The rear of the hearse was cramped and Loewen's knees were under his chin. He watched Sigi open the hinged lid of the casket and gesture with her Luger.

"Now Dieter, you must trust me. Kindly cooperate by climbing inside the box."

A vision from the grave clouding his thoughts, Loewen eyed the casket warily. For several minutes he'd been glaring at Sigi with hate and scorn, but now he shot her a look of pained incredulity. "I am a German officer, entitled to proper——"

"Do not resist me," she interrupted. "Kapitan, you'll be comfortable enough. You see? The coffin is padded and lined with satin. And the French undertaker was considerate enough to provide air holes for breathing. You are of no value to us dead, I assure you. Quickly now, climb inside."

Loewen wet his lips and folded his arms across his chest. The Third Reich's sole surviving U-boat ace did not intend to cower inside any coffin—lined with fine purple satin or otherwise. His insistent adversary was determined enough, but was she an accurate shot? The Luger she leveled his way, he noted, rested carelessly on one end of the open casket. Just a brief distraction and he might slam the lid on her hand, deflecting the weapon. But he was too far away. Erika was between them, closer, and in an ideal position, but would she cooperate? She was just sitting there, angular and awkward, as if waiting for him to do something. Together, if she were in fact on his side, they might make a stand of it.

Slowly, a fraction of an inch at a time, Loewen slipped the

slender letter opener from his rear pocket and nudged it toward her.

Glancing down at the sharp stiletto, Erika turned pale. For a long time, like a frightened, trapped animal, she stared back at him. She reached for the would-be weapon and brought it up before her. Forlornly, she said to Loewen, "I'm sorry, Kapitan. Out of necessity, my little performance must come to an end."

"In Faust's name!" Loewen shouted. His face reddened as he bit back the bitterness he felt in his throat. "*You as well*," he whispered. He stared at Erika in disbelief, trying to find in her closed expression some clue to her real identity. Repeatedly he shook his head.

She said softly, "In addition to being a displaced *boui-boui* entertainer, Herr Kapitan, I am with the Dutch Resistance."

Loewen watched Sigi gesture for Erika to hand over the would-be weapon. The distraction, brief enough, was what Loewen had been waiting for. He pounced on the casket lid as deftly and quickly as a mongoose after a snake. The Luger, knocked from Sigi's hand, went off with a sharp click, sending a bullet ripping through the coffin's satin lining. The gun dropped to the floor.

Loewen catapulted across the casket in one fluid, easy movement. Sigi threw up her arms to protect herself but his broad hands grabbed her by the neck, powerful fingers digging into her throat. Loewen had every intention of throttling her, choking out the very last breath, but from the corner of his eye he saw a sudden blur. He was too late to react. His head exploded in fire as the butt end of the Luger crashed against his skull. The darkness was immediate.

Erika hoped she hadn't given their war prize a concussion. Her hand trembled as she handed the gun back to Sigi.

Reopening the casket, they managed to topple the unconscious U-boat ace inside. Together they quickly bound his wrists and ankles with a roll of surgical tape Marie Selva had left in the coffin. Sigi took the letter opener, and despite Erika's sharp glare of disapproval, cut the ribbon which bore Loewen's Iron Cross to his tunic. Without explanation, she thrust the medal into her purse. Erika wanted to say something, but bit back her protest as Sigi slammed the casket lid shut.

The hearse braked to a halt and Erika assumed they'd

reached Marie Selva's undertaking parlor. She heard footsteps in the street and immediately the rear door opened. But now another gun, this time a Walther automatic, stared her in the face. The weapon, she noted, also covered Sigi.

Erika let out a sharp sigh and raised her hands. Sigi did likewise. As they crawled out of the hearse, Erika saw the newly-acquired letter opener fall into the wet street. She watched as the familiar SS colonel ceremoniously clicked his heels on the wet pavement.

"Good evening, *Frauleins*. Ah yes, *Anna Schramm*—or should I say Sigi Petersen?" He turned to Erika, squinted through the rain, and pulled down his cap. "Is that frozen stare of yours only for the gun, or do you recognize me? I believe we've met before, at Wilhelmshaven or Ploen? Erika, yes? Is your last name Vermeer or Krager? I must admit my impatience to find out whom you really work for, young woman." Schiller eyed her uniform. "And I use the term loosely."

Erika stood her ground. "Take a leap, Colonel Schiller."

"American slang? The idiom escapes me, but I fear it's hardly complimentary."

Marie Selva stood cautiously off to one side of the German as if waiting for an opening. Schiller edged closer to the hearse, trying to see into the darkness beyond Sigi and Erika. His eyes narrowed on the closed casket. "*Kaleun* Loewen?"

Erika said calmly, "He's safe enough. Inside the coffin."

Schiller glared back at her, then turned to Marie. "The U-boat ace in one of your French caskets, Madame? A wooden box? Abominable! You'll pay dearly for this later."

Marie bristled but kept her silence.

Erika's gaze remained on the SS colonel and his gun, wondering how she might distract him. Marie Selva, too, appeared to be waiting with the patience of a puma, ready to strike. If only Schiller's gun hand would waver!

Scowling, the German reached for the coffin lid. Erika edged forward, but before she could act, the woman undertaker saw her chance. Marie leaped, managing a quick hammerlock on Schiller's neck from behind. The colonel's gun hand shot skyward, but his grip on the Walther remained firm. Sucking in her breath, tiny Marie fought like a tigress. She climbed higher on the SS man's back, tightening her choke-hold and kicking her feet into Schiller's waist and stomach.

Erika jumped down from the hearse, looking for an opening

to grab the colonel's menacing pistol. She watched Marie gouge Schiller's eyes repeatedly and kick harder until both their struggling bodies tumbled to the cobblestones. The rain increased. Despite her size, Marie fought with a fury, slamming the colonel's hand repeatedly against the ground, trying to break his grip on the Walther. *"Basta!"* she shouted. But Schiller brought up a fist that landed square in her jaw and she rocked backward. Instantly, the much larger German was on top of her and bearing down. Schiller had lost his hat and the rain pelted his blond crewcut. Wiggling like a worm but unable to get away, Marie called out to Erika, "Quickly! On the street, pick up the knife! *Allons*, you must use it!"

Erika fell to her knees behind the hearse and found the stiletto in a pool of water. She found it quickly, but hesitated, caught up in a sudden strange panic. The repercussions would be unbelievable if they killed Heinrich Himmler's right-hand man. Partisans had done it before in Czechoslovakia and an entire town had been wiped from the face of the earth. Erika shook, feeling the ambiguity and reality of the spy business as she'd never felt them before.

Erika saw Schiller fighting to wrench his gun hand free from Marie's grip, trying to bring its muzzle to bear, and he was succeeding. The woman undertaker's eyes grew as wide as a tawny owl's.

The French woman shouted again. *"Mon Dieu!* Please strike now!"

Erika's brain flashed. Thinking again of the children taken from the orphanage to the ovens, her arm came crashing down, driving the stiletto into the colonel's back. The six-inch, shiny sharp blade penetrated the oilskin raincoat and serge jacket but went into the body less than half an inch. She withdrew the weapon and with all her strength thrust it in again. This time the sterling silver hilt with the inlaid swastika came to a halt with a dull, sickening thump. Sweat coarsing down her face with the rain, she turned back to Sigi, as if seeking approval. The Norwegian woman had gone back inside the hearse to retrieve the Luger, but now it wouldn't be needed.

Marie Selva rolled aside, gasping for air.

Bewildered, his face stiffening with pain, Reinhard Schiller dropped his gun and spun around, clutching at his back as if stung by a hornet. A sudden convulsion went through the SS colonel's body. Erika backed away and watched Schiller collapse, cough up blood, and stare back at her with veiled eyes. "You cannot succeed—the great invasion force is doomed to——" The German's voice faltered. "I personally may have failed the Fuehrer, but others must succeed. You are outnumbered." His voice trailed off into an unintelligible whisper.

The pain Schiller felt from the letter opener, the pain that preceded death, had reached Erika. She suddenly felt confused. A tremor began in her shoulders and spread rapidly over her body until she was shaking like a punished puppy. She looked away, feeling a twinge of regret for the man who had pursued her for so long. The SS colonel was too clever to die, but knew too much to live. She picked the Walther off the street and tossed it into the hearse.

Marie Selva still lay on the ground catching her breath.

Ignoring her, Erika watched Schiller as if mesmerized. His face suddenly fell sideways into a puddle of water as he gave up an unpleasant grunt that was half moan and half rattle. With dreadful understanding, she knew SS Colonel Schiller was dead.

"More trouble now," Sigi called to her. "Another body on our hands and an important one at that."

The little Frenchwoman, apparently put out that they had moved too slowly to help her, cursed several times, wiped the mud from her face, and climbed unsteadily to her feet.

Erika bent over the dead German. Withdrawing the stiletto from Schiller's back, she rolled him face up. The dead man's glazed eyes stared up her. Erika's thoughts ventured back over Schiller's chase—from Holland, through Germany, and Paris. The flashbacks—discomforting memories Erika couldn't share with the others—wandered so far that the effort to bring them into focus was a physical ordeal, a brutal tug on her brain.

The storm became a downpour, washing the recollections away. Erika vaguely heard the woman undertaker shouting at her.

"Yes, Madame?" The rain ran down her cheeks and off her chin in a river that connected her to the ground.

"Hurry. We must carry the Gestapoman's body into the house!" Marie turned to Sigi, whose eyes remained strangely fixed on the casket inside the hearse. "Don't concern yourself with the U-boat ace now," she cried, closing and securing the vehicle's rear door. "You two did bind him well, I assume?"

Erika nodded. Shaking the rain from her face and putting away her downcast mood, she helped Marie and Sigi carry Schiller's body into the building. They struggled with it down the long hallway to the embalming chamber. Marie Selva took off her wet coat and immediately went to work. She said with concern, "I worry about our friends in the sewer."

"If anyone can accomplish the job, I'm sure it's Skeet Merrill," Sigi countered, making a half-hearted attempt to be buoyant. She, too, took off her soaked outergarments. Nervously lighting a cigarette, she blew a long column of smoke toward the ceiling.

Erika for the first time was concerned about the vulnerability of the American. She made up her mind to put dislike aside and do what she could. Had events taken a different turn, she would have the code, not Sigi. Erika knew that without Hugh Cummings in the picture, the American would be a big help in getting Sigi and the sub ace out of France. Still, if worse came to worse, Merrill, like Dieter Loewen, would be expendable.

Erika once more stared at Sigi, trying to read her thoughts. The Norwegian woman knew well enough that the document stashed inside her blouse was worth any price that might have to be paid to see it safely to England.

Dieter Loewen, his brain still reeling from the blow to the head, lay still in the darkness of the coffin listening to the sounds around him. He'd heard agitated voices and the sounds of a fight and at the conclusion the terrible silence of death. Wriggling his bound hands, Loewen felt the tape bite into his wrists. He cursed, berating the closeness of the casket and the dark power of circumstance holding him so helpless.

Straining against his bonds, he again felt a chafing pain and he gave up the struggle. Loewen's mind wandered erratically. He thought of U-boat crews drowning at sea, and of his wife and daughter buried in the bombed-out rubble of Dusseldorf. Why had God taken their innocent lives instead of his guilty one? He pondered the possibility of being better off dead himself. The desperate thought sank into him repeatedly, and his mind could go no further.

Chapter 38

IT HAD ALL gone wrong for Erika, and it was Sigi's fault. But they were on the same team and now Erika felt an urge to go up to the Norwegian woman, touch her lightly, and offer congratulations. Sigi had removed her blouse and was changing out of her wet clothing; her breasts were plainly visible through her soaked brassiere.

Erika watched all this, then closed her eyes, thinking: She's not only smart, but sensuous. I would like to make love to her but it is impossible.

Except for the small metallic sounds Marie was making at the embalming table, the silence in the room grew ominous. Erika put her admiring gaze at Sigi away and turned to the woman undertaker. "If no one else has a solution, I suggest we truck Colonel Schiller's body to the forest outside the city."

Marie looked up from her work. "Too dangerous! The pouring rain would turn any burial effort to mud. The discovery of a fresh grave in the critical days ahead would compromise our mission."

"I say the river," insisted Sigi. "Less chance of discovery."

The French woman shook her head vehemently. "Far too risky for us. The waterfront is heavily patroled. Discovery of a high-ranking SS officer's body in St. Nazaire would result in horrible reprisals. A very important corpse indeed, this Schiller." Marie pointed to the cuff markings on the German's blood-stained uniform. "Heinrich Himmler's personal staff, I regret to say." She continued to work feverishly on the lifeless form, stretching it across the stainless steel table, folding the hands at waist level. She looked at them again. "Demonical as it may sound, I believe I have the answer."

Erika and Sigi both sent her a quizzical look.

Marie smiled at them. "Time, my dears, we desperately need time."

With mixed curiosity and apprehension, Erika watched the short woman stand on a stool, roll up her sleeves and fasten a hand pump to a large container of formaldehyde. Marie then calmly proposed, "There is a way we can *delay* discovery of the colonel's incriminating remains. Erika, out back, in the storage shed. There are several empty wine barrels. Select the best one, along with a lid to seal it properly, and bring it inside. Sigi, if you'll be kind enough to help her. Go quickly now."

Erika was anxious to end the death watch and be rid of Reinhard Schiller's oppressively silent company. Immediately, she darted outside. Sigi reluctantly followed. Erika's mind started to spin again. Might she lightly embrace the Norwegian woman in the darkness? *No, keep to the task at hand.*

They worked silently and quickly in the shed. By the time they returned with the barrel the Frenchwoman had already drained the remainder of the blood from the SS man's body.

"Please hurry, Madame," Sigi pleaded. She retreated into a corner, slumped down on a stool, and lit another cigarette.

Erika looked at her and said softly, "You smoke too much."

Suddenly the telephone rang in the outer hallway.

"Undoubtedly business," said Marie, not looking up from her work. "They expire at all hours. We can't risk being interrupted now. My assistant is off duty, so I will ignore the call."

The telephone continued to clamor for what must have been two minutes, agitating the three of them by its persistence. The Frenchwoman took on a look of sharp concern. At last there was silence.

For a long time Sigi gazed blankly at Schiller's lifeless form on the embalming table. Then she rose, went to her purse, and withdrew Dieter Loewen's Iron Cross. Turning it over in her hands, she examined it casually. Erika said to her, "Colonel Schiller knew all along we were taking the sub ace to England."

Marie Selva frowned, padded across the room, and took the medal from Sigi. "This souvenir is a bad omen. It would only bring you bad luck, Mademoiselle." Marie returned with it to the body. Shrugging, she calmly tied its red, white and black ribbon around Reinhard Schiller's neck. "*Aux morts*," she intoned. "*Aux grands morts*—to the dead, so be it. After his hard work, the colonel must not be sent back to the Fatherland unrewarded, no?" Propping the dead SS officer upright, without ceremony she let the body plummet head first into the empty wine barrel.

Erika looked away, repelled by the scene.

Sigi, too, wrinkled her face in disapproval. "Your humor does not move me, Madame Selva," she said soberly. "Such a squalid scene."

Marie ignored them, struggling to push one of Schiller's feet into the barrel.

Erika watched with mixed scorn and curiosity as the woman undertaker began transferring the pale yellow contents of a nearby steel drum into the barrel.

"Formaldehyde," Marie explained with calm indifference. "He'll be as well-preserved as a laboratory fetus. A more tidy job, mind you, than the British did on Lord Nelson when they shipped his body back from Trafalgar in a cask of brandy!"

Sigi winced. "This makes my blood run cold." Her voice was higher and more intense than it had ever been before.

Marie shrugged and continued to work the pump. Her eyes flashed like the shiny swords on Loewen's Iron Cross as she said, "I'm sorry, but death is my business. Under the best of conditions, the work hardly appeals to feminine sensitivity. I have learned to be thick-skinned out of necessity." She smiled and pointed to the side of the wooden barrel. "Look at this, my dears."

Erika noted the large black stencilled letters that read MUSCADET.

"Our fine Breton wine, made only from grapes grown near Nantes," Marie emphasized. "A barrel of this vintage would be extremely welcome back in Germany, yes? I suggest we ship it as far as we can, by the slowest possible means. To Berlin, perhaps? To Schiller's superior, the notorious Heinrich Himmler? No, better yet, to the Fuehrer himself."

"You're a bit of a sadist, Marie," Sigi scolded.

"The situation demands heartless expediency, *mon cher*. It's imperative the Gestapoman's body not be discovered in Brittany. Retribution would be horrendous." Marie sniffed the palms of her hands, thought for a moment, then placidly continued, "If God is with us, our consignment will not arrive at its destination until after St. Nazaire is liberated."

The telephone began ringing again, insistent.

Sigi was tired and had a slight headache. The streets were slick with rain as she drove the hearse to the *gare*. Beside her, Erika sat silently. She, too, had changed into dry clothes, abandoning the sailor's uniform for some civilian clothing rounded up by Marie Selva. It was the first time any of them had seen Erika in a skirt. The woman undertaker had remained behind to make her radio contact with London at the prescribed hour.

Peering through the windshield, a pulse of concentration pounded in Sigi's temples as she fretted over the French-woman's explicit instructions for shipping the wine barrel. *Distance. They needed to buy time.* When they arrived at the station, Sigi backed the hearse out of the rain, under the protective cover of the freight dock. She turned to Erika. "You can't risk being seen at the shipping office. Remain in the cab." Sigi knew her own face at the consignment desk hardly mattered, for with any degree of luck she'd be out of France in a matter of hours.

Waving his clipboard, a well-fed Frenchman wearing a green eyeshade came out of the darkness and greeted her at the rear of the hearse. "Closed! Closed!" he bellowed.

"Do you speak German?" Sigi asked with impatience.

"A little," the freight clerk replied, surprised to discover his customer was not French. "But I am sorry, Fraulein. No shipments or deliveries are permitted after dark."

Sigi threw open the back door of the hearse and emphatically thrust a twenty Reichsmark note into the attendant's palm. "For you. This is a very special consignment, Monsieur." She paused, permitting her voice to become a measure more respectful of his authority. "How long will it take this barrel of vintage to reach East Prussia? Rastenburg?"

Guardedly, the Frenchman eyed first the wine barrel, then the coffin in the back of the vehicle. He thrust the money back toward her, but she deliberately ignored it. "Fraulein," he stammered, "both the French and German railroads are national disasters. There is every probability your consignment will never reach its destination, and if by miracle it does get through after rerouting and delays of higher priority military cargo, the shipment would take almost a month. I'll give you some advice, yes? Carry a bottle or two of Muscadet with you back to Germany."

Sigi's manner became harder, more insistent. "This wine is not for me, Monsieur." Not blinking an eye, she fabricated, "The Muscadet is a favorite of the Fuehrer." She hesitated, kicking herself for this worst lie of all, wondering if the freight man knew that Hitler didn't imbibe. "I'm sure my Gestapo superiors would take a dim view of your refusing me."

An unsettling laugh, not unlike hiccups, rattled in the Breton's throat.

"Must I call them?" The timbre of her voice didn't invite further discussion.

The overweight Frenchman stopped laughing. Beneath the green visor she could see his eyes dilate. Immediately he hand-trucked the wine barrel into the freight shed and waited while Sigi filled out the necessary papers for the shipment to Adolf Hitler's redoubt near Rastenburg. She addressed the consignment to the Fuehrer himself, in care of his aide Martin Bormann, then paid the bewildered attendant the freight fee in French banknotes.

"I must tell you, Fraulein, this is a gamble of good money, for there's no way of insuring whether this shipment will, at this stage in the war, reach its destination."

Sigi could have cared less; the man inside the barrel was dead, of no use to anyone. *Now or later*. She said goodbye to the attendant and headed back to the hearse. Smiling sagely to Erika, they quickly drove off.

The *Gare des Voyageurs* was on the opposite side of the tracks, but Sigi made the distance in quick time. Her plan now was to let Erika go without ceremony, but an awkward silence seemed to submerge the two of them. Shutting off the hearse engine to conserve petrol, she looked at Erika, pressing her fingers lightly against her cheek. The young lesbian woman gazed back with a startled look. For several minutes they stared at each other in silence.

Finally Sigi said simply, "Good luck, Erika." She grabbed the Dutch girl's hand, squeezed it, and held on.

Blushing lightly, Erika looked troubled.

"You're trembling," Sigi whispered. "Why?"

Erika hesitated for a moment, then said in a dull voice, "The night grows colder."

Sigi studied her, then asked bluntly, "Have you ever been with a man, Erika?"

The Dutch girl's eyes widened. She stared back at Sigi for several seconds, then finally smiled with effort.

In her hand Sigi felt Erika's pulse begin to pound rapidly. She immediately regretted her question. It wasn't fair to mock or taunt the young woman. "No matter," she sighed. "You've time enough."

"You're wrong. I've been with several men, and all were distasteful. Including Hermann von Wilme in Paris."

Stunned, Sigi stared at her, trying to decide what to say next. No thoughts came. Reaching into her purse, Sigi withdrew a handful of francs and handed them to Erika. "You may have need of these back in Paris."

The Dutch girl nodded, thanked her, and gazed out into the rain. Opening the passenger side door, she prepared to make a run for it. "Goodbye, Sigi," she said uneasily.

Sigi looked across the truck cab at her as if thoughts long submerged had begun to gnaw into the present. She felt strangely compelled to touch Erika's forehead and gently brush her fingers across the younger woman's mouth and eyes. Very softly, Sigi said, "Goodbye and good luck, *Erika Krager*."

A troubled contrition replaced Erika's innocent smile. "For the past few years I've become used to the name Vermeer and have heard no other." Smiling, she let go of Sigi's hand and turned away.

Sigi watched for a long time as Erika ran off at a masculine trot into the darkened station.

Realizing that she was finally alone in the hearse with the U-boat ace, Sigi sighed with impatience. She turned and looked through the glass slider at the casket in back, debating whether this was the moment to open it and confront Loewen. There were private things that had to be said, the sooner the better.

Before Sigi could make her move, she was startled by a sudden tap on the passenger side window. She turned and saw Pierre Roger throw open the door. His beret and coat were soaking wet.

Roger slid quickly inside and said to her, "Something is wrong. Maurice Duval ran off. Disappeared."

Sigi stared at him. "The mute isn't inside the station, waiting?"

"Duval came with me to the *gare*, but he wandered off and has not returned. I'm accustomed to his quiet coming and going, but this time I fear trouble." Roger glanced in the back of the hearse. "I saw you leave Erika off, but where is Madame Selva?"

"She waits for me at the undertaking parlor. Tell me, Pierre. Where is Lieutenant Merrill now?"

Roger looked cheerless. "We left him in the sewer to set off the dynamite. By now he should have been on his way back to Marie Selva's, but I've heard no explosion. We must go look for him."

"Hardly necessary for you to come, Pierre. You'll miss your train to Paris."

He looked at her, stiffening. "There will be no departure for two hours. You must find Merrill and I have to find the mute. Let's go."

Sigi gave him a reluctant look. "As you wish." She started the engine and shifted into gear. Without further conversation they headed back to the undertaking parlor, driving slowly down Boulevard Paul Leferme and skirting around the U-boat base perimeter.

"Still no explosion," she said to Roger in a subdued voice.

"Peculiar. The explosives were intact and ready. The American was almost ready with the detonators when we left him."

Turning up rue d'Anjou toward Marie Selva's, Sigi felt a sudden, sharp uneasiness. The door to the undertaking parlor was ajar, swinging unchecked in the rain-driven wind. A bright stream of light from the hallway violated the St. Nazaire blackout as it shimmered on the wet pavement. Sigi shivered with discomfort. She turned and saw that Roger too, appeared apprehensive, his small mouth tightening as his eyes examined the dead-end street.

"Odd," she said to him.

Roger rubbed his chin. "I suggest, as a precaution, we park the hearse a few blocks away. You must protect your prized cargo in the back, at all costs."

Sigi nodded. They drove away from the funeral parlor in silence. Instinctively, she groped in her purse, feeling for the Luger. Then she remembered. *Not there*. She'd left it with

Marie Selva earlier. The SS colonel's Walther was still in the back of the hearse, but as a precaution she'd leave it there—an insurance policy for later. For the present she'd rely on Roger and his weapon. "You do have your gun, Pierre?"

Roger patted his coat. "Of course." There was a faint mocking tone to his voice.

The hearse edged left on the wet street and Roger held on. Sigi straightened the wheel, peering through the wiper's fast flickings. She needed to concentrate on the driving.

Finding a secluded spot in the shadow of a bomb-damaged building, she pulled the vehicle up to the curb. As they climbed out, a dog ran from a gap in the structure and began barking loudly. Ignoring the animal, Sigi gestured for Roger to quickly follow her down the deserted street. When they turned the corner into the ominously silent rue d'Anjou, Sigi again saw the light from the entry. The door was still open, swinging in the wind. The house was quiet enough. They hesitated. Sigi said, "I suspect Skeet Merrill's still back in the sewer trying to make his detonators work. Wait here, Roger, while I get Marie. We'll all go for him."

She stepped inside and closed the door against the wind, securing the loose latch. *The door had blown open on its own*, she assured herself. "Madame Selva?" Sigi's summons was met only by her own echo from the far end of the tile corridor. The house was strangely hushed. She called out again, but there was no answer. Guardedly, Sigi pushed open the double doors to the embalming room.

Her breath caught in her throat. She drew back instantly, both hands pressed against her face in disbelief. The room was demolished.

For a full minute Sigi's eyes swept over the destruction. Drawers were torn from their cabinets, pictures ripped from the walls, chemical drums overturned and leaking. The room had the cloying odor of formaldehyde—*and death*. The heavy embalming table lay on its side, the broken model of the U-boat base scattered from one end of the chamber to the other. Sigi moved around the table and saw, in one corner of this orgy of destruction, the inanimate form of Marie Selva.

Sigi could almost smell the blood. It was everywhere! She instinctively wanted to back away from the obviously tortured Frenchwoman and run outside for Roger, but a slight, barely discernible movement of Marie's foot caught her eye. Sigi bent over her. The woman undertaker's face was grotesquely distorted, the swollen orbs that passed for eyes were dull and unmoving, but her lips quivered.

"*Je suis fini*," she managed to spit out with difficulty. The words seemed to toll in the room. "I am finished," she repeated, summoning her strength. "But the soul of France is not broken." Gasping for air, she added, "The Gestapo—they saw—my shoe——" She wasn't able to complete the sentence; there was a final cough and her labored breathing trailed off. Sigi felt Marie's pulse diminish to nothingness. The Frenchwoman's once lively eyes, now a dull brown, stared back at her in the blind reproach of death. A pain throbbed in Sigi's throat and she felt a numb despair. Looking nervously around the room, she remembered the radio transmitter. Had Marie been able to get through to London?

Scurrying to the lavatory, Sigi found the wooden medicine cabinet splintered and hanging from the wall. What had once been a powerful transceiver was now a mass of crushed metal and broken glass tubes. Several hard blows from the butt end of a rifle had ended its usefulness forever. Sigi felt one of the shattered tubes. *Still warm.* Had Marie been caught while transmitting, or after?

Telling herself not to panic, Sigi hurried back to the body. What had been Marie's dying rattle? Something about *her shoe*. Sigi bent over the Frenchwoman's still form. There, barely visible, protruding from the heel rise was a folded piece of paper. She quickly retrieved it and read the scrawled notation:

8:00 A.M.—TEN MILES OFF LE POULEGEN— FISHERMAN FELIX—REPEAT 24 HOURS IF NEC- ESSARY

This was followed by the coordinates. Sigi frowned and thought for a moment. Feeling a measure of encouragement, she tucked the message inside her brassiere next to the other important documents. Once more her eyes flashed around the room, thinking of the silencer-equipped Luger pistol she'd left with Marie. Little chance it would be here now.

Suddenly from outside, there was the noise of automobile brakes rapidly applied, then several gunshots. Sigi ran back down the hallway, turned out the lights, and peeked through the narrow entry window at the street below.

Diagonally blocking rue d'Anjou at the corner was a black

Mercedes and protruding from its rear window was a hand clutching an automatic. *More gunfire*! Sigi looked out on the stoop and saw Roger fall. Hit in the side and bleeding, he started to crawl toward the door, then abruptly turned and began firing again. Throwing open the door, Sigi grabbed Roger's arm, summoned her strength, and pulled him inside. More bullets struck the front of the house, then there was an unsettling silence.

Sigi ventured a look out the window.

Beside her, Roger clasped his bleeding side and battled to regain his feet. Stumbling to the window, he gasped, "There are only three of them. An unarmed driver and two men in back. *Mon Dieu*! Look!"

Sigi saw a short, balding man jump out of the rear of the Mercedes, grab a pad of paper from the uniformed SS officer inside, quickly examine it, then dash off down the street. *Maurice Duval!* Sigi's mind raced in confusion. Was the mute actually on the German team or was he a plant?

Without consulting her, Roger broke the window and leveled his Luger at the Mercedes. He got off three shots before the entry was plastered by return fire. Roger reloaded and fired again.

Pressed against the wall, Sigi looked at the shattered entry window, then down at her arms, now covered with Roger's blood. She felt like a wounded mermaid who had met her first tiger shark. If she ever admitted to needing Skeet Merrill, she needed him now. To make matters worse, Roger now clicked an empty gun.

"No more ammunition," he admitted with a faltering voice. "I suggest we get out of here—while there's still time. Knowing the *boche*—they'll wait—for reinforcements—with automatic weapons—before storming the building."

Something in Sigi's mind snapped, then shouted, move! *Move quickly*! There was only one direction they could flee, back to the embalming chamber and Marie Selva's secret exit. If it was still intact. Pulling Roger's arm over her shoulder, they struggled down the hallway.

Chapter 39

SIGI HAD STRONG doubts that Pierre Roger would make it. His eyes were glassy and disoriented, and the bleeding from his side had not abated despite the towel compression she'd given him.

Hurriedly, she sized up the solid wood door to the bathroom. It appeared durable enough to defy strong shoulders, but she knew the ancient barrel lock, made for decency purposes only, wouldn't stand a chance against a volley of bullets. Still, it might slow them down. Sigi slammed the door and struck home the rusty bolt. Trundling the ancient bathtub away from the wall, she hastily peeled back the linoleum and flung open the trap in the floor.

"Go ahead—it is safe," said Roger, with difficulty.

She immediately dropped down the ladder into a cold and foreboding pit, smarting at the dank smell that closed in around her. Roger closed the trap door and struggled halfway down the ladder after her, but he lost his footing and fell the rest of the way. She tried to help him but he waved her away.

Sigi's foot struck a small wooden container. In it, she found the emergency items Marie Selva, at her earlier indoctrination, had promised would be there: a powerful flashlight, two hand grenades, several tins of military rations, and a first aid kit. Sigi grabbed the flashlight. Her heart hammering in her throat, she surveyed the dirt tunnel in both directions.

Sigi saw Roger scramble to his knees, his face a worsening, contorted mask of death. She watched him crawl unevenly toward a slender, upright metal box with a wooden plunger— the detonator, with its copper wires leading back up to the

embalming chamber! Roger's trembling hands struggled to pull
the handle up, arming the mechanism. He looked at her, smiled
thinly, and murmured, "*Adieu, l'amie.*" Clutching his side and
grimacing with pain, he fell on top of the plunger.

The next thing Sigi knew she was sprawled on the floor of
the tunnel, her nose half-buried in rubble. Her flashlight still
glowed, but illuminated nothing but settling dust. In her
twilight state, it was several moments before her brain sorted
itself out and everything began to make sense again. Roger had
evidently known about the location of the charge and that they
would come out of it safely, though thoroughly shaken. Sigi's
eardrums ached from the thunder of the blast overhead and her
lungs were choked with dust and smoke. She crawled over to
Roger, who lay motionless beside the detonator. Her flashlight
found the gaping bullethole in his side and she knew it was no
good; blood continued to ooze steadily from the wound. She
turned his face toward her and edged back, startled. Roger's
eyes were open, staring back at her in endless stupefaction.
Sigi felt for a pulse, but there was nothing.

Fighting back the dizziness, she shook the dirt from her hair
and felt for broken bones on her own body. There were none,
only more bruises than she cared to count. She struggled with
her brassiere and felt inside; thankfully, the code and escape
rendezvous notation were still intact as were her other assets.

When the dust finally cleared, Sigi saw that the ladder and
trap door had disappeared, buried behind a mass of splintered
timbers and bricks. The only noise now was the diminishing
trickle of dirt and debris from above. Her trail was neatly
sealed off, with no way to go back if she wanted to. And Roger
was dead. She'd now have to go it alone.

Sigi waited until the high-pitched clangor in her ears
subsided, then took her bearings. She had to find her way out
of here, rendezvous with Skeet Merrill, and get back to the
hearse and Dieter Loewen. She thought of Maurice Duval who
had so effectively messed up her plans. *Damn the deaf-mute!*
She wondered how much Duval knew about the code phase of
the operation.

The only sound now in the oppressive silence was her own
heart drumming in fear. Sigi had no idea where the underground shaft led, for Marie Selva had not explained these
details. Remembering the location of the undertaker's house off
rue d'Anjou and the position of the lavatory, she could

calculate one thing: the escape burrow—for the present at least—led off in a general southerly direction, toward the ship turning basin and the River Loire.

Trembling from the cold and dampness, Sigi examined the scattered inventory of the emergency supply box. She concluded that if her luck held she'd have no use for the first aid kit; if it didn't, the two grenades would be infinitely more valuable. She hooked them carefully to her skirt belt, then, flashing the light before her, she cautiously began crawling down the tunnel.

Gradually the dizziness and the sick feeling went away. She could think more clearly now. Her predicament had taken on all the qualities of a grotesque dream, for it hardly seemed possible that the tenor of her activity, until now unchallenged and blessed with luck, could change in so short a time! Roger's ill-timed gun battle with the Gestapo had reduced her to a frantic mole, burrowing an escape. She first cursed to herself, then aloud. If she made it, her scratched, filthy knees would never look the same.

The dirt shaft was about three feet high and shored at intervals by wooden posts. From somewhere up ahead Sigi heard the sound of water. Advancing with caution, she came upon an iron-barred grate, beyond which was another sewer gallery, this one larger. Running with over a foot of turbid water, the new tunnel was high enough for a person to walk through standing erect. Someone, she noted, perhaps the undertaker, had sawed off the bolts to the heavy grate. Sigi kicked and it fell easily away. She remembered Selva's warning about the rain and how the sewer system could flood in a flash. Had the storm above abated or worsened? She'd have to take the chance.

The cross tunnel appeared to run east and west. Flashing her light beam downstream, she hesitantly began to follow the swift current. The water penetrated her shoes, its fetid odor making her nauseous. She searched overhead for manholes, but saw none. Swallowing an urge to be sick, she waded on. Her head brushed against something clustered overhead—a small squadron of bats that exploded in flight, disappearing quickly into the darkness.

After traveling underground for what seemed a good two city blocks, the sewer abruptly cascaded into an even larger cross chamber filled with much deeper and swifter water, but this time equipped with a foot-wide dry ledge along one wall. Sigi edged slowly along the walkway, glad to be out of the muck. In the tunnel's disarming solitude, disturbed only by the running sewage and storm water, every sound magnified its importance. Her own footfalls seemed ominous; a rat's sudden flight along the ledge charged itself with absurd significance.

The water, she noted, appeared to be rising rapidly. A dim yellow light appeared up ahead; it turned out to be a pump control pilot lamp at the foot of a steel ladder. Sigi's pulse quickened. Directing her flashlight beam overhead, she saw a large manhole cover. She climbed the ladder and pushed, but the cast iron was too heavy. Reluctantly giving it up, she shivered in the cold and continued to explore along the ledge.

Up ahead her flashlight beam caught several pinpoints of red light that flickered, came briefly toward her, then halted. *More rats*! They scuttled toward her, stopped, and sniffed her scent. Were they, too, fleeing the rising water? Sigi was terrified. Despite her panic, there was no retreating. She stiffened, counting eight of them, all good-sized. Moving forward slowly, she kept the flashlight leveled like a gun on the rats until, whiskers twitching over their teeth, they let out a high-pitched squeal, turned, and pelted away.

Sigi had probed less than a hundred yards more along the larger tunnel when she heard the sound of voices. *German voices*, and very close! There was another junction in the sewer system just ahead, and from it light streamed in from the right. Stealthily, Sigi approached the intersecting shaft. With infinite caution, a fraction of an inch at a time, she pressed her face against the wall and peered around the corner. No one blew her head off.

Sigi's eyes widened as she recognized the area. Less than six yards away was a familiar broad platform with a wooden ladder leading to the street, and still hanging from the ladder's middle rung was the kerosene lantern she'd placed there herself hours earlier. It was the same sewer access through which her associates had lowered over two dozen kegs of dynamite!

A bored SS trooper with a machine carbine slung over his shoulder, pained at standing the duty in an odious sewer, was bantering with someone above ground just outside the manhole. "SS Major von Wilme and the deaf-mute take their time," the listless trooper grumbled, gazing upward through the opening.

"Too long," came a gruff response from above. "But if you are smart, Heinie, you will stay close to the prisoner. Things won't go well for us if he should get away."

Sigi's heart skipped a beat at the mention of the word *prisoner*.

The trooper in the tunnel laughed and began climbing the ladder. "You're like an old woman, Klaus! The Ami is well bound and the corridor is dead end. Maybe you want to smoke down here with all these explosives, eh?" He climbed out of the manhole.

Sigi sensed he was offering a cigarette to his partner on the street.

"You're lucky," snapped the voice of the second guard. "Up here I have the rain and cold wind."

Sigi heard the conversation fade off. The two sentries had probably sought shelter in a nearby entryway to light their smokes. A sharp tingle ran up her spine. Their live prisoner had to be Skeet Merrill. Entering the side gallery, she waded quietly past the opening overhead. Her entire body ached and she itched; God, how she'd like to take time out for a hot bath.

Merrill was around the corner, bound, gagged, and helplessly waiting.

He looked up at her, eyes brightening and nose sniffing as she went to work on his bindings.

Chapter 40

SIGI PETERSEN'S HAIR was filthy and tousled and her dirt-smeared face reflected a measure of fear and uncertainty, but to Merrill she was still an angel from heaven. When she removed the gag, he ran his tongue over his sore lips, at the same time allowing his eyes to patronize the full, round breasts heaving over him. Sigi came closer, working feverishly at his wrist bindings. She was helping him to escape, frantically rushing against time, yet Merrill found the unexpected sensation of her breasts brushing against him strong and deliciously exciting. The scent of her body, above the fusty smell of the sewer he'd come to endure, had a warm, animal tang that charged him with excitement.

Once more the blood started reeling in Merrill's veins. When his hands were free, he flexed them. He let his fingers slowly tighten around her knee, then relax and climb the smooth slope of her thigh.

She responded with a quiver of delight, but at the same time frowned. "Your sense of timing leaves much to be desired," she said firmly.

Merrill grinned. "All my life needed at this point. A *First Class* Girl Scout who knows her knots. Under the circumstances, I'll shelve my baser instincts." He winked at her. "But only for the moment."

Sigi ignored him, going to work on his ankle bindings.

Merrill asked, "How did you get in here?"

"The sewer. Can't you smell it?"

"Sorry. Merely thought you changed perfumes." Merrill thought for a moment, remembering the plastic explosives set to go off at midnight. "What time is it? Those souvenir-hunting goons outside took my watch."

"Eleven-thirty," she replied.

"We've got to clear out of here." He shook himself to clear his brain, smiled at her and grumbled, "A timely rescue. Up until now, I thought I was the one riding shotgun on this stage line."

"I thought the same. But our Gestapo friends apparently don't understand your predictable Hollywood Western scenarios." She tore away the rest of the rope. "Now, for God's sake, let's go!"

Merrill stretched and clambered to his feet. His legs felt weaker than a newborn pinto's. "Where's our captive hero? And the Dutch girl?"

Sigi seemed to hesitate. "Loewen's secure, hidden in the casket as planned."

"Secure? Where? I wouldn't count on it. A fox will bite off its own leg to get out of a trap."

"I'll explain it later," she said calmly. "Erika's waiting for a Paris train at the *gare*. Let's pray she's got a better chance escaping this mess on her own."

"Pierre Roger and the mute will take care of her."

"Sorry. Not a chance. Roger is dead. And so is Marie."

Merrill stared at Sigi. "Then we have to pick up the mute and Erika. If they're picked up by the Germans, they could be forced to spill the beans. Especially Erika—she knows about the damned code. So far, the enemy may think we're purely a sophisticated demolition team."

Sigi nodded in agreement. "I know it's a risk, Skeet, but I say let her go alone."

Shaking his head, Merrill interrupted, "That tough little Dutch girl is a cross between a frightened rabbit and a clever coyote. I say you're wrong. She has to go back to England with us—provided she is in fact on our side. The other traitor possibility is Duval."

Sigi quickly interjected, "No possibility, a fact. I saw Maurice with the Gestapo."

"Traitorous cocksucker! What next?" Merrill's spirits sagged.

"Please Skeet, let's get out of here. How do we get past the guards?"

Merrill knew they'd be easy targets the minute their heads

popped out of that manhole. The only way was to get the two
guards down into the tunnel, fight them on his terms. But he
had no gun. Merrill's eyes focused on the grenades Sigi carried
at her waist. Dangerous, but better than nothing. But first he'd
need a ruse, a noisy distraction.

Leading Sigi back down the tunnel to the overhead opening,
Merrill grabbed the kerosene lantern that hung on the ladder.
He pulled Sigi around the corner into the intersecting gallery,
blew out the flame in the lantern, then swiftly lobbed it back
down the darkened tunnel. It struck the wall beneath the
manhole with a resounding clatter.

They waited, listening carefully for the sound of alarm, of
hurrying footsteps on the street above, but there was only a
guarded, muffled coversation, followed by stillness. It was an
inactivity Merrill wasn't ready to accept. He continued to wait
patiently, reasoning only a cretin or a foolhardy hero would
stick his neck into the darkened manhole at a time like this. He
and Sigi listened as the voices from above grew louder and
agitated. The two sentries were arguing.

Merrill knew the guards were considering their predicament.
They were elite SS troopers who had been given an assignment
and they knew there would be hell to pay if they didn't return to
their duty stations and investigate. Conceivably, the lantern
could have slipped off the ladder rung. The cigarettes had
already been a breach of discipline and they could ill afford
another. The men above delayed the inevitable as long as
possible, but finally, after some additional argument, Merrill
saw the probing flashlight and the first pair of jackboots appear
through the manhole and slowly descend. The second trooper
followed quickly on the ladder.

Merrill reached for the grenade clipped to Sigi's waist, but
she balked and convulsively slid away from him.

"More noise?" she whispered, restraining his hand. "Isn't
there another way? The dynamite is too close by."

Merrill suspected that she, too, knew a measure about
sympathetic explosions. A remote possibility, but they had to
chance it. "Relax, boss-lady," he whispered back. "I'm still
the expert at this, remember?"

Still she edged away and wouldn't let him have the grenade.
It was dark, but Merrill started to see red. He shuddered with
annoyance as he heard the two Germans drawing nearer. They

were approaching the junction in the sewer, their flashlights probing ahead of them, guns held in readiness.

No time to argue with Sigi, Merrill flashed. Snorting like a bulldog, he ripped the grenade off Sigi's belt, pulled the pin, and counted to himself. Timing would be critical, super critical. He heard labored breathing around the corner as the guards drew closer. Merrill swung his arm, trying to lob the grenade around the corner, up on the dry platform, but Sigi struck his arm, disrupting his aim. "No!" she shouted. "The explosives!"

The grenade was deflected into the deep trough of sewage water. It all happened quickly.

Merrill covered his ears and pressed himself against her body. Panicking, the two sentries dove into the protection of the side tunnel. The sharp blast went off underwater a short distance away, splattering the walls with sewage and filling the chamber with acrid smoke. One of the Germans was wounded and dropped his automatic carbine. Merrill leaped through the billowing smoke and before the second guard could recover, retrieved the weapon and covered him. An instant later, coughing violently, both Germans had their arms in the air.

Merrill shouted to Sigi. "Time to make with the Girl Scout knots again, and work fast." He led the SS captives several yards into the side tunnel where they'd be reasonably safe from the midnight explosion. Everyone's eyes burned with tears, but thankfully the overhead manhole had created a strong draught and was pulling the suffocating blue smoke away.

When the two SS sentries were securely bound and gagged, Merrill and Sigi hiked back to the manhole overhead and listened carefully. No noise. Merrill's head still throbbed from the concussion and his eyes felt like they were on fire. He knew Sigi had to be suffering the same agony. Merrill thought quickly. Though time was running out, he still had some interrupted, unfinished business back in the dead-end tunnel. He'd come too far not to finish the job.

"Wait here," he said to Sigi. He didn't dare consult her on this one. Merrill dashed back to the hole they'd cut through to the abandoned tunnel. Von Wilme's SS men, when they'd captured him earlier, had removed the fusing leading to the dynamite kegs inside the opening. But they had not had time to remove the explosives that were still neatly stacked beneath the snorkel facility!

Merrill remembered that minutes before the Germans had confronted him he'd removed his tunic and tossed it aside. Recovering the jacket, Merrill found in the breast pocket what he hoped might still be there: three pencil igniters. *Hallelujah*. Once more the adrenalin coursed through his body. Merrill reached through the jagged hole in the brick wall, propped up his flashlight, and broke the vials on each pencil. Taking careful aim, he tossed them one at a time. He cursed as the first missed its mark, but the two other pencil igniters landed neatly inside an open container of cordite.

There wasn't time to enter the abandoned tunnel and go to the far end to check the timer mechanism on his underwater charges, but Merrill felt reasonably sure they were still intact and the Germans knew nothing about them. Merrill ran back to where he'd left Sigi. "Finished," he said to her with finality. "Now let's get the hell out of here."

Merrill could sense his tone frustrated her. It was neutral enough, neither friendly nor unfriendly, but it didn't invite conversation. Merrill looked up at the open manhole, then over to the shattered wooden ladder; the grenade blast close by had made kindling of it. Propping the broken, two-foot remaining section against the wall and gaining purchase on the manhole rim, Merrill hauled himself up effortlessly, thankful he hadn't neglected chin-ups as part of his daily monkey drills.

Outside the rain had stopped and the air smelled cool and clean. Merrill quickly scanned the street. Even though it was a quiet industrial area, with all the noise coming from the sewer Merrill was surprised to find it still deserted. He reached down and pulled Sigi up easily. Climbing to her feet, she glanced keenly in all directions like a mother fox taking the scent.

"Our friends down below were kind enough to leave us some transportation," she said, nodding toward a three-wheel patrol motorcycle parked nearby.

Merrill wasted no time kicking the BMW to life. Discovering a woolen greatcoat in the gondola, he wrapped it around Sigi's bare shoulders, at the same time gently kissing her on the ear.

They sped off, the roar of the motorcycle shattering the strangely muffled silence of the city. A bright, three-quarter moon suddenly poked through the remaining storm clouds, its light filling the bomb craters with ugly dark shadows. Squeezing the throttle, Merrill spared no rubber as he dodged the bomb holes, skidded around the corners, and rattled over the slippery cobbles toward the *Gare des Voyageurs*.

Looking up at Merrill with alarm, Sigi shouted, "My stomach feels like a cage of squirrels!"

"Stop complaining and grab tight!" he cried back.

Sigi did hold on, with white knuckles as though her life depended on it, which, under the circumstances of Merrill's spectacular driving, it may well have. A hair-raising bike ride was the least of Merrill's concerns now; his own fears were rooted in a far more serious danger that lay elsewhere. He gave the engine more gas and the BMW leaped ahead even faster.

Events of the past hour had shaken Merrill more than he would admit, even to himself. The mission was up for grabs, depending on who reached Erika Vermeer and Dieter Loewen first. Both knew too much. As for Erika's talking, and despite her stubborn nature, Merrill had no doubt that if a mixture of scopolamine and mescaline failed, Hermann von Wilme's slow, sadistic torture methods would eventually break her. All this, assuming the girl was in fact on the Allied side.

It suddenly occurred to Merrill that he'd made a serious mistake. He swore loudly. "Crap!" In his haste to pull Sigi out of the sewer he'd forgotten to haul up the guard's automatic carbine. "We're unarmed, Sigi!" he called down to his partner. "And no time to go back now!"

She gestured to her waistband, shouting, "I still have another grenade! And if we can get to the hearse, there's a gun in the back!"

Merrill smiled feebly. Neglecting to latch on to the sentry's Schmeisser was an unforgiveable mistake, his first big one. He would have returned for it were it not for the impending explosion. Suddenly, as an exclamation point to that fact, the street beneath the motorcycle heaved. A terrible, convulsive explosion rocked the city. *The kegs of dynamite*.

"What time is it now?" Merrill shouted.

Sigi strained to check her watch. "Twenty past midnight!" She sent him a congratulatory smile.

Beaming in self-satisfaction, Merrill made a mental note that the corrosive acid in the pencil fuse had run two minutes slower than expected. At least there'd be no more snorkel refitting in France and they could chalk up success for one phase of the mission.

Merrill swerved, missing a German supply truck by inches.

Occasionally he would lay his finger on the horn and leave it there. *Ooo-gah! Ooo-gah! Ooo-gah!* Several sailors crossing at an intersection scattered before the charging BMW. Merrill smiled, musing that the only way he might make Germans move faster would be to drop a skunk in the middle of one of their Oktoberfests. Again he accelerated.

Merrill began to wonder about the twelve-volt electric timer on the underwater charges. Late or faulty? Immediately, he had the answer as a series of sharp, muffled explosions could be heard in the distance. The molded plastic on the U-boat hulls, wired in relays, had detonated, as planned, in nine fierce concussions. Sigi looked up at him with a frown, but Merrill ignored her, savoring his exhilaration. He knew that more than fish had been blown out of the water back in the U-boat pen. Keels broken and gaping holes torn in their hulls, nine submarines would rest on the bottom, blocking the use of the berths for incoming U-boats.

Alarmed by the mysterious concussions, townspeople and German servicemen came pouring out into the streets. Sigi again looked sharply up at him. Merrill knew she was perplexed by the unexplained second series of explosions, but he deliberately ignored her. When they found a minute's peace and quiet, then he'd try and explain. But not now. There wasn't time.

The black Mercedes in front of the *Gare des Voyageurs* and the smartly tailored SS major alighting from it were self-explanatory to both Merrill and Sigi. It was Hermann von Wilme and they were too late! Merrill once more felt a disquiet that wasn't about to be shaken off. The SS was a step ahead of them again. Another leak. How did the SS know Erika would be at the St. Nazaire railroad station?

Barely slowing the BMW, Merrill skirted around the command car and swerved up a brick road that led off behind the *gare*. When the paving ran out near a railstop there were only tracks, and for several hundred feet the motorbike jounced along the ties until Merrill stopped and took his bearings. The moon laid a broad, milk-gray swath across the railyard. He saw Erika, almost at the end of one of the concrete platforms, sitting alone at a bench, her head slumped. She was asleep. Opposite her on Track 3 was a passenger train, but it was engineless and unattended. In the distance at the station end of the platform, Merrill saw three black uniforms saunter through the passenger gate and head in the Dutch girl's direction. From where Erika was sitting, Merrill knew she'd never spot the approaching SS men until it was too late.

"She doesn't have a chance," said Sigi.

"Never say die," Merrill muttered. He gunned the motorcycle and raced down the far side of the parked train. He counted the passenger cars aloud. Without a gun, Merrill could only account for his actions as madness, but it was worth a try. The motorcycle rattled and bounced its way over the washboard ties, finally slamming to a halt at a spot he hoped would be opposite Erika. Merrill left the engine running and leaped from the BMW to the deserted coach. Once inside, he glanced out the far side of the darkened car to check his position. He was right on the money, for her seatbench on the platform was less than a coach length away.

Erika at first thought someone was calling to her in a dream. She slowly opened her eyes, blinking in owlish comprehension. Less than four meters away and beckoning to her from the shadows of the train vestibule was the American, Skeet Merrill!

"Look at me, baby doll. That's it. Don't look behind or to your left! Not a word, just easy-like, get on your feet and step up into the train—very calmly, like you were about to depart on a long trip."

Erika suddenly felt wide awake. It was either some deep premonition or the sound of approaching hobnail boots that made her obey the American without a moment's hesitation. As she climbed the coach steps she heard a familiar voice back along the platform calling out to her.

"You there, Fraulein Erika Krager!" the voice shouted, "Stop!"

She was about to glance back over her shoulder, but Skeet Merrill didn't give her a chance. He slammed the vestibule door closed and pushed her bodily into the coach. "Let's go!" he barked. "Move your ass and follow me like your life depended on it!"

Erika gulped in a lungful of air and sprinted after him, as agile as any male athlete.

It was only after she'd jumped from the opposite side of the train and squeezed into the sidecar with Sigi Petersen that Erika placed the voice back on the platform. *SS Major von Wilme!*

He'd obviously been alerted earlier by Colonel Schiller and
knew. For the first time, Erika's festering dislike of the Paris SS
officer was mixed with fear.

The motorcycle roared away, but already excited voices
were shouting after them. She could hear footsteps running in
pursuit, then a fusillade of pistol shots rang out over the
railyard. Erika crouched lower as bullets whistled through the
air. Beside her, Sigi's face and flaxen, windblown hair were
only a pale blur in the darkness, but leaning over the older
woman and shielding her as best she could, Erika felt a strange
sensation. She not only experienced a masculine urge to be
protective, but she felt warm, secure, and unafraid herself.

Chapter 41

OBERLEUTNANT GUNNAR HERSCH ROLLED over on his cot and buried his head in eiderdown. The insistent rapping on the door to his officer's billet was part of a bad dream, he reasoned. The pounding became louder and his name was being shouted. Hersch shook himself awake, stretched like a snail, and padded to the door in his naval underwear. His early morning visitor, a stranger in a black uniform, stood in the center of the hallway glaring at him.

"Oberleutnant Gunnar Hersch?" The SS major's implacable gray eyes bore in on him like high-beam headlights.

"Yes," replied Hersch, unenthusiastically.

"It is an early hour, I realize, but the welfare of the state is a twenty-four-hour-a-day matter."

Hersch looked at his uninvited guest, not caring about the state of anything except another hour's sleep. All he wanted was for the SS man to promptly state his odd-hour business so he could return to bed. Like everyone else at the sabotaged U-boat base, Hersch had been up most of the night.

"I am Major Hermann von Wilme, from SS Headquarters in Paris." Swiftly withdrawing a folded document from his pocket, he thrust it forward. "Your orders, Oberleutnant. Indeed, from most high and very special authority."

Hersch blinked and scrutinized the document under the hallway light. Orders? From an SS major? Hardly likely, he thought. But what Hersch saw brought him instantly to his senses; even before he'd finished reading, the SS officer before him began to enlarge on the significance of the orders.

Von Wilme, who appeared agitated and pressed for time,

entered his quarters without being invited. "As you can see by that document, I need a ship. Ordinarily, a small surface vessel would suffice, but my intended mission is fraught with uncertainties. With the state of enemy air patrols what they are over the coast, a U-boat will be a distinct advantage."

Hersch's room was dark except for the light shining inside from the hallway. Von Wilme struck the switch by the door. "I need your submarine, Oberleutnant Hersch," he said, smiling thinly. "Or should I say the Lion's boat?"

Suddenly realizing that his jaw had dropped in blank astonishment, Hersch quickly closed his mouth and swallowed with difficulty. Finally, he said, "But Herr Major, I regret that will be impossible!"

Von Wilme's eyes were on him, hard and dangerous. "Nothing is impossible!"

"These orders—they state you need a U-boat for tomorrow!" Hersch stood there, numb and frozen, as though his sub's lead ballast were chained to his feet. "I don't understand."

"Put on your trousers, Oberleutnant. It's impossible for a military officer to think clearly in his underwear."

"Yes, it is cold," said Hersch, completely dashed.

Von Wilme promptly renewed his attack. "Tomorrow, my Reichskriegmarine friend, is already here. Luckily—and I might add *curiously*—the U-601 is the only vessel that was not sabotaged. Your U-boat is completely intact, and they haven't as yet started your snorkel installation. Obviously, with the catastrophe tonight, that work will be delayed for months, if not out of the question. Correct me if I'm wrong."

Hersch reluctantly nodded. "Under the circumstances, we intend to finish painting the hull and put out to sea as quickly as possible."

"The primer is dry," snapped von Wilme. "I assure you my little mission won't keep you out long. If things go well, we'll return in a matter of hours, a full day at the most."

"But the crew. I have only half a complement."

"For my particular requirements, that will suffice. I will be bringing some of my own SS men as well. Now, I suggest, Oberleutnant, that you prepare for sailing. I have already checked that you have ample fuel, but your decks are a snarl of air hoses and electrical umbilicals."

Gunner Hersch was dumbfounded, disappointed, and just

plain angry. His was the only operational submarine in St. Nazaire. And now, his first mission as a commanding officer of the U-601 and the Reichskriegmarine lends his vessel to Himmler's police force! Was it all a bad dream?

Von Wilme didn't appear to be finished. "Tell me. Your former commander, the illustrious sub ace Dieter Loewen. I met the Kapitan in Paris and I understand he returned to St. Nazaire. He seems to be missing. Have you had any communication with him whatsoever?"

"We met this afternoon in the officers' wardroom."

Von Wilme glared back at Hersch, expecting more.

"He was entertaining guests from Berlin."

"So I understand," said von Wilme, gritting his teeth. "Any suggestions as to where I might find him at this early hour?"

Hersch wished that right now Dieter Loewen were here beside him. He, if anyone, could comprehend these strange orders and know how to handle a rank-pulling SS major. After a long pause, Hersch said, "I suspect he has returned to Paris and gone on to Versailles. Kaleun Loewen is on leave, prior to reporting to the Fuehrer."

"I am aware of that," sighed von Wilme. He straightened his shoulders and headed for the door. "A pity. I would like to have him with us on board at dawn."

"Dawn, Herr Major?" asked Hersch, unhappily, checking his watch. It was an hour away.

"We'll leave then." Von Wilme smiled coldly at him, gave the Nazi salute, and disappeared into the hallway.

Gunner Hersch wasted no time ringing up the duty command on the hallway telephone. He gripped the receiver as if it were his only possible escape from hell itself. Indeed, things had come to a sorrowful state if the Kriegsmarine had begun knuckling under to Himmler and his SS minions. Unfortunately, the calm voice at the oppisite end of the line assured Hersch that his sailing orders for the U-601 were very legitimate. Karl Doenitz himself had approved them by wire from Berlin. Furthermore, for the next hour, making the U-601 ready for sea was to have top priority over all operations at the badly damaged St. Nazaire base.

Hersch sighed, slowly replaced the telephone on its hook, and went searching for his shoes.

Chapter 42

UNDER A SKY the color of tarnished silver and a veil of rain, the Left Bank stretched, flung open its shutters, and reluctantly greeted the new day. When the baker Brion changed the soiled numeral cards on the calendar behind his counter, Dominique Roger gave the new date, June 3, 1944, only a casual glance. Tucking the morning's *baguette* inside her coat to protect it from the rain, La Reine Bleue's *patronne* hastened out the *patisserie* door. Across the street Lefaucheux's produce stall was preparing to open. Tightening her shawl, Dominique hurried across the cobbles, eager to be first in line when Lefaucheux rolled back his gate, for she knew the day's vegetable selection would be sparse.

Minutes later, as she picked through the produce, a perspiring, agitated young man suddenly burst into the stall and cried out to her. "Madame Roger!"

Dominique turned, to be confronted by Sebastien, La Reine Bleue's plump female impersonator. "You must come quickly," he pleaded, frantically tugging on her sleeve. "German soldiers are rummaging through the bistro!"

Sebastien's words cut her with the force of a guillotine. The turnips in her hand fell to the floor as she bolted for the street. Dominique Roger's first impulse was to go in the opposite direction from La Reine Bleue, to run away, but curiosity gripped her and Sebastien waited impatiently.

"You must come and vouch for all of us," he wailed.

Elbow-jostling her way through the queues outside the food shops, she hurried the several blocks back to the bistro. Sebastien trotted along behind her, panting like a dog. His

road hips shook like gelatin as he lamented, "My costumes!
They will ruin them!"

When Dominique turned into rue de' Seine she saw a crowd
gathering. Braving the light rain, the people looked on
helplessly as a truckload of SS troopers swarmed through La
Reine Bleue like fire ants.

Indicating for the *patronne* to follow him, Sebastien brusquely pushed his way to the front of the curious spectators. At
the bistro's entry a square-chinned SS trooper with several
chevrons on his tunic stopped the obese entertainer with an
outstretched arm. "Did you find her?" the German snapped.

"Yes," replied Sebastien quietly. "Did you doubt me? You
have my money now, yes?" He stared back at the trooper with
wide unfrightened eyes, like a fat sheep before a butcher. The
street crowd glared at them both. When Sebastien turned, fully
prepared to point a finger at the *patronne*, his face turned
gaunt.

Dominique, smelling betrayal, had moments earlier disappeared in the crowd.

The SS sergeant stiffened and called to one of his men just
leaving the building. He wagged his head toward the plump
entertainer. "This one will go along for questioning. Take
him—or her—to the truck."

Sebastien withered. He'd helped the Germans and this was
his reward? In desperation, he tried another ploy. "But it won't
be necessary," he stammered. "Colonel Schiller or Major von
Wilme will surely vouch for me."

The SS man sneered. "And who do you think gave us our
orders, you fat toad? Into the truck!"

The crowd grew increasingly restless. For the night people
of St. Germain des Pres, La Reine Bleue, from all appearances, was now history. *The final curtain*. A white poodle
came out of the bistro, barking sharply without let-up until
silenced by the butt end of a rifle. Let loose by the rummaging
SS men, the magician's panic-stricken parakeets fluttered off
seeking an uncertain freedom, and the crowd disappeared with
them.

Farther up Rue de Seine, a shawled woman hurried on, also
unsure of her freedom. Dominique Roger slowly shook her
head in dismay. *Sebastien!* Only a fool, her husband Pierre had
insisted. The *collaborateurs* were everywhere! The implications of the Gestapo raid on the bistro became clearer to her. As

comprehension filled her mind, abject fear followed swiftly
Dominique could no longer stay in Paris; there was only one
place now, her sister's farm near Lille.

Tears welled up in Dominique Roger's eyes. Unchecked
they cut long streaks through the white powder on her cheeks
A deep-seated, ugly premonition told her that she would neve
see her husband Pierre again.

The road between London and the south coast of England
was nearly impassable, even for Winston Churchill's Humber
sedan with its siren-equipped motorcycle escorts. The lorries
tanks, and gun trailers stretched for miles, and the appalling
weather made driving even more difficult. The PM was bound
for Admiral Ramsey's naval headquarters at Portsmouth, bu
before that he would have a late breakfast with Eisenhower
The American general had set up a temporary SHAEF
headquarters in a country house behind the high wall of a
coastal estate.

Churchill's entourage passed through the tall gates of the
manor a little after nine, and less than fifteen minutes later he
was seated with Ike in the spacious dining room. Both men ate
quickly; outside in the hallways, Churchill could hear the
frantic activity of the D-Day preparations. Churchill liked the
charged atmosphere of the scene; the mood here at Portsmouth
was definitely one of impending action and vitality, rather than
the stuffy bureaucratic tension he'd felt back at Whitehall.

The PM had purposely brought his wire recorder along and
had chosen this moment to play for Eisenhower a copy of
Edward R. Murrow's latest CBS report to the American
people. Ike sipped his coffee and listened with interest.

Finally, Murrow concluded: "Having thus far survived the
V-1 buzz bomb, the people of this island nation now fear a new
terror. Intelligence has revealed the ready-to-launch status of
the larger V-2 rocket. But are these weapons a sign of future
German technological strength, or will this new reign of terror
merely be the death rattle—the last agonized thrashings of a
dying, demonic monster? Beware, Mr. Hitler, the allied cause
is only beginning its counterattack. This is Edward R. Murrow,
reporting from London."

An aide turned off Churchill's recorder. Eisenhower solemnly asked, "Can your British fiber withstand these new terrors until we destroy the launching facilities at Peenemunde?"

Churchill looked at him with impatience. "The buzz bombs are a tragic roulette game, but the odds for survival are imminently better than under the saturation bombing of the blitz. Provided the Germans don't devise a way to plant the nasty devices on *specific* streetcorners, where and when they choose."

"Perhaps another of your *finest hour* speeches may be in order. Or shall we say a *grin and bear it* pep talk?" Eisenhower smiled thinly, then abruptly stiffened. "The armada's ready to sail. We've contained the Luftwaffe and we'll work on the rockets when we get a foothold on the continent. My only concerns now are the shore batteries at Normandy, the German panzer divisions, and the U-boats. Regarding the latter, is there any action at G-10 on this Operation Storm Tide affair?"

Shifting uncomfortably, Churchill swallowed a mouthful of scrambled eggs. "Yes, indeed, action. I prefer it any day to dull planning and cockcrows."

Eisenhower sent back one of his impish grins. "Each in equal measure. You avoid my question, Prime Minister."

"Not avoiding. *Delaying,* parleying for time, General. God knows, each hour counts." Churchill paused uncomfortably. "Perhaps, at this point in the operation, it's a matter of each *minute* counting. We may be short on feed-back but it won't be for long; Colonel Foster's en route to Brittany to help wrap up the mission."

"Wrap up or clean up? You're confident of the success of our operatives?"

Churchill smiled sagely. "You did select the American naval lieutenant, General."

Eisenhower wasn't about to be outscored. "And you, Mr. Prime Minister, stubbornly insisted on bringing this German war hero out as a part of the package."

"Goebbels' penchant for nonsense propaganda is insane and we must fight fire with fire." Churchill sat back in his chair and grinned. "I understand there is even a kiosk on the Wilhelmplatz outside his office where souvenir postcards picturing his own family can be purchased."

Eisenhower looked at the PM, unmoved.

Churchill resolutely continued: "Dieter Loewen's capture is

a minor consideration in our scheme of things now, but time
will prove me out. Damnation, but I'm eager to find out what
kind of man this German war hero is!" Churchill chortled and
pointed a fork across the table. "I want to hold the blighter's
Iron Cross with Oak Leaves in the palm of my hand, General.
And I'd like a picture taken of that scene and sent, by whatever
means necessary, to the Fuehrer himself. Let them print that in
their *Signal* magazine! We'll use leaflets, if need be, showered
on Berlin!"

Eisenhower remained stoic. "Nazis are not noted for their
objectivity. I suggest they hear only what they want to hear."

Churchill finished off the rest of his coffee. "True, true, but
in the Fatherland, *realpolitik* and individual soul-searching—
especially at this point in the struggle—are different things.
The majority of Germans did not vote for Hitler."

Eisenhower leaned forward. "But thirteen million did and
the rest looked the other way. And now, the lot of them
obediently follow him over the precipice."

Churchill calmly added, "Or, in the case of the U-boat fleet,
to the bottom of the sea."

At the Reich Chancellory on Vosstrausse, Adolf Hitler
stared at the jagged holes in the wall as workmen hurriedly
built scaffolds to board them over. Martin Bormann stood
beside him with a grave expression.

"The American and British bombers are like an insufferable
plague of locusts," Hitler complained, his voice shaking with
anger. Again, by a stroke of luck, his own spacious wing of the
chancellory was undamaged.

Both men proceeded down the Long Hall to Hitler's
sumptuous office that had now become little used.

"When do you return to your headquarters at the Eastern
Front, my Fuehrer?" Bormann asked.

Hitler paused before the sixteen-foot high, massive mahogany doors leading to his private quarters. He looked at
Bormann narrowly. The guards on each side of the magnificent
marble-framed entry visibly stiffened. Above them loomed the
massive shield bearing the initials AH. Architect Speer had
designed the intimidating bronze plaque—over a yard wide and
taller than a man—at a canted angle and it appeared as if it
might fall at any moment. Martin Bormann considered it an

architectural abortion and had a habit of nervously glancing up
at it each time he went through the entry.

Hitler finally answered Bormann, his tone brisk. "I cannot
go back to the *Wolf's Lair* until the matter of the U-boat ace is
resolved. And there is the matter of the invasion. I would like
to speak to General Rommel in person. Arrange for him to
come back from France immediately, a meeting here in
Berlin."

"As you command, Fuehrer."

"As for the damage to the Reich Chancellory, repair it
quickly and have all the windows boarded over except those in
my office." Hitler shook his head, his voice rising several
decibels with each new sentence. "Churchill and Eisenhower
have become international incendiaries. Madness, absolute
madness! They will never learn. They try to convince the
British and American people that the Third Reich is exhausted,
completely spent! A hundred German bombs, a hundred
V-rockets, for every cowardly aerial attack on our civilian
population!" Hitler hesitated, trying unsuccessfully to mute his
rage. "Bormann, get Himmler on the line again. I won't accept
his evasive answer! Impossible that he cannot immediately
locate Dieter Loewen! I demand a personal report from our
counterspy Viper!"

The Reichsleiter nodded and padded off. Hitler turned,
raised a trembling hand in a casual salute to the white-
helmeted, white-gloved SS bodyguards, and entered his office.

At ninety by fifty feet, the chamber of ebony and dark red
marble was big enough to be a ballroom. Not as large and
imposing as Mussolini's palatial quarters, but just as overpow-
ering and capable of putting a visitor in his place. Hitler
avoided his massive desk and stepped across the carpet to the
broad marble fireplace beneath Lenbach's classic portrait of
Bismarck. Hitler sat in a wingback chair, his dull gaze
alternating between the oil painting and the lofty, coffer-work
ceiling of rosewood. The anger from his outburst with
Bormann had dissipated, but still the entire left side of his body
trembled out of control. And the persistent pain at the back of
his neck had begun again.

Enduring the brief moment of solitude, he sat there, deep in
thought. He suddenly wished he had studied to become a
doctor, not only to cure his own pains, but Germany's. A
physician's occupation was like his own; the doctor tried to

arrive at the truth, then prescribe a remedy to living and survival.

Remedies, solutions. Hitler thought again of the wonderful V-2 rockets at Peenemunde that were almost ready to supplement the V-1's. He suddenly remembered what Grand Admiral Doenitz had told him when they had both watched the first test launch: "My Fuehrer, I am impressed. Imagine what warfare would be like if we could launch such rockets from submarines." *Some day*, Hitler thought. *Sooner than the world expects*.

The chamber's doors opened suddenly and Martin Bormann entered with a pained expression. What he had to say next was superfluous, for Hitler could hear the air raid sirens sounding in the distance.

"I'm sorry to interrupt, my Fuehrer, but the enemy aircraft come earlier today. They will be over Berlin in twenty minutes. I suggest we return to the concrete bunker immediately."

Hitler shrugged and looked glumly at the sumptuous surroundings he'd been forced to permanently abandon. Without hesitation he followed Bormann, heading for the massive shelter and personal quarters that had been built beneath the Chancellory garden.

Chapter 43

LOEWEN WAITED HELPLESSLY in the dim void, dividing his attention between reminiscing over his military career and listening for any exterior signs his ears could pick up from outside the casket. All he could hear was the steady purr of the hearse engine. Loewen knew only that they had started at dawn and the vehicle was somewhere on an open road. His brain was spinning; he had to think and keep his mind occupied, to fight off the claustrophobia. But as Loewen tried to reconstruct the curious chain of events that had placed him in this disastrous predicament, nothing made sense to him—not his adversaries' motives, not even the war.

From inside the confining box the war and the upcoming invasion, in fact, seemed a long way off. Like millions of his countrymen, Loewen had done his job faithfully. He'd served with distinction under two different German flags: the black, red, and gold of the short-lived Weimar Republic, and the Swastika of the Third Reich. He'd sworn allegiance to both. And to Adolf Hitler as well. But now he privately wondered if this holy Houdini in Berlin—who had pulled so many rabbits out of his hat by personal magnetism alone—could produce a few more and win the war by some spectacular, surprising trick. If Loewen really believed in anything, it was that beyond politics, he knew the Fatherland would survive this conflict and the next. Whether he himself survived or not, there would be other fleets, more advanced submarines, and another generation of sailors to sail in them. National legend, folk hero, U-boat ace, whatever—the fact remained that he was completely expendable. The Norwegian bitch had caught him with his pants down in more ways than one, and the insolent American—a submariner himself—was making it even more miserable and embarrassing for him. Never before had Loewen felt so much contempt for the enemy.

The vehicle hit a rut, slamming Loewen's head against the side of the casket. The blow shook his meandering brain back to the present. *Reality.* Where were they taking him? Surely, it had to be only a matter of time until they came upon a German checkpoint or roadblock. In the meantime, Loewen could do little more than swear to himself.

"Cree-aw! Cree-aw!"

Diving out of the cold morning sky, the curious gulls repeatedly swept down from the clouds, examined the old hearse purring along the coast highway, then tacked back over the maritime forest toward La Baule Bay.

Hunched over the wheel, Skeet Merrill reconstructed in his mind the luck that thus far favored them. Though it had been marginal luck the night before, they'd made it out of St. Nazaire, thanks to a ponderous freight train that separated Sigi, Erika, and himself from their SS pursuers. Returning to the hearse and finding the sub ace undisturbed, Merrill had armed himself with the Walther PPK and driven the vehicle some nine kilometers outside the city. Hiding in the woods and taking turns standing guard, they'd slept fitfully, but remained undetected. Dieter Loewen had been permitted to walk and stretch his legs, but they'd found the German totally uncommunicative and filled with rancor. Merrill had also kept a speculative eye on Erika, but the Dutch girl did nothing suspicious, save a surprising interval of comradery and repeated eye contact with Sigi. Merrill resolved to learn a little about lesbian behavior if he ever came out of this mission alive.

The new day had begun as an umbrella of gloom. Murky gray nimbostratus clouds, the remnants of a storm over the English Channel, scudded overhead. The picture-postcard seafront Merrill followed in the hearse had been one of Europe's favorite summer playgrounds before the war. But now the splendid rocks of Pornichet—favored by fishermen and painters alike—and the immense beach and oceanfront boulevard of La Baule, with its promenades, hotels, and shuttered casinos, meant only one thing to him. The scenic route afforded their only hope for escape from occupied France.

Everywhere Merrill looked he saw resort hotels requisitioned by German troops and sailors, and many of the early risers were already on the streets. Luckily, the hearse had come across no sign of military roadblocks or civilian checkpoints. Merrill began to wonder if the SS had blundered or if they were being deliberately lulled into a false sense of security. He'd no more than dismissed the thought when Erika shouted a grim warning.

"*Boches* following us," she cried, looking backward.

Merrill checked the side mirror. Rapidly gaining on the hearse, their faces hidden by massive goggles and helmets, were two armed *Feldgendarmen*.

Merrill withdrew the Walther pistol from his pocket and placed it on his lap. They were on the outskirts of La Baule now and the road ahead was deserted.

The lead *Feldgendarmen* roared up beside the hearse, looked in the cab, and gestured quickly with his thumb for Merrill to pull over. Merrill thought fast. If he stopped now they wouldn't stand a chance.

He accelerated and the German did likewise. But now the biker raised his goggles, glared menacingly at Merrill, and shouted. Getting no response, the *Feldgendarmen* reached for the pistol on his belt holster.

"Steady the wheel!" Merrill shouted to Sigi, who sat in the middle of the cab. Swiftly, holding the PPK with both hands, he aimed it at the patrol motorcycle's front tire. The gun roared twice before the German could bring his own weapon to bear.

Merrill tramped the accelerator and grabbed the wheel. Just behind them the German motorcycle went out of control and overturned, flinging the rider to the side of the road. The second *Feldgendarmen*, hardly as lucky, slammed into the wreckage at full speed, his ruptured gas tank exploding into flames.

Wincing, Merrill mopped his sweating forehead and kept his eyes on the road. Sigi and Erika both sat in tight-lipped silence as the old hearse sped on, unmolested.

At last they arrived at Le Pouleguen, a small fishing port of whitewashed houses just north of La Baule's broad beach. The contact on the dock was Felix, a lean, hawk-nosed fisherman in

his late thirties. The Breton's chocolate-brown eyes were cold
and expressionless as they peered out from beneath two wiry
thickets that were his eyebrows. Felix wore a dirty yellow raincoat and his wavy black hair was ruffled by the brisk wind from
seaward. He was unusually tall for a Frenchman and reminded
Merrill of a frigate bird.

Felix examined the coffin in the back of the hearse, then
lifted his gaunt, rugged face skyward and studied the inclement, rapidly moving storm clouds. "Not enough room for
four," he told them, viewing the unanticipated face, Erika
Vermeer, with little pleasure.

"Sorry. A change of plans," replied Sigi. "You'll have to
make room."

Felix spat off the dock. "You'll be pinched up, then." He
pointed to the hearse's fuel tank. "Any petrol left?"

"Some," said Merrill.

"Two or three liters will make the difference," Felix
grumbled. "Let's get on with the siphon. Back the hearse
behind the net shed out of sight. You, Monsieur!" He pointed a
grease-covered finger at Merrill. "It is best you wear this
priest's frock and hat." He handed over a bundle of black
clothing.

Without questioning the Frenchman, Merrill took the gar-
ments and gestured for Sigi to follow him into the shed. Erika
proceeded to move the hearse.

When Merrill was alone with Sigi, she smiled serenely,
unfolded the frock, and held it up to him. "Does wonders for
your character." When he gently pinched her rear and pulled
her closer, she edged away, declaring, "You're a lunatic, and I
don't make love to priests."

Merrill promptly threw the frock over his head, straightened
the waist and pleats, then grabbed her again, this time firmly.
He drew her close, looking at her for a long time before gently
kissing her ears, forehead and lips. She acquiesced briefly, then
pulled away. Sigi's eyes were on the doorway, where Erika
stood awkwardly with a gasoline can, staring at them in
silence. Wordlessly, Sigi went out to join her on the dock.

Merrill bit his lip and followed them. He still wondered
about Erika, and couldn't put his finger on why. The night
before she'd seemed grateful enough for her rescue from von
Wilme, but something in her behavior that Merrill couldn't
pinpoint was still running counter to her friendliness.

Sigi watched Felix siphon the last drop of petrol from the hearse, then asked, "Have you enough to make it to the rendezvous point?"

The fisherman shrugged and spat again. "One way, possibly. Both directions, no."

"We have to chance it," insisted Merrill. "Whoever picks us up out there should be able to come up with a jerry can of gas for your return." Looking over the dock at the decrepit *Antoinette II*, Merrill sniffed and shook his head. Never before had he set his eyes on such a foul-smelling, waterlogged specimen of a boat.

Erika, too, was staring at the vessel with concern. "This goes to sea?"

Sigi broke in harshly, "It's better than swimming."

"Let's pray the worms are holding it together." Merrill was thankful for one thing: sheltered by the high, overhanging dock and net shed, the twenty-eight-foot trawler was berthed inconspicuously enough. No one saw them load Dieter Loewen's casket on board.

Inside the coffin, Loewen angrily stared into the nothingness, his mind calculating escape and retribution, but his body feeling only helplessness. Again, his thoughts wandered. A pleasant vision flashed by: a chalet in the Bavarian Mountains at the shore of Lake Tegern, surrounded by fragrant pines. A retired Reichskriegmarine officer in lederhosen and a leather-trimmed, gray flannel jacket, playing with a dog and feeding cheese to the trout.

Then outside the casket, Loewen heard shouts, a boat's engine sputter to life, and knew the dream would never come to pass.

"Foul weather out there," Felix again complained, as he tied down the ends of the wooden coffin to the deck. "Barometer's rising. Wouldn't mind waiting an hour."

Sigi nervously glanced at her watch. "Impossible to delay," she said, not sparing him a second to consider the idea. "We have to go now. Sorry, Monsieur. Time is critical."

Felix rapidly pulled in the *Antoinette II*'s dock lines, then lifted the lid from a large wooden container that extended across the stern of the trawler. "Be sorry for yourself, then. As I warned, you'll be pinched for space. There's a *boche* patrol launch five hundred meters out that monitors the fishing fleet. Only the priest must be on the deck with me." Felix looked from Sigi to Erika, then insisted, "Into the box, please. Both of you."

Sigi wrinkled her nose in displeasure. She waited while Erika, mouthing masculine Dutch obscenities at the fisherman, settled herself first on the fetid-smelling bottom. Sigi reluctantly squeezed in beside her, grimacing at the combined aroma of fish and fuel oil that permeated the confined space. Felix closed the vented lid and covered it with eel netting.

Seven minutes later in mid-channel, as Felix had predicted, the harbor patrol launch heaved alongside. Ignoring the German inspectors, Merrill sat on Dieter Loewen's coffin, mumbling in fractured French as he pretended to read from the prayer book.

Listening to the bogus priest's eulogy for the dead, Dieter Loewen stared into the darkness with feelings compounded of curiosity, hatred, and shame at his predicament. His mouth was sore and hurting from the thick gag they'd inserted. Hearing German voices, Loewen repeatedly kicked at the side of the casket, but the thick padding muffled the noise and apparently it was lost in the wind. Loewen flared with anger. Help so close by and yet so far away! For a man of his supposed achievements, this helplessness and nothingness were hard to grasp and terrifying to accept. It was an odd, convoluted twist of fate that had put him here and he suspected it would have to be another twist that would save him.

Merrill smiled in relief. The German inspectors made no attempt to board the *Antoinette II*. Felix was a familiar face and he had the proper papers for a burial at sea. A priest was a priest. As they'd evidently done countless times before, they held their breath against the trawler's odious smell, glanced quickly inside one of the forward cabin ports, then nodded for Felix to proceed.

Wet-nosed and slavering, the *Antoinette II* plowed ahead through the quartering sea. Not until the boat was three miles

out and hidden from shore by the deep running troughs did
Felix remove the eel netting from the fish storage box and lift
the lid. Sigi and Erika poked their heads out of the box,
blinking their eyes and gulping in fresh air by the lungful. They
quickly tested their cramped legs on the trawler's heaving
deck.

The casket, too, was opened, and Dieter Loewen permitted
the freedom of the deck. Only his wrists were kept bound.
Stiffening his shoulders in rigidity and gazing silently shoreward, the fresh air seemed to energize him.

To Skeet Merrill, the *Antoinette II*, her engine rattling on its
bed bolts, seemed to be hanging on to some old dream of
herself. For the duration of the war, Merrill figured, she was
apparently just adequate for Felix's dream of himself. He
watched the tall, wiry fisherman sniff the air. The wind was
already decreasing noticeably, the trawler taking less spray
over the bow.

"Better go down below until it calms. All of you. It's dry
there," advised Felix.

Merrill threw off his priest's frock and gestured for Loewen
to move forward in the cabin. Sigi followed them below. For
several minutes they all sat in silence, then Merrill became
restless. He felt in his shirt pocket for his harmonica, but
suddenly remembered he'd left it in the front seat of Selva's
hearse. Merrill swore to himself; for sentimental value alone,
had there not been a war on, he'd have swum back to shore for
it.

Loewen sat apart from the others, calmly waiting for the
final denouement without emotion. Despite the circumstances,
he felt his sailor's honor was intact, for he'd never surrendered
a ship to the enemy. But the fate of the Reichskriegmarine
code—here was a different blot on his name. Loewen let his
eyes alternate between the fisherman out on deck and the
American guarding him with the Walther pistol. He made up
his mind to remain silent and alert, for they were not infallible.
If only his wrists were not bound. And how could he strike?
His mind raced back and forth, but the only answer he could
come up with was to wait, to sweat it out.

                    *   *   *

Merrill looked at the Lion of the Atlantic and saw the bitterness. Bored with the silence and spoiling for an ad-hoc debate, Merrill parried, "The war in the Pacific would be over if we had more officers like you in our navy. A shame you're on the wrong side, Kapitan."

The German glared back at him, steely-eyed. "I'll see you roast in hell."

"Fine. We can enjoy each other's company there and swap pigboat stories."

Loewen wasn't amused or in the mood to be friendly. "It amazes me, Lieutenant, that you Americans fight us so valiantly when not one German bomb has yet to fall on your soil."

"Call it sympathetic virtue."

"Like wild west cowboys, you're determined to put Adolf Hitler on the gallows, whatever the cost."

Merrill shrugged. "Now cowboys I know just a little about. But in rebuttal to your remark, I'll wager my discharge pay when the war's over that none of us will have to lift one finger to prosecute your Fuehrer."

Loewen stared at him.

Merrill shrugged. "Adolf Hitler, the bullying coward that he is, will probably kill himself if your own German leaders don't wise up and do it first."

Loewen glared back. "Nonsense. Absolute nonsense."

"The Greeks call it *hubris*——the sin of overweening pride, fancying oneself to be more than a man. An arrogant over-estimation of genius always leads to self destruction and defeat, mark my words."

Sigi smiled sympathetically at Loewen. "Relax, Dieter. Even if what Lieutenant Merrill claims should come true, your Fuehrer will have an important place in history."

Merrill looked at her. "Sure. Next to Attila the Hun, who bragged that the grass would never grow over the places he rode his horse over."

Loewen smiled for the first time. "I'm impressed that an American fighting man is so well versed in history. I'd heard otherwise."

"Your war machine had us figured all wrong from the beginning, Ace. A *mongrelized nation*, right?" Merrill shook his head. "I suggest you stop fighting us, Kapitan, and cooperate."

"I will fight you to the end, for I am an honorable man. Prepared to die, if necessary, for the Fatherland."

Merrill said quickly, "A foolish enterprise at this point in the war. All that's left of Germany is Hitler's cesspool of self destruction." Merrill leaned forward and quietly asked, "You a member of the Nazi Party?"

"No," Loewen said flatly, his eyes softening. "And what party do you belong to, Lieutenant? Does that make a difference, or for most Americans is it simply my country, right or wrong?"

"I hold the gun, so I get to ask the questions. Were you in the Hitler Youth?"

Loewen smiled. "Come now, I'm a trifle old to have been through that."

Merrill's curiosity wasn't about to be dismissed. "How about the party's organizations? Who are you trying to bulldoze?"

"No again." The ace looked back at Merrill, weary but firm. "Sorry to disappoint you. The German navy does not recruit from any political group. I am a graduate of the Naval Academy at Flensberg. I've done my duty and stand by it. Now if you don't mind, this conversation annoys me."

Merrill exhaled sharply. He felt an aura of complete desperation coming from the man. Angry, nervous energy that wanted to explode, but was carefully, stubbornly held in check. Merrill looked away, out of the cabin hatch. He saw Erika detained at the stern rail. Out of all this assaulting of their senses, it was inevitable that someone had to be sick.

When Erika finally came staggering into the shelter of the cabin the U-boat ace sent her a slow, sad smile that conveyed neither malice nor contempt. But the Dutch girl ignored Loewen and found a place for herself in the corner. Erika's usual tough-as-nails demeanor had oddly disappeared; she seemed insecure and edgy. Probably her seasickness, Merrill thought. She squinted out the porthole, then her eyes scanned the others one at a time, her focus finally coming to rest on Merrill's gun hand.

Merrill felt threatened by Erika's silence, the sensation alien and disturbing enough for him to say things to her now he wouldn't have said otherwise. "So how well did you know the deaf-mute Duval?" he asked gruffly.

Erika shrugged and met his eyes. "I not only have a stomach

full of squirrels to contend with, but I'm very tired." She turned to Sigi. "Sorry, do what you will, but I'm through taking orders from your partner."

"Back to being uncooperative?" Merrill asked the question through clenched teeth.

She yawned in his face. "What have I to lose? The mission's almost over." Leaning her head against the bunk, she turned away, as tight and reserved as Loewen.

Merrill didn't like being ignored, but words, under the circumstances, would have to wrung out of her. Erika would tell him about Duval only when she was ready. There was plenty of time, he knew, for once they were picked up it would be a long boat ride back to England. Merrill estimated that they were still two miles short of their rendezvous point. The cascading seas had diminished to an easier, rolling chop and they were making better time. Glancing out the hatch, he saw that overhead the ominous gray clouds had begun to disperse; here and there small open spaces of blue appeared.

Merrill heard an aircraft. It was somewhere overhead, trifling with the breaking cover. He visibly flinched, wondering if the Luftwaffe was out sniffing around.

Loewen also, heard the plane and with a sense of expectancy, let out an audible sigh of relief.

Chapter 44

FELIX, TOO, HEARD the single engine aircraft but couldn't spot it. Then the noise was lost, and only the sounds of the wind, the breaking sea, and the *Antoinette II*'s three-cylinder engine remained.

Ker-chug, ker-chug, ker-chug, ker-chug.

"Monsieur!" Felix shouted, suddenly.

Merrill poked his head out the forward cabin and followed the fisherman's alarmed stare.

A slender gray shaft cut through the water, parallel to and less than a hundred yards abeam of the trawler. Then gradually emerging from the depths like some amphibious creature from primeval time, the sinister outline of a long gray shape took form.

Seconds later the U-601 surfaced close by. With all the ballast tanks blown the partially-repainted hull rode easily up and down the waves like a cork. Sailors emerged like ants from the conning tower and stern hatches and ran to their surface stations.

Merrill cursed, exchanged swift glances with Felix, and shouted down to the others, "Everyone up on deck! We have unfriendly company."

Erika stood frozen in the hatchway, suddenly forgetting her seasickness as a different kind of discomfort gripped her. Sigi, peering over the young girl's shoulder, seemed the least surprised of all.

Merrill looked up at the U-601's bridge. Among the crewmen was a determined face he hardly expected to see

again after Paris—the Gestapo major, Hermann von Wilme!
"Cunning devil after all," Merrill said gloomily.

Sigi came out on deck. "And with our hospitable U-boat
base *tour director*, Gunnar Hersch."

They all winced as they saw another familiar face peering
down from the conning tower.

Erika stared at the short, balding figure and exclaimed, "The
mute—Maurice Duval!"

The instructions from Oberleutnant Hersch's bullhorn, carrying across the water loud and clear, were backed up by a
zealous crew who appeared more than eager for a chance at
target practice with the sub's three-inch deck gun. "Come
alongside immediately," bellowed Hersch. "Approach our
starboard, downwind! And *drop your weapons!*"

Felix looked at the U-boat's gun, slowly shook his head, and
spread his hands in a gesture of defeat. Reluctantly, he turned
the wheel over.

Merrill gave a soft hoot of incredulity, aware that for the
U-boat, it was a turkey shoot. Obediently, he dropped the pistol
to the deck, but his eyes focused again on the grenade still
fastened to Sigi's belt. Merrill glanced back into the cabin to
see if Loewen was watching.

The U-boat ace felt Merrill's eyes on him, but he didn't look
out on the deck. Instead, peering through the porthole,
Loewen's expectant stare was fixed on the submarine. He'd
never seen his own boat at sea from another vessel. The
partially repainted U-601 was a shabby sight, but the peeling
gray, the partially obliterated lion emblem, the ugly streaks of
rust all went unseen by Loewen. Like a father of a cross-eyed,
overweight daughter, he saw only her beauty.

For once Sigi stared back at Merrill blank-faced, offering no
suggestion as to what his next move ought to be. For lack of
anything better, Merrill again considered the grenade; it just
might be worth the old college try. The German sailors on the
U-boat, however, were watching him like a clutch of vultures.
They were joined by four of von Wilme's SS troopers aft of the
conning tower, and these men held persuasive machine
carbines.

Sigi looked up at Merrill with a secret, female smile. She asked bluntly, "What now, genius?"

He winked back and whispered, "That grenade's our only chance. Don't look at me, just sit down slowly and slide it under the fish net beside you."

Beaming in satisfaction, Loewen stepped out on the trawler's deck and thrust his wrists toward Felix. "Monsieur fisherman, if you will, please. I'm uncomfortable."

Felix gazed blankly at the German, looked over to Merrill and the others, then reluctantly severed the ace's wrist bindings with his bait knife.

Rubbing his sore hands, Loewen glared at Merrill, the bitterness that had festered in him while in the casket at last bubbling over. Angrily, he said, "In America, you say *the table is turned*, am I correct, Lieutenant? Your mission, apparently, has turned out to be a fool's errand."

Clichés, Merrill thought. But clichés were as good as freshly minted cleverness when the damned reality they pressed bore as much weight as the ace's remark. Once more luck was with the bastard.

At first Merrill couldn't think of anything to say to Loewen; words now seemed superfluous. But he couldn't resist one final barb: "Taking you captive wasn't my idea. It would have been easier to have shot your body out through the tube with your diving officer back at the pen."

Loewen stepped forward, pushing Sigi aside. Eyes blazing, he landed a fist on the side of Merrill's face. Stumbling back awkwardly and rubbing his chin, Merrill was ready to hurl himself back at the U-boat ace when Felix grabbed his shoulders and gestured toward the German guns on the U-boat that were now leveled at him.

"That was for Mueller. And the indignity of the casket," Loewen said with contempt as he stood rigidly before Merrill. The two war heroes eyed each other steadily.

Dieter Loewen saw a rapidly swelling face and a look of defeat and bitterness, but no trace of fear. Skeet Merrill saw a perfect model for a painter who wanted to portray the essence of steel-willed, Teutonic heroism.

"You lose, Lieutenant," said the German, finally, with a trace of a grin. Loewen's eyes, for the first time, sparkled with something other than hate.

Despite his sore jaw, Merrill tried to continue the flip mood.

"Scratch the mission but not the war, Ace," he replied calmly. "History will pass an ugly enough judgment on your U-boat packs."

Loewen's face sobered. "In the froth and fury of battle, I focus only on victory. There's no time, none whatsoever, to consider the judgment of history. From your submarine experience, you should know this. *Auf wiedersehen, Herr Kapitan*. Better luck next time."

Merrill's eyes held on the German. "It's all bullshit and you know it."

Loewen rubbed his chin and shrugged. "Yes, historians will probably take that view. They will undoubtedly label the acts of submarine commanders—your acts and mine, Ami—as obscene. But in the meantime, we have no choice but obedience and duty."

Merrill looked away, avoiding Loewen's stare and the others' as well. He faced failure as he would probably face death—with cynical bitterness and a need for solitude.

Though the water was calmer on the lee side of the U-boat, the *Antoinette II* jolted repeatedly against the heavy steel hull. As two sailors struggled with boat hooks fore and aft of the trawler, Hermann von Wilme, followed by Maurice Duval, descended from the conning tower bridge to the sub's weather deck.

"*Herr Kaleun!*" von Wilme called to Loewen in a mocking tone, "the SS extends its compliments. I bring you your man-of-war!"

Not bothering to acknowledge the SS major, Loewen grabbed a boat hook from one of the sailors and heaved himself to the U-boat deck. Ignoring von Wilme, quick-stepped and confident, the ace headed for his familiar place on the conning tower.

Merrill looked at the others beside him. Erika was as pale as a white moth. She sat down on a mound of eel netting and gazed disconsolately up at the German SS major who was about to leap to the crazily rolling deck of the trawler. Sigi—her own face expressionless—sat down beside her. Felix stood quietly near the stern with a look of angry defeat.

Merrill waited taut-lipped, to be confronted by von Wilme.

The SS major jumped easily to the fishing boat's pitching deck. Recovering his balance, von Wilme quickly withdrew his Luger and pointed it at his captives, unnecessarily, for his prey were already adequately covered by a bevy of automatics from the U-boat.

Maurice Duval promptly joined von Wilme on the trawler. He retrieved Merrill's Walther off the deck and tucked it in his belt.

"*So*," von Wilme snapped. The Gestapoman wasn't about to waste time with contrived pleasantries; the unwinking eyes and immobility of his mouth served to emphasize, not mask, his determined implacability. "Down to business then!"

"Just one question, Major," said Sigi, forlornly. "How did you know we were here?" She leaned back against the thwart, her skirt drawing across her thighs in a way that might have titillated other men.

Von Wilme wasn't about to be distracted. "The hour, the latitude, the longitude—were carefully extracted from the woman undertaker *before* you returned to her parlor, Fraulein. The shoe, remember?" He slowly shook his head. "You were thorough in the demolition, which I admit caught us by surprise. Madame Selva and her house were barely recognizable when we investigated. Sordid. Thankfully, we did not venture inside moments earlier." Von Wilme turned to Merrill, observing that he was eyeballing Duval with undisguised contempt. Patting the mute on the shoulder, the SS man said to Merrill, "The physically handicapped make effective double-agents, do you agree?"

"So it appears."

Von Wilme turned his piercing gaze on Erika and gloated, "For the time being, Fraulein Krager, you afford the SS more entertainment alive than dead. For some reason—I suspect you've done mischief elsewhere—SS Colonel Schiller requests that you be sent directly to him. Unfortunately, I cannot find the colonel. I don't suppose any of you have seen him in the past twelve hours?"

They all remained silent except Erika. Glaring up at the SS officer with mixed fear and hate, she said quickly, "Fuck yourself."

Von Wilme slapped her face. He then turned back to Merrill. Moving with the careful precision of a well-oiled machine, he began speaking in heavily accented English. "As for your excellent German, Lieutenant Merrill, I believe it was one of your American writers, Mark Twain, who said, *You have the words, but not the tune*. You are not only a submariner yourself

but a talented explosives expert; that much Duval here has con-
firmed.

Merrill looked at the mute. "Prick!" ˙

Smiling thinly, von Wilme continued, "As for our charming
Fraulein—I suspect that she is Norwegian or Dutch. Indeed,
there appears to be a real Anna Schramm from Berlin, but this
journalist was killed in a train accident over a year ago." He
paused and turned again to Merrill. "Very effective sabotage
for so small a team. Indeed, nine U-boats immobilized. But
why not this one, Lieutenant?" Von Wilme gestured toward the
U-601. "I'm not sure demolition was the real thrust of your
mission. And there is also the matter of the U-boat ace—
Kapitan Loewen taken hostage."

Von Wilme was jabbing at them like a surgeon gone mad,
sadistically toying with the exposed nerve endings. He gazed
inquiringly from one to the other, but his eyes finally remained
on Merrill, not Sigi. "Now then, what is your contact just a
mile farther out? A submarine? A surface ship? If you remain
silent it will be simple enough to accompany you to your
rendezvous and wait. You'll find I'm as patient as I am
persistent. Our U-boat will submerge and follow at periscope
depth; you'll succeed at nothing but delaying the inevitable,
and many additional lives will undoubtedly be lost in the
process."

Time itself had become a dimension of Skeet Merrill's
anxiety. All he could do was stall for more of it. He slid his
hand across his forehead in a travesty of a salute, smiled
mockingly, and said, "Steven Keith Merrill, Lieutenant,
United States ‚Navy. Serial number A-407——"

"Enough of your insolence," von Wilme interrupted. "The
code for captured prisoners does not apply to spies! You take
me for a fool?"

"Since when has the SS cared a lick for the Geneva con-
vention?"

Ignoring Merrill, von Wilme looked at Sigi. "And you,
Fraulein, have you anything to say?"

"Absolutely nothing."

Merrill wondered how long their continued silence would
make a difference. It was all a matter of time. Dieter Loewen
was free and he knew the real purpose of their mission to St.
Nazaire. Merrill's troubled eyes darted up the U-boat's conning
tower. He saw that already the ace was conferring in hushed

tones with Gunnar Hersch on the U-601's bridge. Within minutes a radio report would be on its way back to Berlin.

Looking down from the U-boat, Loewen knit his brows, smiling uneasily as he observed Hermann von Wilme confronting his captives. The helpless enemy agents on the little trawler appeared bleak, suddenly gone tired. Even the rangy, tough-hided American had a look of defeat on his face. Loewen's eyes locked on Skeet Merrill's again and he saw, beyond this enemy's initial outrage and bitter disappointment, a flicker of envy—the common look of a sailor dispossessed of his ship. Loewen had seen that numb, helpless expression before.

Instead of his usual practiced indifference to the enemy's plight, Loewen felt a sudden twinge of pity for them at the hands of the Gestapo. He looked away. Always before when he'd considered his own fate and good fortune he'd nervously fingered his Iron Cross which was either around his neck or in his tunic pocket. But now it was missing. They had managed to get away with some part of him after all.

Despite his continued threats, von Wilme gained nothing but stony silence from his captives. He gave Sigi another hostile stare. "Very well, Fraulein, enough gentle persuading." He turned, waved his Luger at the fisherman, and shouted: "Lay off a course as before, and make no errors in your reckoning! One moment. The two women will go aboard the U-boat."

Erika needed no urging to jump from the wildly rolling *Antoinette II* to the more stable deck of the U-601. It was the break she needed, for no one—not even her companions—had seen her slide the grenade from under the fishnet and bury it in her blouse. But she had no sooner landed on the sub's corrugated steel deck when a lookout above on the bridge suddenly cried out a warning. Sigi Petersen didn't have time to follow her.

"*Alarm! Flugzeug!*" the sailor on watch screamed, dropping his binoculars.

Instantly, more from instinct than authority, Dieter Loewen took over command. It took him only a fraction of a second to follow the lookout's pointing finger before pulling the diving alarm. Gunnar Hersch and the watch men popped down the hatch into the hull. Harried by Loewen's frantic shouting from the conning tower, the startled SS troopers on the weather deck and three sailors manning the deck gun broke for the aft hatch.

The curious gulls circling the submarine, responding to the frenzied activity on the deck below with plaintive cries of their own, caught the steady northwest wind and held their wings motionless. But there was one determined bird headed straight for the U-boat, holding its wings far more rigid than the others.

"Mustang on the horizon!" shouted Loewen to the last two men scrambling far too slowly into the stern hatch. "Move your asses and dog that cover!"

Already the whine of electric motors had replaced the idling diesels.

"Dive! Dive!" Loewen shouted. Frantically, he glanced off to starboard. The trawler, with Major von Wilme and Maurice Duval suddenly left alone to guard their prisoners, was making off as fast as its three-cylinder engine could take it away from the vulnerable U-boat.

The last man dropped down the stern hatch and the bridge was clear. Leaping for the tower ladder, the ace failed to see the young woman climbing over the bridge rail behind him. Nor did he hear her anguished shout.

"Wait!" Erika screamed in her coarse, mannish voice.

There were more desperate voices below and louder sounds from the U-boat itself. Loewen did not hear the plea from beyond the hatch.

"*Achtung!* Flood!" bellowed the diving officer, signalling his men to pop the vents.

Straddling the top of the ladder, Loewen pulled the heavy bronze cover overhead closed. It slammed to within three inches of the deck and stopped. In blank astonishment Loewen stared at the foot jammed between the hatch and the deck sealing ring!

Erika wanted to cry out for the searing pain, but there were worse perils impending than a crushed foot. She heard the air expelled from the tanks and the sound of water rushing into the hull. Already the U-boat was tipped forward in its rush to the depths. In less than thirty seconds it would be underwater, but before that, she sensed by the increasing angry drone behind her, the airplane would have caught the U-boat. *A sitting duck!*

Heaving open the hatch cover, Dieter Loewen stared at Erika in disbelief, his face as white as tissue and twice as thin. Suddenly, .30 caliber bullets hit and beat a metallic tattoo from the bow all the way to the conning tower.

Erika looked at Loewen, her brain reeling. Quickly, she triggered the grenade and dropped it into the round opening past the ace's startled face.

Seconds later, two devastating explosions rocked the hull of the U-601. The first, a direct hit on the stern by the aircraft's bomb, ripped open the pressure hull and finally triggered in the aft torpedo room. The second blast was the smaller but lethal stroke Erika's grenade had made on the sub's control room and the personnel in it. In the concussion, Loewen had fallen somewhere below. Only blue smoke filtered out of the hatch. The bridge suddenly went awash with water and tons of foaming sea water surged through the opening.

Erika Krager couldn't swim. It didn't matter. Nor need she have feared a smashed foot would keep her a cripple for life. A sharp fragment of steel from the explosion aft had stuck Erika in the back of the neck, plunging her into immediate, mortal blackness. The pain in her foot was gone.

U-boat ace Dieter Loewen, likewise, didn't suffer long. As the water closed in and the blackness folded over him like the wings of a great vulture, he had a flashing vision that the sea war was lost. He heard the U-boat's death rattle, but it came to him that he'd at least saved a good part of himself. Once more he briefly heard the English woman—Vera Lynn's voice singing to him, calling him from London—"I'll be seeing you, in all. . . ."

Then the thoughts faded away, dwindling to black. Endless, nothingness, black. Inside the ace, the enigma that had inspired him, relentlessly driven him, and somehow blessed him with incredible luck, remained unsolved as he passed the gate of oblivion.

Chapter 45

SOME 200 YARDS removed from the stricken U-boat, Skeet Merrill stood on the rolling deck of the *Antoinette II* and stared at the disaster confronting him. He glanced at Sigi and saw her eyes closed in thought.

Across from Merrill, Hermann von Wilme bore a look of disbelief; his usually quick eyes were dense and vague and small beads of perspiration formed on his cleanly chiseled forehead. Maurice Duval, too, had a harried look. But both their guns had not wavered. Merrill searched desperately for a sign of weakness, a chance to strike at them, but saw none.

The grim-faced SS officer warily scanned the horizon for the Mustang, then once more considered his captives.

The fighter finally returned, but, ignoring the fishing trawler, it hung over the death-rattled U-boat like a great buzzing fly. It circled the area three times, then disappeared in the clouds.

Merrill watched the bow of the U-601 shoot out of the water, point despairingly at the sky, then slip backward, its downward suction taking with it assorted bits of flotsam and a lone body on the surface. A gradually expanding white ring of foam was all that remained.

Sigi opened her mou*'. n an effort to speak, but the words didn't come. Waiting for the tight knot in her throat to dissolve, she finally whispered, "They didn't have a chance." The air suddenly seemed cooler and she edged herself along the thwart to be nearer Merrill. Having witnessed death compounded in all its horribleness, they both felt a need to seek out the living.

Merrill had seen Erika struggle up the conning tower ladder with the grenade in her hand and he now felt guilt for having

334

doubted her. On top of this, the sight of the sinking submarine
was like witnessing a roll call of the dead. As a pigboat man
himself, he couldn't dislodge from his brain the terrible truth of
what would occur inside that plunging steel tomb in the next
several minutes. The bottom was a long way off, and he knew
that those crewmen who were spared from drowning by a
watertight compartment would suffer a slower death by suffo-
cation.

Remembering the awesome ship-sinking statistics Dieter
Loewen had boasted over just the night before, Merrill fought
off his submariner's sympathy for the U-601's crew. He knew
that in a matter of seconds the ace's infamous boat would lie
broken on the bottom of the Bay of Biscay, in the same alien,
unyielding world to which it had unmercifully consigned far
too many Allied merchantmen.

Merrill looked back at von Wilme, eyeing again the Luger in
his hand. Eyes glazed, the SS major appeared suddenly
desperate, shocked almost to immobility by the incredible
collapse of his carefully planned trap.

It was Sigi who broke the oppressive silence. "You're a
lucky man, Major von Wilme," she said lightly. "By a matter
of seconds only you missed death yourself."

Merrill looked at her, arching his eyebrows. "You've never
heard the proverb 'He that is born to be hanged shall never be
drowned'?"

Von Wilme glared at Merrill icily, but didn't respond. He
turned to Felix, who had cut the trawler's engine without
consulting him.

"We must conserve petrol," said the fisherman, bluntly.

The choppy sea, as if alerted by some ominous cue, had
changed to gentle, rolling swells and the *Antoinette II* drifted
aimlessly.

Sigi looked away from the spot where the sub had
disappeared and turned her eyes skyward, apparently searching
for the airplane.

Merrill followed her gaze. Already, he noted, the sea birds
had deserted the area. He knew it was a common phenomenon
for the lingering odor of disaster to keep flying creatures away
for days, sometimes weeks.

Von Wilme finally pulled himself together. "The odds
appear to have reversed themselves," he said guardedly. "Your
rendezvous, whatever it was supposed to be, is off. No matter,

Lieutenant Merrill, my superiors will still insist that you be
brought to Berlin.'' The German turned to Felix, a hint of
defeat in his blustering voice. "Very well, fisherman, return
this stinking barge of yours to Le Pouleguen immediately!''

"Can't be done. Not enough petrol,'' growled the Breton,
taking on a sudden defiance.

"Liar!'' retorted von Wilme. "You will turn us back now!''

Merrill shouted angrily. "What's the point? You're beating a
dead horse, von Wilme!''

The SS man turned his deadly gray killer's gaze back to
Merrill. "I still make the decisions here.'' He waved his Luger
back and forth between Merrill and Felix. "We'll get under
way now. Start the engine!''

Merrill was never to know whether it was Felix's slow,
deliberate movement away from the engine controls or the
spittle of the fisherman directed over the gunwale that suddenly
triggered von Wilme. Merrill grimaced as the red-faced SS
major squeezed his finger on the Luger. The gun bullet struck
home with a sickening thud.

Felix staggered as if he'd been slapped in the side by a
whale; he reached out shakily to grab the stern rail, but instead
folded in half over it. A second later, rolling with the trawler,
his lifeless form slipped off into the sea.

Sigi and the deaf-mute blanched.

Von Wilme, showing no hint of remorse, waved his gun at
Merrill. His eyes bore the look of animal hunger, rapt and
possessed.

"Bastard!'' Merrill spat out the word without fear.

"All right, Ami. You claim to be navy, yes?'' Von Wilme's
tone softened, his venom suddenly honey-coated. "Be productive and get us back to port immediately!''

"Impossible, Major,'' Merrill said flatly. "Unless it's a
mirage, your fishing expedition is about to be interrupted by
the Royal Navy.'' Merrill pointed beyond the German's
shoulder, off to the northwest.

Maurice Duval turned, following Merrill's finger to the
horizon.

Von Wilme didn't blink an eye. "I am not the fool to fall for
the oldest ruse in the world,'' he said gruffly.

"He's telling the truth, Major,'' said Sigi with a sharp sigh.

Merrill shrugged. "Then don't look. Just tune your ears.
Sounds to me like a couple of souped-up Fairmile gunboats. If

I remember nomenclature, they're equipped with two 850 horsepower supercharged engines and can push along at twenty-six knots. You still want me to fire up this potboiler?''

Cheeks twitching, von Wilme stole a glance over his shoulder. His eyes widened as he saw the two enemy gunboats. They were approaching at high speed, hurling great white sheets of spray into the air as their chined hulls planed through the sea.

Brief as it was, the curious backward glance proved costly for both von Wilme and Duval. Instantly, Merrill struck with the brass belaying pin he'd withdrawn from the gunwale beside him. The mute was closest. Caught just behind the ear, Duval toppled against von Wilme, then slid unconscious to the deck. Merrill immediately went for the SS man, who had been momentarily thrown off balance in the scuffle. The brass pin struck von Wilme's gun hand. The Luger, firing just before it was knocked from his grip, flew over the stern of the boat into the sea. Merrill was a fraction too close and caught the stray lead. Cursing, he clutched at a grazed, bleeding shoulder.

Despite the agony his hand caused him, von Wilme clenched his fist and planted it in Merrill's stomach. Merrill fell backward over the empty casket and thudded on the deck. Sigi helped him struggle to his feet.

Searching for another weapon, von Wilme found what he was looking for beside the bait box. Grabbing the fish gaff and raising its sharp, five-inch hook in the air, he waited for Merrill's rush.

Catching his breath, Merrill had no intention of moving in on the German. Not yet. Instead, he propped his winged shoulder against the forward cabin and with his good arm started gathering up eel netting. When Merrill had an armful, he moved back slightly and waited, watchful as a gladiator. The trawler's deck rolled and it was difficult for both of them to keep their balance.

Several seconds passed. The roar of the British gunboats grew louder. Suddenly, furiously, von Wilme came at him, bearing down with the menacing gaff. Merrill flung the net. It caught, managing to deflect the menacing hook, but the gaff's handle came on to strike Merrill's wounded shoulder. He grimaced with pain and stumbled to one side, clutching at his upper arm. Biting back the agony and mustering his remaining strength, Merrill catapulted forward, Texas longhorn style, and tackled von Wilme's legs.

The German swore and sharply brought up a knee that caught Merrill in the chin. Falling backward, Merrill's head struck the wooden casket hard; as if in a dream, he felt the SS man kicking his ribs as he lay there. Then the sharp, painful blows to his side stopped. Merrill rolled over groggily, slowly climbed to his feet, and brought his eyes into focus.

"Stop the useless fighting. It's too late," cried Sigi. She was heaping eel netting over von Wilme faster than the German could claw out from under it.

Regaining his wind and seething with retribution, Merrill ignored her plea and moved in again, this time using his good arm and fist to land several blows through the net to the SS major's face and chin. Von Wilme groaned, covering his bruised and bleeding face with his hands. Sliding to the deck, he squirmed like a snake at the end of a forked stick.

Pulling the eel netting off von Wilme, Merrill backed off, figuring his beaten adversary would wilt until he lay sprawled flat on the deck. Instead, the Gestapoman stubbornly braced himself, lifted his tortured face, and pulled back his shoulders in wooden rigidity. He looked over at the deaf-mute's unconscious form then up to Merrill, his eyes bearing mixed fear and malevolence. "You are in German-controlled waters," he whispered. "You will not escape."

"Remains to be seen," rasped Merrill, hurting for air himself. "That remains entirely to be seen."

Maurice Duval began to regain consciousness.

Merrill looked down, startled by the moaning and grumbling coming from the mute. He quickly withdrew the pistol from Duval's belt and watched the confused Frenchman open his eyes. They were small, darting, confused, as though something had abandoned him for the moment.

"*Qu'est-ce qui arrive?*" Duval slowly asked.

Skeet Merrill and Sigi Petersen exchanged looks of pure amazement.

"He spoke!" Sigi shouted.

Von Wilme, too, looked on as if he were thunderstruck.

Merrill shook his head. "Surprise, surprise."

Chapter 46

SIGI HURRIED INTO the forward cabin and tore a piece of linen from the bunk. She had Merrill's wound securely bound by the time the British gunboats drew alongside.

A line was sent flying from one of the MGBs. Sailors in the blue sweaters and caps of the Royal Navy grinned as they worked their hooks to bring the *Antoinette II* alongside. Beside them at the rail, wrapped in a wool peacoat and puffing on his briar, stood Colonel Stuart Foster.

"I say," he shouted, "neither of you looks too bad off, all things considered! Can't say the same for those of us aboard these flimsy plywood skiffs. Took a hellish beating crossing the Channel in a storm to reach you!"

"Damned decent of you, Colonel," replied Merrill as he pulled von Wilme to his feet. "If one of your chaps would kindly keep a Sten gun trained on our Schutz-Staffeln friend here, I could rest my damaged wing a bit." Merrill turned to his suddenly tight-lipped captive. "Say goodbye to sauerkraut, von Wilme. Where you're going, they call it victory cabbage." He paused, studying the German. "Just a minute, please." He stooped, checked inside both boots of the SS man and from one withdrew a stick grenade. Merrill handed it to the wide-eyed sailors on the MGB. "A tradition of the SS, Colonel, carrying these nasty calling cards inside their jackboots."

Von Wilme shrugged and smiled at Merrill. "It is a shame, Lieutenant. By a twist of fate, you have missed a rare opportunity to have an audience with the Fuehrer himself."

Colonel Foster grinned. "Appears you've missed your moment in history, Skeet, old chap."

Merrill scowled. "A trip to the zoo I'm pleased to have avoided."

His face reddening with rage, von Wilme glared back at Merrill for long moments, then looked bleakly at the MGB and the guns trained on him. Not one, but two armed British seamen hustled him on board the waiting gunboat.

Foster tugged on his moustache, considering the German's black uniform. "I dare say, this chap doesn't resemble a Reichskriegmarine war hero. Why the SS man?"

Sigi leaped to the deck of the MGB, shook Foster's hand, and set him straight: "Sorry, Colonel. Unfortunately, Dieter Loewen's dead. He was on the wrong boat when your air support flew over. The SS major, here, by a sheer stroke of luck, is your consolation prize."

Merrill prompted, "You've struck intelligence pay dirt, Colonel. Our friend Hermann von Wilme is adjutant to the Commander of SS and Police in France."

Foster's moustache twitched in the wind like a tassel on an ear of ripe corn. He looked inquisitively at the saturnine German, then back to the two operatives confronting him. "Interesting, very interesting. The PM should be pleased after all."

Merrill hustled Maurice Duval over to the MGB's deck and thrust him up before Foster. "And here, Colonel, is that intelligence leak you were concerned about. Our counterspy here is a long way from being deaf and dumb, or even French. Although it now appears he speaks it well enough."

Foster eyed Merrill with puzzled severity. "*Marty here?* I dare say; of course he's not French. Best double-duty man we have at G-10." Smiling easily, Foster let the shock die out of Merrill before continuing. "Hardly thought it necessary for him to give up his cover for your mission, however. Hoped he had a little time left in Paris. Sigi, Skeet, meet Martin Devon—on the continent known as *Maurice Duval*."

Von Wilme stiffened with anger. "Swine!" he shouted.

Sigi's eyebrows quivered in anticipation.

Devon rubbed the back of his bruised head and stretched out a hand to Merrill. "Curious kind of war, isn't it, chum?" he asked, in a rich, cockney accent. His innocent, slouched facade was gone now, replaced by an alert, postured, and very determined manner.

Merrill's face was still frozen in shock. Unable to smile or speak, he numbly shook Devon's hand and returned his pistol.

"Sorry, Guvner, I couldn't have been a trifle more helpful beyond ringing you up on the tely." Devon shrugged. "We've all got our own special jobs to do."

Sigi shook her head slowly in amazement. "And roles to play," she added, forlornly.

Devon glared at her, then turned to Foster. He grinned. "For a while, Colonel, even you were suspect. Thank God you were wise enough to avoid contact with those distant German relatives of yours who showed up in Stockholm."

Foster smiled. "I made a point of spurning their inquiries."

"A wise move. They were planted by the Nazis to incriminate you."

Already the sailors were setting the *Antoinette II* adrift. The colonel shouted to the gunnery man on the MGB's stern. "Sink the trawler! And put some dispatch into it!" Foster turned back to Merrill. "Sorry, where were we? What happened to Hugh Cummings?"

Merrill shrugged. "It's a long story. I'll explain it on the way back. Right now I suggest, Colonel, that your men take von Wilme below and strip him completely. If he runs true to SS form, the coward's probably carrying one of those damned cyanide cure-all pills."

"Take the smarmy Gestapo chap forward and search him. Top to bottom," Foster shouted to the men with the Sten guns. "Afford him not a fraction of an inch of privacy."

The Rolls semi-automatic aft began hammering away at the ill-fated *Antoinette II*. The rotting timbers of the trawler didn't stand a chance against the two-pound shells and in less than two minutes it was quiet again. Foster knocked the ashes from his pipe over the rail. "Best we sneak out of here and make time. Clouds are breaking up and that means the Luftwaffe will be out sniffing around. May I have the code now? We'll duplicate it and send one copy back on the other MGB by another route. Too bloody important to risk its transmittal in one boat."

"One burden I'm relieved to get off my chest," Sigi announced, fishing inside her brassiere for the neatly folded documents. She handed them to the colonel.

Merrill noted that her hands were trembling.

Foster turned to the gunboat's bridge. "Sub Lieutenant

Smythe! Take this below and make a copy. And triple-check for accuracy!"

"*No need*, Colonel. No need at all to waste your time on that lot." The calm, matter-of-fact voice was Martin Devon's. His words were somewhere between a request and a threat.

Foster's eyebrows arched like caterpillars. He turned and looked at Devon quizzically. The scene that followed might have been a freeze-frame from a movie. Sub Lieutenant Smythe, halfway through the hatch, stood poised in mid-air, expectant. Merrill's mouth was half open. Sigi looked frightened.

The feisty double agent reached inside his jacket and withdrew a book covered with blue leather. The cover bore a gold-embossed swastika and the words *GEHEIME—SECRET*. "Glad to be rid of this," Devon told them. "The blasted thing's weighted with lead."

Merrill frowned and slowly shook his head. He'd seen the book before, all too recently.

Sigi pursed her lips and gave Devon a speculative look.

"Clever, clever *counter-espionage*," Devon murmured. "Ingenious. And the Heinies—almost, within a hair's breadth, bloody well got away with it."

Colonel Foster looked dazed, completely uncomprehending.

Devon eagerly proceeded: "Sorry, Colonel, to burst your sacred G-10 bubble, but you wanted to know if there was a traitor among us. Indeed there is. Not Marie Selva, Erika Krager, or Pierre Roger, whom you suspected, Colonel. And hardly our well-meaning American hero here. The most dangerous, most successful double-agent of this war or any war, you'll be forced to admit, can be described by another superlative." Devon's accusing eyes flashed to Sigi. "She is also the most beautiful. Gentlemen, *there is your traitor*. Meet Viper!"

The only sounds were the idling of the Fairmile's engines and the gentle wash of the waves against the hull.

Sigi's face drained of color, but she didn't bat an eyelash. "Nonsense! The man's gone mad, Colonel," she said smartly.

"Now there's damned cheek for you," Devon grumbled.

Merrill felt as if he'd been sandbagged. "What the hell are you talking about?" he asked, wishing immediately that he hadn't interrupted. The question, under the circumstances, subordinated him to Martin Devon.

But the little Englishman was too caught up in the moment, too anxious to be relieved of his startling revelations to be patronizing. Avoiding Merrill's query, he turned to Foster. "The code documents she gave you are worthless, Colonel. At least from the Allied point of view. It's a special German operative code, right-o, but if Section 8-S pays a lick of attention to it, your big invasion fleet is in for rafts of trouble. She almost had it neatly planted, but unfortunately the lady left one bun in the oven—*me*." Devon patted the volume in his hand and thrust it at the bewildered Foster. "Here's the real merchandise, fresh off the U-601, compliments of my itchy fingers." Devon winked and rubbed two fingers together. "Watching the Dutch safecracking girl often enough, I picked up the knack." Now he turned to Merrill. "You needn't have worried about the U-601 missing out on all the sabotage back at the base, chum. Remember last night, the missing plastic from the suitcases? It wasn't easy with von Wilme nearby most of the time, but I was able to plant enough of it on that U-boat this morning to do it in properly. I set off the pencil igniters just before boarding the trawler with von Wilme." Devon frowned and glanced at his watch. "Unfortunately, the bloody Mustang upstaged my efforts by ten minutes."

Sigi Petersen took an angry, hesitant step toward Devon, then changed her mind and turned to Foster. "What in God's name, Colonel!" she cried, "What is he saying? That I deliberately——"

"Precisely," snapped Devon. "My, you really are going the pace, aren't you?"

Stuart Foster grimaced, leafed slowly through the code book in his hand and shook his head. Finally recovering his composure, he signalled Sub Lieutenant Smythe with a sharp nod of his head. Smythe withdrew a pistol from his hip holster, and although he wasn't sure whom he should point it at, held it in readiness.

"She's a Nazi?" Merrill prodded.

Devon nodded. "Women often make the proudest Nazis, Guvner. It's a political philosophy closely tuned to the emotions." He winked at Merrill. "And this lady, from what I understand, is not without emotion."

Merrill turned to Sigi. She stood erect and defiant, but in her face—slack and sullen as if slapped—he saw the truth.

Devon's watchful eyes held on Merrill. "Too bad, Lieutenant. She never told you about her contact, SS Colonel Reinhard Schiller, did she? One of Himmler's right-hand men, assigned to work with Admiral Doenitz at OKW. Intelligence firecracker, this Schiller. He was dogging your operation even before you dropped out of the sky. And thanks to Sigi, he was one step ahead of you at St. Nazaire. To make matters worse, the Fuehrer himelf was keeping tabs on the operation."

Merrill exhaled tremulously. "Never heard the name Schiller nor saw the man," he admitted.

Devon turned back to Colonel Foster. "She and Schiller made doubly sure of that. Our unfortunate young lesbian friend knew about him. Sorry neither Erika nor Schiller are here to back up my story, but the facts will soon enough speak for themselves. Fraulein Petersen's jolly-well had that *false code* long enough. Ever since that first night at the Clarice-Almont Hotel. Schiller gave it to her then."

Merrill's mind shot back to the door that had abruptly closed in his face, Sigi sending him padding to his room for a cold shower.

Devon wasn't finished. He turned to Merrill. "I took a chance then, hoping she might have left the false code hidden in her room. The next night, while you and the lady were tipping cognac with the Lion at La Reine Bleue, I got to cracking inside the room. Unfortunately—rotten luck—I got caught in the act and recognized by the nosy desk clerk, a stinker I'd already spotted months back as a Nazi sympathizer and informer. As you saw, I had to get nasty with the bugger. Pierre Roger joined me minutes later, warning me that you and the Fraulein were headed back to the hotel. Obviously, there wasn't time to get the room in order and dispose of the clerk's body. On top of that, I still hadn't found the code and figured it had to be there somewhere. More likely, however, she had it on her. Probably got all the way to St. Nazaire stashed in that damned brassiere. I suspect the copy act in the U-boat, Merrill, was just that—an act."

"When you are quite ready for the truth, Colonel, I'd like to begin," said Sigi, coldly.

Merrill felt a dazed incredulity as he stared at her.

"Begin?" asked Devon. "You're finished. Just a ride back to Old Bailey and the gallows now. I suspect even our SS man down below will fare better than you. Blood all over that blighter's hands too, but the man's in uniform. Geneva code and all that rot."

"Blood?" asked Merrill bluntly. "Who did she do in?"

Devon shook his head. "Before Operation Storm Tide, who rightly knows how many, mate? A dozen? A score? You nearly took the deep six yourself."

Colonel Foster's face was wooden, transfixed.

Devon's eyes remained on Merrill. "She twice tried to kill you."

Merrill looked at him doubtfully. "But the *Metro* incident. She couldn't have. I left her at the hotel, with Loewen."

"A fat female impersonator named Sebastien did that. The dandy collaborated with the Nazis for the money," explained Devon. "Sigi was the one who pushed you over the balcony and shot at your ass during the parachute drop."

Stuart Foster sighed and quickly added, "Three tries, Devon. It now makes sense that she's the one who bribed a scurrilous lorry driver—a known assassin—to run Merrill down his last night in London."

Merrill grimaced. The enormity of the conspiracy was coming into sharper focus. "Go on, Devon," he urged, "Why?"

"There wasn't any big need for a nosy, meddling American along to queer their plan, was there? You were the fly in the ointment, so to speak. The clever lady knew a spot of trouble when she saw one all right. With not only Himmler, but Hitler himself breathing down their necks, neither she nor Schiller had any intention of permitting Dieter Loewen to be taken back to England." Devon smiled thinly at Merrill. "And for G-10 if she could write off her failure to blow up the U-boat pen to your early demise and French OCM inefficiency, so much the better." Devon turned back to Foster. "You, Colonel, and the Prime Minister were hardly likely to reprimand an agent who brought back—single handed, mind you—what you believed to be the Reichskriegmarine code!"

Noting Merrill's continued look of skepticism, Devon smiled and added, "Initially she was out to get you, chum. Unfortunately for Fraulein Petersen, you survived. But more unlucky yet for our cunning double agent, Major von Wilme of the Paris SS office blundered into the picture. Marie Selva, Pierre Roger, and I tried to put the SS major and Schiller out of the way on the Paris highway, but we failed. All this was meddlesome, confusing interference that our friend Sigi hadn't anticipated. And that's where I came in—the lady just couldn't be sure if I was working for the Allies or the Germans. For a while, Lieutenant, you had similar ideas about Erika."

Devon met Sigi's icy glare. "Terrible nuisance, weren't we, Fraulĕin? You suddenly had to revise your plans. You needed both a witness and a foil, for there were now three sides to the espionage coin."

"One moment, Devon," Foster interrupted in a careful sort of voice. "In all your blethering you haven't explained why she didn't try to get rid of Merrill later?"

Merrill, too, was wondering why he was still alive. Quick flashes of their visit aboard the U-601 came back to him: the torpedo tubes that had so conveniently disposed of Leutnant Mueller's incriminating body! Breaking cover and enlisting Dieter Loewen's support, she could have easily eliminated both Erika and himself, no one the wiser.

"Colonel," admonished Devon, "this one's a clever tart. Eliminating Merrill late in the game wouldn't have stuck. Her anticipated ticket out of St. Nazaire, Hugh Cummings, was killed by the Germans. Plus she knew you were suspicious of a traitor, a double-agent. That, supposedly, was me, or one of the others. She knew she could count on Lieutenant Merrill to back her up, keep the name of Sigi Petersen in the clear. Most important, once her SS contact Schiller unexpectedly bit the dust, she was miserably, completely on her own and badly needed help to get out of the fire." Devon exhaled wearily. "Have I missed anything?"

Foster slowly shook his head. "No, no. If I hadn't known you for ten years, Devon, I would say your accusations were the inventions of a raving madman. Absolutely incredible!"

"What's incredible, sir, is what would happen to the great armada if our anti-sub forces and your cryptographic specialists relied on a code they believed to be broken, while in fact it was a skillfully prepared strategic trap, a devious stunt supervised by Hitler himself. Wolf packs of U-boats, most of them with snorkels, in all the wrong places! A suicidal gesture, call it what you may—the dying gasp of the German navy—but the blokes would still have set the D-Day invasion back weeks, if not months, not to mention the thousands of troops and supplies sent to the bottom of the Channel."

* * *

Sigi had retreated slowly, an inch at a time, to the corner of the MGB deckhouse, her eyes on the grenade a sailor had placed near the binnacle some five minutes earlier.

Finally she was able to make her move. Instantly, the weapon was in her hand and she held it up before them, her fingers hovering over the detonator release. She gestured to Lieutenant Smythe. "I have nothing, absolutely nothing to lose. We all go up together unless you cooperate."

Chapter 47

THE MGB COMMANDER stared at Sigi and tightened the grip on his pistol, but he was waiting for Foster to tell him what to do.

"Go below," she ordered him, an annoying smile dancing on her lips. "And bring the SS major back up on deck."

Martin Devon's hand reflexively clutched at the Italian automatic in his pocket. He hesitantly withdrew it but made no attempt to threaten her.

Merrill said quickly, "Stay where you are, Lieutenant Smythe. We'll leave von Wilme below, where he belongs." Merrill turned and glared at Sigi, measuring out his rage a little at a time. There was no use in trying to contain his disappointment and contempt for her; the personal pain would be written on his face, obvious to the others.

She focused on him. "You aren't arguing with me, Skeet, but with this German grenade."

Merrill felt himself sliding. *Careful*, don't fall into the pit of pandemonium. Call her bluff! He gestured to Martin Devon for his gun. Taking it, Merrill slowly brought up his trembling hand and leveled the barrel at Sigi's heart.

She showed no fear whatsoever.

"Lieutenant Merrill, think twice," warned Foster in an unsteady voice. "We need to question her."

Merrill didn't respond, but his anger gradually ebbed. Shrugging, he handed the gun back to Devon, straightened his shoulders, and purposefully stepped toward her.

"You leave me nothing, Skeet. I will not be degraded back in a London prison like a common whore. Stand back or I'll release the detonator. I have my duty."

Unafraid, Merrill moved relentlessly closer. "*Ein Volk, ein Reich, ein Fuehrer*, is that it, Sigi?" He grabbed her wrists, but she kicked and managed to pull the arming mechanism.

Merrill flinched. He took the long slender grenade away from her as easily as taking a lollypop from a child. The others looked on in white-faced amazement as he held both her and the weapon. Merrill brought the grenade just under Sigi's chin and pulled her closer. "Count," he whispered softly.

They were inches away from each other, so close Merrill could smell her fear-induced sweat. She stared back at him like a winged, helpless sparrow returning the hypnotic gaze of the snake that would swallow it. The seconds ticked by too swiftly. Small beads of sweat formed on both their foreheads.

At the last possible instant Merrill flung her back, at the same time heaving the grenade to the far side of the MGB. It went off a split second later, barely underwater, with a muffled roar. The boat shuddered and lifted slightly, but the blast was just far enough away so that no shrapnel penetrated the hull.

For the first time Sigi Petersen looked defeated. Her angry eyes locked on Colonel Foster for several seconds then darted away to the French coastline off in the distance.

Merrill could almost read her thoughts. Having made it through the dank, miserable sewers, she now faced a sudden narrow turn in a pipe and there was no way to force herself on through! Nor was there room to back up. He watched as she slowly inched her way along the rail toward the stern of the gunboat, away from all the incriminating stares. Her hand withdrew from her pocket the small silver piano he'd given her earlier. She opened the lid and let it play, at the same time trying to unobtrusively withdraw a tiny glasss ampule she'd stashed inside. Sigi had it halfway to her mouth, but Merrill leaped toward her, his hand grabbing the wrist and spinning her around. The cyanide capsule and tiny silver piano fell overboard, the tinkling sound of *Celeste Aida* ending abruptly.

Merrill slowly shook his head. "You never give up, do you?"

Sigi wearily sat down on the deck, alone in her sin. Her eyes moved like a robot's, searching the other faces. Slowly, painfully, she said, "Whether or not I am the Nazi zealot you believe, Skeet, is irrelevant. I have no choice but to work for the Germans. They may pay me well, but it is more than money and my personal politics. My brother is not dead, but alive in special internment, as is my father. Both are foolish, outspoken socialists and are now hostages, walking a tightrope with death. I have visited them in Germany. They live only as long as I am loyal and useful to the Third Reich. I owe you foolish Americans and the arrogant British absolutely nothing. Under the circumstances, I owe everything to the new Germany." A mystified silence followed her words.

Merrill looked at her wearily, his entire body tightening. Passion had been big in his heart for this confused beauty, but now he felt only bitterness. He should have let her swallow the capsule; who was he, playing God? Merrill looked away, feeling suddenly suffocated. He could hear the gunboat's commander talking softly to Foster, and Martin Devon again expanding on his discoveries, but the words no longer registered.

Merrill's mind was strangely detached. Once again, he was inside the U-601, where he could clearly see the doomed faces of the men who manned it. He saw Loewen, Gunnar Hersch, all the crewmen; and he saw the death-white faces of others who had nothing to do with the U-boat. He had a vision of the Dutch girl, the bistro owner, the woman undertaker; there was also the fisherman Felix and the Scot Cummings, hanging grotesquely by the neck. Merrill's mind spun out of control. He'd aged in the last several days, and now suddenly he was lonely. Merrill wondered if the shapely young brunette, the country maiden turned WRNS officer who had fed him, poured his bitters, ironed his clothes, and slept with him under the blitz, would be waiting for him when he got back to London. *Molly.* God, he not only wanted her, he desperately needed her.

"Lieutenant!" Foster shouted. "I say, Merrill, are you with us?"

Merrill shook himself back into the present and nodded.

"The others?" Foster asked, "Roger made it back to Paris? Is Erika en route to Holland? And Madame Selva? She hasn't blown her cover in St. Nazaire?"

"No." Merrill didn't hesitate to give it to him candidly; indeed, he awaited Foster's reaction with some curiosity. "Sorry, Colonel, they're *all dead.*"

The older man's face sagged from weariness, as if he'd heard similar reports one too many times in his career. "All?" he asked.

Merrill nodded.

"Devon's told me about the base explosions, and as for the U-601, we heard the Mustang's report. Ten U-boats? I dare say, you're a miracle worker! Congratulations!"

Merrill grunted. "Colonel, things might have gone a little easier for all of us had you leveled with me back in London."

Foster's eyes narrowed. "Sorry, Merrill. Shouldn't wonder you'd be miffed. But too much depended on keeping the Jerries off balance and distracted from the real intent of the mission. As riddled as we were, new faces and new cover were in order. An American war hero who could be trusted was a new pitch, but the fewer people who knew what we were about, the better. *Three operatives* who knew were far too many."

"Three?" Merrill's expression was painfully humble and alert. "Who besides Sigi Petersen and Devon here?"

"Erika Krager had the assignment to go after the code first." Skeet Merrill felt a dull, thudding relief surge through him. Now, in some convoluted way, he was given the full particulars of the seventy-two hour crap shoot with his life. Foster's explanation along with Devon's revelations were like tonics after the fact.

The Colonel continued: "Erika tried eight months ago back in Holland and Germany but her luck didn't hold. Even managed to get her into the Reich's sub training school at Wilhelmshaven, posing as a boy, but Schiller caught on to the scheme. Then our cipher boys back in London finally broke the Enigma machine code. Erika was sent to Paris for other work. Did a good job there too. God knows she compromised herself feeding us information on the SS. When the Germans changed the naval code again last month, Eisenhower and the PM put a top priority on breaking it, stealing it, or whatever, before the big invasion."

Merrill pressed the Englishman. "Operation Storm Tide, and enter yours truly."

"Precisely. As for the Lion of the Atlantic, he would have been the frosting on Churchill's cake. Shame about Erika. She was tough, very tough."

Merrill's thoughts went back to the Dutch girl and her heroic stand on the U-601's conning tower.

"As I see it, Lieutenant, you're the real hero to come out of this. Ten incapacitated U-boats. I'm sure the PM's going to recommend a medal for this one."

"Skip the medals, Colonel. If the Prime Minister wants to do me a favor, replace my lost silver harmonica. He can engrave a message and his name on it if he likes."

"I'm sure that can be arranged."

Merrill looked at Foster thoughtfully. "I'll tell you something, Colonel. Back in the States, when I was a kid I remember a cowboy philosopher named Will Rogers. Popular guy, a legend of sorts himself. He came up with some down-to-earth statements, like claiming 'the thing about being a hero is knowing when to die.'" Merrill slowly shook his head and pointed to the rolling sea. "Like Loewen, I suspect. Rogers also said, 'we can't all be heroes because someone has to sit on the curb and clap as they go by.' Colonel, I've seen enough blood spilled for a lifetime. Now I'd just like to sit on that curb. If you insist, I'll wave Old Glory or the Union Jack and applaud, but damn, it would feel real good to just park my ass and rest."

"Buck up, Merrill," said Foster. "You've displayed plenty of bottom. More than bought your way out of the European war. You'll be on the Jerries' most-wanted spy list from now on and needless to say we can't risk your capture. I'll wager you'll be a Lieutenant Commander before you get back to the States."

Merrill's face hid whatever feeling of gladness he had. So much for *post mortems.* For a long time he looked back toward the coast of Brittany, woozily shaking his head.

Foster followed his intense gaze. "Sorry about the others. Marie Selva and Pierre Roger will never hear the poem on the BBC."

"*Blessent mon coeur d'une monotone,*" volunteered Sigi, dully, from her spot by the rail. She too, was staring moodily at the distant French coastline.

"Good God! She knew it all! Everything!" Foster grimly shook his head, then translated. "Wound my heart with a monotonous languor. The long sobs of the violins of autumn," he whispered quietly, staring back at her. "The second part of Verlaine's poem." Foster's eyes darted back to Merrill. "You've earned the right to know. It's the secret invasion alert. The BBC will air the message tomorrow night to the French Underground. We'll have a thirty-one hour run to Falmouth, so you'll be back just in time to witness the departure of the largest armada the world's ever known. The crossing we've jolly well waited long enough for—D-Day."

"I say, Colonel," said Devon, sprightly, "what's the bloody 'D' mean?"

"D is for *Dammerung*—the twilight of the Nazi gods." Foster smiled effusively. "There's other good news as well. We expect Rome to be liberated in a matter of hours."

Merrill gave up a long, resigned sigh. "Colonel, it's been three days of hell. I could use a little pad duty." Three days, four lives gone, not to mention the enemy's staggering loss, he reflected. Like everything else in the rotten war, the German code had its appalling price which the other operatives had paid in full. The events of the past seventy-two hours had been lived in terrible and disastrous clarity, yet already, looking back, the entire affair seemed not real, not real at all. Merrill suddenly felt very cold. He turned and saw that Martin Devon, too, felt the chill. They both pulled up their collars against the brisk wind and looked uneasily back to the horizon, the place where Germany's great U-boat ace had been summarily committed to Neptune's locker.

"Almost forgot, Merrill," said Foster, withdrawing a small envelope from his pocket. "Before I left the Admiralty one of the Wren warrants who prepared your cover package asked me to give you this. I thought it a bit irregular, but she insisted you would definitely understand." Foster handed over the unsealed envelope and watched as Merrill removed a delicate sheet of blue stationery and sniffed its fragrance. Foster winked and added, "An attractive brunette indeed, Warrant Officer Tremayne. Naturally, under the secrecy circumstances of the mission, I was obliged to read the message."

Merrill nodded. He silently read the note twice, the second time aloud, translating it from the German.

"Here's the rest of that Cornish ballad, Skeet, if you've now a mind for it:

Back home she stands alone on the strand
    Still clutching her handkerchief fair, oh,
Crying where is my sailor who plows the deep sea
    Hasten back to your maid on the shore, oh."

Shoving Molly's note in his pocket, Merrill looked up at the Colonel and exchanged grins.

Foster said to him, "Molly Tremayne's a very pretty young woman."

Merrill lowered his eyes. "Yes, I know. I've been blind." He felt warmer now, much warmer. But his wounded shoulder ached and his brain was tired, dog tired. He would go below and try for sleep, allowing the fast-moving events of the past few days to settle in the last layers of his mind.

Merrill looked solemnly at the silent female standing by the rail, her flaxen hair fluttering in the wind. Foster's gaze, too, was on her. Sigi Petersen had become an expendable liability that painfully weighted the heaviness both men felt in their chests. She shivered convulsively and smiled back at them.

"Take her below," Foster instructed Smythe.

Sigi hesitated in the hatchway, cooly returning Merrill's stare, exactly as she'd done the first time at the embassy reception in London almost two years earlier. But now Merrill saw that her blue eyes no longer sparkled brightly like a sunlit fjord. They were intense, brooding eyes, lost in a murky lake, deep in the forest of Faust. Churchill had spoken of the war as blood, sweat and tears. Clearly, Sigi was a woman who would never cry, who knew no tears.

Merrill looked at her for the last time and wondered about the madness in the world that would take her permanently from him. It was over. He wanted to say something profound to this intelligent, beautiful woman he'd briefly admired, but there was really nothing to be said, only foolish, hateful, small talk the moment didn't deserve.

Suddenly feeling solitary and lonely, Merrill looked away. He felt a sudden need to be back on a pigboat with men of his own stamp. Dieter Loewen would have understood this—he was the greatest submariner of them all.

The sky was clearing fast, the few clouds remaining only small fragments disintegrating into long, pale threads. The MGB's came together and a parcel was quickly passed. Then they separated and accelerated on slightly different courses to the northwest, leaving great frothing wakes behind them.

Epilogue

In 1950, DURING the postwar reconstruction of Germany, a *Weinstube* opened for business in the small town of Andernach. Mounted conspicuously in the masonry wall of the establishment was a barrel of vintage wine the owner claimed to have salvaged from a pre-surrender, bombed-out train wreck near Aachen. Since the stencils on the end of the keg indicated the wine was consigned to one Adolf Hitler, the prize of war was left untapped, a conversation piece of the community.

When the *Weinstube's* owner passed away in 1980, his less nostalgic heirs, out of curiosity, opened the barrel. They found it did not contain aged Muscadet, but instead formaldehyde, along with the well-preserved body of SS Colonel Reinhard Schiller—easily indentified from the armpit tattoos. An Iron Cross, First Class, with Oak Leaves and Crossed Swords of Silver, engraved with Dieter Loewen's name on the back, was also retrieved from the barrel. The World War II curio was sent to the Bundesarchive.

Shortly after being brought back to London, Sigi Petersen was interrogated and it was learned that prior to her role as the counterspy Viper she'd been a well-paid Norwegian *Quisling*. Employing her usual charm in the English docket, she reiterated her story of relatives in a German concentration camp. Despite a vigorous, unsympathetic prosecution demanding the death penalty, after a lengthy trial she was finally sentenced by an Allied tribunal to life imprisonment. Appalled by such a lenient sentence for traitorous conduct, Norwegian

activists in Britain ambushed the police van carrying her to
Marston-Tyne prison, shooting and killing her.

Martin Devon remained in Britain until after the war.
Remembering the many friends he'd made during his three
years in France posing as the deaf-mute Duval, he took his
accumulated espionage earnings and immigrated to that country in 1948. He backed his former employer, Dominique
Roger, in a small *patisserie* in Lille and married her younger
sister. Dominique wrote her memoirs of the Paris Resistance
movement, the work receiving several printings in France and
Britain. She died in 1985, while Devon is now retired and still
lives in the south of France.

SS Major Hermann von Wilme was traded, through Portuguese intermediaries, for an important RAF squadron commander held prisoner in Germany. After the Nazi surrender,
von Wilme, like countless other SS men, went underground,
changing names, trying to bury the snout of the Gestapo beast.
Years later he emerged as a successful security manager for a
German aircraft parts manufacturer. Israeli investigating teams
discovered his infamous background, and under harrassment
von Wilme retired in Spain, again under a new identity. He was
killed in a freak Costa Brava auto accident, a head-on collision
on a rain-swept highway. The other car, oddly enough, was
driven by a Frenchman whom von Wilme had personally
consigned to torture and imprisonment at Compeigne in 1943.

V. Levec, the produce man whose fields were used for one
too many underground-movement airdrops, was shot by SS
investigators only three days before General Patton's Third
Army liberated the area around his farm near Meaux.

The female impersonator Sebastien was sent to a concentration camp in Germany, along with several other homosexuals.
He was never heard from again.

* * *

Rather than face the certain vengeance of the victorious Allies who captured him, SS head Heinrich Himmler commited suicide by cyanide capsule in May of 1945. Up until the moment of his death, and despite a relentless investigation and terrible persecution of countless innocent individuals, he was never to learn what had become of his trusted assistant, Colonel Reinhard Schiller.

On retirement from G-10 and the Admiralty, Colonel Stuart Foster purchased a country place, a shotgun, and a champion English Springer Spaniel. He set up housekeeping less than a mile from Chartwell, Winston Churchill's country home. Together, as often as possible, the two men enjoyed reminiscing on Admiralty adventures during two World Wars. Foster lived several years beyond his beloved friend, and at the time of his own death in 1978, had accumulated one of the largest private collections of the former Prime Minister's paintings.

Winston Churchill did make it to Normandy aboard a destroyer in the relative safety of D-Day plus six. While most of the British Prime Minister's wartime goals came into satisfying fruition, Section G-10's plan for shattering U-boat ace Dieter Loewen's credibility with the German home front went unrealized. Dr. Goebbels' propaganda experts went ahead with a stunning article on the U-boat commander for *Signal* magazine, even using a few of the photographs they'd found in a camera abandoned by Skeet Merrill. Later, they cleverly conspired to have Loewen die a martyr to Hitler's cause. *Missing in valiant action,* read the newspaper obituaries, though the ace's officially recorded disappearance was kept from the German people for five months. The postage stamp with the U-boat hero's face on it is still a collector's item.

But Winston Churchill was gratified to have broken the operational code, and thanks to his steel-willed determination and Eisenhower's foresight, not one ship in the invasion fleet was reported lost to a German submarine. In the Prime Minister's memoirs, considering the many trials facing the Allied cause, he wrote: "The U-boat attack was our worse peril. It would have been wiser for the Germans to stake all on it."

*   *   *

Shaken by the D-Day events at Normandy and bitter for weeks after hearing of U-boat ace Loewen's death, Adolf Hitler's further disintegration came after the military conspiracy to end his life in July, 1944. Week by week, he saw his megalomaniacal dreams for a thousand-year Reich crumble. A sick man weighed down with defeat, he cowered in the depths of the *Fuehrerbunker*, becoming no more than a hunted animal marked for death. The end came by a self-inflicted bullet to his mouth on April 30, 1945. Hitler's body was incinerated by associates in the Chancellory Courtyard.

For the Third Reich, too little came too late. Even at the time of surrender, seventeen sleek, new-generation U-boats, the technological promise of the future, lay incomplete on the Bremen shipways. From the morning the Allied troops pounded ashore at Normandy, Grand Admiral of the Fleet Karl Doenitz was resigned to both the fate of the German navy and the impending doom of his Fatherland.

The Fuehrer's will appointed Doenitz his successor. Accepting this tattered mantle, he presided over Germany's surrender. At Nuremburg, the Allies sentenced Doenitz to prison for ten years, charging the admiral with waging aggressive sea war and violating the laws of war at sea, all this despite the fact that U.S. Naval authorities admitted that American submarines in the Pacific waged the same form of unrestricted warfare. Among the former U.S. sub commanders called to testify was Lieutenant Commander Skeet Merrill.

After being released from Spandau prison, Doenitz wrote his memoirs and lived in modest retirement in a small apartment near Hamburg. A model of one of his World War II submarines was prominently displayed there, along with a portrait of Frederick the Great, but no photographs of U-boat ace Dieter Loewen or Adolf Hitler. Karl Doenitz died in 1980 at the age of 89.

Skeet Merrill, as predicted, picked up another medal, this one from Churchill himself. Following VE-Day, he married Warrant Officer Molly Tremayne. Molly was one of the eighty-thousand-plus English brides who went off to a new life in the USA. Remaining in the military service, Merrill was promoted rapidly and retired as a vice admiral. But he never again commanded a submarine, nor did he return to his native Texas; the balance of his illustrious naval career was spent in the nation's capital at the Pentagon until his retirement in 1970. Since then Merrill has been raising quarter-horses in Colorado on a ranch a few miles from John Denver. Merrill politely refuses lecture opportunities, interviews, and repeated invitations from the VFW to participate in 4th of July parades, preferring instead the quiet solitude of his ranch, the company of his family and two Labrador retrievers.

Vera Lynn, the velvet-voiced English songbird, continued to entertain and broadcast to the troops through the end of the war. Countless numbers of fighting men on both sides of the battle, by the time of the Nazi surrender, had committed her many songs and messages to memory:

I'll find you in the morning sun,
    And when the night is new,
I'll be looking at the moon
    But I'll be seeing you.

"This is Vera Lynn saying goodnight and good luck to all my armed forces sweethearts. May God bless all our fighting heroes on the land, in the air, on and under the sea."

ABOUT THE AUTHOR

Douglas Muir is a graduate of the University of Washington. He was a Hollywood film and TV writer-director prior to turning his hand to full-time novel writing. Over the years his cinema work has won numerous international awards. His credits include TV commercials, several network projects, and a stint as associate producer and writer for the acclaimed "Undersea World of Jacques Cousteau."

Muir made his debut as a thriller writer with the novel *American Reich*. Currently, he divides his time between work on an MFA degree at UCLA and final polishing of a novel about a defecting Russian who marries a Hollywood actress.